I0574573

VICAR BREKONRIDGE

VICAR BREKONRIDGE

A VICAR BREKONRIDGE NOVEL

RICHARD HELMS

First published by Level Best Books/Historia 2023

Copyright © 2023 by Richard Helms

All rights reserved. No part of this publication may be reproduced, stored or transmitted in any form or by any means, electronic, mechanical, photocopying, recording, scanning, or otherwise without written permission from the publisher. It is illegal to copy this book, post it to a website, or distribute it by any other means without permission.

This novel is entirely a work of fiction. The names, characters and incidents portrayed in it are the work of the author's imagination. Any resemblance to actual persons, living or dead, events or localities is entirely coincidental.

Richard Helms asserts the moral right to be identified as the author of this work.

Author Photo Credit: Elaine Helms

First edition

ISBN: 978-1-68512-352-9

Cover art by Level Best Designs

This book was professionally typeset on Reedsy.
Find out more at reedsy.com

To Elaine
Because she drives me insane with love.

Preface

A small portion of this novel was previously published in the July/August 2019 issue of *Ellery Queen Mystery Magazine,* under the title *"The Cripplegate Apprehension."*

Praise for Vicar Brekonridge

"Helms just keeps on making up new and interesting private eyes, but *Vicar Brekonridge* may be one of his more intriguing creations… For all his rough-and-tumble manners, cynical bravado, mercenary motives and sliding scale honesty, in a shady profession not particularly known for its integrity, (Brekonridge) struts through the streets of London, a cloud of hemp in his wake, hewing to some inexplicable personal code that betrays a startling even-minded empathy for the criminals he hunts down, and a concern for—of all things—justice."—Kevin Burton Smith, *Thrilling Detective*

"In a seamless blending of historical fact and narrative skill, Richard Helms reimagines the sensational case of Daniel M'Naghten, whose 1843 murder trial set a precedent that reverberates to this day. Helms has crafted a thoroughly gripping historical mystery that will leave readers eager to hear more of the "notorious thief-taker" Vicar Brekonridge."—Daniel Stashower, author of *American Demon*

Chapter One

Had Edward Drummond worn a thicker overcoat, he might have lived.

The late January weather in 1843 had been cold and blustery for days, but he was only going as far as his brother's banking house at Charing Cross, a half mile from his office at 10 Downing Street. With such a short distance, he determined to make the walk in a lighter, more comfortable jacket.

Had the bullet deviated a mere inch, Edward Drummond might have lived. Fired upon at point-blank range, the muzzle of a single-shot pistol pressed against his back, it was possible the damage might have been restricted to muscle and flesh only. As the pistol ball struck him, he experienced little pain. It felt as if he had been slapped across the back lightly with a cudgel. Only the thunderous report from the pistol informed him he had been shot.

He rolled and saw his assailant standing over him, holding a pistol, blue smoke curling from its barrel. The man slipped the pistol into his jacket pocket and took another from inside his coat. He leveled the second pistol at Drummond's head and pulled back the hammer. As it fell into its lock, the click sounded like the snap of lightning before the first peal of thunder.

Drummond wanted to close his eyes, but his horror wouldn't allow it. His mind raced to find some sense in what was happening to him. He raised a hand in futility to ward off a second shot. For a fatal instant, the two men's eyes locked. Drummond saw fury and determination in the assailant's face. He tried to form words, to say something—anything—to dissuade his attacker. Nothing came.

As he lost hope for salvation, a uniformed London police officer appeared behind the assassin and grabbed for the man's arms. When the officer jerked the man around, the second pistol went off. The ball whined as it ricocheted off the granite curb, only inches from Drummond's head, and careened away. The gunman struggled as the constable wrestled him to the ground.

A crowd gathered, drawn by the sound of the pistol and the anticipation of excitement. More uniformed officers, alerted by the gunfire, arrived to help subdue the shooter. Two men helped Drummond to his feet. His back throbbed sorely.

"You've been shot, sir," one said.

"Yes," Drummond replied. It was all he could muster. The reality of his potentially mortal circumstances still had not registered with him. "Please help me? I've come from my brother's bank in Charing Cross. Can you assist me in returning there?"

"You need a surgeon!" the other man said.

"My brother will tend to it. I do not wish to remain here, on the street, in the open. There may be more—"

A sudden metallic taste filled his mouth, and his vision wavered and dimmed. His knees felt weak. He was supported by both the men, one under each shoulder.

As quickly as it had hit him, the shock subsided. Drummond waved one weak hand in the air. "It is only a short distance," he said. "Only as far as Charing Cross. I can walk. Please. I will be fine if I can only get to my brother."

* * *

If a surgeon—a real surgeon—had been immediately at his disposal, Edward Drummond might have lived.

At a brisk pace, one could walk from the Prime Minister's office to Drummond's Bank in slightly over ten minutes. Edward Drummond had been halfway between those points when he was shot. A brisk pace out of the question, Drummond and his two Samaritans took almost a quarter hour to make their way to the bank.

Charles Drummond kept private quarters on the third floor of the bank in case he might have to work too late to return to his home. As soon as Edward staggered into the bank, the back of his light winter coat stained with blood, Charles had him escorted to those quarters.

"Please," Edward whispered as they laid him onto Charles's bed, "Summon Anne. If I am to depart this earth today, I do not wish to do so without first laying my eyes on my dear sister's face once more."

"First, let's tend to your wounds," Charles said. "I will send for a surgeon at once." He ordered an assistant to run out and bring a surgeon, and another to fetch Anne Eliza Drummond.

"Can you tell me what happened?" Charles asked, as he knelt next to the bed.

"I have no idea. I was walking toward Downing Street after our visit, when a man pressed a pistol into my back and fired. I can find no provocation or possible conflict that might have instigated such an attack. Thank you..." he took a glass of Madeira wine his brother poured for him, and sipped. "He must surely have been a madman."

Charles ordered Edward to be quiet and rest until medical help could arrive. When it did, it came in the form not of a surgeon, but a local apothecary named Richard Jackson.

"I'm sorry," the assistant said, "All of the surgeons along the streets were otherwise engaged."

"You should have told them my brother is the personal secretary to Sir Robert Peel," Charles said angrily.

"I did the best I could!" the assistant argued.

"Out," Charles ordered. "Your presence here in my emotional state endangers your situation."

Richard Jackson sat beside Edward's bed and examined the wound as the assistant skulked out of the room.

"No exit," Jackson noted immediately. "The ball is still inside him. Where, I cannot say. Please unbutton his waistcoat and shirt. I wish to listen to his heart."

Seconds later, Jackson declared Edward Drummond's fifty-one-year-old heart to be steady and strong. "I see no immediate life-threatening concerns," he said. "The ball must be removed. A proper surgeon might be able to determine with much greater specificity what danger our patient here might face, but I think—for the moment—he is not in mortal peril."

"If so," Edward said, "I wish to move to my own apartment. I can be much more comfortable there and will pose no further disruption to the operations of the bank."

"Perhaps it would be better for you to remain here, at least until a surgeon can arrive to remove the ball," Charles suggested.

"I feel quite strong enough to make the short trip to Grosvenor Street. It is only a little over a mile. If you would summon a carriage…"

"You will take mine," Charles said. "And Mr. Jackson will accompany you."

"I'd better patch you up, first," Jackson said. "The ball might not kill you, but you've already lost a fair amount of blood. Won't help you to lose any more."

* * *

Within an hour, Edward Drummond arrived at his apartment at 19 Lower Grosvenor Place. Richard Jackson assisted him from the carriage and up the stairs. They found his sister, Anne Eliza, waiting for them, after Charles had sent word of Edward's shooting to her. She was distraught, her eyes red-rimmed with tears, and she clutched a dainty linen handkerchief.

She had located two surgeons to tend to Edward's wounds. George James Guthrie, a former president of the Royal College of Surgeons, was accompanied by Bransby Cooper, somewhat more notorious and arguably less skilled than his companion. Cooper had been the subject of a scandal years earlier when his botched surgery on a young man had resulted in the man's most painful and agonizing death.

Edward's sister waited outside as the surgeons examined his wounds. The pistol ball had entered to the left of his spine at a point underneath his shoulder blade. After warning Edward that it would be necessary to probe for the ball, entailing no small amount of pain, the two surgeons explored the path of the projectile. It had ricocheted off one of Edward's ribs, turned downward, and lodged under the lowest left-side rib in muscle near the surface of his abdomen. As they probed, Edward tried to remain stoic, but finally cried out in great pain.

"It can't be stated with absolute certainty," Cooper said, after placing a pad over the wound and allowing Drummond to recline again on his bed, "but there is the potential for severe organic damage. I don't believe the heart was impacted, but I can't say the same for your lung and other vital organs. My recommendation would be to remove the ball as quickly as possible and hope nature will correct any other injury."

"Please do it at once," Edward ordered.

After plying Drummond with almost half a decanter of brandy, the physicians set about the business of removing the pistol ball lodged in his lower abdomen. It took only a few minutes to create an incision and to dissect the muscle beneath the skin. Intoxicated but not insensate, Edward chewed a wadded piece of his linen sheet and grimaced in agony as they excised the lead fragment. They sewed the wound shut and bandaged it, and Edward lay back on his mattress, gasping and wiping the tears from his face.

"Your recovery may be slow," Dr. Guthrie warned him as he cleaned the blood from his hands in a china washbowl. "You are not a young man, Mr. Drummond. The body loses its ability to heal after age fifty. Don't overly exert yourself, allow your devoted sister to attend to your needs, and I believe you will recover in time."

* * *

Later that evening Edward's sister Anne found him resting, however uncomfortably, in his room.

"It was fortunate you were able to locate the surgeons," he said to her.

"You can thank the Prime Minister," she said. "When he was informed of the attack on you, he summoned them immediately."

"I am in his debt."

"Nonsense. Sir Robert would be lost without you, my dear brother. He was only protecting his best interests. Shall I read to you?"

"Please do not bother on my behalf. To be truthful, I am completely exhausted. I do wish you would stay by my side while I go to sleep. Your presence, as always, is such a great comfort for me."

She grasped his hand and promised to remain until he was asleep. His palm was moist, the fingers cool and pale. Her mind involuntarily migrated to thoughts of how she might manage without him. Neither she nor Edward had married. As a result, they were each other's most constant companions since childhood. At forty-four, Anne Eliza's prospects for matrimony were decidedly limited. While she loved her brother Charles, she was utterly devoted to Edward. Charles was married to his beloved Mary, and his life was consumed by work and family. It was unmarried and unattached Edward who escorted her to every social or arts event. In return, Anne Eliza accompanied Edward to government functions. In the absence of spouses or romantic attachments, they had become as dependent on one another as married couples, and the potential loss of her brother would cut as deeply for Anne Eliza as the death of a spouse. She grasped his hand, sensing his weakened pulse, and she willed him to live.

* * *

Edward awoke early the next morning, before sunrise, coughing and in great pain. When he tried to draw breath, his chest ached terribly. Each inhalation was accompanied by raspy wheezing noise. He kept a small bell by his bedside to summon his housekeeper. When he rang it, Anne burst into the room. She had been sitting outside, dozing in her chair.

"What is it?" she asked as she knelt next to his bed.

"I am experiencing great distress," he gasped. "I cannot breathe comfortably. We must summon the surgeons."

Edward lay corpse-like on the bed, afraid to roll one way or the other.

Each movement resulted in tormenting exquisite pain in his left side. It started under his left breast and then radiated all along his chest and abdomen. He found, if he took short shallow breaths, he could suck in enough air to forestall the sense of drowning and the panic that accompanied it.

Both surgeons arrived within a half hour. They went to work directly, examining him carefully but not entirely gently. He moaned in pain as they rolled him over to inspect the wound. Anne stood near the door, worrying the Irish out of her linen handkerchief.

Directly, Guthrie stood and addressed her.

"His condition is much more serious than we first believed," he announced. "Due to swelling along the path of the pistol ball, we were unable to detect that it had shattered his lowest rib on the left side of his chest. It appears, sometime between the shooting and this morning, shards of the rib have irritated his lung, perhaps even penetrating it. The lung is filling with fluid."

"What can you do?" Anne pleaded. "Please, tell me you can save him!"

"We will do everything in our power," he reassured her. "Should he descend fully into pneumonia or pleurisy, we will not be able to do much to save him. He would be in the Lord's hands."

Cooper joined them near the door.

"I would suggest bleeding," he said. "By reducing the volume of blood in his body, we might be able to reduce the fluids in his lungs. The lungs extract these fluids from the bloodstream, after all."

"I am more concerned about inflammation," Guthrie countered. "The fluid in his lungs may be the result of an infection along the path of the pistol ball. There is evidence of putrefaction near the site of the incision we made yesterday. He risks gangrene."

"Bleeding may still be beneficial," Cooper said. "And we could apply leeches to the area of the incision to absorb the necrotic tissue. I have seen this provide some benefit in the past."

Guthrie crossed the bed chamber to Edward. "You heard the conversation?" he asked.

"Every word," Edward stared at the ceiling. "Be about it, Doctor. I fear I cannot survive much longer with this enormous pressure in my chest."

Cooper escorted Anne from the room, explaining that the procedure, however safe it might be, could unduly frighten her, due to the large quantity of blood they would release. After she was out of the room, he returned to the bedside and assisted Guthrie.

First, they shaved the side of Drummond's head to expose the temporal artery. They palpated the pulse from the temporal artery forward of his ear and—after warning Edward to brace himself—cut into it using a razor lancet, being careful not to sever it entirely. Cooper made the incision, creating a fine spray of blood that burst forth under pressure. Guthrie immediately pressed a muslin pad against it to keep from painting the bed chamber walls as they positioned Edward correctly to allow for the free release of his blood.

They allowed the wound to bleed into a chamber pot until they had extracted a little over two pints, then packed the wound with fresh gauze and applied a bandage, winding it several times around Edward's head.

Within hours, Edward awakened, sat up in bed, and requested soup and bread. The surgeons, satisfied that the crisis had passed, left him in Anne's care.

She read to him in the evening. He appeared to be in high spirits, almost giddy at times. At one point, she put down the book and dropped to her knees at his bedside.

"I was so worried," she said. "I cannot bear the idea of being separated from you, brother."

He stroked her hair affectionately. "I have no fear of departing this life, except that it would cause me to leave you with nobody to provide you support or protection. As I have lain here in pain, I have taken account of my life to this point, and I cannot say I am disappointed. True, I might have risen to greater heights had I been a more ambitious man, and yet such achievements seem to me unimportant when I see the sorrow in your eyes. Perhaps, when I am properly on the mend, we might consider a vacation on the continent."

"Your work—"

"I will need a period of recuperation. How much better to regain my strength and vigor in a villa in the south of Italy than here in foggy London? And you will be my companion."

She lay her head on his mattress and smiled at him. "I would be so lonely without you. I wish we could never be separated, not even by death."

"Most assuredly by death," he said. "But not today. And not soon. We will have many years in each other's company yet."

* * *

On Sunday following the shooting, Drummond gained even more strength through the course of the morning. He was still confined to his bed, so Anne asked for a bowl of water and some towels, and she cleaned him as best as she was able. She opened the curtains to his bedchamber, which had been closed since the shooting on Friday, except when the doctors were tending him, and Edward was delighted to find the sun was bright and intense as it streamed in through the windows.

"An excellent omen!" he cried.

She read to him for a bit, until he interrupted her.

"I am hungry. Truly hungry. Might you have cook prepare a proper luncheon?"

Anne had the staff prepare roasted pork with sweet apple sauce and root vegetables since it was January and fresh vegetables were almost impossible to obtain, even for someone with Drummond's highly placed connections. She helped him eat. When he was finished, she left him to rest as she retired for her own temporary room down the hall for a nap.

In late afternoon Drummond awoke, acutely aware that something had changed. It felt as if something inside of him had broken loose and was roaming about his innards like a drunken snake. He immediately reached for the bell but, as quickly as the sensation had struck him, it vanished again, to be replaced with the same dull but tolerable agony he had endured for two days.

Ten minutes later the physical apparition returned, a strange feeling of tension in his abdomen that uncoiled into a flurry of spasms and sharp, penetrating twinges, as if some force were ripping his body apart from its core.

This time, he did ring for help. In seconds, Anne was at his side, her face reflecting his concern.

"Something is wrong," he said. "It feels … different."

"Shall I call the surgeons?" Anne asked.

"Let us hold off for a few hours," he said. "It is possible this is part of the healing process. I am at a loss to say. After all, I have never been shot before. But, please, stay by my side. I find in your closeness a great balm."

* * *

Nine o'clock the next morning found the surgeons Guthrie and Cooper arrive at 19 Lower Grosvenor Place by carriage, having been summoned by Anne not long after first light.

They found Edward Drummond on his bed, his face ghastly pale. His thin fingers fumbled with the bedclothes. His breath smelled foul and diseased, and his lungs gurgled as he tried to draw in air. He had a fever again. His eyes blinked open and closed, and he hadn't uttered a word since awakening.

"He must be bled again," Cooper stated with authority.

"We took a quart on Saturday," Guthrie cautioned. "And God knows how much when he was shot on Friday. We must take care not to exsanguinate him."

"The risk of inaction is much greater!" Cooper said. "We must be at it at once, or he may not see the end of the day."

"Help me turn him on his side," Guthrie said. He and Cooper delicately rolled Drummond, and they examined the two wounds on his back. A faint smell like rotting meat rose to their nostrils.

"The infection is spreading," Cooper said. "We risk gangrene if we do not act immediately."

Reluctantly, Guthrie agreed. They positioned the nearly-comatose Drummond over the basin on the floor, and reopened the incision into his temporal artery. This time the blood did not spray, but rather bubbled and pooled on the surface of his skull before dropping into the basin. Both surgeons watched as it covered the bottom of the basin and crept up the sides.

"I expect two quarts may be sufficient," Cooper said.

"Certainly not so much!" Guthrie argued.

"It's been two days, and his sister has assured us he has eaten and drunk well. He has replaced almost all the blood we removed on Saturday. The risk of acting is minimal. The risk of delay, great."

"It's on your head," Guthrie said.

"I am perfectly willing to leave him in your hands if you wish. On the other hand, I think the Prime Minister would be much distressed were I to leave this man's bedside and some grave tragedy befell him. I fear we are both in this to the bitter end, sir. Please be sure to keep his head still."

When they were finished, they bound his head again and left him to rest. He did not awaken again until the next morning, Tuesday. He was listless and groggy, but he was able to answer simple questions from Anne.

"The man," he whispered to her as she sat at his side.

"Which man?"

"The one who—" He pantomimed firing a pistol.

She cupped his face in her hands and gazed into his eyes. "He is being held in the jail at Gardener's Lane. The newspapers are vague on the subject, but I am led to understand he believed he was shooting at Sir Robert Peel."

"Ah," Drummond rasped, settling back into his pillow. "Yes. That, at last, makes sense. There would be little profit in erasing me from the Earth, but shooting the Prime Minister makes the picture much clearer. After the attacks on Her Majesty, assassination appears to have become something of a fashion."

Drummond remained stable for most of the afternoon. He was wan and weak. His energy did not resurge as it had following his arteriotomy on Saturday. By Tuesday morning he was scarcely able to prop himself up in bed without considerable assistance from Anne and a servant girl.

Late on Tuesday afternoon, Anne dozed in a soft wing chair which had been brought into Drummond's bedchamber for that purpose. She was roused by mumbling in the bed next to her.

"Foul…waste…hindrance…so frail…"

She leaned close over him, determined to figure out what he was saying. She wiped his brow with a damp cloth. "Is there something you want to tell me?"

He shook his head, his eyes clenched shut, and swiped at the cloth with his hand. He remained in a state of delirium until almost dusk, at which time— desperate for some sign of hope—Anne once again sent for the surgeons. Only George James Guthrie responded.

"Where is Doctor Cooper?" Anne demanded.

"I cannot say," Guthrie muttered as he examined Drummond.

"Edward is declining."

Guthrie thumbed open Drummond's left eye and held a candle up to it. Then he tapped on the stricken man's chest repeatedly. Finally, he checked Edward's racing pulse.

"I am not encouraged," was all he would say. "I shall remain here until the crisis passes, one way or the other."

They sat with Drummond through the night. By first light the next morning, his agitation had resolved, and he slept briefly. When he awoke, he stared at the ceiling almost as if he could not determine its nature.

On Wednesday morning, Guthrie examined him once again. He shook his head and took a seat next to the bed. He stroked Edward's forehead until the man's eyes opened.

"It is with the utmost regret that I tell you this, Mr. Drummond," Guthrie said. "I fear your hour is at hand. I do not believe you will live until midday."

Across the room, Anne gasped and wept softly into her handkerchief—the latest of dozens she had soaked since Friday.

"I understand," Drummond replied. "The sooner the better. I am not presently in pain. If there is no hope, I would as soon pass quickly than wait for my agony to return. I thank you, Doctor. You have given me three more days with my beloved sister. Would you leave us alone for a few moments?"

"Certainly." Guthrie stepped toward the doorway, momentarily placed his hand on Anne's shoulder, and then walked downstairs to the parlor.

Drummond gestured for his sister to come to his side. She ignored the chair and slipped up onto the mattress, placing one hand under Drummond's head. With the other she brushed matted hair away from his brow.

He whispered. "My only regret is parting with you. Perhaps I might have married and had a family of my own, had my life gone differently. I wish you to know, in their absence, I could not have spent my life with a finer companion."

Anne pleaded, "You will get stronger. We will take that holiday to Italy."

He mustered a faint, exerted smile. "You are sweet and kind, but I am afraid the awful French word *malaise* expresses most fully my burden. I am thirsty. Might you bring me a glass of brandy? It will help me rest."

"I am afraid to leave your side," she said.

"I assure you. I will not depart this world in the time it takes to fetch a glass."

She returned only a minute or so later. His breath had become labored. She placed the brandy to his lips, and he sipped.

"Delightful," he whispered, and his body was wracked with a sudden fit of coughing. His back arched, and one hand flew out, dashing the snifter onto the carpet and spilling the brandy across the floor. He moaned as he fought for breath, and she tossed her arms around him and cradled his head to her bosom. His respiration slowed, more a liquid rattle than breathing, and then it stopped altogether.

Anne wailed in despair as her brother's body went limp in death.

Half an hour later, she emerged from his room and made her way to the parlor downstairs, where Guthrie waited for her.

"It is finished," she said. Ignoring manners and custom, she poured a drink from a decanter next to the fireplace and downed it all in a single gulp. She started to pour another, but Guthrie's hand stayed her.

"Courage," he said.

"To hell with courage," she said, her eyes flashing. "All I hold dear has been ripped from me. I shall not accept and I shall not forgive. The man who has done this will pay."

She pushed the doctor's hand away and reached again for the decanter.

"He will pay dearly," she said.

Chapter Two

By the time the two bobbies pulled the shooter up the steps to the Gardener's Lane Station House, word had spread of the attack on Whitehall. The station was crowded with interested officers and some citizens, including one or two reporters who had happened to be in the station when the announcement was made.

The gunman had initially resisted the policemen, crying out as they clapped the cuffs on his wrists, "Do not detain me. I know what I am about!"

However, on the short march toward the station house, the young handcuffed man appeared to be strangely happy. He even chuckled several times. Constable Silver glanced at Constable Stevens as if to ask whether the man might be insane.

"It is done," the man said softly. "He shall not destroy my peace of mind any longer."

Stevens began the process of booking the man, but was interrupted by an inspector named Tierney, who conducted the interview himself. He ordered Silver and Stevens to stand guard outside the room.

"Look at me," Tierney told the man, his words couched in a thick Yorkshire accent. "I wish you to understand your circumstances. You are to be charged with an attempted murder. Do you understand this?"

To Tierney's surprise, the prisoner looked up at him, and appeared to be at peace. He didn't say anything. He was of medium height, with straw-colored hair and scant whiskers. His eyes were a penetrating blue. He was dressed in a black overcoat, with a cloth waistcoat and tweed trousers underneath. He seemed calm and collected, especially for a man who had attempted murder only minutes earlier. What struck Tierney most of all was the man's youth. He appeared to be no older than twenty-five.

"Your name?"

"Daniel M'Naghten," the man said. Tierney noted the man's accent sounded Scottish.

"You're from Scotland?" he asked.

Nothing. The man stared ahead, calm, unchallenging, but also uncooperative.

"What is your address in London, if you have one?"

Nothing again. This man M'Naghten appeared to wish to control the interview, something Inspector Tierney could not abide.

"The penalty will be quite severe," he said, in a clumsy attempt to frighten the man into complying. M'Naghten continued to gaze into Tierney's eyes, seldom blinking, and showed no fear at all. "I suppose you are aware of the identity of the man you shot?"

"It is Sir Robert Peel, is it not?" M'Naghten said with a sly smile. "Have I not shot the Prime Minister?"

"I am happy to say you have not," Tierney informed him. "The man you assaulted was Sir Robert's secretary, Edward Drummond, and you had better hope no greater harm comes to him. The penalty for attempted murder is severe enough. Should Mr. Drummond succumb to his injuries—" He held his hand up, with the index finger pointed down, and waggled it back and forth to suggest a swinging body.

M'Naghten's face clouded over. "I do not wish to say any more," he said.

* * *

After several more attempts to engage M'Naghten in the interview, Tierney left him chained to a table and joined Constables Silver and Stevens outside the room. Stevens still held the two pistols he'd taken from M'Naghten.

"What do you make of these?" he said, handing them to Tierney, who examined them closely.

"Excellent craftsmanship," Tierney said. "The engraving and tooling of the metal, the fine walnut grips, the balance and weight precise. They appear to be almost new. These are a gentleman's pistols. Please assist me in inventorying his possessions. Perhaps we can find some more information about him among the effects he's carrying."

All three officers reentered the interrogation room, where M'Naghten sat serenely, staring at the wall. Tierney ordered him to stand, and Silver and Stevens rifled through his pockets. Tierney wrote each item they found.

"Two five pound notes…four sovereigns…eleven shillings…four silver pence…one copper penny…a pen knife…a key…"

"Hey, now, what's this?" Silver said, as he extracted a slip of paper from M'Naghten's waistcoat pocket. He handed it to Inspector Tierney.

Tierney said, "A deposit receipt from the Glasgow and Ship Bank, made out to Daniel M'Naghten of 7 Poplar Row, Newington. Is that your current address, Mr. M'Naghten?"

M'Naghten stared straight ahead. Tierney picked up the key.

"If I send an officer to 7 Poplar Row in Newington with this key, will he be able to access your lodging there?"

His question was met with further silence. Tierney handed the key to Silver, with instructions to have Tierney's assistant Sergeant Shaw visit M'Naghten's presumed lodgings.

"I suspect, once we have the opportunity to toss your rooms, we will know a great deal more about you, sir," Tierney said to M'Naghten. "This deposit slip intrigues me. Seven hundred fifty quid is an impressive amount of money, enough to sustain you for several years, if one is frugal. You mentioned your intended target was Sir Robert Peel. Were you paid to assassinate him? Is this blood money?"

M'Naghten sat like a statue. If he heard Inspector Tierney, he did not indicate it.

"At the least," Tierney said, "Possessing such a large amount of money, you should have no problems locating extremely able legal assistance. Believe me, you will need it."

* * *

Newington was a short walk from the Gardener's Lane Station House, across the Thames, and Sergeant George Walter Shaw was able to make the trip in a little over a half hour. He crossed Westminster Bridge and followed the Bridge Road into the center of Newington.

Until the middle of the eighteenth century, most of Newington had been farmland. Because of this, the houses Shaw found on his walk were largely newer, with many modern conveniences. Even so, Newington itself, separated from the bustle of government on the other side of the Thames, had a sleepy, almost tranquil quality. Shaw could see the advantage of living there.

Poplar Row was a short offshoot road from Rockingham, lined with row houses. While the area was not affluent, the houses appeared well-tended. Some children played in the street as Shaw rounded the corner, but scattered when they saw him.

He quickly found number 7 and banged on the door. It was answered within seconds by a middle-aged woman with a napkin tied around her neck. Apparently, Shaw had interrupted the landlady's dinner. She stared at Sergeant Shaw as if the policeman had dropped from a cloud.

"Do you have a tenant named Daniel M'Naghten?" he asked.

"Has he done something?"

"There was a shooting near the Horse Guards on Whitehall this afternoon. M'Naghten is a suspect." He held up the key retrieved from M'Naghten's trousers. "This is to his rooms?"

The landlady peered at it, then took out a pair of pince-nez glasses and looked again. "It appears to be the key I gave him," she said.

"Please lead me there. I must search his belongings."

She led him up a flight of stairs to the second floor, where Shaw used the key to open M'Naghten's flat. The first word that came to him as he surveyed the meager rooms was *austere*.

"Your name?" Shaw asked.

"Sarah Dutton."

"How much does M'Naghten pay for these rooms?" he asked.

"Two shillings six a week," she said.

"Seems a bit much for lodgings of this size. Did he bring his own furniture?" Shaw said, noting a single bed, a wardrobe, two chairs and a table in the main room.

"No. The rooms come furnished."

Shaw crossed to the wardrobe, and opened it. He found several shirts, two pairs of wool trousers, a second pair of shoes, and little else.

"You can identify these as belonging to M'Naghten?"

"Yes," she said. "I've seen him wear these trousers many times."

"How long has he lived here?"

"Mr. M'Naghten has lived here twice. He left for a few months, and then returned asking if his rooms were available."

"When was that?"

"Let me think. He arrived here in late October, I believe. He had been gone since April or May. He showed up again, noting I had put a sign in his window to let out the room. He asked whether his old room was available."

"How was he as a lodger?"

"He was quiet."

"And these clothes were all he brought with him when he returned in October?"

"No. You should have seen him when he returned. His clothes were tattered and darned. He looked like some itinerant day laborer. He disposed of those rags almost immediately, and within days was more properly attired, as was his custom."

"He's a bit of a dandy?" Shaw asked.

"Not at all. He is merely particular about his clothes, which is why I was so surprised to see him so disheveled."

"Do you know where he went for the months he was absent?"

"No. I make it my habit not to inquire too deeply into my lodgers' lives. They have a right to privacy, don't they?"

As she spoke, Shaw checked the pockets of the clothing in the wardrobe. In the trousers, he felt two small objects. He pulled them out and discovered percussion caps, used in single shot pistols to fire off the gunpowder in the breech. These Shaw placed in his own jacket pocket to take back to the Gardener's Lane Station.

"Could you expound on Mr. M'Naghten's habits?" he asked. "You said he was quiet. How do you mean?"

"He is an ideal tenant. I have never seen him drunken or even tipsy. He makes a point of delivering his rent directly to me, and he is never late."

"Did he do some sort of work in London?"

"I don't think so. He slept quite late, often until seven-thirty or eight in the morning. He'd rise, take a light breakfast, clean his shoes—he was almost manic about clean shoes—and left the house. Most evenings, I would not see him again until late. He never mentioned any employment. It was my impression he was retired, or perhaps of independent means."

"Did he ever mention the Prime Minister? Or Mr. Edward Drummond?"

"Not as I can recall. You must remember, he seldom returned to his rooms before ten o'clock at night. What he did in the time between leaving this house and returning I have no idea. In fact, I don't recall having any lengthy conversations with the man."

* * *

The next morning, at the same time Edward Drummond was bled by his surgeons, Daniel M'Naghten was transported to Bow Street Police Magistrates' Court for arraignment.

The legal system in London in 1843 was a curious mix of civil and criminal courts. For most miscreants, the first stop after arrest was a Police Magistrate's Court, where charges were read and decisions regarding binding over for holding until trial or the setting of bonds for release were made. Actual trials took place at the Old Bailey, but arraignments, bond hearings, and civil cases tended to be forwarded to Bow Street for disposition.

The Bow Street complex was impressive. Situated northwest of Covent Garden, the building was a huge four-story brick and stone edifice housing several different administrative courts.

Around ten-thirty, the chambers doors opened, and Chief Magistrate Thomas James Hall made his appearance. As was custom in all of the London courts, Hall wore the traditional long powdered wig and dark robes associated with the bench. He took a moment to situate himself at his elevated seat, and called for M'Naghten to be brought in.

All heads turned as the doors to the holding cells opened and M'Naghten appeared in public for the first time since the shooting. He glanced around the court chambers and took the place at the bar where he was directed by a bailiff. He did not appear overtly disturbed or frightened by his circumstances. In fact, M'Naghten's appearance might most accurately have been described as serene and, as a newspaper reported the next day: *"...as if careless about the awful charge about to be brought against him."*

The Chief Clerk of Administrative Court, a man named Burnaby, asked the accused man to state his name.

In a soft voice, difficult to be heard in the back of the chamber, he said the first words he had spoken since the previous afternoon. "My name is Daniel M'Naghten."

Magistrate Hall cleared his throat. "Mr. M'Naghten, I am about to remand you to custody. This is an administrative hearing, and therefore it is not necessary for you, at the present occasion, to make any observations or contributions unless you see fit. I should remind you that any statements you make, under every circumstance, will be taken down and may be used in evidence against you at a future period. Perhaps you had better reserve what you have to say until the next examination."

The court attendees leaned forward, perhaps expecting some dramatic confession from M'Naghten. Instead, the man stood still in the bar and did not respond.

Burnaby addressed him directly. "Prisoner, do you wish to state anything to the magistrate?"

For an instant, M'Naghten looked confused. Then he slowly shook his head. "I am much obliged to you, sir, but I shall say nothing at present."

"Very well, then," Hall said. "Please return Mr. M'Naghten to the cells."

The bailiff led M'Naghten toward the door to the holding area.

As they reached the waiting room beyond the doors, M'Naghten hesitated. The bailiff tried to pull him along, but the prisoner resisted.

"I was mistaken," he said. "There is a statement I wish to make. Could you take me back into the court chamber?"

"As you wish," the bailiff said, almost mocking. He was not accustomed to having his charges make special requests from him.

He led M'Naghten back into the courtroom and placed him in the dock.

"I am informed you wish to make some observations?" Hall said to M'Naghten.

From the dock, M'Naghten glanced around the courtroom, and then spoke in a clear, even voice, as if he had rehearsed this speech a thousand times.

"The Tories in my native city have compelled me to do this," he said. "They follow me, persecute me wherever I go, and have entirely destroyed my peace of mind. They followed me to France, into Scotland, and all over England. I cannot sleep nor get no rest from them in consequence of the course they pursue towards me. I believe they have driven me into a consumption. I am sure I shall never be the man I was. I used to have good health and strength, but not now. They have accused me of crimes of which I am not guilty. They do everything in their power to harass and persecute me. In fact, they wish to murder me. It can be proved by evidence. That's all I have to say."

A hushed silence fell across the room. The prisoner had accused the Tories—the party represented by Sir Robert Peel—of driving him to kill their leader through persecution and harassment. He was making a political appeal, which at the same time took on a tone of irrationality.

Chief Magistrate Hall cleared his throat to speak, but M'Naghten interrupted him. This time, his voice was even quieter, and perhaps a bit more despondent.

"I am quite a different man," he stated, "to what I was, to what I used to be before the annoyance which, for a time, has been practiced towards me."

From the clerk's desk, Burnaby asked, "Do you wish to say anything more?"

M'Naghten dropped his head, and stared at the floor. "I have nothing more to say," he said.

Moments later he was led away, back to the holding cells.

He never spoke publicly about his crime again.

Chapter Three

When Daniel M'Naghten shot Edward Drummond, Thomas James Hall was in his seventh year as a Magistrate of the Police Courts—his fourth year as the Chief Magistrate of the Bow Street Court. It was at Bow Street where he had gained his greatest recognition, and his greatest access to the halls of power in Great Britain.

The exchange with Daniel M'Naghten troubled him greatly. The early years of the 1840s had been a period of social and political upheaval in England and Scotland—and to a lesser extent in Ireland—due to conflicts between two rival philosophies.

A coalition of conservative factions, the Tories had undergone several iterations since the seventeenth century but had found their feet again in 1834 when Sir Robert Peel published the Tamworth Manifesto outlining the fundamental beliefs of the party, which included granting seats in the House of Commons to large cities that had arisen in the course of the Industrial Revolution, and removing seats from districts with tiny electorates. The primary thrust of the Tamworth Manifesto was the necessity for the Tories to reform in order to survive, and in doing so Peel moved the staunch conservatives inches toward the middle of the political spectrum.

The other side of the political conflict was represented by a much newer and occasionally radical faction, a group calling themselves Chartists. The Chartist movement was a populist uprising, intended to vest power in the hands of the working men of Great Britain. The name came from another manifesto, the People's Charter, written in 1838 by a member of Parliament named William Lovett.

The People's Charter had outlined six major reforms to correct inequality in the governing of the empire. Universal suffrage, a secret ballot, the abolishment of land ownership requirements for serving in the House of Commons, and they demanded service in the House of Commons to be paid, enabling even men of simple means to participate in government. Not surprisingly, they expected adoption of these changes to swell the ranks of liberals in Parliament.

The Tories recognized this as well and were not disposed to lose the majority they had only recently acquired. The response on the part of the political establishment in London had been dramatic and swift. They had rejected the Chartists' demands outright.

The conflict between the Tories and the Chartists had devolved in only five years to a war between rich and poor. The rich, who had enjoyed centuries of power, had undertaken to squash what they saw as the Chartists' rebellion against tradition, a process which they went about with great enthusiasm.

In the year before Daniel M'Naghten shot Edward Drummond in the shadow of the Horse Guards on Whitehall, Chartists had staged several disruptions throughout Britain, but particularly in Scotland.

In May, a petition containing three million signatures of working men across England, Wales, and Scotland was presented to Parliament, requesting a vote on the reforms contained in the People's Charter.

Parliament refused to debate the matter.

Believing their political approach would never bear fruit, the Chartists turned to more extreme—some said more radical—means to make their cases.

The working men who made up the Charter Movement recognized in 1842 that the wheels of industry and agriculture in Great Britain were lubricated with their own sweat and blood, and concluded they could most impact their cause by drying up the system. This led to a series of strikes, compounding an economic depression gripping the country. Most of the strikes were undertaken with the demand for the People's Charter to be enacted before workers would return to their jobs.

Some expressions of resistance by working men during 1842 were more extreme, such as the widespread practice of removing the vent plugs from steam boilers powering the machines that symbolized the Tory devotion to industry over manpower. Collectively, these acts of sabotage were referred to as the Plug Plot.

The pushback against the monarchy and Tory-led governance turned dangerously violent, with three different attempts to assassinate Queen Victoria in 1842 alone. In May, a man named John Francis tried to shoot the Queen while she was riding with Prince Albert near Buckingham Palace on two different occasions, missing both times. He was arrested after his second attempt and eventually sentenced to death, but the Queen commuted his sentence in favor of transporting him to Australia, from whence he never returned to England.

A more bizarre attempt took place in June, when a hunchbacked dwarf named John William Bean got within a few feet of the Queen and pulled the trigger on his pistol, which providentially misfired—not surprising since it was later discovered the gun was filled with paper and tobacco. He attempted to escape, and for a brief period no hunchbacked dwarf in London was safe from police harassment. The holding cells in every borough were packed with small, deformed men, held on suspicion of having made an attempt on the Queen's life.

In short, Great Britain in 1843 was ripe for physical and economic conflict, if not outright rebellion. The foundation of the monarchy hung in the balance

All of which troubled Chief Magistrate Thomas James Hall greatly as he made his way to meet with the Prime Minister. He had slept fitfully the night before, his mind roiling with the implications M'Naghten's declaration might carry. His insomnia might also have been impacted by the missive he received upon returning to his home, suggesting it would be to his advantage to pay his respects at 10 Downing Street the next morning.

While the message was couched in the politest terms, its subtext was unmistakable. Magistrate Hall was being summoned to an audience with arguably the most powerful man in the world at the time, British Prime

Minister Sir Robert Peel.

Hall presented himself at the reception area on the ground floor of 10 Downing promptly at nine o'clock. The letter he received had not indicated a specific time, but Hall—an Anglican deacon—had to attend church later in the morning, so he felt it better to address the invitation as early as possible.

Despite the fact it was a Sunday morning, Hall was not surprised to hear Peel had arrived an hour earlier, and was waiting for Hall's arrival. The indefatigable work habits of the Prime Minister were well-established and widely known. Within minutes, Hall was whisked into the Prime Minister's office.

Robert Peel was an imposing figure. Standing slightly taller than average, he was regarded as a handsome and magnetic gentleman, well-read, and a moving and convincing speaker. Hall found the great man standing at his desk, leafing through several newspapers. Peel wore fashionable clothes, since a man in his position in life and society would be expected to be seen in the latest styles. His jacket had been removed and hung carefully on a hook in one corner of the office, but Peel had kept his tight waistcoat on, for no English gentleman would be caught in public in only a shirt and pants. He wore tight trousers, slung low on his hips and cinched with a leather belt, a fashion which had been made popular by the Royal Consort, Prince Albert. His collar encircled his neck all the way to the base of his jaw, with a loosely gathered linen tie knotted around it and tucked under the waistcoat. His boots were polished to a rare sheen.

His nose was slightly beak-like, situated over a cupid's bow mouth and strong chin. His eyes were penetrating, and seemed to move about the room constantly in search of any small detail he might have missed. His hair, only slightly tinged with gray, was swept from left to right, and fell long on the right side with a decided wave, as was also the fashion of the day, and was combed forward over his temples at the sides. In whole, he presented an impressive if not intimidating figure.

"Hall, I take it," he said, as he strode across the office to meet his visitor. Chief Magistrate Hall handed the Prime Minister his calling card, which Peel immediately placed on his desk. "Have you read the papers this morning?"

"I have not had the opportunity," Hall said.

Peel retreated behind his desk and picked up several pages of newsprint.

"From *The Examiner*," he said: " *'M'Naghten's manner and countenance clearly indicates that he was in a state of insanity. But his extremely healthful appearance of body did not at all bear out his statement regarding his health.'* Would you quite agree?"

"I am not qualified to comment on the man's mental state," Hall said. "As to his general appearance, I can confirm he appeared to be well-formed and in excellent health."

"And his comments regarding the Tories. What do you make of them?"

"Again, it is outside my expertise, but the statement does imply a delusion of some sort."

"What do we know about the man? What information about his background have we uncovered?"

"Not much, I'm sorry to say. The attack was only two days ago. The police are still gathering facts about him. A sergeant named Stephens is gathering information in Glasgow as we speak."

Peel sat, and gestured for Hall to take a seat across from him.

"I am concerned with the statements made by his attacker in your court yesterday. Mr. M'Naghten was most explicit regarding the role of the Tories in this unfortunate affair."

"Part of his delusion, surely."

"Perhaps. Perhaps not. The timing could not be less opportune."

"How do you mean, sir?"

"Three years ago, there were two attempts on Her Majesty. Last year there were three more. My secretary has been wounded, perhaps mortally, by a man who presumed him to be me. I cannot escape the conclusion that some radical elements are willing to go to unacceptable extremes to attain their goals."

"You speak of the Chartists, I suppose."

"The frequency of attacks on the Queen have opened the door to legitimizing violence as a tolerable means to an end. Personal or political, the underlying motivations of assassins seem to justify their acts, at least in their minds. Five potential royal murders in three years, and now an attempt on my own life misdirected toward my secretary. We have entered a violent age."

Hall considered what the Prime Minister had said, and replied, "You could be right. However, I may see a way of reversing the course."

"How so?"

"The majority of your Chartist opponents are most assuredly men of honor, but you cannot discount the possibility that interspersed with their ranks are individuals who are driven by more animal natures. Violence can beget violence, if violent people see it as a common and acceptable solution to their woes."

"Yes. Go on."

"We can start by not making this man M'Naghten a martyr to a political cause. Should Drummond succumb…well, the more we can attribute M'Naghten's murderous act to some defect of reason or disease of the mind, the less our political enemies can use his fate to fuel their outrage."

"I cannot say I completely follow your reasoning. Please forgive me, but my degrees are in classics and mathematics, not in the law. I may oversee the making of laws in the Empire, but I cannot say I always understand their execution."

Hall said, "Suppose we find a penalty for Mr. M'Naghten which keeps him out of sight, and out of mind. For all intents and purposes, he would be removed from society. He would not be a martyr for any cause, and his existence would be forgotten. It seems to me this would be the resolution to the M'Naghten case you would find most satisfactory."

Peel ran his hand across the top of his desk, and it came to rest on the stack of newspapers.

"For the sake of clarification," he said, "it sounds as if you are suggesting, in the interests of maintaining public order and a peaceful resolution to the current political conflict, the court should find M'Naghten insane."

"It is a means to an end."

"And if he is not insane, sir?"

Hall brushed a stray strand of lint from his jacket sleeve. "Does it matter, Sir Robert? Does it really matter?"

Chapter Four

On January twenty-sixth, the morning after Drummond died, a clerk knocked on Sir Robert Peel's office door.

"There is a woman to see you, sir," the clerk said when Peel called him inside.

Seconds later, the clerk escorted Anne Eliza Drummond into the office. She was dressed in black, with a black mourning hat and black gloves. Her face was covered with a dark veil.

"Miss Drummond," Peel said, as he took her hand. "May I express my sincerest condolences." He led her to a chair next to his desk and asked her to sit. He remained standing.

"You are most kind," Anne said, as she lifted the veil and lay it across the top of her hat. "I am profoundly bereft, and quite adrift. My brother was my closest companion."

"Have you made funeral arrangements?

"Yes. It will be a private affair. He will be buried in the churchyard at Charleton Church in Woolwich next Tuesday. Our other brother will officiate."

"Lady Peel and I will be most honored to attend."

"I'm sorry, but I will not allow anyone to attend except for family members. Edward loved his country, and he was devoted to his work as your secretary, but I will not have my brother's funeral transformed into an opportunity for political gain."

Peel was surprised, but made every effort to conceal it. "On so solemn an occasion, our concerns would be entirely with your brother."

"Then what is being done about it?" Anne demanded. "There is a hole in my heart. It will never be filled. I will live the rest of my days at once despondent and furious. Is it my understanding, from reading accounts in the newspapers, the monster who killed Edward believed he was firing at you?"

"I have been told so."

"And what will become of him? How will he be made to suffer on account of his actions?"

Peel crossed to his desk and located several sheets of paper, which he held up. "I have this morning received a message from the Magistrates' Court on Bow Street. Mr. M'Naghten's case will be presented to a grand jury on Monday. If they return an indictment for murder, he will be arraigned on Tuesday, and trial will take place at a later date."

"And if he is found guilty of murder?"

"He will most assuredly be hanged. However, M'Naghten, according to my reports, has not spoken a word since the arraignment for assault on Saturday. It is entirely possible he is as lucid as you or me, and his derangement is an act intended to absolve him of responsibility for his murderous assault on your brother. I am not competent to make such a determination, but you can be assured, every effort will be made to ascertain his true state of mind."

"In that case, I would prefer he be found mad."

The declaration came as a total shock to Peel, who sat at his desk to absorb it. "May I ask why?"

"You think I should wish M'Naghten to suffer the most extreme punishment. And what then? His story will have come to an end. Mine will go on, perhaps for decades. I shall wake each morning, forced to face the world without my brother's companionship and support. My entire adult life has been built around my brother. How am I to face each new day knowing he lies moldering under the ground? Killing Mr. M'Naghten would be too easy, too quick. Should M'Naghten be found insane, he would be transported to Bedlam?"

Bedlam was the common name for the Royal Bethlem Hospital, a former monastery endowed to the city of London during the reign of King Henry VIII as an asylum.

"That is the most probable outcome," Peel said.

"And am I misinformed? Is it a most horrifying place, a place where no comfort and solace might be found?"

"In times past, yes. There have been reforms, but my understanding is, despite more humanitarian approaches to dealing with psychic disorders, one would not wish to spend more than a few moments inside the walls of this terrible place."

"So," Anne said, folding her hands on her lap. "Killing him provides only finality. Were he ripped instantaneously from the face of the earth and flung into oblivion, the world might be a safer place, but his suffering would be ended. My brother would still be dead. I would still awake each morning to face the sunlight with dread and remorse. How much more comforting if I could reassure myself, no matter how bleak and depressing my life might be, his would be infinitely more uncomfortable and terrifying. As I take my tea alone in the afternoon, deprived for the rest of my life of my dear brother, I could find solace in knowing the monster who killed him is suffering, moment to moment, a far worse fate."

"What you are describing sounds less like justice and more like vengeance."

"Vengeance? And might I be blamed? Since Edward's passing, I have thought of little else. I don't want this man to die, Sir Robert. I wish him in permanent torment. I wish him to wake up every morning knowing the rest of his unholy existence will be spent in a hole occupied for centuries by men who lived in their own filth. I want him to go to sleep every night to the screams of men whose demons dance around inside their heads like dervishes. I want every bite of food he takes, until the day he dies, to slide down his throat like sewage, and I want every drink of water that passes his lips to be soured by his own stink of hopelessness."

Peel cleared his throat, shocked at the intensity of the hate Anne Eliza Drummond directed toward her brother's killer.

"I think, perhaps, you should seek the counsel of your parish bishop. Perhaps he can help you to feel more charitably toward Mr. M'Naghten.

If the man is truly a lunatic, I would suggest he is more to be pitied than tormented. Adequate treatment could—"

"Restore him to normalcy? And what then? He returns to Scotland to live out his days in peace and contentment? I could not abide such an outcome. As for a parish bishop, I find little comfort in faith, and I have no desire to place my trust in a God who would take my brother from my house and leave vermin like M'Naghten to enjoy the sunshine and stars and the sweet breath of life. I do not trust such a deity to ensure this monster is doomed to the fires of Hell. I would rest much more comfortably knowing he is burning in those fires day by day here on earth, and I helped fan the flames."

Chapter Five

William Corne Humphreys and George Perceval relaxed in Wilton's Restaurant near St. James, after a huge meal of oysters, beef and root vegetables. As a digestive, Humphreys had ordered port for both of them.

Humphreys was in his middle fifties, a little overweight, but otherwise in good health. He had been a barrister for many years in London, where he had enjoyed some small renown as a critic of the grand jury system.

George Perceval had been in a legal partnership with Humphreys for almost three years. Still in his early thirties, his legal acumen was formidable, but he was an incorrigible gambler. It had been said by some of his colleagues that Perceval would wager on whether the sun would rise the next morning. Three times over the previous ten years, he had managed to arrange loans to pay off staggering gambling debt. Most of his creditors now avoided him.

Humphreys was checking his watch when a man of medium height appeared at his side. The man appeared to be in his late fifties, with a broad face, a receding hairline, and thick mutton-chop whiskers. His clothes were several years out of style, but had been carefully cared for and preserved. There was a look of desperation in his eyes.

"Mr. Humphreys, Mr. Perceval, I hope you will forgive my intrusion on your dinner," the man said, his voice thick with a Scottish brogue. "I humbly request a few minutes of your time. My name is Daniel M'Naghten."

Made unusually amiable by his dinner wine and the port, Humphreys gestured toward an empty seat. Perceval appeared annoyed at the interruption, anticipating he was about to be pressed into some bothersome favor by the interloper.

"M'Naghten," Humphreys said, as the man sat uncomfortably. "Why do I know that name?"

"It's been in all the papers," Perceval said. "The man who shot Sir Robert's secretary. Are you related to him, sir?"

"The man is my son. My…illegitimate son. I have raised him since he was a child, after the death of his mother. I am a woodturner by trade, from Glasgow. I trained him, made him my apprentice, and then turned him out in favor of my legitimate sons. Had I brought him into the business, perhaps none of the events of the past two weeks would have occurred. My son was brought before the Grand Jury at the Old Bailey yesterday. This morning they issued an indictment. He will be tried for murder."

"And quite properly so," Perceval said. "Please forgive me, Mr. M'Naghten, but the facts of the case appear most clear. Your son was apprehended by two different police officers in the act of shooting Mr. Drummond. The newspapers have implied your son sought to murder Sir Robert Peel himself, and shot Mr. Drummond by mistake. In either case, it is a tragedy."

"One which I regret wholeheartedly. Daniel isn't a wicked man. He was never violent. I cannot imagine he would undertake such an act of his own accord. I can only explain it by saying he must have been mad. Mr. Humphreys, would you represent him at trial? He will need an able barrister, someone who is intimately involved with the court system."

"I don't know," Humphreys said. "There is a matter of the cost," Humphreys added. "A high-profile trial of this sort would consume a great deal of time and effort in the preparation. It would be expensive."

"My son has a substantial amount of money on deposit at the Glasgow and Ship Bank," M'Naghten said.

"How much money?" Perceval asked.

"I am told it is well over seven hundred pounds."

"What do you say, Mr. Perceval?" Humphreys asked, his face demonstrating sudden intense interest. "Would it be worth the effort to persuade the court to release some of those funds to finance a defense of young Mr.

M'Naghten?"

Perceval settled back in his chair and folded his hands across his belly.

"It is worth contemplating. Mr. M'Naghten, have you dined yet this evening?"

"No sir, I have not. I have been too troubled by my son's circumstances to take the time."

"Then please, have a bite as our guest while we discuss the possibilities of your son's defense at greater length. In the meantime, Mr. Perceval and I will continue to enjoy this delightful port."

Chapter Six

On February 2, 1843, Daniel M'Naghten was transported from Newgate Prison to the Old Bailey for his official arraignment. When his handlers came to his cell, they found him dressed and ready to go. He didn't speak to them as they assembled the manacles and cuffs around his ankles and wrists. One of the men later described the prisoner as unusually calm and collected, considering his dire legal situation.

Sitting on the bench in court were James Scarlett, who went by the baronial title Lord Chief Abinger, and Justice George Maule, who signaled to the bailiff to call the first case. M'Naghten was led from the holding area to the dock, where he stood for the remainder of the proceedings.

"Is the prisoner represented by Counsel?" Maule asked.

A dapper man in his early forties stood and approached the bench.

"I will represent the gentleman," he said. "My name is William Clarkson, Barrister. I have been asked by the solicitors Humphreys and Perceval to appear on their behalf today and represent the defendant, Mr. M'Naghten."

"I see," Maule said. "Well, let us proceed. Please read the charges."

The Deputy Clerk of Assigns stood and read from the indictment issued two days earlier.

"If it please the Court, this Grand Jury has determined after due deliberation that there is probable cause to believe, on the afternoon of January twentieth, Year of our Lord 1843, Mr. Daniel M'Naghten did willfully approach Mr. Edward Drummond, and did shoot Mr. Drummond in the back, resulting in Mr. Drummond's death. The charge in this case is murder."

Justice Maule turned his attention to M'Naghten, and was surprised to discover the man had fixed his eyes on the bench in a manner not unlike a predator on some helpless prey. Yet, M'Naghten's face appeared serene and composed.

"How say you, prisoner?" the clerk said. "Are you guilty of the charge, or not guilty?"

Some people in the rows of seats closest to the dock later said M'Naghten appeared to sigh. After an uncomfortable silence, he finally responded to the question, in a soft, sweet, low voice, audible from only a few feet away.

"I was driven to desperation by persecution," he said.

William Clarkson rose to address the bench. Lord Abinger held up a hand to stop him, and Clarkson took his seat. Abinger speared the air with a wrinkled, wizened finger in M'Naghten's direction, and admonished him.

"That is not a proper answer," Abinger said. "Will you answer the question? You must say either you are guilty or not guilty."

For the first time since being led into the room, M'Naghten appeared to be uncomfortable, as if he were wrestling with some great conflict inside his head. He shuffled his feet, and his gaze dropped to the floor.

"I am guilty..." he said. "...of *firing*."

The courtroom erupted into chatter. Lord Abinger rapped the gavel on the bench several times to restore order. Then he turned back to M'Naghten.

"By that, do you intend to say you are not guilty of the remainder of the charges, that you intended to murder Mr. Drummond?"

M'Naghten replied, in almost a whisper, "Yes. It is my intent."

Abinger leaned over for a moment to confer with Justice Maule. They appeared to reach a rapid agreement, and Lord Abinger then addressed the court.

"The law regarding murder is most explicit. It requires the accused to act with malice and purposeful intent to deprive another of life. The defendant has denied his intent to kill Edward Drummond, which amounts to a plea of not guilty. The court reporter will record this as the plea of record. Trial will commence at the earliest possible venue."

William Clarkson stood again to address the bench.

"Regarding the trial date, I would wish to be allowed to present an affidavit to the court on behalf of Mr. William Corne Humphreys and Mr. George Perceval."

"Regarding?" Justice Maule asked.

"Messrs. Humphreys and Perceval have been retained to represent Mr. M'Naghten at trial. This request was received only night before last, and Messrs. Humphreys and Perceval have not had adequate time to prepare for a full trial. I would beseech Your Honors to grant a delay in this trial, in order to afford Mr. M'Naghten the ablest representation."

"How long a delay?" Maule said.

"I should imagine a proper defense might be mounted in four weeks."

Maule leaned over to discuss the delay with Lord Abinger, then he sat upright and addressed Mr. Clarkson.

"Four weeks appears not unreasonable given the potentially complex nature of this trial. We will grant your request, and set trial for March third of this year."

"If it please the Court," Clarkson continued. "It has come to our attention the defendant has a large sum of money on deposit at the Glasgow and Ship Bank in Scotland. In a case of this magnitude, putting on a proper defense of Mr. M'Naghten should be an expensive enterprise. Defense Counsel would implore the Court to release Mr. M'Naghten's funds into the hands of Messrs. Humphreys and Perceval, to pay for the necessary examinations, subpoenas, and their own fees."

"Has the Attorney General had ample time to review the information in these affidavits?" Lord Abinger asked.

"We have, Your Honor."

"And do you object to the contents contained therein?"

"We do not."

Abinger said, "The Court does not object either, and we feel bound to comply with the request for delay of trial, and the release of Mr. M'Naghten's bank account to Mssrs. Humphreys and Perceval to mount an adequate defense. We will reconvene at this venue on the third of March to hear testimony and arguments in this case."

Chapter Seven

Queen Victoria still had a great deal to learn about the machinations of governments and the workings of social institutions. She was also pregnant with her second child at age twenty-three. She was almost seven months along, and the tribulations of gestation often left her feeling irritable.

After Westminster burned in 1834, Buckingham Palace was pressed into service as the Royal Residence. Renovations were speedy and—by some reports—shoddy. The chimneys, poorly designed, tended to draft smoke back into the palace through the fireplaces. To prevent asphyxiation, the fires in the hearths had to be extinguished. In the winter, this promoted the sense of the palace as an opulent ice house, its residents shivering straight through until Easter. The place could be dark as well, despite the gas lamps installed prior to Victoria's coronation. Because of the inadequate ventilation in Buckingham, the gas lamps often remained unlighted, for fear the gas might accumulate and take out the entire city block with a massive explosion.

When the twenty-one-year-old Queen Victoria married her adored cousin Prince Albert in 1840, matters at the palace improved. The Royal Consort took it upon himself to make all the needed improvements in their home. By 1843, the building was more comfortable and infinitely more inviting, yet still imperiously intimidating.

Sir Robert Peel was ushered into the White Drawing Room at Buckingham. While there was no longer a constant threat of death by suffocation in the palace, the twenty-foot ceilings presented a challenge to even the hottest of fireplaces, of which the White Drawing Room had three, all ablaze in a valiant attempt to ward off the damp February chill. Two rich velvet settees had been placed on either side of the fireplace. Behind one was an ornate hand-painted pianoforte flanked by a small sitting area with a round table for tea.

Near the fireplace at one end of the White Drawing Room, Queen Victoria sat at a roll top desk. She reviewed newspapers placed before her as Peel entered. The usher announced his presence. The Queen rose, with some difficulty, to face him, and—according to custom—Peel affected a deep bow as a show of respect. She extended her hand, and he took it to help her settle back into her chair.

"How might I serve Your Majesty today?" he asked.

"Have you read the newspapers?" she asked. Her voice, as might be expected from her station and upbringing, was refined and clear. Had the Queen been a singer, she would have been considered a lyric soprano—warm, bright, and loud enough to make a royal impression.

"Not all of them," he replied. "The *Times* and the *Standard*, of course."

"I am concerned about this M'Naghten business," she said, getting directly to the point. "The *Times* made a particularly disturbing observation. *'We fear the events surrounding this tragedy represent the abandonment of traditional values, and signals the potential of England to revisit the melodramatic massacres of Young France, or to imitate the Lynch-Lawlessness of the republic in America,'* " she read aloud. *"'It is our fervent hope the soft-headed will not twist and torture minor incidents of peculiar behavior in the life of the accused and interpret them as symptoms of insanity. We must keep in mind those laws are the most merciful which deter men from the most atrocious crimes.'"*

She put the papers aside. "I am inclined to agree with these statements. Regardless of M'Naghten's mental state, he should be held legally accountable for his act."

"I cannot speak to his mental state. Such determinations are beyond my expertise and training," Peel replied. "A Sergeant Stephens was dispatched to Glasgow the day after Mr. Drummond died, and he visited Mr. M'Naghten's lodgings there. The evidence he returned did not appear to endorse madness on the man's part."

"And can we trust this Sergeant's report?"

"It is my tendency to place my complete trust in all of the officers of the London Police."

"It would be, would it not? After all, they exist entirely because of your initiatives. One does so wish to believe the best of one's children."

"In this case, Your Majesty, I believe his estimate of Mr. M'Naghten's mental status is warranted. Sergeant Stephens discovered a seditious publication in Mr. M'Naghten's dresser drawer. Its contents certainly indicated radical leanings."

"I have heard as much from Home Secretary Graham," the Queen said, lifting a sheet of paper from her desk. "He is preparing a brief which might be used at the time of trial to prove Mr. M'Naghten is a Chartist, and he acted out of political motivations."

"I have misgivings," Peel said. "If Mr. M'Naghten is found guilty of his charges, and is required to forfeit his life as a consequence, his name may become a rallying cry for radicals across the country. If, on the other hand, he is found to be deranged, the law is quite specific as to how he should be treated."

"There have been five separate attempts on my life in only five years. As you are aware, the men who attacked me were all transported, imprisoned, or placed in Bedlam rather than executed. In the interest of leniency, I may have erred and instilled a belief amongst the subjects that they might endeavor to harm me with impunity."

"I would not presume to question Your Majesty's judgment," Peel said.

The Queen said, "I have been disturbed for some time over the conflicts between your Tory coalition and the radical elements of the Chartists and their ilk. I would be most interested in a conclusion to this matter which does not provide solace or support to our political adversaries."

"I understand your position completely, Your Majesty. I am not as certain regarding your directive. Are you stating you would consider it a suitable outcome if Mr. M'Naghten were found guilty, and his attack on my private secretary not be attributed to madness?"

"My only desire is to avoid even more frequent attempts on government officials and heads of state. Speaking frankly, Mr. Prime Minister, I am weary of being the target of assassins. I am also in no small measure enraged by the frequency of attempted regicide in the Empire. I wish it to stop. Mr. M'Naghten must be held accountable for his act."

Chapter Eight

Daniel M'Naghten Senior barely noticed the British Museum as he made his way past it in the direction of 119 Newgate Street. He had been sent an invitation to visit the offices of Humphreys and Perceval on the morning of February fifth. Anticipating news about the defense of his son, he had dressed hurriedly and had set out to meet with the esteemed solicitors.

Humphreys and Perceval maintained their law offices on the second floor of a building also housing a printworks. Fortunately, a separate entrance had been provided for clients. M'Naghten found it quickly. He pulled the bell cord and was greeted by a young man who appeared to be little more than an adolescent. M'Naghten, a simple woodturner from Glasgow, was unfamiliar with the practice of carrying and presenting calling cards, so he simply told the young man his name.

"Yes, of course, Mr. M'Naghten. Messrs. Humphreys and Perceval are expecting you. My name is Simon Daughtrey. I'm a clerk with the firm. Please allow me to escort you upstairs. Mr. Humphreys and Mr. Perceval are in a strategy meeting, but they will conclude it in a few minutes. You will be more comfortable waiting in the conference room."

He led M'Naghten up a narrow flight of stairs to the second floor.

"Excuse me," M'Naghten remarked as they trudged up the steps. "I do not wish to offend, but you appear young to be a law clerk."

"Yes," Simon said. "I am. You are not mistaken."

He did not elaborate, and M'Naghten did not press the issue. Simon led him into the conference room across from the barristers' offices and bade him to take a seat.

"Might I bring you a cup of tea?" Simon asked. "The walk from Bloomsbury must have been exhausting."

"Thank you," M'Naghten said. "But, how did you know I didn't take a carriage?"

"It is obvious. Your shoes were recently cleaned and shined, but there is mud halfway up the soles and lasts. It is February, but you have an outbreak of perspiration on your face, indicating you walked here in something of a hurry. There are other indicators, but I do not wish to bore you. I'll return shortly with tea."

Fifteen minutes later, Simon ushered M'Naghten into Mr. Perceval's office. There, M'Naghten found Perceval and Humphreys sitting on a plush, upholstered divan. Perceval rose and greeted M'Naghten as soon as he was let into the room.

M'Naghten shook hands with the attorneys. "I was just conversing with your young clerk. A remarkable laddie!"

"Yes," Perceval said. "He's a student at the Middle Temple. Very bright."

"I take it there is some word regarding my son's trial?"

"Of a sort," Humphrey's said. "Please, take a seat. First of all, I am happy to report the funds deposited to your son's account at the Glasgow and Ship Bank have been transferred to our firm. We are now quite adequately funded to provide your son with the most competent defense."

"I am gratified to hear it," M'Naghten said.

"There is a concern," Perceval said. "I must tell you, with no small regret, that Mr. Humphreys and I will not be able to represent your son personally."

"I...I don't understand. Is there some problem?"

Humphreys replied, "This is no typical murder. Your son's case is taking on a political overtone. His statement, placing the blame for the killing of Edward Drummond on the shoulders of the Tories in Glasgow, has troubled many highly-placed dignitaries in London. I can tell you, without violating any confidences, Mr. Perceval and I have both received communications from Downing Street inquiring as to our plans for your son's defense."

"You see," Perceval continued, "Your son has stated he was driven to shoot

Mr. Drummond by persecution inflicted on him by Tory sympathizers. His stated target was the Prime Minister. This will not be treated like the cases of the poor wretches who attacked the Queen. Nobody was harmed in those incidents. In the event Daniel is found competent and guilty, he will be hanged."

"My son is not a radical," M'Naghten said. "He is confused."

Perceval said, "And, in fact, confusion is to be the core of our defense. It is our intent to quite conclusively prove your son insane."

"What!" M'Naghten cried out. "But…but that is preposterous!"

"There is no doubt he killed Edward Drummond," Humphreys said. "The attack was witnessed by at least a dozen people, including three constables. Had he pled guilty at arraignment, it is possible he might have been subjected to transportation to Van Diemen's Land as an alternative to hanging. Having pled his innocence of all except firing the pistol, and having placed the blame for the murder on Mr. Drummond's—and the Prime Minister's—party, your son has placed himself in extreme peril. The only explanation which might save his life is deranged thinking."

"In order to prove his insanity," Perceval said, "We need the proper barristers to represent him. We propose to act as coordinators of a defense team which will be much better qualified to plead your son's case. Expense at this point is of no consequence. The monies transferred from your son's account will be more than sufficient to attract the highest-caliber barristers."

"In fact," Humphreys said, "I am pleased to say we have enlisted services of Mr. Alexander Cockburn."

"A most esteemed attorney," Perceval said. "Especially considering his relative youth. His grandfather was Sir James Cockburn, the 8th Baronet and an MP from Linlithgow Burghs."

"He's Scottish!" M'Naghten exclaimed.

"Cambridge man," Humphreys added. "Trinity Hall. He seems to dislike London."

"Quite so," Perceval added. "He focuses his practice in the western districts. I hear he seldom sees clients in London. Even so, we believe he is the right man to lead our defense."

"May I ask why?"

"He is a Queen's Counsel. Her Majesty has conferred upon him a most distinguished title, and therefore he is in her favor. In the happenstance we might be required to negotiate a sentence commutation at a later date, his standing with the Queen could prove beneficial."

"And, besides Mr. Cockburn?"

"We anticipate assembling a team including three additional, extremely experienced lawyers."

"Four barristers. Does it not seem…excessive?"

"This is no time for Scottish frugality. It is an exceedingly complicated case. The law surrounding insanity is not written in stone. The last landmark case was over forty years ago, and legal minds still debate the interpretation of the ruling," Perceval said. "Mr. M'Naghten, you approached us asking for help. We did not seek you out soliciting for our services, and in fact I can assure you we would not have done so. London is a Tory city. It is likely to remain so for the foreseeable future. We live in this city, and maintain professional and personal relationships with many men of high standing. It would not do your son any favors to politicize his defense, and we would derive small benefit from it."

"Except for Daniel's money," the elder M'Naghten snapped.

"Shall we return it?" Perceval asked. "We would, of course, retain a small consultation fee, no more than twenty pounds. Then you would be free to approach other barristers. You came to us for advice. We have provided it, and you can do with it as you please. Your son's best chances to keep his neck straight lie in the hands of the men we've described."

M'Naghten twisted his hands, obviously wrestling with his decision. After a long pause, he said, "I apologize for my outburst. I did not intend to impugn your character, or to suggest your motivations were driven by greed."

"But they are," Humphreys countered. "This is not an avocation for us, sir. We subsist on the income from our practice. Even so, seven hundred pounds divided in various proportions among six people will not constitute a windfall for any of us. I can promise you, any strategies we employ will be intended to serve your son in the best possible way, regardless."

"I understand," M'Naghten said. "Is there some contract for your services I should sign?"

"We will arrange for that," Perceval said. "And I will personally schedule a conference so we can plot out our strategies for your son's defense."

Chapter Nine

Home Secretary James Graham waited for Sir Robert Peel at 10 Downing Street when the Prime Minister returned from Buckingham Palace.

Most of his colleagues in Parliament regarded Graham as a sour man, permanently petulant and haughty. He had been privileged with one of the more remarkable political careers in British history, perhaps made greater by the good fortune of frequently and improbably being in the right place at the right time.

Over the years, his political stance had swung, opportunistically, from the liberal to the conservative end of the spectrum.

Tall and erudite, with a handsome face and fair features—if somewhat balding—Graham, at the age of fifty-one, constantly roamed the halls of Parliament with the look of a man who had recently sucked on a lemon. Those who first met him expected a man in his position to be charming and gregarious. Those same individuals invariably left feeling as if they had encountered a tin god with the temperament of an ogre.

His personal shortcomings notwithstanding, Graham had managed to rise to the office of Home Secretary. For that, he could thank Sir Robert Peel. A moderate with occasional political pendulum swings, Graham had found common philosophical ground with the Prime Minister's reluctance to accept a political label. He knew that Peel found him distasteful, even as he also knew that Peel recognized him as an official who inexplicably enjoyed somewhat greater favor at Buckingham Palace. That was why Peel had named him as Home Secretary.

Graham was impatient to find out what Peel had learned from his audience with the Queen. By now, Peel had to be aware that Graham had already made his feelings about the M'Naghten case known to her. He hoped she had found his positions on the case worthy, and he would be able to proceed with the prosecution on his own terms.

Peevish as always, Graham was impatient to put the M'Naghten business behind him and get back to more important matters of state. He fidgeted in his overstuffed chair in the entrance hall of 10 Downing Street. The checkered tile floor annoyed him. He believed it would benefit from a proper woolen rug, especially in the cold days of February. The lack of real warmth from the fireplace in the entrance hall irked him. The delay in Peel's return vexed him.

The Prime Minister arrived at last, and gestured to Graham to follow him as he handed his greatcoat to the doorman. Without speaking, Graham followed Peel up the winding main staircase past portraits of previous PMs dating back to Robert Walpole, until they reached the Study on the third floor. Compared to the rest of the house, the Study was intimate and personal. Long and narrow, with fireplaces at both ends and glass-fronted bookcases lining the walls between high windows and cushioned window-seats, the Study was one of Peel's favorite places to seek privacy.

Having ordered tea, Peel gestured for Graham to take a seat while he shuffled through some papers on a desk in the corner.

Since entering the house, Peel had not uttered a single word to the Home Secretary. Instead, he appeared to avoid direct interaction. Graham found this disconcerting. It rankled him.

Tea was served, and only after the attendants left the study did Peel—still standing as he drank—address Graham.

"I do not recall directing you to communicate with the Queen regarding the M'Naghten affair," he said. His tone was flat, and Graham could not discern whether Peel intended approval or anger.

"Should I not have?" Graham asked. "The administration of justice in the United Kingdom is my responsibility, is it not?"

"Please, elaborate. Tell me about your interviews with the murderer of my private secretary. I would like to hear what he told you."

"I have made no such interviews. Neither would I."

"Yet, you presume to make pronouncements regarding M'Naghten's mental state. You suggested the man who apparently sought to kill me is feigning madness in order to escape the hangman. You went so far as to link M'Naghten with the Chartists."

"It was a logical conclusion," Graham retorted, the exasperation in his voice unmistakable.

"It was not. The investigation into M'Naghten's motivations is only beginning. We have no understanding of his political affiliations at all. We do not know his associates in London or Glasgow. He has not been examined by alienists or physicians. We have only the scant words he uttered in the dock at the Old Bailey. Drawing conclusions as to his sanity, given the paucity of information we have, muddies the waters and creates confusion. Your deductions are drawn on smoke and supposition. Are you pleased with your position as Home Secretary?"

"I am, sir."

"Then you should recall who was responsible for your office. From this instant forward, all communications to Buckingham Palace regarding Mr. M'Naghten will emanate from my office, and will be transmitted directly by me. Will there be further uncertainty on this issue?"

"None at all, Prime Minister."

"Good. Please brief me on the preparations for M'Naghten's prosecution."

"Yes, sir. As you are aware, the court has set the trial date for March third, almost a month from now. George Perceval and William Corne Humphreys of Newgate Street will conduct the defense. It is my understanding they have secured the services of Alexander Cockburn, the Queen's Counsel."

"Cockburn!"

"Yes. You know the man?"

"My late sister was married to William Cockburn, the 11th Baronet of Langton. Alexander is his nephew. He's slated to inherit the baronetcy upon William's death. Curious he'd wind up defending the man who would have killed me. Of course, he does not care much for me."

"The court released M'Naghten's funds from the Glasgow and Ship Bank to provide for funding."

"Does it not appear to be a large sum for a woodturner from Glasgow? Do we know where he obtained it?"

"My reports indicate he sold his woodturning business almost two years ago. Perhaps the money is the proceeds from the sale. Scotland Yard inspectors are already looking into M'Naghten's associations in Glasgow, and we have received information suggesting he spent some time abroad over the last two years. We did find one interesting fact. It appears, while he was in business in Glasgow, M'Naghten hired as an assistant a young man named Abram Duncan."

"And how is this relevant?"

"Duncan is one of the most prominent Chartist agitators in Glasgow."

"Guilt by association?"

"Smoke, Mr. Prime Minister. It typically suggests fire. What was the Queen's position on the question?"

"She is duly concerned, as might be expected after five attempts on her life. She fears the escalation of violence is a symptom of a deep divide in the country between liberal and conservative factions. It is my impression she would be happiest if the entire M'Naghten affair were simply to vanish."

"Unlikely."

"True. Lacking that, she would prefer that M'Naghten take a trip to Tyburn Tree. Barring sudden amnesia on the part of the entire population of Great Britain, how do we minimize the impact of this murder?"

"I was hoping you would ask. First, I believe the Crown should take the position in prosecution that any suggestions of M'Naghten's insanity are ludicrous. Under no circumstances should we allow the defense to sway the jury into making him another Hadfield."

"How?"

"We will use the same prosecutors who tried the cases of the Queen's attackers. They are the most experienced with this sort of trial. We need to establish a motivation other than political sentiments. The more we can establish M'Naghten acted out of personal rather than political motivations, the more we can isolate him from radical elements and minimize his role as a martyr for the Chartist cause."

"Her Majesty expressed similar opinions," Peel said.

"There is more," Graham said. "M'Naghten might have returned to Scotland last year specifically to be there during the Queen's visit."

"Implying what?"

"Sir, what if you were a secondary target? We should entertain the possibility M'Naghten originally intended to join the growing list of aspirants to regicide and, failing his mission in Scotland, decided to make an attempt on your life instead."

"For what possible reason if not a political one?"

"We do not know, sir. And, at the end of the day, does it matter? We can concoct a reason for his actions out of whole cloth, arrange the facts of the investigation to fit our needs, convince a jury, hang the miscreant, and get on with the business of state without giving the Chartists their scapegoat."

Peel sipped at his tea, which had grown tepid during the conversation, and mulled over his options.

"Make it so," he said at last. "I would advise you to tread lightly. Assign the best inspectors we have available to gather every bit of information on M'Naghten. Keep me posted on all new developments."

"As you wish, Prime Minister."

"And," Peel said, jabbing at the Home Secretary with his index finger, "remember what I told you. No more direct communications with Her Majesty unless you pass them through this office first. Have I made myself clear?"

They were interrupted by a knock at the door. Peel's other private secretary, William Stevenson, stepped inside the office.

"I apologize for the interruption, Prime Minister," he said, "but I have been asked to bid you to return to your home. There appears to be some disturbance with your wife."

Chapter Ten

Julia Floyd Peel, wife of the Prime Minister, was broadly regarded as a rare beauty. The daughter of a renowned general, she was tall for the time, with jet black hair, dark eyes, naturally rosy cheeks, and classic features. Robert and Julia Peel had been married for twenty-three tumultuous years, during which Julia had taken the role of a patient and supportive spouse to her husband's political aspirations. She had stood by his side through his days as a member of Parliament, as the Home Secretary, and two separate terms as Prime Minister.

To the rest of the world, Robert Peel was Prime Minister of Great Britain and the United Kingdom, a master of political gamesmanship and the stalwart epicenter of the empire. To Julia, he was her faithful Bobby, wracked by feelings of insecurity, inadequacy and inferiority. But, at the end of each day, as he fell into bed obsessing he had not done enough, she was there to reassure him.

Robert Peel was the gravitational center of Julia Peel's life.

And, had Daniel M'Naghten gotten his way, her husband would have been untimely ripped from her.

Robert arrived at his home to find Julia in a state of near-panic. She had been crying for most of the afternoon, refusing to allow the household servants access to her room.

"What happened?" he asked Julia's attendant as he approached the closed door to their bedchambers.

"I have no idea," the girl said, weeping. "Lady Julia had a visitor earlier today. Mrs. Marylebone. They appeared to be getting on quite well, when suddenly Her Ladyship became agitated. She retired to her bedchamber. I followed to assist her, but she refused to allow me to enter. I could hear her sobbing and wailing beyond the door. Each time I knocked, she demanded no one was to enter except for you."

"It's all right. Please prepare a pot of tea and bring it up as soon as it is ready. I will see if I can calm Lady Julia."

When the attendant had disappeared around the corner, Peel knocked on the door and turned the knob. "Julia, it's Bobby. I'm coming in."

Hearing no refusal, he opened the door. Julia Peel sat in a chair by the window, dabbing at her face with a lace handkerchief. Her eyes were red and the skin of her face blotched. Her hair had come undone and fell about her shoulders in cascades and wisps.

"I am embarrassed," she said, sniffling. "I fear I have made a scene. Tell me the truth, Bobby. Is it true? Have there been other attempts on your life?"

Peel crossed the room, took her hand, and led her to the bed. She lay her head on her pillow, and he sat at the edge of the mattress next to her.

"Tell me what you have heard," he said.

"Mrs. Marylebone was here. She had dinner the other evening with Lady Theodosia Denman, the wife of the Lord Chief Justice. Lady Theodosia told her the murder of poor Edward was neither the first nor the last attempt to kill you!"

Peel walked over to the window. He looked out over their gardens and sighed quietly. "I had wished to spare you any anxieties over these matters. From my perspective, they seem quite trivial."

"Where your safety is concerned, there is no triviality," Julia said, weeping again. "After nearly a quarter century of marriage, I cannot believe you would hold something this important from me."

Peel walked back to the bed and sat again. He took Julia's hand and stroked it tenderly, as he gazed into her obsidian eyes.

"The kindest and most considerate thing I could have done was keep it from you, my love. If you insist, I will tell you, but I can assure you it is nothing to worry about. About a month ago, in early January, a man arrived from Edinburgh. Sources reported he had arrived with the intent of murdering either the Queen or myself. He was arrested within hours, and is currently in Newgate Prison awaiting trial on attempted treason charges. We are, I assure you, quite safe from him. In all probability, he will be transported to Van Diemen's Land before spring arrives, and will never see England again.

"There was another man, who was behaving strangely, pacing back and forth along Whitehall in a manner similar to the M'Naghten fellow. The police intercepted him because he refused to say to anyone why he was there or what his business was. He turned out to be harmless, an idiot in fact. He was questioned at the Bow Street jail and released to his family, where he is well cared for.

"Finally, police in Glasgow arrested a man three days ago, because he stood in a square and stated openly to anyone who would listen of his intent to travel to London and finish what M'Naghten started. The assizes there found him insane and he was placed in a mental asylum. So, you see, I was never in any real danger. My police department is on top of things."

Julia sat and threw her arms around Peel's neck, holding tight as if to keep him from falling over a steep precipice.

"Is this our lives now?" she implored. "Are we to spend every waking moment in fear some madman might appear out of the shadows? Is this the state of our society?"

"I cannot say," Peel said.

"Then put an end to it. What more is there for you to achieve? You have been Prime Minister twice. There is no higher office for you. We are no longer in the bloom of youth. Would it be so hard for you to step down? You are a baronet, my love. We could live the rest of our lives in comfort in the countryside at Drayton Manor. Let some younger man carry the burdens of state."

"I wish it were that easy," he said wistfully. "The time is not right. There are still reforms to pass before I can go peacefully. The Factories Bill, the Chartists conflict, and many more. To abandon my office now would be irresponsible, and could undo everything I still wish to accomplish."

"And what of this M'Naghten man?" she said. "What will become of him?"

"I wish I could tell you, but I truly don't know."

"When I think what could have happened."

"Darling, I told the Queen his afternoon that I have walked Whitehall without police escort every day since the shooting. I have not experienced the first moment of apprehension in doing so. This M'Naghten business was an aberration."

"As were the five attempts on the Queen's life?" she said, suddenly angry.

"As a matter of fact, yes. We have discussed this before. None of those weak-minded would-be assassins were capable of inflicting the slightest harm on Her Majesty. Shall I tell you a secret?"

"If you wish."

"You can't repeat it to anyone."

"After so many years, you doubt my trustworthiness?"

"The next time we see Her Majesty in public, take a close look at her parasol."

"The emerald green silk one she favors? Why should I?"

"It is a singular parasol. Prince Albert himself designed it, and had it constructed by the armorers in the Tower. It looks like an ordinary brolly, but hidden between layers of silk are several thicknesses of finely woven chain mail. I have handled the item myself, and it is surprisingly heavy, especially for a woman as diminutive as the Queen. So, let's say she and Prince Albert are taking a carriage ride through London, and an armed assailant emerges from an alleyway intent on doing her some mischief. Why, all the Queen needs do is open her sunshade, hold it in front of her, and no ordinary pistol ball can penetrate it."

As he described it, he acted out the scene for Julia, pantomiming opening an umbrella and hiding behind it. For the first time since he had entered the room, she smiled. Then her face grew dark again.

"And what of you, husband? Are you wearing chain mail linens under your suit? Can you stop a pistol ball without harm to yourself?"

He caressed her hand and kissed her cheek. "I have been at this for over twenty years. This M'Naghten business is no more than a loose cobblestone which has temporarily caused us to stumble. But, if it will put your mind at rest, at the next elections, I will not stand for Prime Minister. Please allow me to complete this work on the Factories Bill, and a couple of other matters of great importance to the empire, and then I will step down. We shall retire to Drayton Manor, and live the rest of our days in peace and solitude. Would that suit you, my darling?"

She collapsed into his arms and placed her head against his chest.

"Oh, yes. That would be delightful."

* * *

"I am bedeviled by the women who surround me!" Peel declared the next morning as he breakfasted with Sir Frederick Pollock, the Queen's Attorney General. "Poor Edward's sister demands I do everything possible to declare M'Naghten insane, so she can live the rest of her days enjoying her strange vengeance against him as he languishes in Bedlam. The Queen demands I make every effort to find him sane and competent, so he can be hanged in private as quickly as possible and not become a lightning rod for the radical Chartists. My wife wants me to wash my hands of the matter entirely. I wish I had never heard the name Daniel M'Naghten."

"You damned well nearly didn't," Pollock said, as he speared as slice of link sausage. He was a dour-looking man with a long, sad face, a prominent chin, and large, wide-set eyes. He had been the Attorney General in both of Peel's terms as Prime Minister. "After all, had M'Naghten managed to succeed in his mission, you likely would have died on Whitehall wondering what the devil had happened. What did happen, anyway? How did M'Naghten take Drummond for you? You are of similar size, of course, but your faces are nothing alike."

"A case of mistaken identity, pure and simple. It seems M'Naghten planned his act for some time, loitering about Whitehall to determine the times of my coming and going. At one point, as Drummond and I strolled toward Charing Cross, according to the police investigation, he pointed us out to an officer and asked whether he was actually seeing the Prime Minister. But, M'Naghten pointed to Drummond instead of me. M'Naghten made an incorrect assumption, and in the course of it condemned Mr. Drummond."

"It's sad," Pollock said. "You say he took great pains to identify his victim, over the course of some days. Does that not imply premeditation and purpose?"

"I suppose it does," Peel said absently, as he slathered a roll with butter and preserves.

"The act of planning and premeditation suggests M'Naghten had all his faculties about him. He went about his business of assassination methodically, developing a plan, properly, if incorrectly, identifying his target and arming himself for the assault. What greater indicator for sanity could you ask? In any case, you already have the answer to your conundrum. The Queen demands M'Naghten pay the ultimate price for this murder. What Drummond's sister or your wife wish are inconsequential. You have a duty to fulfill Her Majesty's wishes."

"And what a convoluted path that will be," Peel said. "Somehow, we are to prove M'Naghten was not mad, and at the same time divorce his act from any political motivation, when he himself has already blamed the Tories for the murder. Fortunately, I will not be required to navigate the labyrinth. That, I'm happy to say, falls on your shoulders."

"About that..." Pollock said.

"Yes?"

"You recall Feargus O'Connor and fifty-eight other Chartists were arraigned in Lancashire for the uprisings last August? It seems their trial is scheduled for March first there. I anticipate it will continue for at least a week. Perhaps longer."

"Are you saying you cannot prosecute M'Naghten?"

"My office will do so, but my priorities lie elsewhere. Making Mr. M'Naghten climb the steps of the gibbet seems an appropriate response to his crime, but putting an entire band of Chartist rabble-rousers behind bars will have much more profound impact on the movement. If we can successfully convict O'Connor and his horde of malcontents, it may negate any support their movement might receive from a M'Naghten conviction. Logically, the O'Connor case carries the greater weight."

"Who will prosecute M'Naghten?"

"The Solicitor General."

"Follett? He's an able barrister, but as an orator, he's…well, boring."

"Notwithstanding, the true chore in this case is to convince the jury of M'Naghten's sanity. The rest follows as a logical progression. Motive is relatively unimportant in this case. Too many people witnessed the shooting, so the facts are indisputable. We may be able to sidestep the Chartist business entirely and hang the wretch. Wouldn't that put Her Majesty in a jolly old mood!"

Peel took a sip of his tea and leaned back in his chair.

"We do wish to keep the Queen happy," he said.

Chapter Eleven

William Corne Humphreys surveyed the men assembled around a conference table in the offices at 119 Newgate Street which he shared with George Perceval. If some disaster were to strike the building—say, an explosion or a fire—Great Britain might be deprived of almost half of its most brilliant legal practitioners.

It was an amazing team he and Perceval had brought together, led by Alexander Cockburn. Considered a rogue and an iconoclast by his legal brethren, Cockburn nonetheless was known to be an astute legal scholar, and something of a forensic scientist. Small and slight, but with a head seemingly too large for his body, Cockburn was also known as a ladies' man. Despite his legal acumen and undoubted academic achievements, his critics still regarded him as far too possessed with a desire for frivolity and corporal pleasure.

Cockburn reveled in his own notoriety. Perhaps to reinforce his image as an firebrand, he had made it his habit to avoid practice in London. He did not need the money that practice in a major city might afford, since he enjoyed an enviable family fortune and was expected to acquire the title of Twelfth Baronet of Langston on the death of his uncle William. So, instead, he focused his practice in the western regions of England and in Wales, where he had nurtured his deserved reputation as an expert litigator.

Despite his reputation as a reprobate, he had managed to curry the favor of Buckingham Palace, and two years earlier had been made a Queen's Counsel. It was largely for this recognition that Humphreys and Perceval had determined Cockburn should be the lead counsel in Daniel M'Naghten's defense.

An Irishman from County Galway, a second colleague, Henry Bodkin, had acquired an enviable reputation as a litigator through his practice in the courts of the Home Circuit, as well as practice in the Central Courts at the Old Bailey. Having won a seat in Parliament by the barest of margins, he was the House of Commons representative of Rochester, Kent, for the Conservatives. Bodkin also had acted as a defense attorney for Edward Oxford on charges of attacking the Queen in 1840.

Taller than Cockburn, Bodkin was balding and tended toward the comfortably rotund. As age crept up on him, a slightly wandering right eye had become more pronounced, and as a result Bodkin had developed the conceit of addressing most of his friends at an angle, favoring his left side. Bodkin presented as the most stable and reliable among his colleagues. His devotion to the poor and his generous nature were well-known. He was as proper as Mr. Cockburn was degenerate.

A third man, William Clarkson, had represented M'Naghten at his arraignment, and had arranged for M'Naghten's funds to be disbursed to fund his defense. His greatest contribution, like Bodkin's, was his experience. He had assisted in the defense of John Francis the year before, on charges of attempting to assassinate Queen Victoria and Prince Albert. As an associate with Humphreys and Perceval, and with little prospect of eventually making partner, he led a frugal but comfortable life. Easily the tallest of the men at the table, he was slender and fragile-looking, with a head of dark hair he tended to keep short for practicality's sake.

The fourth man was John Monteith, an attorney from Glasgow, where he was respected as an able barrister and litigator. Short and as solidly built as a bare knuckles prizefighter, Monteith was known more for his scholarship than for bombast in court. His command of legal precedent was unrivalled, as it was rumored he had the most amazing capacity to instantly digest almost any volume of material presented to him, and to recall it verbatim weeks, months, or even years later. His primary role, while he would examine selected witnesses, was to feed ready information to the other barristers to bolster their arguments before the bench.

It was likely there were no four individuals in the empire better suited to mount a defense of Daniel M'Naghten. Certainly, no more formidable legal team had been assembled in the memories of anyone in the room.

Perceval opened the discussion. "I would like to express my gratitude to all of you for making time to meet with us today. Especially you, Mr. Monteith. I know you were in Glasgow when you received my message, and I appreciate you making the journey to London. As I wrote to each of you, it would appear our best hope to save our client from the gallows is to prove he was insane at the time he assaulted Mr. Drummond. I presume we are all in agreement on this point."

All of the heads around the table nodded.

Perceval continued. "I would like to ask Mr. Monteith to draw on his remarkable stores of information and expound on the current state of the insanity plea."

Monteith cleared his throat, and launched in. His accent was thicker than the muck at the bottom of the Thames, but the assembled crew discovered they were able to follow his main points.

"Thank you, Mr. Perceval. Forty years ago, James Hadfield conspired to assassinate King George III. His esteemed barrister, Mr. Erskine, maintained that injuries Hadfield had acquired in battle, while not incapacitating him completely, did leave him in a sufficient state of complete derangement to justify acquittal on grounds of insanity. As you may know, Hadfield was confined to Bedlam for both his and the community's safety."

Humphreys said, "Mr. M'Naghten does not appear to be laboring under such a complete delusion. He seems to have acted with definite premeditation, carrying out a murder he planned with some precision. I am concerned as to whether we can convince the court he was insane under that standard."

"I have anticipated that," Monteith said. "The Hadfield decision was written in 1800. Doctor Pinel had only begun to reform the practices in the Salpêtrière and La Bicetre asylums in Paris eight years earlier, and his grand experiment was still underway by the turn of the century. We know a great deal more about diseases of the mind now than we did then. The prosecution intends to demonstrate Mr. M'Naghten is sane, because he does not meet the standard *under Hadfield*. Our task, daunting as it might be, is to prove the court erred in the Hadfield decision four decades ago, and that *partial* insanity may serve to excuse an accused man of responsibility for any crime, up to and including murder."

Monteith's words echoed briefly, and then the room was silent as each attorney weighed exactly what the Scot was implying.

"You are suggesting this case should set a new precedent," Perceval said at last. "A new standard for insanity."

"I am," Monteith said with a sly smile. He placed both hands on the tabletop and scanned the faces of the other men in the room. "Under the current circumstances, I see no other way to keep our client from hanging."

"May I ask," Clarkson said, "precisely how do you propose we accomplish this extraordinary feat?"

Monteith pulled a sheath of papers from the inside pocket of his jacket, and distributed them around the table.

"I have prepared a list of physicians acquainted with the most modern practices in the diagnosis and treatment of diseases of the mind. Since the Hadfield decision, there has been a sea change in the understanding of the extent to which even partial insanity might cloud a man's reason to the extent he might not completely comprehend the nature of his acts. In our case, I believe our most effective option would be to demonstrate conclusively that, at the time he fired on Edward Drummond, Mr. M'Naghten was possessed of a delusion of persecution so strong, he truly believed he was engaging in an act of self-defense."

"But only if we can convince the court Hale was wrong, and partial insanity renders a man as incapable of reason as full insanity," Bodkin added.

"Yes," Monteith said, "In order to save M'Naghten's hide, we need merely rewrite four hundred years of English Common Law."

Perceval stood and crossed the room to an opened japanned liquor cabinet and reached for a decanter. "Don't know about you fellows," he said, "but I could use a drink."

"Might as well bring the entire decanter, and snifters all around," Cockburn suggested.

After they had all served themselves, Cockburn said, "We are like Hercules facing the Augean stables. What you advocate, Mr. Monteith, is no mean task. I endorse your proposal to recruit the services of your list of physicians, but none of them have interviewed or examined Mr. M'Naghten. Your esteemed physicians might diagnose him as delusional today, but they can have no idea of the degree of his reason on January twentieth."

Perceval said, "We need to know more about M'Naghten than we do today. We need to find out everything we can about the man *before* he returned to London to commit his crime. If we can establish a pattern of mental deterioration over the months leading up to the attack, we may be able to state to the court with assurance that his stability on the day of the attack diminished his capacity to understand the nature of his act enough to demonstrate insanity."

"The Metropolitan Police are already interviewing his associates in Glasgow, and some of the people he knew here in London," Bodkin said.

"And, if M'Naghten's statements are to be believed, his actual target was Sir Robert Peel, Perceval countered. "Scotland Yard owes its existence to the Prime Minister, and its loyalty to him is unquestioned. Given the deceased was his private secretary, I would bet the Prime Minister has every intention of seeing M'Naghten go to the gibbet."

"You would bet on whether the sky is blue today," Humphreys said, gesturing to the brilliant sunlight streaming through the conference room window.

"Nonetheless," Perceval continued, smiling at the truth in Humphreys' accusation, "if we are to acquire useful information we can trust, we should conduct our own interviews in London and Glasgow."

Cockburn said. "As it happens, I know a man perfect for the job. He's a former Metropolitan Police officer. Before that, he was a Bow Street Runner."

"What is the man's name?" Humphreys asked.

"Vicar Brekonridge."

"A clergyman?" Clarkson asked.

"Far from it," Cockburn replied, a sly smile on his face. "You could say Mr. Brekonridge and grace are not on speaking terms."

"I know that name," Monteith interjected. "I remember reading about his exploits in the *Times*. Is he not the officer who assaulted Sir Martin Barbury's son three or four years ago?"

Cockburn answered, "In the version I heard, he found young Barbury strangling a prostitute in the East End and was protecting her. A review of Mr. Brekonridge's history indicates he was frequently disciplined by his superiors due to his predilection to resolve differences using violence. He was particularly likely to engage in aggressive enforcement when the honor of women was at stake."

"I fail to see how such a man might be of assistance in our circumstances," Perceval said.

"When he isn't throttling nobility, he is known to be a thorough investigator. During his days with the Bow Street Runners, he was reputed to have one of the highest apprehension rates among his peers. He is regarded as bright, perceptive and observant. More importantly, he is almost certainly available. I should note he is Scottish and well-known to support Chartist causes, which may be of some benefit should it turn out, as I suspect, that many of M'Naghten's acquaintances share those sympathies. I suspect the real reason he was cashiered at Scotland Yard was more political than anything else. The police tend to be a rather conservative lot. Mr. Brekonridge's social sensitivities likely made him supremely unpopular. Even so, if it were not for his unfortunate accident, I believe he might still be wearing a uniform."

"What unfortunate accident?" Bodkin asked.

"A fire. If you should meet the gentleman, you will see what I mean. With your permission, I would be happy to approach Mr. Brekonridge and inquire as to whether he might assist us in building a case to save Daniel M'Naghten."

"You say he is almost certainly available. What did you mean by that?" Monteith asked. "In what sort of employment is your Mr. Brekonridge presently engaged?"

"Ah," Cockburn said. "Well, you see, Vicar Brekonridge is a thief-taker."

Chapter Twelve

Vicar Brekonridge pulled his thick wool greatcoat closer around him as he strode in two inches of snow past St. Alphege's Church near the Cripplegate in Islington. He was headed toward the Whitecross Street Market on a gloomy Sunday morning. The Market was only held on Sundays, when vendors erected booths and tents to sell wares ranging from food, to beer and ale, to miscellaneous sundries including baskets, scarves, refurbished boots, woolen stockings, root vegetables in the winter and fresh produce in the summer, poultry, mutton, discarded furniture, and linens from the beds of the recently deceased.

Despite his name—a smirking conceit by his parents—Vicar Brekonridge was no clergyman. Brekonridge was looking for something other than grace as he turned onto Whitecross Street from Beech and plunged immediately into a sea of barkers and fishmongers. He bought two parcels of hot roasted chestnuts from a vendor for a penny, and immediately stuffed them into each of his greatcoat pockets to keep his hands warm. A block further down Whitecross, he purchased a dozen oysters wrapped in oiled parchment paper and perched himself on a wall in front of a decrepit church to eat them.

Brekonridge would have been a striking figure even if he hadn't stood almost a head above the men who surrounded him wherever he went. In public, he favored a conventional—if shopworn—beaver felt John Bull hat that added another half foot to his stature.

His hair, still remarkably jet black as he neared fifty, was pulled into a queue, but thick strands of it evaded the ribbon he used to tie it back and fell sloppily over his ears. His watery blue eyes seemed to miss nothing around him. Even as he pried open and slurped the briny oysters, his gaze darted back and forth, scanning the crowd.

His most notable feature was one he dearly wished he could hide. His left profile, dominated by a long, pointed nose and strong chin, was attractive enough. At times in his life he had even been regarded as ruggedly handsome. When he turned, the right side of his face revealed a congealed mass of bubbled scars extending from what remained of his ear down across his jaw line, up into the hair, and down the back of his head into his neck. The stray locks of hair hid some of the deformity, but not enough for him to look at himself in the mirror with comfort.

He had earned his scars nobly, rescuing three small children in an apartment fire in which he had also lost all his earthly possessions. During the winter, he tried to conceal them by wrapping his neck and lower face in a long, moth-eaten wool scarf. In the summer, there was no way to adequately hide the disfigurement, so he simply endured the looks on people's faces when he walked abroad.

He finished the oysters, dumped the shells into a growing pile behind the vendor's tent, and went in search of ale. He pulled out his white porcelain pipe filled with hemp and lighted it with one of Ashford's new phosphorous friction matches. The acrid smoke wafted around his head. Within seconds he relaxed and became completely focused on the crowd around him.

On any Sunday, Whitecross Market might contain as many as fifteen hundred vendors, and three times as many shoppers who loaded up on staples and non-perishable foods for the coming week, or simply strolled from booth to tent inspecting the newest wares. Children played in the snowdrifts piled up along the road and slid precariously on patches of blackened ice they found on the rare hard surface.

Brekonridge stopped at an ale booth and ordered a pewter flagon, which he drank standing there. He placed the container back on the wooden plank that served as a bar, wiped his mouth with his scarf, and resumed his search for the man who had brought him out on such a wretchedly cold day.

As he strode the length of Whitecross Street, cries from salespeople and artisans rang in his ears.

"Old for some but new for you! As little as tuppence for fine linens!"

"Roast chestnuts hot and sweet, a penny a score!"

"Fresh guinea fowl! Mutton! Joints of beef! Buy, buy—bu-u-uy!"

"Lovely bonnets, only fourpence! Two for six!"

"Bootlaces! Three pair for a ha'penny! Bootlaces!"

"Fresh and succulent whelks! None finer in all of London! Penny a lot!"

Men, hunched at the back after years of laborious hauling, struggled past shoving barrows piled high with shellfish, trying to urge the wooden wheels through the snow. A man walked by with two muslin sacks over each shoulder, one in front and one in back, loaded with loaves of bread baked fresh that morning. A shivering woman sat on a sun-bleached milk box in front of four baskets filled with dried flowers. The din of commerce went on block after block as vendors desperately endeavored to make enough money to survive until the next Sunday market.

Brekonridge's pipe had gone cold. He tamped the cinders into a snowbank and stuffed it into his inner jacket pocket. He knew the face of the man he sought, and he continued to scan the street, every darkened booth, every alleyway, and every doorway for the man's features. He was able to screen out the ruckus of the crowd and focus only on locating his quarry.

Vicar Brekonridge was a thief-taker.

It could be a surprisingly lucrative line of work, with bounties as high as a hundred pounds for some miscreants, in an age when the average working man was fortunate to see three hundred pounds in an entire year. He would make nowhere near that sum with the man he was pursuing in Cripplegate on this particular Sunday in February, but Brekonridge had amassed an enviably tidy bank account ten or twelve pounds at a time.

The newspapers were dominated by the assassination of Prime Minister Robert Peel's private secretary Edward Drummond. Assuming the heightened police activity around Buckingham, Downing Street, and the Admiralty would result in a privation of constables elsewhere in the city, and therefore an increased number of warrants for arrest, Brekonridge had ventured to the Bow Street Assizes where such warrants were posted.

He found the usual collection of sneak-thieves, cutpurses, highwaymen, cheats, and swindlers, along with a smattering of anarchists, agitators, and everyday ne'er-do-wells.

One warrant in particular caught his eye, not so much because of the bounty, but because he knew the man.

January 29th, 1843. A warrant for arrest has been issued for MATTHEW MARK LUKE JOHN MAYHEW, late of 46 Bishopsgates-street. Five feet, two or three inches in height. Pockmarked complexion, thinning hair, sometimes wears a beard. Absconded, charged on a warrant with stealing monies. Well-known to the London Police as a pickpocket and embezzler. Five pounds paid directly to the man who delivers him to the Bow Street Magistrate's Court, and a bonus of ten pounds in gratitude from the theft victim.

Mayhew had been hired by a tavern owner to keep the floors and tables clean and the cuspidors emptied in return for three shillings a week, a cot in the back room of the tavern, and free access to sandwiches and pottage put out for the customers. Mayhew had repaid the barkeep's generosity by raiding a moneybox after the tavern closed and vanishing into the night.

Fifteen pounds was far from the largest reward Brekonridge had chased in his highly successful career as a private policeman, but it would keep coal in his firebox and food in his belly for weeks.

He had apprehended Mayhew on two other occasions and had spoken about him in passing with another acquaintance only a day or so before. That acquaintance, Jericho Pratt, most likely knew of Mayhew's whereabouts.

Jericho Pratt was a pure-finder. He sought his fortune in the world by roaming the streets of London with a barrow, one hand clad in a heavy leather glove, collecting dog waste to sell to tanners who used the chemicals in the feces to produce leather.

If Jericho Pratt had an idea where to find Mayhew, Brekonridge figured he could complete the job in a few hours and have Mayhew in irons before dinner. He claimed the warrant and set out from Bow Street to begin his hunt.

Brekonridge marveled at how much of his business was conducted in the East End, with its industrial population, dense greasy fogs, and horrid odors. His first stop was a tanner's shop on Morocco Street in Bermonsey. Pratt was a freelance pure-finder, so it was likely every tanner in the district knew him. The shop proprietor was a man named Bouton. He greeted Brekonridge as the thief-taker ducked through the short doorway of the tannery office.

"I'm looking for Jericho Pratt," Brekonridge announced.

"Haven't seen him in days," Bouton said. "Word has it he's in Newgate Prison. Can't tell you why."

* * *

The last time Brekonridge had been on the Newgate Prison grounds was on a brutally hot July day in 1840, when he had joined an estimated forty thousand other Londoners to witness the widely-publicized hanging of Francois Courvoisier for the murder of Lord William Russell. The execution was of no small interest to Brekonridge, whose role in the investigation of the unfortunate Courvoisier had been swept under the rug by the Home Office. Among the forty thousand in the sweltering throng, only a few knew the entire story behind the Russell murder. Brekonridge was one of them.

Adjoining the Old Bailey Courthouse, Newgate was an imposing place, and in fact had been designed for the purpose of frightening would-be criminals away from their intended acts. For centuries, dating back almost to the reign of King Henry II, the building had been regarded as a place of horror and torture, from the dungeons in which men had been shackled to walls for years to the outdoor public space for executions, the *architecture terrible* design was intended to drive thoughts of malfeasance from the minds of potential lawbreakers.

Not everyone heeded the warnings. The prison was typically full to overflowing, its inmates divided into two populations. The first—the

Commoners—were street thieves and blackmailers and common ruffians who could not afford better accommodations, and likely never would. They tended to be housed in groups, chained to walls and standpipes to prevent them from attacking one another, living in communal filth and degradation, eating from a common trough filled with tavern slop each evening.

The other population was housed in the State wing. These were offenders who had the means to afford slightly more comfortable quarters—the term "comfortable" in this case was more relative to the Commons area than to everyday life. Even so, State inmates enjoyed the dubious luxury of being jailed one to a cell.

Brekonridge stepped up to the massive front door and lifted a large black iron knocker. He had been there enough to know one knock was sufficient to draw the attention of the gatekeeper, who arrived quickly and swung the door open. Brekonridge presented the Bow Street warrant.

"My name is Vicar Brekonridge. I am attempting to apprehend a thief, and I believe one of your inmates, a man named Jericho Pratt, can point me in his direction."

The gatekeeper ushered him in and closed the outer door with a dramatic crash. Brekonridge, no stranger to violence, and generally resistant to fear, could not stifle a shudder. He comforted himself with the knowledge that—unlike the unfortunate Mr. Pratt—he could leave any time he wished.

The gatekeeper fished through his ring of keys and opened another door at the opposite end of the Keeper's House, which led into an atrium. As the turnkey escorted Brekonridge beyond heavy iron doors into the ward where the prisoners were held, the thief-taker's nose wrinkled at a sudden sour smell. It was a combination of damp earth, mold, sweat, human waste, and a brief whisper of decomposition, an odor Brekonridge knew only too well from his wartime days.

To Brekonridge's surprise, Jericho Pratt's cell was in the relatively comfortable State wing, near the end of a long, second-level catwalk, accessed by stairs from a central hallway. The door to the cell was constructed of heavy cast-iron plates and straps, brazed and fastened with massive iron bolts.

The room was twice as long as it was wide, the walls and arched ceiling built of kiln-fired bricks and heavy mortar, many inches thick. An iron bed covered with a thin blanket was bolted to the brick and concrete floor. A small table with a single chair had been provided, where Pratt could eat his meals and write any letters he might wish to send. At the end of the cell, some eight feet above the ground, was a glass window with a mildly arched top, bars and steel mesh attached to the inside to prevent prisoners from getting to the glass. At midday, sunlight streamed into the cell. There were no candles or gaslights. Brekonridge could only imagine how dark the place must become after sundown. A covered bucket in the corner served as Pratt's sanitary facilities.

Pratt looked up as Brekonridge filled the doorway. An expression of alarm crossed his face. He was a slight man, rail-thin and pale. The top of his head was entirely bald, ringed by a long fringe of colorless, wispy hair. The turnkey reappeared with a second chair.

"I wish to be alone with the prisoner," Brekonridge said. "You may close the door and leave us here."

"I don't know, sir," the turnkey said. "This one is a murderer, you know."

"Look at me. Look at him. I will be perfectly safe. In any case my interview with the man will be fruitless if he believes he is being spied upon."

"It's your neck, sir," the man said. "I do feel obligated to report this to the Superintendent."

"Yes. Please do. I would not wish you to be remiss in your duties."

The turnkey retreated, locking the door behind him.

"Jericho," Brekonridge said, shaking his head. "Who did you kill?"

"I didn't kill anyone, Mr. Brekonridge. This is all a horrible mistake. Nobody has told me anything. All I know is some police officers barged into my rooms two nights ago and dragged me off. I haven't seen another person since they slammed that door. When you walked in, I thought maybe you had some news."

"I'm sorry. I don't know anything. How did you arrange to be housed in the State wing?"

"It's a long story, and in truth I can't tell you the answer. I have means.

I was born into a good family. I'm an educated man, despite my lowbrow employment. Times are difficult, and my affection for wine and ale has quite undone me, I'm afraid. Were it not for them, I might still be a gentleman. One takes the work presented. Someone must have told the authorities that I had resources the prison could attach to pay for my accommodations." He swept his hand in the air to indicate his quarters. "Are you here investigating my case?"

"I'm on a different matter. A few days ago, we spoke of Matt Mayhew. I'm looking for him."

"I can't help you. As I mentioned the other day, I haven't seen him in weeks. There is a man, though. He is closer to Mayhew than I. I'm told he's come to visit me several times since I was incarcerated, but they won't allow him back."

"His name?"

"Not so fast. I'm innocent, I tell you. I have no idea whom the authorities think I've murdered, but I swear to you I haven't harmed anyone. If I tell you the man's name, you must agree to help me. I have some money. Not a lot, but you will not go uncompensated for your endeavors on my behalf."

"Agreed," Brekonridge said, happy for the opportunity to add to his bounty for apprehending Mayhew.

"His name is Albert Camp. He's another pure-finder, but he grew up with Mayhew. If anyone can point you toward Mayhew, it's Camp. Don't forget me, though. You promised to help me."

"And my promise will be kept. As soon as I catch Mayhew, I'll return."

"Bless you, Mr. Brekonridge. You may have the face of a devil, but your heart is angelically pure."

"Don't count so much on my heart. I have to eat like everyone else."

Chapter Thirteen

Brekonridge stopped on the steps of Newgate prison to wrap his face—and his egregious scars—with his woolen scarf. He began to walk toward Newington, and then stopped when a motion in his peripheral vision caught his attention. It could have been a shadow, but he was certain he had seen a man duck into an alleyway ahead of him, on the other side of the street.

He sat on a bench and pulled the ceramic pipe from his jacket. He had already packed it with a pinch of the new East Indian hemp he had acquired from his chemist, so he lighted it and began to puff idly, staring seemingly off into space.

He saw the movement again, at the corner of his eye. He tilted his head back, as if trying to catch as many of the sun's meager February rays as possible, but in doing so he also turned his head so that he could get a better view of the alley.

A small, gnarled man emerged from the space and walked briskly down Newgate, affecting a slight limp. As Brekonridge watched, the man stopped at the Cross and Key Public House and stepped inside.

Brekonridge tamped out the pipe and walked back to the prison. A few seconds after he rapped at the door again, the gatekeeper opened and peered out at him.

"I am sorry to disturb you again. A moment of your time? According to Jericho Pratt, a man has visited him several times since Pratt was jailed. Do you recall the man's physical features?"

"I should say so."

"Was he, then, a short man with a balding head, and a thick upturned nose, face lined with wrinkles, and a club foot?"

"That's the man, precisely! How can you know all that?"

"The description fits the features of a person I've run across quite recently. Thank you, sir."

* * *

The transition as Brekonridge entered the Cross and Key Public House was jarring. It was like walking into a dreary cave. A small bar stood in one corner of the main room. The owner had installed two gas lights, one on either side of the bar, and some of the tables had burning tapers. Behind the bar was a doorway to a back room where, no doubt, food and barrels of stout and wine were stored. The walls were ancient brick painted many times over, the floor thick oak planks with spaces between them wide enough to sweep the crumbs at the end of the day to keep the rats happy and out of the tavern proper. Tables were scattered around a fireplace in which a few logs crackled and spit. A black iron cauldron of Welsh cawl hung on a hook at the inglenook, its savory contents simmering heartily and filling the otherwise dingy room with a delightful aroma.

Brekonridge quickly surveyed the five or six men sitting lazily around the pub. The short man he had observed ducking inside sat alone on an L-shaped bench built into a far corner, still bundled in his thick winter coat.

Brekonridge walked to the bar and ordered a tankard of cider and asked for a bowl and a spoon. He crossed to the hearth and ladled from the cauldron until the bowl was three-quarters full. Cawl was the Welsh equivalent to the ancient pottage that had maintained British and French families through most of the middle ages. It was a never-ending stew made from various meats, root vegetables, cabbage, herbs and spices. The cauldron had likely not been completely empty in years. Something—a bunch of chopped carrots, a handful of parsley, the remnants of a roast guinea hen, a head of cabbage, or any other variety of foodstuffs—was added every day, along with enough water to keep the stew from boiling down to sludge. It was particularly popular in public houses because it was cheap to make, cheap to maintain, and eating it kept the customers ordering beer and ale. He cut a thick slice from a huge loaf of soda bread and dropped it into the bowl.

Brekonridge took his meal to the corner where the little man sat nursing an ale, and he sat at the next table, taking care to ensure that his mass prevented convenient egress. The little man stared at Brekonridge, though it was impossible to tell whether it was due to suspicion or the fact that Brekonridge, by design, had sat with the ghastly scars facing him. Brekonridge began to attack the cawl, shoveling large spoonsful into this mouth, and making sounds of contentment.

"Like my mother used to make," he said to the little man. "Would you believe I grew up in a tavern?"

The man looked at him but didn't respond.

"You should get some of this to go with your ale," Brekonridge said. "This is a meal to warm the soul, it is."

And, in fact, it was. Partial to public houses, Brekonridge had sampled pottage, stews and cawl all over the British Isles. The example he enjoyed now was superlative. It was nice not to have to feign delight while forcing back swill. He smacked his lips as he stuffed in another spoonful, then wiped his right hand on his jacket and extended it.

"Brekonridge," he said.

The little man recoiled slightly, then caught himself, and leaned forward. More out of curiosity than cordiality, he put out his own hand.

"Camp."

"Nice to meet you, Mr. Camp. Yes, I've spent many a happy hour in public houses like this one, recalling the warmth and comfort of my childhood. One thing about growing up in a tavern, it ain't like being the cobbler's barefoot children. There's never a shortage of food. What can beat the sense of contentment a child enjoys when his belly is full? Am I right?"

"I suppose," Camp said. He had lost interest in the conversation, and in Brekonridge, who made a show of slurping down the cawl, alternating it with sips from the cider. When Brekonridge was convinced the man had begun to ignore him, he took out the Bow Street Magistrate's Court warrant for apprehension on Mayhew and slid it across the table. Camp glanced down at it, at first disinterested, and then he read the text.

"You must be burning up," Brekonridge said, the bonhomie suddenly missing from his tone. "Take off your coat. Stay a while."

Camp's expression grew panicked. He stood to run, but the only route he had from his corner seat meant getting by Brekonridge, who kicked out his leg and slammed his boot into the wall, effectively blocking the man's exit.

"No. Really. I mean it," Brekonridge said. "Take off your coat and have a seat, Mr. Camp. Do not be alarmed. I have no interest in harming you, but I believe you can tell me things I would like to know."

Camp tried to protest, but Brekonridge noted he did not do so enthusiastically. He saw Camp glance toward the barkeep, and then back at Brekonridge, who shook his head and gave Camp his most intimidating scowl. The little man sat back down. He unbuttoned his coat but did not remove it.

"Your first name, Mr. Camp?" he began.

"Albert," the man muttered, defeated.

"Jericho Pratt sends his regards."

"You've spoken with him?"

"Within the hour. You've attempted to visit Jericho Pratt in Newgate Prison?"

"What matter is it of yours?"

"Mr. Pratt has just enlisted my assistance in proving his innocence. You've been trying to visit him. If you have information that will assist me, I recommend you share it."

"He's a friend! Isn't that enough?"

"He's been charged with a murder."

"I know."

"Who did he kill?"

"Jericho didn't kill nobody," Camp whined. "They say he stabbed a man named Fenwick, but he didn't."

"Who did?"

"I don't know."

"Who do you suspect?"

"Not a clue. I swear to you, sir. This man Fenwick is a tanner in Bermonsey. He and Pratt got into a fight because Fenwick was underpaying for Pratt's dog dirt. The next night, Fenwick turns up dead on the floor of his tannery, a knife in his chest. Someone saw him fighting with Pratt and told the bobbies. Now you know as much as I do."

"Not entirely. I understand you are close to Matt Mayhew. I need to find him. Where might he be?"

"I don't know for sure. Last I heard, he was down in Cripplegate. He's a cutpurse, Mr. Brekonridge. You want to find him? Market Day is the place. He's sure to be there, plyin' his trade."

* * *

"They say you killed a man named Fenwick," Brekonridge told Pratt after returning to Newgate.

"Fenwick! He's dead?"

"A knife in his chest."

"I see." Pratt settled on his bed. "Fenwick and I argued. Loudly. He was cheating me. It's bad enough that a man of manners in his cups must resort to pure-finding to avoid destitution, but when a customer shortchanges you, the pain is almost unendurable."

"Did you make threats toward the man?"

"Probably. Who can recall exactly what they say during a pique of anger?"

"Did you strike him?"

"Of course not! After venting my spleen, I told him I would never do business with him again. There is a surfeit of tanners in Bermonsey."

"And you can account for your whereabouts in the day or so before you were apprehended?"

"Not all of it. I'm afraid, after I got into it with Mr. Fenwick, I went on something of a tear. There are parts of those two days I don't recall accurately, and some I cannot retrieve at all."

"But you are certain that—in your inebriation—you did not return to Mr. Fenwick's tannery and do him in?"

"I cannot swear to it, but I cannot imagine a state of mind, impaired or not, in which I would undertake such violence. It is not in my nature."

"All right, then," Brekonridge said. "I have a man to apprehend, and once I've deposited him at Bow Street, I shall turn all of my attention to your situation."

* * *

Matthew Mark Luke John Mayhew's name was longer than he was tall. The adopted son of an Anglican priest whose teachings were wasted on the boy, Matt Mayhew had grown up to be an accomplished sneak-thief, shoplifter, pickpocket, and—when the need arose—arsonist. Never murder, however. Mayhew had his principles. When he couldn't make ends meet through criminal pursuits, he hired himself out to any business that would take him and was in the rare position of being unaware of his larcenous nature.

The midday bells had barely stopped chiming in the belfry of St. Giles Cripplegate when Mayhew emerged from a stable, with the apparent goal of picking pockets. Mayhew was no more than five feet tall, and skinny as a fence stake. His rat-like appearance included a protruding brow, squinty eyes, overly long and upturned nose, recessed chin, and buck teeth you could use to dig a trench. Brekonridge caught sight of him within seconds after he stepped out into the street and watched from the shadows, amused, as Mayhew stalked any well-dressed man he could spy in the crowd, looking for an opportunity to make off with a few shillings or even a pound or two. Brekonridge probably could have apprehended the little man immediately but preferred to catch him in the act of theft, on the off chance the charges against him at Bow Street fell apart. It had happened.

Within two minutes he watched the wretched little man lift one wallet, surreptitiously grab several coins from a wool-merchant's money box when the man was briefly turned away, cut the strings to a coin purse on an oyster-barrowman, and cadge two apples from a fruit stand.

A gentleman accompanying a lovely and much younger woman stepped out of a cab near the corner of Whitecross and Roscoe and helped his companion to the street. The man was dressed in the latest fashion from Paris, the woman clad in a bell-shaped dress in silk and satin, cinched furiously under the bodice. She grasped the man by the hand and directed his attention toward a booth selling bolts of brocade and lace. He tossed the hack driver tuppence to wait.

Brekonridge imagined Mayhew was unconsciously drawn to the gentleman the way southern climes compel geese to migrate in the winter. Even from a distance, he couldn't miss the outline of the man's wallet in the inside breast pocket of his greatcoat.

Brekonridge increased his pace and rapidly closed the distance between himself and the brocade merchant's booth. He stood behind Mayhew, careful not to draw the thief's attention, and waited for his move.

It didn't take long. While the man's attention was directed by the woman toward a silhouette artist snipping away at black paper with scissors at potentially dismembering speed, Mayhew grabbed a bucket and silently slid it behind the man's heels. Momentarily, as he turned to move along, the man stumbled over the bucket and tumbled into a pile of snow at the edge of the street.

Mayhew was upon him in an instant.

"I say, Guvnor, are you all right? That's a right nasty fall you took. No, please, don't try to get up too quickly. Me cousin tripped over a bucket once't and he was bedridden for days. Here, allow me to brush some of this snow off your lovely coat."

He made a show of straightening the man's jacket and helping him back to his feet. The man offered his thanks, and the woman took his arm in a nurturing fashion, and also thanked Mayhew for his kindness.

"Think nothin' of it, my lady," Mayhew said. "It's the Sabbath ain't it? No better day to do a fellow traveler a favor. Please enjoy your afternoon."

He waved and turned to walk away. Instead, he ran straight into Vicar Brekonridge, his rodent nose crushing against the thief-taker's chest.

"If you break my pipe, you'll buy me a new one," Brekonridge said, his voice gravel-like, with a hint of a Scottish accent.

"Oh, damn," was all Mayhew could manage. "Brekonridge. Beggin' your leave, sir. I had no intent of violating your person."

Mayhew tipped his cloth cap and tried to sidestep Brekonridge, who grabbed the man by his collar.

"Matthew Mark Luke John Mayhew, there's a warrant for your apprehension at Bow Street. I'm to deliver you to the jail to await arraignment. I would appreciate it if we could handle this with as little resistance as possible."

"What resistance could I possibly offer? You're a bloody giant, and a right ugly one."

"Give me the wallet you took off the gentleman."

"My hearing ain't so good, Mr. Thief-Taker. I didn't catch what you said."

"You lifted the man's wallet while you brushed off his jacket. I should be charitable and offer it was a right masterly job of it you did. You are an artist, if I may be permitted to say so."

"I am gratified at your appreciation of my craft. Is there any way we can come to an agreement that don't include you delivering me to the assizes? I have no desire to return to Newgate. It is a poor place for a soul to pass a winter."

"Give me the wallet," Brekonridge repeated.

"I see," Mayhew replied. "I see perfectly. I can't say I am enamored of the idea of parting with this delightful prize, but if it is the cost of my freedom, it's cheap indeed. You can have it."

He reached into a slit cut in the lining of his scuffed greatcoat, withdrew the gentleman's wallet, and handed it over to Brekonridge. As he extended his hand, Brekonridge grabbed it, slipped an iron handcuff over the thief's hand, and screwed down the lock.

"What's this then? You're going to rob me and still turn me over to the magistrate?"

"Not at all," Brekonridge said, as he attached the other end of the cuff to his own wrist. As soon as they were securely yoked to one another, Brekonridge dragged the little man up Whitecross Street toward the intersection with

Roscoe, where the gentleman's cab waited.

Moments later, the gentleman walked into view, looking distraught as he rushed the young woman back toward the silhouette booth. Brekonridge pulled on the cuff, bringing Mayhew to his feet, and forced him to walk toward the same booth. Halfway there, the gentleman saw them and pointed a finger as he stumbled through the snow in their direction. Brekonridge held up the man's wallet.

"Good afternoon, sir," he said. The woman caught up to them and then recoiled when she saw the right side of Brekonridge's head. "My name is Vicar Brekonridge. The gentleman chained to my wrist is Mr. Matthew Mark Luke John Mayhew, a wanted thief. I am hired to detain him and deliver him to the Bow Street Magistrate's Court. However, as I approached him to apply the irons, I saw him take this from your coat. Please allow me to return it."

The gentleman grabbed for the wallet and inspected it as if it might contain the secrets to existence itself. Satisfied, he slipped it back into his pocket.

"I thank you, Mr. Brekonridge. A less scrupulous man might have kept it as the spoils of war."

"The spoils you speak of are most often bitter compensation for the loss of your soul. I could have kept your wallet, but nothing comes for free. I'd have had to give up something more precious in compensation for it. I'll take my leave of you, sir. Please do have a pleasant afternoon."

He started to turn, but the gentleman hailed him. Brekonridge looked over his shoulder. The man held out a gold sovereign.

"For your trouble, Mr. Brekonridge. And for your honesty."

"I'm not proud, sir, I will accept your gratitude." Brekonridge pocketed the coin. "And good day to you, sir." He led Mayhew away toward Banner Street and tried not to think about the way the woman had shivered as she turned from him.

"Are you demented?" Mayhew demanded as he tried desperately to keep up with Brekonridge's long stride. "There was twenty quid easy in the man's wallet. You gave it up for a sovereign. What kind of fool are you, anyway?"

"One who sleeps at night. Turning you in will net me a reward of fifteen pounds. Added to the gentleman's largesse, I'd only be out four quid, and my conscience will not torment me over it. Be quiet or I'll walk more rapidly."

"Wait, wait," Mayhew said. He pulled gently against the handcuffs. Brekonridge stopped and scowled at him. "An idea has occurred to me. Do you realize, in the last ten minutes, you've made a sovereign?"

"You noticed."

"And you didn't have to cut a purse or put the cosh to anyone. A sovereign! This idea only now formed in me mind. We could team up, you and me. I pick the pockets, you catch me and tell the victim you're taking me to justice, we return the goods, and split the rewards. It's brilliant, I tell you. Brilliant. And legal!"

"Except for the thievery," Brekonridge said.

"We give it back! Why, at the worst it would be borrowing, and there's no ordinance against borrowing is there? Why, we could do the act ten, maybe twenty times a day. Think of it, Mr. Thief-Taker. We could be living like lords in a few weeks' time."

"Forget it."

"It's the opportunity of a lifetime. The opportunity of a lifetime, I say!"

"Not my lifetime," Brekonridge said, and continued the long trudge toward Bow Street, Mayhew's short legs churning in the snow to keep pace. "Besides, I have enough on my plate. As soon as I drop you off at Bow Street, I must return to Newgate Prison, where a man awaits my services."

Stop!" Mayhew said, and dug his heels into a snowbank. "Would you be talking about Jericho Pratt?"

Brekonridge glared down at him. "You know Pratt?"

"We are of long acquaintance, the pure-finder and me. We've bent elbows in many a tavern over the years. Only yesterday, I heard Pratt had been transported to Newgate for the murder of the unfortunate tanner Fenwick."

Brekonridge continued walking. "What do you know about it?"

"More than you, I'd guess. People talk, Mr. Brekonridge. Secrets are passed across the tables of taverns and public houses. A man who keeps his eyes low and his ears open can hear things."

"Such as?"

Mayhew stopped and shook his head. "Not so fast and not nearly so easy. Everything has a price."

"I suppose you wish me to forget about the warrant for your arrest and allow you to go free."

"I ain't so foolish. We have a history, you an' me, and I know you are incorruptible. However..."

"Yes?"

"If I am to pass the cold months chained to a standpipe in Newgate Prison, I see no reason to share my information with you. To think, a single sovereign could buy me a bed—however humble and mean—in the State wing. I believe that would make my inevitable incarceration tolerable."

Brekonridge pulled the sovereign he had received as reward from the gentleman and held it above Mayhew's head. It sparkled in the sunlight. Mayhew made a grab for it, but Brekonridge lifted it above the little man's reach.

"If the information is good," he said.

"Yes," Mayhew said. "Since my unfortunate departure from my last employment, I have been sleeping in the loft of the stables on Whitecross. There is no warmth in a stable loft, so I found it necessary to fortify my blood with a few glasses of Irish whisky. I was in the St. Ives tavern several nights ago, biding my time. I overheard a conversation between Fenwick and another tanner named Bouton."

"I've met Mr. Bouton," Brekonridge said.

"Then you know him to be a sizable and powerful man."

"He seemed pleasant enough."

"He was sober. Bouton has a reputation for being a nasty drunk. On the night I saw him and Fenwick, they were arguing."

"About what?"

"Jericho Pratt. It seems Mr. Pratt has been a longtime provider of dog dirt for both Mr. Bouton and Mr. Fenwick. However, Fenwick tried to cheat him, claiming the product Pratt sold him was of poor quality. Come on, Mr. Brekonridge. It's shite. How good could it be? Am I right?"

"Go on."

"I heard Fenwick attempt to conspire with Mr. Bouton to cheat Pratt. It seems Pratt refused to sell his product to Mr. Fenwick, and said he'd take all his business in the future to Mr. Bouton. Fenwick suggested that he and Bouton fix the price, so Pratt would have to continue selling to both. Bouton went into a rage at the suggestion. I asked the tavernkeeper about them, purely out of curiosity, and was told Bouton and Fenwick have a troubled past. Seems they have been at loggerheads for years over some woman. So, I'm talking to the barkeep, minding my own business, when Bouton slams his mug into the table, stands, and roars, "I'll see you dead before I throw in with the likes of you!" to Fenwick.

"You know the name of the tavernkeeper?" Brekonridge asked.

"Smythe. Tolerance Smythe. A big, round man. You can't miss him."

Chapter Fourteen

They arrived at Bow Street, where Brekonridge presented Mayhew to the magistrate for arraignment and transport to Newgate. As he turned to leave, reward money newly lining his pocket, Brekonridge was stopped by Mayhew.

"What about my money?" Mayhew asked.

"I will speak with Smythe," Brekonridge said. "If he corroborates your story, I will return to Newgate and pay for a room for you on the State wing. If you're lying…"

"I'm a cutpurse and a pickpocket," Mayhew protested. "Don't make me a lying man. Everything I told you was the truth."

"In that case, you can look forward to a winter that is only mildly tolerable, compared to the miserable, unbearable season you faced otherwise. Good fortune to you, Mr. Mayhew. I have no doubt, one way or another, we shall meet again."

"Until that time, Mr. Brekonridge. Until that time."

* * *

The St. Ives Tavern on Roscoe Street was dim and quiet when Brekonridge entered. It was middle afternoon on a Sunday, not the peak time for public alehouses. He stepped to the bar and rapped on the wooden top twice. Seconds later, a rotund man almost as tall as Brekonridge emerged from the back rooms. Brekonridge ordered an ale. As the man drew it, Brekonridge said, "You'd be Tolerance Smythe?"

"I would. And I believe you to be Vicar Brekonridge."

"Have we met?"

"No, I am happy to say. If we had, it might mean I had run afoul of the magistrates. I'm an honest man, sir. However, your reputation among some of my customers is well-established. I recognized you by…" he pointed to the right side of his head.

"Only this afternoon, I apprehended a sneak thief named Matt Mayhew. Do you know the man?"

"Indeed I do. So they finally nipped Mayhew? Can't say I'm happy. I've pocketed a great deal of his money over the years. Always has cash and lots of it."

"Someone else's cash," Brekonridge corrected.

"All money has been or will be someone else's money," Smythe said, smiling. "Shite's no good unless you pass it 'round."

"Do you also know Jericho Pratt?"

Smythe shook his head. "Only by name. Word has it he killed the poor tanner, Fenwick."

"Whose word?"

"Nobody in particular. Word on the street. Heard he was picked up by bobbies and transported to Newgate for the crime."

"Mayhew tells me Fenwick was a customer here."

"Indeed he was."

"And the tanner, Bouton?"

"I know the man."

"According to Mayhew, Bouton and Fenwick argued in this tavern two nights before Fenwick was murdered."

"Now that you mention it, I believe they did. Refresh your tankard?"

"Thank you." Brekonridge handed it to Smythe. "From what I heard, during that argument, Bouton threatened to kill Fenwick."

"Yes." Smythe slid the pewter tankard back across the bar. "I recall threats being made. Didn't think much of it at the time, or since. As long as it doesn't come to blows or cause damage to the tavern, I let it go. Men in their cups say things they later regret. Especially those two."

"So, otherwise, Bouton and Fenwick were friends?"

"Far from it. They've been bickering for years. As is often the case in stories like theirs, there is a woman involved."

"A romantic triangle."

"Not anymore. Years ago. Both Fenwick and Bouton were interested in the same girl, Ivy Cornwell. Bouton won her but realized quickly she was no prize. The girl was a shrew, only Bouton didn't discover that until after they were married. Fenwick later told him he had learned her true nature early and had voluntarily relinquished her to Bouton's arms. Bouton always believed he'd been cheated into an unhappy marriage. He thought Fenwick should have warned him about his intended spouse. He blamed Fenwick for all his various woes."

"And Mrs. Bouton? I would like to know her location."

"In a churchyard somewhere, I should think. She died several years back. Can't remember how many."

* * *

Brekonridge set out for Bermonsey and Bouton's tannery. As he strolled, he lit his pipe again and allowed the smoke to focus his mind, as he tried to see how all the pieces of the story of Fenwick's demise meshed.

On a hunch, he stopped in at the Bermonsey constable station of the London Metropolitan Police. He was fortunate. An officer manning the main desk recognized him from his days wearing a badge.

"As I live and breathe, it's Mr. Brekonridge!" the constable, Caleb Toll, said. "I haven't seen you in five years." He shook Brekonridge's hand vigorously.

After they hurriedly caught up with each other's lives, Brekonridge became serious. "I'm in the midst of an apprehension, perhaps," he said.

"Perhaps?"

"As it happens, a man is already in Newgate awaiting trial for the crime, but I believe he may have been accused falsely. Are you familiar with the murder of the tanner, Fenwick?"

"Am I? I was among the officers who took Jericho Pratt into custody."

"How did you find him?"

"Nearly unconscious with drink. We could have nabbed him with a single officer. One of the smaller ones."

"And how did you determine Jericho Pratt was your prime suspect in the murder?"

"We had a tip. A man reported he had seen Pratt in a horrible row with Mr. Fenwick, during which Pratt said he would kill the man. Made a promise, he did, and two days later Fenwick was dead. Seems an open and shut case to me, if you ask."

"If it would not violate a confidence," Brekonridge asked, "Could you divulge the name of the man who informed on Mr. Pratt?"

"Wouldn't violate confidence at all. After all, I reckon the man will be called to the dock during Pratt's trial."

He said the name. Brekonridge was not surprised.

* * *

Brekonridge arrived at the tannery, and his eyes watered at the stench. Clouds of ammonia-laden air were oppressive and nauseating. Outside, piles upon piles of bound tree bark awaited rendering for tannic acid. Inside, large wells of stinking chemicals roiled and churned, skins undulating in the foul liquid as they were preserved and softened. Workers, dressed in loose linen shirts and trousers rolled to the knee, waded in the tanks with long poles, continuously pushing the skins deep into the tanning solution. Other workers tied the treated skins to drying racks, sweat pouring off their faces and arms as they hefted the hides.

Brekonridge found Bouton in the same office he'd visited earlier in the day. The tanner was a large man, thick through the waist, with shoulders and biceps swollen from years of wielding a tanning pole and lifting sodden skins from vats. He sported a full beard, which he had allowed to grow lusciously over his lower face to the point that his mouth was barely visible through hair. He looked up as Brekonridge walked through the door.

"Mr. Brekonridge! Did you locate Jericho Pratt?"

"I did. As you suggested, he was at Newgate Prison. I was distressed to learn you had lied to me."

"Lied? In what way?"

"When we met earlier, you told me Pratt was in Newgate, but you also said you had no idea why."

"So?"

"In fact, you knew quite well why Pratt was incarcerated. You were the person who told the police that Pratt was in a horrible fight with Mr. Fenwick, and you told them where Pratt could be located for arrest. I also checked in at the Dove and Turtle public house down the street. You are familiar with the establishment?"

"I've visited a few times over the years."

"According to the tavernkeeper, you and Pratt drank heavily there the night before Fenwick was murdered. More precisely, he told me Pratt drank heavily, and you paid for the ale. He said you had to carry Pratt out of the pub, because the man could barely walk. The next day, after Fenwick's body was discovered, you turned Pratt over to the constables. Perhaps you could explain how a man who couldn't stand upright managed to plunge a knife into Fenwick's chest."

"I have no need to explain anything," Bouton said. "I merely told the police what I saw."

"Did you witness Pratt threaten to kill Mr. Fenwick before or after you made similar threats yourself?"

Bouton cocked his head and glared at Brekonridge.

"Say that again."

"It may well be the case that Jericho Pratt argued with Fenwick. He might even have threatened the man. However, the only witness the police have to such a confrontation is you. I have two witnesses who saw you threaten Fenwick in the St. Ives Tavern in Cripplegate, two nights before Fenwick died. You and Fenwick have been enemies for years, after he tricked you into wedding Ivy Cornwell. Trapped in a horrid marriage, you blamed him for all your troubles. I think you heard about the threats made toward Fenwick by Jericho Pratt. I think you got Pratt dead drunk, so he could not account for his time, deposited him in his lodgings, and then set out for a final showdown with Fenwick. I think you drove the knife into Fenwick's heart, and then blamed the murder on an insignificant, innocent pure-finder."

"You have no proof," Bouton stammered.

"Don't need it. I'm not a magistrate or a judge. It appears to me, however, that the preponderance of evidence against you far outweighs that against poor Mr. Pratt. I recommend charging both of you. Let Bow Street sort it out."

Brekonridge was prepared when Bouton launched himself from his office chair, fists clenched, and arms raised to strike. The two grappled in the office. Bouton tried to grasp Brekonridge's head and struggled to gouge the thief-taker's eyes with his thumbs. Brekonridge broke his grasp and slapped at one of Bouton' ears with his open hand, rupturing the man's eardrum. Bouton fell to the floor, howling in pain, but had the presence of mind to lash out at Brekonridge's knee with his heavily booted foot. Brekonridge tried to sidestep the kick, but still caught the boot on the outside of his knee. He collapsed to the floor, rolling to get away from his attacker, as Bouton gained his feet and ran toward the door exiting the tannery.

He ran directly into the waiting arms of Constable Caleb Toll and two other London bobbies. They wrestled him to the ground and were applying the irons as Brekonridge limped outside to join them.

"As I suspected," Brekonridge huffed. "When confronted with the evidence against him, he attacked me and attempted to flee. It's as strong an indicator of guilt as I've seen."

"I didn't murder nobody!" Bouton protested. "It was self-defense, it was. I fought with Fenwick, sure, but he was the one who drew the knife. I took it from him, and he came at me with a length of chain. I had no choice but to stab him. It was him or me."

"If so, you may be spared Tyburn Tree," Brekonridge told him. "But I wouldn't count on it."

Chapter Fifteen

J ericho Pratt, a free man, walked out of Newgate Prison with Vicar Brekonridge.

"I cannot thank you enough," Pratt declared, shaking Brekonridge's hand ferociously.

"Fortunately," Brekonridge said, "your information led me to Mayhew, whose apprehension in Cripplegate will cover my expenses for some weeks to come. The payment you promised for freeing you is extra, and thanks enough. Oh. I almost forgot."

Brekonridge returned to the imposing front door of the prison, struck the knocker, and waited for the gatekeeper to appear. When he did, Brekonridge pressed a gold sovereign into the man's hand. "This is to pay for a cell on the State wing for Matthew Mark Luke John Mayhew. He earned it. Please see to it that he is moved to Mr. Pratt's old cell as soon as possible. I will return in several days' time to ensure my wishes have been carried out."

Back on the street, Brekonridge lit his pipe and started his long walk to his rooms, when a carriage pulled alongside.

"Mr. Brekonridge," a man said from inside.

Brekonridge stopped and peered through the window.

"It's Mr. Cockburn, is it not?" he asked.

"Indeed. May I offer you a ride?"

Alexander Cockburn turned the latch and opened the carriage door. Brekonridge stooped and pulled himself up in to the seat facing the barrister. His John Bull hat nearly touched the velvet-covered headliner.

"You need a man caught?" Brekonridge asked.

"He's already been caught. You are familiar with the case of Daniel M'Naghten?"

"Who isn't? A man kills another, thinking he's shooting the Prime Minister? Word gets around. May I presume you represent Mr. M'Naghten?"

"I am among a team of barristers working on his case. His trial is on March third."

"Four weeks away."

"Yes. The team met on Friday and discussed how we should approach the defense of this poor man."

"Insanity, I reckon."

"And why do you say that?"

"It makes sense. I've given it a little thought as I've read the accounts in the papers. If he's found guilty and sane, his neck gets stretched. If he is found guilty due to his political views, his neck gets stretched and the streets will be full of angry Chartists avenging their martyr. The only option sparing both the man and the city is insanity."

"The prosecution is going to bring witnesses, including medical doctors, who will attest M'Naghten is as sane as you or me."

"Speak for yourself, sir."

"I think not. Your reputation precedes you, Mr. Brekonridge. You are a perceptive man, a man of remarkable resources, and you are pragmatic. We have a short time to build our defense, and you could provide the key pieces for it."

"How so?"

"Familiar with Glasgow, are you?"

"I've passed out in a public house or two there."

"We would like you to act as an investigator for our team. You would interview M'Naghten's acquaintances. Gather as much information on the man as you can. We need witnesses who can testify to a general and steady decline in Mr. M'Naghten's faculties over time, leading to a loss of reason, ultimately possessing him to fire upon poor Mr. Drummond in a fit of delusion."

"And you want me to go to Glasgow."

"Yes."

"Mind if I smoke inside your lovely carriage?"

"Make yourself at home."

Brekonridge pulled out the porcelain pipe and a phosphorous match. Cockburn's nose wrinkled as the smell reached him.

"Is that hemp?"

"Yes," Brekonridge said.

"Would you mind at all if I give it a try? My apothecary recommended it to me some months back. Said it was quite soothing. I am a tobacco man myself, on the rare occasions on which I indulge, but it is difficult to smoke frequently and still maintain the cleanliness associated with being a gentleman. I have, of course, occasion to enjoy a fine cigar or a pipe."

Brekonridge wiped the end of the pipe with his scarf, and passed it across the carriage to Cockburn, who inhaled from the pipe, and immediately broke into a paroxysm of coughing.

"It can be harsh," Brekonridge said. "One gets used to it."

After a few seconds of choking and coughing, Cockburn passed the pipe back. "I believe I will stick to my Staunton shag," he said, his eyes brimming with tears.

Brekonridge shrugged and drew again from the pipe. The smoke curled in the enclosed carriage as he exhaled from both his mouth and his nose.

"I'm not sure I want the job," Brekonridge said.

"May I ask why?"

"We may not share the same hopes for the outcome of this trial."

"Even with the potential for social outrage and riots?"

"A riot or two might be good for this city."

"Surely you do not think so."

"Shake it out of its complacency. I take it you are a Tory."

"My sympathies lie closer to the Liberals. I still believe in the rule of law. It is obligatory in my profession. Fomenting rebellion, which to this point appears to be the end goal of the Chartists, appears to me to be counterproductive to their cause..." He stopped. "Oh. My. What a strange sensation."

"The hemp," Brekonridge said. "The effect takes a few moments to manifest itself."

"Not at all displeasing. May I try some more?"

"Not too much," Brekonridge said, handing the pipe over to him.

"Why? Is it dangerous?"

"Not at all. It is, in fact, practically innocuous. I'm simply in short supply. I was paid for my latest apprehension only an hour ago. Haven't had the opportunity to drop by my apothecary."

"I see. Now, what was I saying? It seems to have slipped my mind."

"You were extolling the benefits of the rule of law."

"Ah. Yes. I fail to understand your point of view, sir. I have been confused for some time as to the motives of the Chartists, and their methods." He handed the pipe back to Brekonridge, who tamped it out and placed it back in his coat pocket.

"Have you been to America, sir?" Brekonridge asked.

"I am sorry to say I have not."

"So you have never seen a slave."

"Certainly not. Slavery has been outlawed throughout the empire."

"But not in America. I was there sir. I served in His Majesty's Navy for a number of years. I fought against the Americans in the Battle of New Orleans, and I returned several times after hostilities ceased. My last visit was to the port city of Charleston. I had the sad occasion there to witness a slave auction, as the guest of a plantation owner there whom I had befriended. An otherwise agreeable fellow, he was sadly entrenched in his views on the ownership of other humans."

"A distasteful business," Cockburn observed.

"You cannot imagine. Humans, dark as coal, paraded across a platform, stripped of their clothes and every shred of dignity, their teeth examined as if they were plough horses. Families torn asunder. Men with whip marks like strings of steel cable covering their backs. Humans whose only crime was to be born of a different race in a pagan country, humiliated, laughed at, and spat upon. It was inhumane. It was disgusting."

"I could not agree with you more."

"My companion then asked if I would accompany him to his plantation for a day or so, and I was happy to do so if only to escape the fetid obscenity in the city. The first night at his home, a young slave boy who could not have been older than twenty attempted to escape. He was captured almost immediately, and returned to the plantation, where my friend ordered him tied to a tree and whipped until he was unconscious. I feigned illness and left that evening to return to the city. It seemed there was no quarter from the horror of the system the Americans persist in maintaining."

"I am sorry, but I do not see—"

"Would you support a return to the feudal system of the Middle Ages, Mr. Cockburn?"

"Assuredly not."

"Neither would I. On the other hand, is our system so terribly different today? Do our social castes not bear some resemblance to the abominable slave system still practiced in our former colonies?"

"You are well-spoken for a thief-taker."

"When you walk the Earth with a visage out of Mrs. Shelley's novel, you learn to spend a great deal of time in your own company. I read voraciously. My formal education may be meager, but I know a thing or two."

"No doubt."

"I was disgusted by some aspects of life in America, such as the owning and mistreatment of their slaves, but there were attributes of the country I admired. For a country made up largely of lawless wilderness, the Americans have discovered an infinitely more civilized method for self-governance than we."

"But they are not a monarchy," Cockburn countered.

"And neither should we be. How can we claim civility in England when so many of our resources are concentrated on so few people? The Chartists are made up of tradesmen, tenant-farmers, laborers, journeymen, the spine of our culture, and yet most of them have no say in how the culture is governed, any more than a slave does in Charleston. They are disenfranchised, not because of a fault in their character or the lack of intelligence, or even because they have been convicted of some crime. They are excluded from the process of governance through accident of birth or failure to acquire property. Does such a system appear to be fair and equitable to you, Mr. Cockburn?"

"As a gentleman of liberal leanings, I may sympathize with your disenfranchised. However, what would happen if we did throw the voting doors wide open to any and all comers, regardless of their social status?"

"Freedom, I suspect."

"Or anarchy, which it appears you endorse."

"Hardly. If you would have you driver turn left at the street ahead, we are nearing my lodgings."

"Will you take the job, Mr. Brekonridge?"

Brekonridge fell silent and stared out the window at passersby. Presently, he shook his head.

"I must be mad," he said. "I could walk into Bow Street today and take my pick from any number of warrants. I do not need to go to Glasgow to make my way and fill my belly. I do not care for travel beyond the streets of London. I grow weary of the expressions of strangers when they first see my disfigurement. I prefer solitude. However, I will take this case on one condition."

"Being?"

"I wish to meet with Mr. M'Naghten first. I want to look in the man's eyes."

"He will not speak with you. He's said barely ten words since his arraignment."

"I should prefer to meet with him all the same."

"He is presently held at Newgate. Perhaps tomorrow afternoon would suit?"

"I will be there. And what compensation are you offering for this contract?"

"What do you require?"

"Passage, lodging, food, and a stipend of one hundred pounds."

"Quite a lot of money."

"Greater than the value M'Naghten places on his head? The newspapers say the courts turned the proceeds of his bank account over to the firm of Humphreys and Perceval. I presume they have employed you as their surrogate."

"That is true."

"I will meet with Mr. M'Naghten tomorrow afternoon. Get the approval for my terms from Humphreys and Perceval and I can be off for Scotland tomorrow evening."

Chapter Sixteen

At Brekonridge's direction, Cockburn let him out near Bloomsbury Street. Brekonridge waited until the carriage turned the next corner before he set off for his lodgings on a side lane. First, he stopped in at his apothecary's shop, two blocks from his home.

"Mr. Brekonridge!" the chemist greeted as Brekonridge opened the door. "Running low on hemp, I suppose."

"Yes," Brekonridge said. "I may be away for several weeks. I'd like to purchase enough for that time."

"And how is it working for you?"

Almost reflexively, Brekonridge lifted a hand to his ruined features. "My doctors suggest any pain I experience is psychically derived, and my scars are incapable of any sensation whatsoever. I have suggested they try living inside my skin for a day. The hemp attenuates the pain and has the side effect of opening my mind to possibilities I had not previously considered. And it does not dull me as opium and laudanum do."

"Our new shipment of ganja from Bombay should suit your purposes excellently. I'll prepare a package for you."

Brekonridge stuffed the parcel into his greatcoat pocket as he left the apothecary shop and stopped in at a tavern five doors closer to his apartment for dinner. By the time he had finished, the sun had set.

He stopped in at a dry-goods' merchant and purchased two containers of chamomile and lavender soap, which he stuffed in his coat pockets, and then made his way over three streets to the nondescript building where he maintained three rooms on the third floor, with a distant view of the

British Museum from his largest window.

Mrs. Langtry greeted him as he entered the building. "A successful outing today?" she asked.

He pulled one of the paper-wrapped bars of soap from his pocket and handed it to her. "A most successful day, madam."

"I have cleaned your rooms, lighted the gas-lamps, and I have filled your tub halfway with water from the pump downstairs. I have kept a stock pot of water heated on the hearth in your rooms."

He thanked her and she followed him up to his lodgings.

Mrs. Langtry had inherited the building from her husband when he had been mercilessly set upon by robbers in Whitechapel four years earlier. They had beaten the man horribly, and he had succumbed two days later from his injuries, but not before Brekonridge had tracked down all three of the murderers and delivered them to the assizes at Bow Street. Mrs. Langtry had shown her gratitude by deeding him the third-floor apartment in her boarding house.

Mrs. Langtry was only in her early forties. Her hair was flaxen and her eyes deep brown. From an ancient Salisbury farming family, she was tiny, standing no taller than an inch or two below five feet. She was sturdily built but not overtly plump. As the proprietor of her rooming house, she was in charge of all the maintenance and upkeep, which had left the muscles under her voluptuous pale skin taut and sinewy. She kept her hair up in a bun most of the time, but when it was untied it fell nearly to her waist in golden rivulets.

The rags Brekonridge wore on the streets were a disguise intended to blend in with his surroundings as he conducted his searches. As he walked into the rooms, he hung the stained and scuffed greatcoat and the moth-eaten scarf on a coat tree by the door, along with the weather-beaten John Bull hat.

Brekonridge had discovered the compensation for a thief-taker, inconstant as it might be, could be generous. With rewards for apprehension and delivery of local ne'er-do-wells reaching forty pounds or more, Brekonridge had enjoyed a considerably elevated standard of living compared to his former peers on the London Metropolitan Police force. The previous year, he had been awarded over six hundred pounds in bounties and rewards, and this year promised to be even more successful. Even so, his work took little of his time. This was partly due to Brekonridge's own tendency toward indolence. Keeping his own company in his rooms in Bloomsbury preserved his dignity, and he preferred to remain there. Necessity and survival required him to occasionally don his thug's rags and inconveniently pass among other humans to hunt human quarry. Between his exploits, there was plenty of free time to indulge his curiosity and personal education.

The furniture in Brekonridge's rooms was new. The walls were lined with bookshelves overflowing with the volumes Brekonridge collected with an almost compulsive fervor. Indoor gas lights were still a rarity in London but, having seen them in one attorney's lovely Covent Garden home, Brekonridge had determined to have them installed in his rooms. Mrs. Langtry did not object since Brekonridge had arranged for every improvement in his rooms to be duplicated in hers on the first floor.

As Brekonridge stepped into his rooms, the gas lights drove off the gloom from outside. A fire waited in the ornate brick fireplace on the outside wall, and a huge cauldron of water simmered over it. Mrs. Langtry crossed the room to the cauldron and ladled the hot water into an oaken bucket kept by the hearth.

Brekonridge pulled off his hobnailed boots, stockings, trousers, and muslin shirt, and then peeled off his linen underclothing as Mrs. Langtry poured three buckets of scalding water into the already half-filled copper tub built into the tile-floored third room. After dipping a finger into the water to check the temperature, and finding it to his satisfaction, he settled into repose as the hot water rose around him. He had read that Beau Brummel had bathed every day, so he had taken to the habit himself while he was still a uniformed officer.

"I will likely be out of the country for a few days," he called to Mrs. Langtry.

"An important case?" she asked as she entered the room, carrying the unwrapped lavender soap and a cloth, which she handed to Brekonridge.

"You are familiar with the murder of Sir Robert Peel's private secretary,

Edward Drummond?"

"I am," she said, as she reached up with both hands and loosened her hair.

"I have been asked by the killer's attorney to investigate his background in Glasgow."

"I presume they offered you an admirable retainer," she said, as her dress dropped to the floor. She laid it across an upholstered chair at the door to keep it from wrinkling. Out on the streets she might have worn a corset and layers upon layers of crinolines. While maintaining her house, she wore only linen pants beneath her dress. She untied those also.

"My demand was a hundred pounds, plus expenses. I made sixteen today, including a reward from a grateful gentleman whose wallet I returned after a pickpocket had liberated him of it."

"A good Samaritan's efforts are never unrewarded," she said, as she slipped over the rounded edge of the tub. She floated to the head of the tub to lie face-to-face with him. She was so tiny that there was plenty of room for both of them. For reasons she never explained, Mrs. Langtry did not find his disfigurement revolting or disgusting. She took the cloth from him, rubbed some soap on it, and washed his chest.

"I left two sovereigns on the table by the door for you," he said.

She said nothing, but lathered his shoulders.

After Brekonridge had found the murderers of Mrs. Langtry's husband, and after Brekonridge had moved into his rooms in Mrs. Langtry's house, they had slept together for several weeks, until the fire of her passion seemed at last to be quenched. They had become so familiar with each other's nakedness, they no longer even feigned modesty. They only infrequently engaged in intimacies anymore.

Brekonridge grabbed the bucket she had placed next to the copper tub, and emptied it around them, causing convections of tepid and scalding water to swirl around their bodies. She slid her hand down his belly and cupped him with it, stroking gently.

It was going to be one of *those* nights. Brekonridge relaxed and sighed as she aroused him with her fingers and mouth. He allowed his hands to explore the curious combination of her hard muscles and soft, glowing skin. After a minute or two, she stopped, and resumed bathing him with the cloth. She seemed to revel in teasing and drawing out her seductions.

That was fine. He had no other place to be, and could think of no more enjoyable pastime. When they were finished, he lifted her from the water, silvery droplets falling back and rippling in the tub, dried her with a heavy towel, and carried her to his bedchamber.

* * *

Mrs. Langtry left before midnight, as had become her custom after their initial fiery affair. He had asked her once why she no longer stayed for the night. She had explained that, once sated, she preferred to be alone. It was simply her way, and he respected her wishes.

After she returned to her rooms, Brekonridge washed again in the now lukewarm water, wrapped himself in a large heavy quilted satin robe, filled his football pipe with hemp, and sat in his favorite chair to review the newspapers. As always, he began with the *Times*, and went directly to the agony columns. It was his daily habit to peruse the descriptions placed there by people seeking lost relatives or friends, especially if they offered a monetary reward for returns.

He paused for a moment to think about what Alexander Cockburn had told him. M'Naghten had not spoken since his arraignment. If the man would not speak, how the devil was Brekonridge to interview him the next day? He took a few more puffs from the pipe, and turned alternative strategies over in his head.

And then he found his solution.

Chapter Seventeen

aniel M'Naghten was held in the State facilities at Newgate Prison, which would make Brekonridge's interview with him somewhat more tolerable.

"Mr. Brekonridge!" the gatekeeper said. "Are you here to check on the cutpurse Mayhew? I can assure you he was moved to the State facilities last evening."

"You have my gratitude. I am to meet Alexander Cockburn here this morning to interview the prisoner Daniel M'Naghten."

"Yes," the man said, as he scanned Brekonridge's devastated face. Brekonridge had reverted to his street clothes, including the battered beaver hat and the wormy scarf, because he was about to interview a prisoner whom he estimated had probably seen enough fine clothes on the barristers and judges who had surrounded him since the shooting. Brekonridge had dressed to put the man at ease.

"Mr. Cockburn has already arrived," the gatekeeper said. "Please step inside."

The gatekeeper fished through his ring of keys and opened another door at the opposite end of the Keeper's House, which led into an atrium where Alexander Cockburn and a young man waited. As soon as the gatekeeper opened the door to the atrium, Cockburn and the boy rose to their feet.

"Mr. Brekonridge," Cockburn said. "I am gratified you are here. I would like to introduce you to Simon Daughtrey, a clerk with Humphreys and Perceval."

Simon offered his hand, and Brekonridge reluctantly took it. The boy's hand was light and tiny in Brekonridge's hardened paw.

"A pleasure, Mr. Brekonridge," Simon said. "Mr. Cockburn has told me about your exploits."

Brekonridge turned to Cockburn. "This is a place for the boy?"

"Clerk," Simon corrected. "I am young, true. But I have already been admitted to the Middle Temple."

In the absence of formal schools of law in nineteenth century England, aspiring barristers sought admission to one of several informal law training academies, where they were exposed to common law, legal history, and were afforded the opportunity to practice their nascent skills in moot courts. Schools included the Inner Temple, Grey's Inn, and Lincoln's Inn. Of the four, the Middle Temple was regarded as the most advantageous. Only the most promising of students were admitted there. If Simon was a Middle Temple member, his sponsors must have held the highest expectations for his professional future.

Today, Simon Daughtrey was merely a lad of minor importance, and therefore of no real interest to Brekonridge.

"I would speak to Mr. M'Naghten alone," he said.

"I would not advise that," Cockburn said. "Anything he tells you could be of potential benefit at trial. Simon here has accompanied me to take down M'Naghten's statement."

"Won't be necessary," Brekonridge said, without looking at the boy. He tapped his temple. "Mind like a steel trap. I'll remember everything M'Naghten says, and I'll recount it when I am finished."

"I'm afraid that is unsatisfactory," Cockburn argued.

"As you wish," Brekonridge said. "Gatekeeper! I wish to leave now!"

The gatekeeper appeared in the doorway, as Cockburn put out an arm to restrain Brekonridge.

"Wait!" Cockburn said. "You underestimate your importance to this case, Mr. Brekonridge."

"I work on my terms. I may be a common thief-taker and not a gentleman, but it appears you need me more than I need you."

He saw a desperate look in Cockburn's eyes, and understood at last how poorly Cockburn evaluated his case for insanity, and how badly the defense team needed the information Brekonridge could provide.

"Alone, then?" he said.

"Alone. But you must relate everything M'Naghten tells you. Nothing is unimportant."

"Nothing is what you already have, sir," Brekonridge said. "I cannot promise it will be useful to your case, but when I have finished we will know more than we do now."

"I can ask for no more. We will wait for you here." He turned to young Simon. "I hope this will be a lesson to you, young man. Sometimes you might win by losing."

Brekonridge affected a shallow bow to convey his respect for Cockburn's decision. "I am ready," he said to the gatekeeper. "Please take me to see Mr. M'Naghten."

* * *

M'Naghten looked up as Brekonridge filled the doorway. An expression of curiosity crossed his face, but nothing more. The turnkey reappeared with a second chair.

"I wish to be alone with the prisoner," Brekonridge said. "You may close the door and leave us here."

The turnkey, having learned his lesson the day before, closed and locked the door behind him.

"Good day," Brekonridge said to M'Naghten. He pulled the second chair up to the small table and sat. He reached into his jacket pocket and drew out a book. Without taking a second look at M'Naghten, he opened the book and read silently.

As he read, he could see a blurry image in his peripheral vision. M'Naghten stared at him from the bunk. Brekonridge was careful not to make any contact. Instead, he feigned total absorption in the novel. It took almost ten minutes, but finally M'Naghten, who had grown increasingly agitated, broke the silence.

"Excuse me, are we waiting for someone?" His voice was soft, the intonation benign.

Brekonridge peered over the top of the book. "No. It is only me," he said, and returned to reading. M'Naghten worried a corner of the blanket. Brekonridge could hear his breathing increase in frequency. M'Naghten glanced at the door and back at Brekonridge. Even so, it took him several more minutes to speak again.

"May I ask what you are reading?"

Brekonridge held up the spine. "American writer. Poe. *The Narrative of Arthur Gordon Pym of Nantucket.*"

"I've not heard of it," M'Naghten said.

"Well, it is his only novel."

Brekonridge returned to reading. He had acquired the novel at a second-hand bookseller a couple of weeks before, having a passing acquaintance with Mr. Poe's short stories in *Burton's Gentlemen's Magazine*. To his pleasant surprise, he realized he was enjoying the book almost as much as he enjoyed taunting M'Naghten.

After another several disquieting minutes, M'Naghten said, "What's it about?"

"Seafaring tale," Brekonridge mumbled without looking up. "Whaling."

"Ah," M'Naghten said. "I see."

The prisoner laced his fingers and rocked back and forth at the edge of the bunk, trying not to stare at his visitor but largely failing. He started to speak on two occasions, but stifled the impulse, as if he had not completely decided what he intended to say.

Brekonridge had reached a part of the novel describing a mutiny, almost an hour and a half after entering the cell, when M'Naghten broke.

"Damn it, man, must you torment me so?" The formerly soft voice had turned menacing and growling.

"Pardon?" Brekonridge asked, barely lifting his gaze from the book.

"You are no better than the Tories in Glasgow, who follow me openly and taunt me in the streets, and who molest my person in the guise of carrying out their police duties! I have no wish to endure more persecution!"

"Persecution? I'm only reading. I have said almost nothing to you."

"And why not, then? For what purpose have you come, except to exact some revenge on behalf of the Prime Minister?"

"Never met the man," Brekonridge said. "I am employed by your defense attorney, Mr. Cockburn. Persecuted you, sir? Nothing of the kind. I have no reason."

"I fear the same is true of me," M'Naghten said, sagging onto his bunk. "My reason has quite deserted me. To do what I did, I must have had fair reason, but would a reasonable person engage in such an act? Would a man in possession of reason ever consider something so vile? Perhaps if he had good enough reason to do so. Do you believe it is possible for one to temporarily divest himself of reason, if the reason to do so be sufficient?"

"I have an active imagination," Brekonridge said. "I can conceive of a great many things."

"Then a man, molested and abused sufficiently, could possibly abandon moral convictions and social obligations, and, in essence, quit reason altogether."

"I have seen men in war do as much."

"In war, yes. Under conditions in which your own demise is imminent, any behavior might be excused. It's a matter of self-preservation, is it not? Is it not human nature to protect oneself from harm?"

"I believe it is one of our basic instincts," Brekonridge said.

"And, it stands to reason then, if a man discovers a plot to undo him, to eradicate him from earthly bounds, he is justified in taking any necessary measures to subvert those plans?"

"Any sane man would do so."

"I thought as much." M'Naghten sat back on the bunk. "I was not deluded then?"

"I cannot say. I am unaware of the pressures put upon you."

"The Tories in Glasgow. They beset me. They followed me, harassed me, taunted me, even threatened me. I was hounded day and night."

"All of them?"

"What?"

"All the Tories in Glasgow? Or were there specific individuals?"

"Do you mock me, sir?"

"Farthest thing from my mind. Do you know the names of any of the Tories who hounded you?"

"It can be proven by evidence!" M'Naghten said.

"Yes. You said the same thing at your arraignment. You claimed there was evidence to support your contention of harrying by the Glaswegian Tories. I would like to hear that evidence. In fact, I would like to go to Glasgow myself and confront your oppressors directly."

"They would destroy you, as they have me."

"I would take my chances. Alas, it is impossible."

"And why?"

"I don't know who they are. I have not been to Glasgow in years. I have no old friends there who could guide me toward the men who drove you to your act. I would be as a stranger in a strange land."

"I could give you the names of men who betrayed me."

"You inspire me," Brekonridge said. "Armed with such information, I would be bound for Scotland on your behalf before the sun rises tomorrow."

"You could do that?"

"As I said, I was employed by your attorney. It would be my duty to get to Glasgow and gather all the information for your defense."

"Please, sir," M'Naghten said. "do take care. If the Tory factions in power get wind of your intent, they will treat you as badly as they have me."

"I can deal with them," Brekonridge told him, "Give me their names."

Chapter Eighteen

"The man tells a good story," Brekonridge said, as he was escorted into the chapel meeting room where Alexander Cockburn and Simon Daughtrey waited. "As to his madness or lack thereof, I am not qualified to speak. He did engage in some interesting wordplay, the nature of which I have observed in poor street beggars who have taken leave of their senses. I can tell you he questions his own reason, but that could be guilt speaking."

Cockburn said, "Did he give you information useful for your investigation?"

"He gave me some names, and described some isolated episodes of harassment by the officials in Glasgow. It isn't a great deal, but it will provide a starting place. As I dig deeper, more information will emerge. It always does."

"You will take the case?" Cockburn asked.

"Yes. Would you be so kind as to arrange passage for one to Glasgow late this evening?"

"We have booked passage for two on the London, Midland, and Scottish line from the Euston Railway Station. That will get you as far as Edinburgh, where there's a new line to Glasgow."

"You said passage for two?"

"Yes. The defense team has decided to send young Simon here with you."

"Absolutely not," Brekonridge said. "Out of the question."

"Be reasonable, Mr. Brekonridge. Your skills as a tracker and thief-taker are renowned, but you are not trained in the law."

"Neither is the boy."

"Not completely, but he is making rapid progress. In addition, we need a member of Humphreys and Perceval's staff to maintain records of your interviews in Glasgow."

"It doesn't work like that," Brekonridge argued. "What do you believe I intend to do? Open a storefront on High Street and advertise for volunteers to tell me all they know about Daniel M'Naghten? My inquiries will be discreet, and my contacts furtive. It may be necessary to engage in deception. Mr. M'Naghten has implicated the Tories in Glasgow as his tormentors, and Glasgow is heavily controlled by Tories. The people I need to speak with may be reluctant to cooperate. We will likely need to meet covertly. I know how to do this. I can't haul a lad too young to have a beard around and still be effective at my work."

"My role would be administrative only," Simon interjected. "We trust your memory, at least for the time it would take you to report back from your investigations. All I will do is collate the information and organize it in a way that will be useful for our barristers."

"You may find young Mr. Daughtrey an asset in other areas," Cockburn said. "His ability to analyze circumstances outstrips his years. His observational powers are remarkable, and his memory is top shelf. You may find his presence advantageous."

"Unlikely," Brekonridge growled, but the surrender in his voice was unmistakable. "I will not be responsible for his safety, and I will not answer for his conduct or should any harm come to him. I did not ask for a companion or an assistant, and I do not believe I need either. If you insist the boy come along as a condition of my employment, you do so at his risk."

Cockburn extracted a wax-sealed envelope from his jacket pocket. "Here are your tickets. Mr. Daughtrey has already received his. He will meet you at the Euston Railway Station this evening at nine o'clock. You will arrive in Glasgow sometime after lunch tomorrow. I trust that will give you sufficient time to acquaint Simon with the names of the people M'Naghten told you to interview."

"I will be there. My bags are packed and ready to go. I need only stop by my lodgings in Bloomsbury to pick them up on the way to the station."

* * *

It took Brekonridge nearly an hour to make his way to Newington and Number 7 Poplar Row, where M'Naghten had kept his room until the day he shot Edward Drummond. The housekeeper and landlady, Sarah Dutton, answered the door seconds after he rapped on it.

"Oh, my," she said, peering up at Brekonridge, who towered over her. He had purposefully turned his face toward the street to hide his burn scars. At the moment, his stature alone was enough to unsettle the widow, and he had no desire to compound her distress.

"My apologies for not sending word of my visit," Brekonridge said. "I am working for Mr. Alexander Cockburn, a barrister defending your former tenant, Mr. M'Naghten."

"In what capacity are you working? You do not look like an attorney to me."

"Indeed, I am not. I am a former Metropolitan Police officer. I now earn my living finding men of interest to the court, and sometimes finding information that might be useful to attorneys. That is my capacity today. I was wondering if I might ask you a few questions about Mr. M'Naghten."

"I've already told the police everything I know," she said, tentatively. "I can't imagine what new information I might be able to add."

"The police are seeking information that will lead to Mr. M'Naghten's conviction. They are a dependable, trustworthy lot, but not terribly imaginative. They are likely to selectively ignore information that does not conform to their mission. I am open to all sides of the question, though I should inform you that my employers do intend to spare Mr. M'Naghten the noose by having the court find him insane."

"Insane! I should think not."

"On what basis, madam?"

"I know the man. He has lived under this roof long enough for me to have recognized any madness on his part."

"Please, madam, may I enter? It is cold at your doorstep, and I have a number of questions I would like to ask you."

She hesitated, and then she opened the door wider. Brekonridge thanked her and entered the building. Mrs. Dutton led him down the hall to her rooms, and bade him enter. It was only as he passed her that he heard her gasp quietly as she saw the burn scars on his head and neck.

"My apologies," he said. "I should have advised you of my injuries. I acquired them rescuing children from a fire several years ago. Sometimes, I forget that they are there. Please do not be alarmed."

"Yes," she said. "Would you like some tea?"

"That would be very kind of you. May I ask you about Mr. M'Naghten while you prepare it?"

She did not object, and withdrew to a small alcove where she kept a kettle on a small woodstove.

"According to the information I have acquired through Mr. M'Naghten's attorneys, as a consequence of your interview with Sergeant Shaw of the Metropolitan Police, your lodger recently returned from a trip to Scotland."

"In November. Yes," she said, as she prepared two cups from her small but efficiently organized pantry. "He had been gone for several months, and had not provided a forwarding address, so after a reasonable period I put his room up for let. Several days later, he appeared at the door asking whether he might return. As he had always been a dependable tenant, I had no objection."

"And when he returned, you reported that his clothes were in disarray, torn and patched, and soiled, and that he himself was disheveled. Did he offer any explanation for the condition of his clothing, or for his personal appearance?"

"Not at all. In any case, he was more properly attired within a day or so of returning."

"And you told Sergeant Shaw that Mr. M'Naghten had followed the Queen around when she visited Scotland last summer?"

"That's what he told me."

"Did he ever mention the Queen in any other context?"

"I don't understand your question."

"Did he ever refer to her activities here in London, or discuss any governmental or legislative issues?"

"Mr. M'Naghten was a quiet man who kept to himself. When he did mention world events, he did not appear to do so in a state of agitation or excitement. The few discussions we had always left me with the impression that he was a man of quiet and closely held convictions, and he was always reasonable and even-tempered. There was nothing in what he told me that would lead me to believe he was a madman. In fact, he was most responsive to my own problems."

"What problems are those, if I may be permitted to ask?"

"Nothing overwhelming. I had a tenant who left in the night and did not pay his rent. It left me financially embarrassed for a short time. I approached Mr. M'Naghten several weeks ago and asked whether he might make me a small loan of two or three shillings until I could collect all the rents at the end of the week. He was happy to comply."

"He gave you money?"

"Not all of it. When I asked, he checked his immediate funds, and said he could only spare me one and six, but that he might be able to advance me more in a few days after he received money he was expecting."

Brekonridge stopped the pencil he had been using to transcribe notes to a sheet of foolscap.

"He was expecting a windfall?" Brekonridge asked.

"I don't know if it could be described as such, but he did anticipate receiving some money."

"When was this?"

"I don't recall, exactly. I have it in my books—I keep meticulous records on all the household transactions. Give me a moment."

She stepped across the room to a small pine desk, where she withdrew a cloth-bound ledger. She riffled through several pages, and then ran her finger down a column of figures.

"January fourteenth," she said. "I recorded it right here. 'One shilling sixpence received from Mr. Daniel M'Naghten as a loan, to be repaid at the end of the month.' And he did lend me the remainder. Another notation here, 'Two shillings received from Mr. Daniel M'Naghten as a loan,' etcetera."

"What was that date?"

"January seventeenth. I recall it well. Mr. M'Naghten received a package that afternoon by a courier. It was a Monday, as I recall. He appeared to be overjoyed to receive it, though he did not tell me what the letter entailed. He did make me the rest of the loan later that afternoon."

"Three days before the murder of Edward Drummond," Brekonridge observed.

"Why, yes, it was. Do you believe the two were connected?"

"Not in any way that would be of benefit to your former lodger. You are aware that Mr. M'Naghten, when apprehended, had on him a receipt from the Glasgow and Ship Bank in the amount of seven-hundred fifty quid?"

"Did he? Dear me, that is a great deal of money."

"And, he went from being able to afford lending you only one shilling six on the fourteenth of the month, to being able to give you two more shillings on the seventeenth, after he received this message. You had no idea he was in possession of such a large amount of money?"

"Certainly not! I am confused. A man with that sort of wealth certainly need not resort to a two shilling and six room in Newington. With those resources, he would easily afford to live in Covent Garden or Piccadilly."

"Perhaps he needed a place that was out of sight, where he would not draw attention to himself."

"For what reason?"

"I can think of several. I believe if we knew what was in the communication Mr. M'Naghten received on January seventeenth, we should understand a great deal more about his motivations than we do now. You told Sergeant Shaw that M'Naghten never had any visitors."

"I have no recollection of Mr. M'Naghten ever receiving a caller."

"And did he mention any of his London associates by name?"

"Not in my memory. As I said, he kept very securely to himself. We did not pass the time sitting by the fireplace downstairs. He rose early in the morning, dressed and breakfasted, and then left the house and did not return until late in the evening. It was rare for him to take supper here."

"This was his regular schedule?"

"It was."

"Even during his first tenure as your lodger?"

"I beg your pardon. I don't understand the question."

"Mr. M'Naghten lived here twice. The first time until approximately April of this past year, and then from November to the present time—I presume you have not already let out his room?"

"Of course not. For all we know, the courts will absolve him and he will return here."

"I somehow doubt that, madam. Again, forgive my candor. First-hand witnesses saw him shoot Mr. Drummond. Mr. M'Naghten will be executed, committed, or transported. There are no other options for him. You may feel free to box his belongings and rent out his room. He will not return here. As a matter of fact, would it be possible for me to inspect his room?"

"The police have already done so. They removed most of his things."

"I would beg your indulgence. I have made my career for many years as a finder of lost objects and missing men. I have the greatest respect for my former colleagues in the Metropolitan London Police, but a uniformed officer may not possess the knowledge and experience to properly conduct such a search. Would it be possible to examine his room now?"

She led him up the stairs to the second floor.

"The door is unlocked," she said, as she gestured toward it. "The policeman who searched the room took the key, and it has not been returned."

"And I doubt it will be. You would do well to employ a locksmith to change the lock on the door."

Brekonridge pushed open the door, and peered inside the room. It was spartan. The wooden plank floor was bare, the firebox cold, and the thin draperies closed. Mrs. Dutton hustled across the room and opened them, letting loose a shower of dust motes in the faint sunbeam that invaded the room.

There was the bed, barely wide enough for a grown man, with its mattress folded double on top of bare wooden slats. The table and two chairs sat forlornly in the corner, no tablecloth or cushions to cover the fading paint and the worn varnish. Another smaller commode table held a dry washbowl and an ancient water pitcher crazed with craquelure. The door to the wardrobe hung open, the interior devoid of clothing or other haberdasheries.

"I perceive it will not take long for you to prepare this room for its next tenant," Brekonridge remarked. "The police took everything?"

"Such as there was."

"Nice of them to leave the drapes."

"Yes."

He peered out the window into the street, at the buildings on the other side of the pavement, and at the sea of rooftops and trees that separated the boarding house from the Thames, a little over a mile away.

"What are you looking for?" Mrs. Dutton asked.

"What there is to see," Brekonridge said softly, almost a whisper. "The police pulled everything they could find out of this room, but they did not look beyond it. Mr. M'Naghten took this room for a reason. As you correctly stated, he could have afforded much more luxurious lodgings. Instead, he came here, whether to hide, to plot, or to escape persecution, or—perhaps—this room placed him in proximity of something he wanted to watch closely. If the latter is the case, I am at a loss as to what it might have been. I see nothing of apparent interest."

He clapped his hands and stepped back from the window.

"Costs nothing to try," he said. He crossed the room to the cherry wardrobe, its dark lacquer already blackened with age, and swung the already-opened doors wide. He rapped on the back wall with his knuckles, listening for any sound of hollows or concealed compartments. He did the same on the base of the wardrobe. The drawers on either side of the interior were empty and had been left partially opened. He pulled each one from its rails and examined it closely, turning it upside down to see if anything had been secreted underneath. Then he checked the rails and stiles inside the supports for the drawers, both visually and by running his hands along the structures.

"If you will allow me," he said to Mrs. Dutton, and he tipped the wardrobe over and lowered it to horizontal on the floor. After examining the underside, he lifted it back into place.

"You must be very strong!" she remarked, as he wiped dust from his hands.

"And my heart is pure," he said, smiling. "The wood in the armoire has long since dried to tinder. It was not all that heavy."

He turned to the bed, with its upended mattress, and examined it. Again, he ran his fingers along the frame, pulled up the slats and checked to ensure that nothing had been attached to their underside, and then he began to feel the mattress.

"I knew a man once," he said as he probed the down and straw stuffing through the thin outer cloth. "He had embezzled a great deal of money from his employer. He was afraid to put it in a bank, as his station in life was not so fortunate that he could easily explain a windfall of that magnitude. In order to hide his ill-gotten gains, he systematically removed the stuffing from the mattress in his room and replaced it with cash. In the course of a year, he managed to squirrel away something over three hundred pounds. Never know what you'll find if you root around inside a mattress."

"And what became of him?" Mrs. Dutton asked.

"Who?"

"The man who stuffed all that money in his mattress?"

"Ah," Brekonridge said. "Burned to death. Smoking in bed, probably in response to his anxiety over possibly being caught. Sought the solace of tobacco, and it killed him. He fell asleep with his pipe still burning. Set the entire apartment building aflame."

He reflexively palpated the congealed scars on the side of his head.

"Hell of a fire, it was. Killed three, but many were rescued. The bills in his mattress burned, of course, but the silver and gold coins were largely undamaged. He was found out far too late for any worldly punishment."

He walked to the other side of the room, his boots clomping on the bar plank flooring, and he gently turned over the table to examine its underside. He did the same with the chair.

"Did Mr. M'Naghten bring any furnishings of his own?" he asked, as he righted the table.

"No. All he had was what I provided."

"Could I trouble you for a broom?"

She looked at him quizzically for a moment, and then nodded and left the room. She returned moments later with a broom. He upended it and began tapping at the floorboards with the hard wooden stick. As he did, he turned his ear toward to floor to listen for voids.

"There is a tenant downstairs," Mrs. Dutton cautioned.

"My apologies. I will be brief."

He continued to tap at the floor, until he reached the side of the room where the commode table and the pitcher and basin had been placed. He again checked underneath the table, and peered down the neck of the pitcher. Then he tapped the floor beneath the table, and was rewarded with a duller thud.

"What's that?" she asked.

Brekonridge knelt next to the wall and examined the floorboard there. He pulled a folding knife from his jacket pocket, and probed the edges of the floorboard with the blade.

"Loose," he said. He pressed the blade into a gap and twisted the knife enough for it to grab, then pulled it quickly upwards. The floorboard popped up, revealing the gap between the floor and the ceiling below. Inside the gap was an envelope. Brekonridge grasped it and placed it on the table.

"Is it important?" Mrs. Dutton asked, as Brekonridge pulled two sheets of linen bond paper from the envelope.

"It could be. It's a list of names. I recognize one or two of them from newspaper accounts and from M'Naghten himself. It would appear that Mr. M'Naghten was compiling a registry of his Tory persecutors in Glasgow."

Chapter Nineteen

Vicar Brekonridge's carriage pulled to the curb near Euston Station around nine o'clock. He retrieved his single valise bag and paid the driver.

Travel by locomotive being a relatively new conveyance, the Euston Station was equally new. Constructed only six years earlier, it was the first of London's grand rail terminals. It had been designed in line with the current craze for Greek revival architecture, the entrance demarked by the Euston Arch with its four huge fluted Doric columns and massive stone and brick corner blocks.

Construction had only recently been completed on the terminal itself, a grand open hall, five stories high, a hundred feet wide by two hundred long, the ornate coffered ceiling unsupported by any interior columns or visible buttresses. Huge windows placed inches below the ceiling illuminated the interior of the Great Hall during the day. Windows could not be designed into the walls on the ground floor because each wall was covered with arched doorways to various rail and carriage platforms. Strategically placed gas lights drove away the gloom at night. The Euston Station was one of the greatest architectural achievements of its day.

And, Brekonridge mused as he walked into the Great Hall, overtly optimistic. The designers counted on this new and sometimes frightening mode of transportation catching on with the masses. If one was traveling much farther than the next city, the costs of rail travel could be prohibitively expensive. In fact, the train he would take with young Simon to Glasgow would include only two passenger cars—a First Class car and a Second Class car. Third Class, had it been included, would have been an open car with benches for seating. In the frigid winter of 1843, Third Class passengers would freeze to death long before they saw the Scottish border. First and Second Class carriages were enclosed.

Brekonridge was in First Class. He sat on a bench near the grand double staircase leading to the Great Hall, pulled out his pipe, lighted it, and waited for his traveling companion to arrive.

He glanced at the clock over the south entrance. Nine-forty. He dared to entertain a glimmer of hope the young law clerk had encountered a mechanical misfortune with his carriage on the way to the station, and would miss the departure. It was a pleasant fantasy.

His reverie was interrupted when Simon appeared at the top of the stairway. A porter behind him hauled an impressive portmanteau on a hand truck. Simon saw the thief-taker at about the same moment and waved at him. Brekonridge stifled a grimace and waved back amiably enough. As the porter struggled to wrestle the huge trunk down the stairs, Simon rushed to greet Brekonridge.

"We aren't *moving* to Glasgow, boy," Brekonridge said, pointing toward the porter. "Was it necessary for you to bring all your earthly possessions?"

"That? Not at all. Only the necessities. We do not know how long we will be away, after all."

"Probably longer than if I had undertaken this assignment alone."

"Please believe me, Mr. Brekonridge. I did not ask for this. I will do my utmost to stay out of your way. My only duty is to ensure all the information you retrieve is conveyed directly to Mr. Cockburn. I will make every effort not to be a nuisance."

"I believe we depart on Track Six," Brekonridge said, as he gestured toward one of the arched passageways, and as the porter arrived with Simon's luggage. "We should make haste."

The initial plans for the Euston Station had called for twelve different train platforms. However, only two had been completed. Track Three was for incoming trains, and Track Six was for departures. The train was already at the platform, but only a few passengers milled about. Brekonridge checked as they approached, and was happy to discover that, perhaps because of the late hour, few of the carriage windows revealed people sitting behind them.

"Carriages" was an appropriate term in this case, since the First Class cars resembled nothing so much as three or four stagecoaches grafted to one another nose-to-tail. Each coach compartment, save the first, had facing bench seats and could seat up to six people comfortably. The seats were luxuriously upholstered in plush button-and-tuck velvet. The doors featured drop-light glass windows, which could be lowered in the summer for ventilation, or kept tightly closed in the winter to avoid freezing to death. They also featured fixed quarter-light windows which were placed so passengers need only turn their heads to view the passing countryside.

The exterior of the First Class carriages, owing to their heritage in stagecoaches, featured tumblehome design with swept lines and valances to hide the wheels and prevent sparks from the steel wheels igniting brush along the train's route.

Even the size of the individual compartments was nearly identical to that of stagecoaches. This was understandable, since the width of the track on which the trains traveled was based on the usual width of horse-drawn carriage wheels, called "Standard Gauge."

The First Class carriages had been placed at the rear of the four-car train. This was a safety measure. Since First Class cars were typically engaged only by the wealthiest of patrons, it was of utmost importance that passengers be afforded every possible convenience. Steam engines still had the occasional predisposition to explode unexpectedly, inevitably showering the cars they were pulling with flaming coal and iron shrapnel. The railway companies placed the Second-Class passengers between the engine and better-heeled First Class to act as a buffer.

Cockburn had reserved the entire forward compartment in the First Class carriage for Brekonridge and Simon. As the porter wheeled their luggage away to be stored for the trip, Simon pulled open the door of the forward compartment and hopped in. Brekonridge stepped in behind him, and they settled into their seats.

"I have to say, I'm excited to be making this trip," Simon said.

Brekonridge did not reply.

"I've never traveled a great distance by rail. In fact, I've only been on one train in my life, and it only ran from the Euston Station to Birmingham. And it certainly was not First Class. I have heard, on a long grade, these engines can get up to sixty miles per hour! Imagine!"

"Yes."

"That's twice as fast as the winner of last year's Derby. Wouldn't you say?"

"Undoubtedly."

"It must be safe, or people wouldn't take the train, would they?"

"Boy, betting on human nature is a fool's errand. Sometimes people do what is contrary to their well-being, with no reasonable explanation."

"But if it weren't safe, certainly the Queen wouldn't ride on a train, and I hear she has done so many times."

"I have heard the same."

"Of course, the word is she is actually frightened of them herself, and demands any train on which she is a passenger may not exceed forty miles per hour."

"I suppose queens can do that sort of thing. Look, boy, it's almost ten o'clock. We have a long journey ahead of us, and I hope to hit the streets as soon as we arrive. Best if we both get as much sleep tonight as we can."

As if to squelch discussion on the subject, he wrapped his wool scarf around his face, lowered the brim of his John Bull hat, slid down in the seat, stretched his legs across the car, and crossed his arms over his chest.

* * *

Simon awakened to a smell like a smoldering ship's halyard. He opened his eyes and blinked as the sun, cresting the horizon, burned into them. He turned his head and saw Brekonridge puffing on a pipe and gazing, fixated, at a sheaf of papers in his hand.

"I don't think you're supposed to smoke in these carriages," Simon said.

Brekonridge, without lifting his eyes from the papers, reached up and opened the droplight window. Immediately, frigid winter air blasted in.

Simon reached across and closed it again.

"That was unnecessary," he said, as his eyes adjusted to the exterior light. "What is that smell, anyway?"

"Hemp," Brekonridge mumbled, without removing the pipe from his mouth.

Simon peered out the window on his side of the coach. The land outside had taken on a more distinctly craggy appearance.

"Have we entered Scotland?"

"About an hour ago. We should be in Edinburgh shortly after lunch. Quite a laundry list Mr. M'Naghten assembled here. Not sure what to make of it."

He handed the list he had received from M'Naghten to the clerk, who read over it.

"Sheriff Bell. Sheriff Alison. Police Commissioner Hugh Wilson. Alexander Johnston, MP for Kilmarnock. Sir James Campbell, Lord Provost of Glasgow. Robert Lamond, Esquire, Barrister." He stopped and looked up at his companion. "The priests at the Catholic Church of Clyde?"

"There are others. It appears Mr. M'Naghten had a quarrel with almost every prominent Tory in Glasgow. Now, either he is right and there is a vast Tory conspiracy to rob him of his reason, or—"

"He's stark raving mad."

"That would be happy news for your employers. I have given this list some thought. Were we talking about any ordinary citizens, it would be a matter of no consequence for me to pay them a visit, intimidate them a little, shake their trees, and see what fruit falls to the ground. We are, however, not talking about any ordinary citizens. Mr. M'Naghten has accused Glasgow's most prominent officials of driving him to murder. What in hell are we to do with that?"

"I see your problem," Simon said. "According to the Municipal Corporations Act, the Town Council in Glasgow is responsible for all the police operations there."

"And the Town Council in Glasgow is dominated by Tories."

"Which means the Tories control the constabulary, commerce, streets and buildings, public works—"

"Almost everything. If they wanted, they could make life miserable for anyone who does not share their political philosophy. There are even some of the Council members listed here. If M'Naghten truly is aligned with the Chartists, it could be a difficult place to live."

"It stands to reason other Chartists are also being made a target of discrimination and harassment."

"Hmm." Brekonridge stared out the window. "While you slept, I reconsidered your role in our little expedition. I would imagine you have papers identifying you as working for Humphreys and Perceval?"

"It's common practice to give them to all employees working abroad."

"Do you think the police and sheriff's offices in Glasgow know M'Naghten is being defended by your firm?"

"It was mentioned in a few newspaper articles around the time M'Naghten was arraigned. It's possible they aren't aware, unless they are paying close attention."

"I agree," Brekonridge said. "There's no point in me walking into their offices and asking questions. If they are guilty of hounding our client, they will be put on warning should I start probing without any credentials. If you approach them, dressed like a gentleman, carrying bona fides on your person in the form of an introductory letter from a London law firm, and sell them some cock and bull story about researching properties, you could disarm them. Even if they know Humphreys and Perceval are the solicitors in M'Naghten's case, they'd never expect the firm to send a boy to investigate it."

"Excuse me," Simon said.

"What?"

"My name is Simon."

"Never suggested otherwise."

"But that's the fifth or sixth time you've called me *boy*. I don't think I care for it."

"You are a boy, boy. What are you? Eighteen?"

"Nineteen," Simon corrected. "And seven months. I'm among the youngest men ever admitted to the Middle Temple."

"Congratulations. The operative word here is *young*. The police and sheriffs would never consider you a threat. Enjoy your youth, boy. Revel in it. You can only use it to your advantage for so long, and getting old hurts like hell. You'll present yourself to the gentlemen, provide your credentials, get in their favor. Then, you can surreptitiously ask how people are reacting toward their local celebrity."

"And what is your role?"

"I think I'd like to start with the people who knew him best. Surely, among them must be individuals who can tell whether he was immersed in the Chartist cause to the point he would kill for it, or whether he was simply another sympathetic party on the fringes of the movement. If M'Naghten is quite mad, they should know."

Chapter Twenty

Glasgow in 1843 was a study in contrasts. Ships plying the River Clyde brought goods from around the world, and the Glaswegians in response had built massive edifices to accommodate the trade along the waterfront, including a new Customs House. The port on the Clyde was constantly in a state of commotion, with ships hastening to unload their cargo before reloading and putting back to sea, sailors taking the opportunity of a brief shore leave to drink copiously and lay with women of easy virtue, stevedores transferring goods to waiting carriages, and the inevitable assaults and murders that always seemed to flourish in cities where a major portion of the population was in transit from one point to another.

One would be required to walk only a few blocks, however, before the large buildings gave way to narrow streets, dozens of church spires, dark alleyways even the bravest of men dared not enter, and a bustling economy of another sort—shops of all kinds, street vendors plying wares from cockles to Oriental silks, houses hundreds of years old still managing to stand at a list, bankers, bakers, counting-houses, milliners, woodturners, hair salons, tanners, dry goods stores, public houses, and public privies.

Simon Daughtrey lived in one of the greatest cities in the world, but found himself captivated by Glasgow. Having never visited, and being completely unfamiliar with the area, he constantly craned his neck to look upward, especially in the areas where churches with their high steeples flourished.

Simon had always been fascinated by churches—the grander the better. He recalled how his father had taken the family on an excursion to

Paris, where they had visited Notre Dame Cathedral. The immenseness and grandeur captured young Simon's imagination immediately, and his excitement was only compounded when they had returned to London and he realized they had never seen the inside of Winchester Cathedral, an oversight which was likely due to the relatively nonreligious views of his parents, but which Simon corrected within days of returning.

His captivation was such that, at a younger age, he had entertained notions of going into the ministry. People had told him he had an unusually empathetic and perceptive character, qualities which Simon felt must be essential to being a successful shepherd to his flock. His primary motivation, though, was the opportunity to be associated with one of these grand structures.

His intellect had betrayed him. As he did with most notions that grabbed his fancy, he had immediately seized upon every reference volume on religion he could locate. He found a neglected Bible in his father's study, and began to read. He pored over commentaries in the library near his home. He went so far as to attend a few services, since it had occurred to him it might be useful to know exactly what goes on inside one of those buildings.

And, in the end, he found himself empty. Through the reading, the exploration, the hours spent trying to soak in the pageantry of worship, he awoke one morning with a realization. As spectacular as the entire process was, he was devoid of the single most important factor he needed.

He did not believe.

He realized he could have gone to divinity school. Intellectually, he was undoubtedly up to the rigors of the study, and he might easily have attained the status of a parish priest or a minister. In the end, though, it would all be play-acting. He would put on a costume and recite lines long committed to unconscious memory, and write sermons of earnest and academic perfection, but lack the passion to make them digestible for the masses. He would have to perpetrate a fraud as the price of his life in the temples of faith he adored for their elegant architecture and mathematic precision and their artistic beauty. He would be condemned to a lifetime of reciting the lyrics but never comprehending the music.

In the end, he had decided to admire his churches and cathedrals from a respectable distance. Glasgow gave him ample opportunity to do so.

Hugh Wilson had been on the Police Commission for almost five years. Like most members, he had a background in the practice of law, and as such he maintained an office on Argyll Street. Simon stepped up to the front door and knocked for admittance.

The door opened fully a moment later. A man peered out at him.

"Do I have the pleasure of addressing Mr. Hugh Wilson?" Simon asked.

"Most certainly not," the man said. "Does Mr. Wilson expect you?"

"I am here on behalf of my employers," Simon said, reaching into his jacket to retrieve the letter Perceval had provided him. "I have a letter of introduction from Humphreys and Perceval, Solicitors, Newgate Street in London."

He held out the letter. The man looked at it as if it might contain a pestilence.

"Please wait here," he said. "I will inquire as to whether Mr. Wilson is able to see you."

He closed the door, leaving Simon on the shallow marble landing. The street, while wide enough, was lined with buildings as high as five stories, many of them set apart by nothing more than blind alleyways a foot or two wide. The effect was to funnel the cold February wind across the River Clyde and down the canyons of brick and stone like a killing fog. Simon pulled his coat closer around him.

The door opened again, and the man greeted him with slightly more ebullience. He was still not overtly friendly, but at least the scowl had disappeared from his features. He led Simon up a walnut flight of stairs to the second floor. The man rapped on a door, and opened it without waiting for a reply, gesturing for Simon to enter.

The room was clean and bright, owing to the large window overlooking Argyll Street and floor to ceiling bookcases. Wilson's desk was simple and small for the space. More interestingly, it faced the wall, as if Wilson was loath to place anything between himself and his visitors.

Wilson stood another half head taller than Simon. He had evidently led an abundant life judging by the broadening around his middle. His nose was bulbous and reddened, his eyes dark and quick. He had a head of black hair shot through with gray, thinning a bit toward the front. He had shed his overcoat and dress-coat, and wore his waistcoat and tie. Simon realized, had he been several years older, Wilson might have shown the courtesy to don his dress-coat. That meant Wilson did not consider him to be of much importance. Simon could use that to his advantage.

"Mr. Hugh Wilson?" Simon asked, trying to throw a little timidity into his voice.

"Yes."

"My name is Simon Daughtrey. I have a letter of introduction here from Messrs. Humphreys and Perceval, Barristers, of Newgate Street in London. May I present it?"

"Please do."

Wilson reviewed the letter and handed it back to Simon.

"And how may I be of service to Messrs. Humphreys and Perceval?"

"Please forgive me, sir, but this is my first time working out in the field, as it were. I am not yet admitted to practice, but I am admitted to the Middle Temple. My employers have asked me to assist them in a matter of no particularly great urgency, as the client in question is recently deceased."

"A matter of a will, I take it?"

"More precisely, the lack of one. You see, we represent the estate of Robert Sturbridge, Fourteenth Baronet. Were you aware of his passing?"

"I was unaware of his living, and therefore his passing would have been of only passing interest to me," Wilson said. He chuckled at his little pun.

"The Fourteenth Baronet may have achieved great success in business, but at the neglect of his duty to produce a Fifteenth Baronet. The gentleman died both single and intestate."

"A great inconvenience to his estate, not to mention a burden on the nobility, leaving a baronetcy to go fallow."

"One might imagine. Mr. Sturbridge's oversight is a boon for our practice, however, as Mr. Perceval was named executor for the estate. It is his obligation to attempt to locate as many distant relatives as possible, to identify the proper heir to the baronetcy."

"And extract a handsome commission for doing so, no doubt."

"It is not so handsome a commission as to allow them to send anyone more senior than a clerk to do this job. Mr. Sturbridge's mother was from Glasgow. We believe there may be relatives here."

"Which is why you have come to our fair city. But it does not explain why you have come to my office."

"I was about to get to that, sir. I am from London. I know almost nothing about Glasgow, its topography, its people, or for that matter how precisely to get back to my temporary lodgings on Clyde Street. Mr. Perceval spoke of the Glasgow Police in the most glowing terms. He suggested, as I uncover the possible names of heirs to the unfortunate baronet, I might enlist your aid in locating their whereabouts. Mr. Perceval was aware of your work as a Commissioner, and suggested I approach you."

"Is that a fact?" Wilson said. "He singled me out, did he?"

Simon realized he had overplayed his hand. "You've found me out, I'm afraid. I was asked to enlist the aid of *a* Commissioner, but not necessarily yourself. Upon my arrival in Glasgow, I investigated the names of public officials, and among the Commissioners of Police your name was the closest to my location. If you believed Mr. Perceval held you in particularly high esteem, you might be more easily swayed to assist our firm. I hope you will consider this an error based on my youth and inexperience rather than a reflection on our agency."

"Of course. I was young once myself. In fact, I am relieved you are here on a matter of an abandoned estate. Did I not read in the *Herald* that Messrs. Humphreys and Perceval have been retained to defend Mr. Daniel M'Naghten, late of this city?"

"That is true. They have retained a countryman of yours, Alexander Cockburn, to head of the defense in that case. Have you met Mr. Cockburn, sir?"

"Once, some time back. He appeared to be a most engaging fellow. Bit of a rogue, I hear."

"I could not say one way or the other."

"You intend to plead insanity, I presume?"

"May I ask why that would be a likely presumption?"

"Because, in my estimation, your client would benefit most from a stint in the asylum."

"You know the gentleman, sir?"

"Oh, yes. For some years now. I believe I first met the lad a little over a decade ago, while he was apprenticing for his father."

"He was a woodturner, I believe?"

"The elder M'Naghten? That is correct. A most competent and facile craftsman. He turned the posts on my bed. I daresay his work has graced the bedrooms of half of Glasgow at one time or another. A good man, the father. I've known him most of my life."

"And the son?"

"A load of trouble, that one. You know he's a bastard. Probably never would have met him, I dare say, except his mother died when the lad was eight or nine. Daniel took the boy in, raised him as if he had lived under the roof from birth. Took him out of school at the proper age and taught him a trade."

"He worked for his father?"

"No. There was a falling out. I have no idea why. Young Daniel went to work for himself. Bought a shop and a couple of lathes, and started taking work. He was an adequate craftsman himself. Those candlesticks are from his shop."

He pointed to two walnut candlesticks on either end of the mantel over his office fireplace. Simon crossed the room to examine them. They were turned on a spiral, and polished to a gleam.

"They're beautiful," he said.

"As I said, he is a craftsman. His father taught him well. Sadly, the boy fell in with the wrong people."

"Criminals?"

"Might as well be. Chartists. Socialists. Anarchists. They warped his mind. You are familiar with the Mechanics Institute?"

"I am not."

"An educational organization. Been around for about twenty years. Their initial mission was noble enough, I suppose. Workers and craftsmen would spend their evenings drinking and gambling, which is not consistent with civic order, so the founders of the Anderson College decided to open a school for tradesmen, to keep them busy and productive. They could go to class in the evenings or at leisure, study subjects like anatomy, science, literature. Bunch of damned foolishness, I reckon. What need does a carpenter have for poetry? How does it help him make a joint squarer?"

"You do not approve of the Mechanics Institute?"

"Waste of time and money, but it isn't *my* time or *my* money. My complaint is it brings together large numbers of men in one place who may feel some discontent with the social order. Next thing you know, they aren't content to be governed by those with the intelligence and capability to do so. They want autonomy. Self-governance. They want to vote and hold public office. The Mechanics Institute is a hotbed of insurrection waiting for a reason to spill over into rebellion."

"And you believe M'Naghten was caught up in it?"

"Poisoned by it, I'd say."

"So you believe M'Naghten is sane, and the murder was politically motivated?"

"Did I say as much? No. Trust me, M'Naghten is definitively not sane."

"How can you say that?"

"He came to me, perhaps a year and a half ago. Said he wanted to file a complaint, but the police had rejected him as deranged. He did not look particularly unhinged, so I asked who had offended against him. He said he was being persecuted by priests."

"Priests? You mean Catholic priests?"

"Aided by Jesuits. He declared they followed him wherever he wandered, in stores and in restaurants. He said they hid under his bed at night, and he found them lurking in privies and alleyways. He went on with the most florid delusions."

"How did you answer them?"

"I told him I'd look into it, and he should return in a few days. I assured him I would investigate, and he seemed satisfied."

"What did you find in your investigation?"

"There was no investigation, lad. The man was out of his mind. I sent a message to his father, in hopes elder Daniel could talk some sense into his son, but the visits continued. He returned a few days later and charged the Tories had joined in with the police and the Catholics. Had he remained in Glasgow, I suspect he would have added the entire population of the city to his complaint by summer's end."

"He left the city?"

"Sold his shop and moved away. He did return almost a year ago, however briefly. I presume you also intend to visit Sheriff Bell and Sheriff Alison during your visit to Glasgow?"

"I do not understand."

"Young Mr. Daughtrey, you are obviously an intelligent lad, perhaps overly intelligent. You comport yourself well in the company of others, and you know how to ask a question. You are a bit young, however, to have been properly schooled in the practice of artifice. You did not happen on my office by blind chance. I was not the most convenient Commissioner of Police to Clyde Street. You came here specifically to ask me about young M'Naghten. I congratulate your employers on their guile. If they had sent a seasoned attorney, it would not have been as disarming. Since Mr. M'Naghten registered a complaint with me, and by all accounts did not receive satisfaction, I presume you intend to interview the other officials in Glasgow to whom he complained. Sheriff Bell and Sheriff Alison are among those officials. If it would assist you in your investigation, I can give you other names as well."

"I suppose I should apologize for attempting to deceive you. And I would be indebted to you for your assistance."

Wilson turned around to his desk and dipped a quill into an inkpot. Then he scribbled some names on a loose sheet of paper.

"I do appreciate your help," Simon said. "However, I must ask. My employers, as you surmised, intend to make a case for Mr. M'Naghten's insanity. Would you appear as a witness for the defense? You appear to be most sincere in your belief the man is not possessed of his reason."

Wilson surveyed him carefully, and crossed his hands over his rotund belly.

"I will not answer now," he said. "Have your employers contact me through more formal venues. I am an elected official. I suspect a subpoena would remove any suspicion from my motives for testifying."

Simon thanked him again and excused himself. The man who had greeted him led him back to the street. There, Simon pulled the paper Wilson had given him from his jacket pocket. The names on the sheet startled him.

The list was almost identical to M'Naghten's list of persecutors.

Chapter Twenty-One

From the shadows, across from Commissioner of Police Hugh Wilson's Argyll Street office, Brekonridge watched as Simon stood shivering on the doorstep.

He half expected the boy would wait for a bit, having been abandoned by Wilson, and eventually would wander away. Instead, the door opened again after a few moments and Simon was ushered inside.

Assured Simon would at least get to meet the Commissioner, Brekonridge set out on his first interview of the day. He found a close—or alleyway—that traversed the land between Argyll and Clyde Street, which ran alongside the Clyde River. Immediately as he exited the close, Brekonridge's olfactory senses were assaulted by a repellant aroma. Much of the waste of Glasgow flowed through the gutters, ditches, trenches and sewers, and ended here, within sight of the arched stone Bishop's Bridge that had provided passage over the river, in one iteration or another, for over six hundred years. The effluvia flowed into the Clyde, where most of it was swept on down toward the sea by the current. Inevitably, some portion of it became attached to the banks of the river, or sank to become part of the muddy silt, and added its odor of decay and corruption to the smells of dead fish and other garbage dumped along the banks.

Reflexively, Brekonridge pulled his woolen scarf up to cover his mouth and nose, lest he might inhale some particulate bit of refuse that would make him ill and compromise his mission in the city. He was all too aware of the typhoid outbreak in Glasgow since the previous summer, and he had no desire to become one of its victims.

He checked the address plates on Clyde Street. His destination was Number 90, a boarding house where Daniel M'Naghten had resided. It was three stories high, made of stone, and had likely stood in its spot for three hundred years. Brekonridge could tell the façade had received architectural attention more recently, and no doubt there had been modifications inside to make room for modern conveniences like gas lights and perhaps even water, but otherwise the building cried out fifteenth century.

He removed his John Bull hat and draped his scarf over his head, hiding as much of the scar tissue as possible, and wrapped the tails around his neck before putting the hat back on. He mounted the two steps to the front door, and rapped the knocker a couple of times.

He could hear footsteps from inside. A tall, thin woman with wiry prematurely gray hair opened the door and peered out at him.

"No vacancies," she said.

"I'm sorry to disturb you, but I am not looking for lodging," Brekonridge said. "Am I speaking with Mrs. Jane Patterson?"

"You are. What's your business here?"

"I am from London, working for the law firm of Humphreys and Perceval. They are representing a former tenant—"

"M'Naghten again. I already told the policeman everything I know."

"I understand, and I regret asking you to go over it again, but you should know the police officer—while I am certain he is an honorable, industrious man—was not looking for the same information I am. If I might trouble you for a few minutes of your time…"

She surveyed him from head to toe. Finally, she stepped aside to allow him in. He thanked her and, taking a seat in the main room, he removed his hat and undid the scarf.

"I apologize for my appearance," he said. "I encountered an unfortunate accident a few years back."

"I've seen worse," she said, as he removed the scarf from his head. "Looks like burns."

"Aye."

"You say you're from London. You sound Scottish."

"I was born in Edinburgh. Most people tell me they can no longer hear the accent."

"There's enough there. Have you met with Mr. M'Naghten?"

"I have, madam."

"Is he well?"

"He appears to be unharmed and healthy. It is my impression he experiences great mental anguish."

"If you ask me, that's a permanent affliction. It was never *my* impression Mr. M'Naghten was straight in the head."

"He showed signs of mental distress while he lived here?"

"Seven years," she said. "From 1835. He was a dependable enough lodger. Paid his bills on time. Never caused much of a commotion. Seems he was always reading. Never met a tradesman who took so strongly to books. But he was always a little off."

"Dangerously so?"

"Goodness, no. How many men do you run across who carry scraps of stale bread in their pockets to feed birds?"

"Not many."

"Each day, before he departed for his shop, he'd ask if I had any hard bread unfit to serve the lodgers here. Loved those birds, he did. How can a man who loves dumb animals so much commit a murder? That reminds me. Strange. I don't think I told the policeman about this."

"About what?"

"When I found the pistols in his room. I demanded to know what he planned to do with them."

"You found pistols in his room?"

"Why, yes. One long one and one short one. They looked perfectly new."

"When was this?"

"Sometime last summer. I don't recall the exact date, but it was unusually warm. I was going from room to room, opening windows to get the breeze flowing through the house, and I came across the pistols in Daniel's room. I have no rule against firearms under my roof, but I couldn't for the world imagine why he might need two. I asked where he got them. He said they were from Martin the gunsmith in Paisley. I demanded to know what his intent was in owning them. You know what he told me?"

"No."

"Said he planned to shoot some birds. I laughed, and he acted insulted. *'Look at you,'* I said, *'a man who hoards stale bread for birds, telling me you intend to shoot them. Keep your little secret then, but I'll thank you not to have those things loaded while inside the house.'* I didn't see the guns again. Tell me, sir. Did he use those guns to kill that poor man in London?"

"Yes. I'm sorry to say he did."

"You don't think I might have had some part in that, do you? By allowing him to keep those things here?"

"Not at all. Believe me, Mrs. Patterson, you are in no legal jeopardy. We are simply gathering all the information we can. Could you tell me a few things about Mr. M'Naghten as a tenant?"

"Initially, he was a fine gentleman. Quiet. Kept to himself. As I said, he read a lot. I could tell he had some difficulties. He couldn't sleep at night. I would hear him pacing back and forth in his room, sometimes talking to himself. It sometimes sounded as if he were having some sort of argument."

"When did he show these disturbing signs?"

"I suppose I first noticed how far he had dropped in early 1841. He was ill, and I was tending to him by bringing him broth and such. I mentioned to him, as he had recently sold his wood-turning shop, he might consider upon his recovery going out and finding a new situation. He got the wildest look in his eyes. He grabbed me by the wrist and squeezed until it became most uncomfortable, and then he released me and collapsed back on the bed. It wasn't long after that he started raving about being followed. That's when I asked him to leave."

"Who did he say was following him?" Brekonridge asked.

"At one time or another, everyone. First it was priests and devils. Then it was the Tories. He said they were all citizens of Glasgow. He told me he tried to escape once by sailing to France, but he got off the boat there and immediately saw one of the figures who had tormented him, so he returned directly here. It got so bad last September, I went to speak with the sheriff about him."

"Which sheriff?"

"Sheriff Alison. I wanted to ask whether there might be some help, to rid him of his delusions."

"And M'Naghten left shortly after you discovered the pistols in his room?"

"He did. Returned to London. It wasn't long after the Queen was here. I recall he made a special trip to see the Queen and the Prime Minister. He seemed quite fascinated by them. When he returned he was upset. Said he could not get close enough to get a good view of either of them."

"Was this before or after you found the pistols in his possession?"

"After, I'm sure. It was not long before he left here for good. Walked out one day with the clothes on his back, a few belongings in a bag, and left everything else behind—books, clothing, shoes, and even some tools."

"Did you store them?"

"Dear me, no. If I tried to keep every article left behind by lodgers, I should need another entire building. No. I disposed of most of it within a few weeks. Gave the clothing to the poor."

"Did M'Naghten have any friends who visited him here?" Brekonridge asked.

"He kept mostly to himself. There was one young man, though. Forrester."

"Do you know his first name?"

"Joseph, but Mr. M'Naghten never referred to him as anything but Forrester. He's a hairdresser. His shop is on this street, if you'd like to speak with him. This fellow Forrester visited Daniel on several occasions. They seemed close. I never liked the man, myself."

"Why is that?"

"He has shifty eyes. He was overly friendly, and didn't like to answer questions about himself. Perhaps it was because I didn't know him, but something about the man put me on edge. Now that I recall it, he tried to go to Sheriff Alison with me the day I went there."

"How did that happen?"

"As I reached Argyll Street, he fell into step beside me. At first, he seemed to be passing the time of day. Tipped his hat, greeted me by name, asked me how I was feeling and where I was headed. I told him. He asked me whether this was about Mr. M'Naghten. *'I don't blame you,'* he said. *'The man is daft.'* That's what he told me. His friend was daft. He asked if he could accompany me to Sheriff Alison's and provide more information to add to my complaint. I didn't like him. He made me nervous, so I told him I had a couple of other stops to make beforehand. He said goodbye, tipped his hat and went on his way."

"May I trouble you a bit further, Mrs. Patterson? The attorney defending M'Naghten is planning to claim insanity. Your testimony would be of huge benefit."

"I will testify. Bless him, I did like the young man. I would hate to see physical harm come to him for an act he could not control."

"My employers will be in touch with you to deal with the details of getting to London. One more quick question. Have you seen Mr. Forrester since Mr. M'Naghten left for London last year?"

"Frequently. He still maintains his shop here on Clyde Street, only a couple of doors down. Number Eighty-eight. Perhaps you will find him there."

Chapter Twenty-Two

I f Brekonridge had wondered why M'Naghten might live in an aromatically objectionable house on the River Clyde, he would have found the answer at his next stop.

From 1835 until 1841, Daniel M'Naghten operated a woodturning shop in a squat row of faded brick shops only a half block away, at 79 Stockwell Street. Apparently, M'Naghten had seen the economy of keeping home and work close to one another.

Brekonridge stepped inside the shop and saw three different operations taking place at once. Against a far wall sat a long cast iron spindle lathe powered by a massive flywheel put into motion by a foot treadle. A boy who could not have been older than ten stepped on the treadle rhythmically to keep the flywheel turning at a constant speed. Bent over the workpiece—in this case a billet of walnut—a turner rested a gouge on a cast-iron stop, and slowly fed the gouge into the spinning beam. Chips flew through the air, bouncing off the turner's leather apron and glass goggles. Brekonridge presumed he was copying the bedposts standing against the wall next to the lathe.

At a smaller lathe against a side wall, a lone worker had to pump his own foot treadle as he carefully hollowed out maple to make a large serving bowl. Against the other wall was a duplicate lathe, where a third turner burnished a candlestick with a handful of shavings. Nobody else was in the shop. Each corner of the room had piles of shavings and sawdust swept into drifts. Brekonridge watched, and waited for someone to notice he was there.

There was a loud clatter to his left as the bowl turner's workpiece shattered on the lathe sending shards of wood in every direction.

"Damn and blast!" the turner shouted. Immediately, the two other workers looked around at him.

"Another void," he said, at the same time he saw Brekonridge. He brushed the shavings off his arms and stepped up to the thief-taker.

"I'm so sorry, sir. I didn't see you there. It's a void in the wood, you see. A sap pocket, or some such thing. The gouge hits it, digs in, and…well, shards everywhere. We call it a blowout. Most frustrating. Is there something we can do for you, sir?"

"This is the woodturning shop that belonged to Mr. Daniel M'Naghten?"

"It is, sir. Perhaps you should like to talk to the current owner, Mr. Carlow?"

"That would be excellent."

The man turned around and shouted, "Billy!"

The man working on the bedposts signaled to the boy to stop kicking the treadles. He removed his goggles and looked at Brekonridge. "Something I can help you with, sir? I'm William Carlow, the owner."

Carlow was a tall, well-built man with green eyes and red hair. His face and hands were a mass of freckles. His forearms were massive, his hands thick and calloused. When he smiled, Brekonridge saw one of his top front incisors lapped over the other. It gave him a rustic, carefree look.

"He was asking after M'Naghten," the first man said.

"Ah," Carlow said. "I see. Perhaps we could go someplace quieter."

He led Brekonridge to the back of the workroom, and through a doorway into a storeroom where long, short, and fat billets of wood sat waiting for the turner's gouge. At one end of the room was another door, which led to a smaller room with a circular dinner table and few Windsor chairs.

Carlow said, "Now, what's this about M'Naghten?"

"You are aware of his circumstances?"

"Don't suppose there are ten people in all of Glasgow who aren't aware of Danny's circumstances. Made this place right popular, you know. I can't complain."

"Have the police been by to interview you about him?"

"Almost right away. I hadn't even heard about it myself, when the constables showed up and started asking questions. Wanted to know whether Danny ever showed any signs of sedition. Like I'd know what a sign of sedition looks like."

"I work for the barristers in London who will defend M'Naghten. I'm gathering information on his acquaintances and their memories of him. Could you spare a few minutes to answer some questions?"

"Why not? Breaks the tedium, doesn't it?"

"When did you purchase the shop?"

Carlow scratched at his chin. "It was in the second half of 1841. Around August, I believe. To be completely truthful, Mister…"

"I'm sorry. My name is Vicar Brekonridge."

"Really?"

"It's only my name. I'm not truly a man of the cloth."

"I might have guessed. Well, to be completely truthful, I didn't want to buy this shop. I mean, take a sniff. Who wants to be right down by the river? Danny made me the most excellent terms. I had turned him down several months earlier, and then he came to me and said he was done with the whole thing. I got the whole operation, with tools and machines, for only eighteen quid."

"That's all you paid for the business?"

"I'm lucky they didn't have me in the assizes for larceny. But Danny wanted to rid himself of the business."

"Did he say why?"

"Danny said a lot of things."

"You keep referring to him as Danny. Were you close?"

"Not like brothers, but I've known him ever since he returned to Glasgow from his acting career. Since at least 1835."

Brekonridge was suddenly alert. "Acting career?"

"Before Danny owned this shop, he tried his hand at the stage. Was completely wrapped up in it, I'd say. Fancied himself another Edward Kean or William Macready. Started off doing skits at the Trades Hall, and decided he had a knack for it. He was in a touring company for a few years. They appeared all over the West Highlands, performing classics. It all fell apart during the recession. Can't very well go out for spot of *Hamlet* when your belly's empty, can you?"

"Was he a good actor?"

"Good enough, I'd say. I've seen him, on the spur of the moment, launch into one of those Shakespeare monologues, waving his arms about and bellowing at the rafters like a wounded ox. He was particularly fond of *King Lear*. Talked about seeing Macready himself in the role some years back. Danny idolized Macready. But, it was not meant to be. He came back to Glasgow, bought this shop, and settled in."

"Did you ever see any signs of derangement in him?" Brekonridge asked.

"He was eccentric, and he had some big ideas. For a long time I defended him. That is, until I saw him act strangely myself. Then he went to France, and everything began to crumble."

"What about France?"

"I saw him after he returned, maybe a year ago. I wasn't there, mind you, but Danny told me the instant he got off the boat in Boulogne he saw spies lying in wait for him. When he got back from France, he was a changed man."

"Was he a political man?"

"Only in the last five years, perhaps. You are aware of the Mechanics Institute?"

"A sort of school for tradesmen?"

"Yes. A way for men who work with their hands to exercise their brains. Danny was in regular attendance there. Over the last decade there has been a movement afoot to transform the mission of the Institute to reflect the goals of the Chartists. Danny was part of that movement. I think it was because of his experience getting the vote."

"I don't know about that," Brekonridge said.

"It was quite a row at the time. Here in Glasgow, whether you can vote is based on your income or the rent you pay for your business. Around 1838 or 1839, his rent went up to twelve pounds a year. The increase qualified him for suffrage, and he immediately applied for the vote. There's an attorney in town named Robert Lamond. A true-blue Tory toady he is, too. There's a reason why the Tories control this city."

"And that is?"

"They control the vote. Registration Courts can challenge applications for suffrage for all sorts of reasons. The process, for poor working men who only want to vote, is crushing. There are court appearances and papers to file and fees to pay, and the smart men hire a barrister to represent them at the hearings, which can cost dearly. I'd dare say there are hundreds, maybe thousands of tradesmen in Scotland who meet the requirements for suffrage, but don't apply because they know they will be challenged, and so they're discouraged. The Tories suppress the vote of Liberals and Whigs and Chartists every chance they get."

"And this Lamond character blocked M'Naghten?"

"He did. With exceptional vigor. I suspect it was because of Mr. Duncan."

"Who is Mr. Duncan?"

"Abram Duncan is a Chartist instigator. He was employed in this same shop. I dismissed him shortly after I purchased the business. He was far too busy with his political activities and too infrequently at his lathe. A good craftsman, but not dedicated to his craft. He's rabble-rousing around the countryside these days, trying to raise support for the Chartists. That's why I mentioned the Mechanics Institute. Abram Duncan was at the forefront of the movement to turn it into a political instrument for universal suffrage. Danny was swept up in the movement. Duncan enjoys the attention of being a rebel. Danny was likely challenged because of Abram Duncan."

Brekonridge said, "Do you believe M'Naghten is insane?"

Carlow drew a circle in some dust on the table. For a moment, Brekonridge thought he might be evading the question. Then Carlow said, "I cannot say he is insane. I do believe he is changed. That much is apparent."

"Are you aware of any other people close to M'Naghten, who may be able to provide information on his mental state?"

"There's Forrester. Joseph Forrester. He's a hairdresser. He and Danny spent a great deal of time together. You might also speak with Bill McLellan, the blacksmith. I believe he has known Danny for over fifteen years. And there's John Gordon. He works for Laing and Son Foundry. I recall he employed Danny from time to time. You could also ask around the Mechanics Institute. That's all I can tell you, sir. It's not as if we were truly close."

"And this Abram Duncan fellow? Any idea where I can locate him?"

Carlow chuckled. "The man dotes on attention. Go to any Chartist rally. He'll be there."

Chapter Twenty-Three

s Simon approached 212 St. Vincent Street, the offices of Henry Bell, the front door opened and a young boy stepped out to a narrow landing, seven steps above the street. A portly man with a bulbous nose appeared behind the boy and handed him a couple of pence, which he stuffed into the pocket of his thin woolen coat. He tipped his hat to the man and trotted up the hill.

The man, who appeared to be in his early forties, remained in the doorway as Simon reached the steps and checked the house number, set into the block stone three-story façade.

"Mr. Henry Bell?" Simon said, as he looked up at the man.

Henry Bell was the sheriff depute of Lanarkshire, an area including part of Glasgow. Born in Glasgow and educated in Edinburgh, he regarded himself as more an academic than an ideologue. He was a short, round man—rounded brow, rounded shoulders, rounded belly—who sported long thick side whiskers and wore pince-nez glasses. His prominent nose only drew attention to his weak chin, and his teeth were bad. He was, overall, a physically unattractive person, for which he attempted to compensate by dressing like a dandy and exhibiting his intellect at every opportunity. Bell's charm, however, disarmed everyone around him. He was among the best-loved of Glasgow's officials.

"Would you be Mr. Simon Daughtrey, of London?" Bell inquired.

"I am, sir."

"Ah. Your coming has been foretold me," he said with a jovial tone, as he pointed to the boy who had already reached to top of the hill. "He did not beat you here by much. Please, come in. The fire in my study is much more agreeable than the February wind in Glasgow."

Simon took the steps up to the door and followed Bell inside. The house was cheery and light, despite the gloomy sky outside. As promised, the fireplace in the study crackled and warmed the room. A man took Simon's coat and hat. Bell gestured for Simon to sit near the fire on a new Duncan Phyfe sofa, made from walnut veneers and fine deep blue velvet and satin upholstery.

"The boy was sent by Commissioner of Police Wilson?" Simon asked.

"Yes. Mr. Wilson advised me of your possible visit."

"For what purpose, might I ask?"

"I couldn't say. What do you think? Should I be warned against you? Perhaps he only wished to let me know you'd be around to ask for help finding a dead baronet's relatives. That *is* your purpose here, is it not?"

Simon reviewed his options. The baronet was decidedly dead, and he had died intestate. There was no lie in that cover story. The fact Wilson had accused him of artifice implied the ruse had failed.

"A youthful ploy, Mr. Bell. Chalk it up to inexperience. Undoubtedly, Commissioner Wilson has already advised you of my inquiries regarding Daniel M'Naghten." He produced the letter from his firm, and Bell inspected it. "My employers have been engaged to provide Mr. M'Naghten's defense next month. It was my intent to gather as much information about M'Naghten as I could, in hopes this information would support the defense strategy of my employers and their litigators."

"That strategy being?"

"Mr. M'Naghten was insane at the time he shot Edward Drummond."

Bell, who had continued standing by the fire, smiled widely, then walked to a chair facing Simon and sat, slapping his thighs as he did.

"Well! If that is your goal I think you should encounter little difficulty. I concur young Mr. M'Naghten is mad as a man can be."

"You know the gentleman?"

"Not to any great extent. I was unaware of him before he came to my office."

"When was that, sir?"

"Must have been last summer. I was about to pour a glass of sherry to take off the chill. Might I interest you in some?"

"That would be most generous," Simon said.

Bell continued the discussion as he crossed to a cabinet at one corner of the study, extracted a decanter and two small glasses, and filled them with a tawny liquid.

"He appeared in my office in May or June, in a state of exasperation. His face was red, his eyes tearful. He shook as he spoke. He claimed he was the target of persecution, and he had not been able to find relief anywhere. He sought the service of the sheriff-depute office to bring the harassment to a halt. I told him I would do whatever I could to help him to achieve redress for his grievances, but first it would be necessary to understand exactly who was persecuting him."

Bell handed Simon the glass and sat at the opposite end of the sofa.

"He launched into an almost unintelligible litany of multiple agents acting in conspiracy against him," Bell continued. "Priests, police officers, businessmen, Tories. They had joined together for the express purpose of spying on his every movement. By the time he finished, it was impossible to determine whether there was any group in Glasgow not in league against him. I, of course, recognized his condition at once as monomania."

"How perceptive," Simon said. "You are trained to diagnose such conditions?"

"Not at all. I have simply read widely and recognized the symptoms. Are you familiar with the disorder?"

"I am not."

"It describes the presence of troubling ideas which persist over time. The individual becomes fixed on an idea that one thing or another is true, when it, in fact, is not so. No amount of logical persuasion can dissuade the individual of his notions. I am sad to say, according to the writings of those who know far more about such things than I, it is most likely a permanent affliction."

"How did you respond to his complaints?"

"I referred him to the Procurator Fiscal. Told him if he wished to file criminal charges against any residents for invading his privacy, it would have to go through that office first. He was distressed at the notion and asked if there was any other option for relief. I told him he might try a civil action against those pestering him, but he would likely need to find a local businessman to finance the lawsuit. He left, and I did not see him for a few weeks."

"But he did come back?"

"Yes, and he was even more agitated than ever. He made the same complaints and said the Procurator had been of no help to him at all. He appeared to be most beside himself. His delusions had become only more florid between his visits here. I'm no medical authority, Mr. Simon, but it is my fervent belief M'Naghten was not in his right mind."

"May I ask, sir? Would you be willing to testify to your impressions of Mr. M'Naghten's behavior in court?"

"If I were summoned, I would appear. Perhaps your employers may wish to reconsider their strategy."

"How so?"

"Have you been inside one of the various asylums scattered across the country?"

"I have only anecdotal accounts to inform me of them," Simon said.

"Horrible places. The hospitals in France and some here in Great Britain, such as the York Retreat, have shown marked advances in treatment of the insane since the turn of the century, but spend even an hour confined to these human warehouses and you will never want to set foot inside one again. A hanging is a quick thing. Compare that to a lifetime shackled to a wall or trying to sleep with the braying of dozens of madmen surrounding you. Imagine the discomfort and the deprivation and the inedible food, day after day, month after month, year after year. Please believe me, Mr. Daughtrey, when I tell you I would not wish such a life on myself, and I would gladly choose the gibbet over it. Your employers may save your client from the gallows, but in doing so condemn him to Hell."

Chapter Twenty-Four

Brekonridge and Simon sat at a table in the Clutha Vaults public house. Each had a tankard of ale and a bowl of fish chowder. It was shortly after dark, but the pub was almost empty.

The Clutha Vaults was situated at the far end of Clyde Street, next to the ferry docks. The ferry ran only a couple of times after dark, due to lack of demand. The Clutha Vaults depended on the traveler customers for the bulk of its business. The hard part of the day, for the barkeep, was over.

Simon looked around the room with distaste. "I'm only saying there were perfectly nice restaurants closer to our lodgings. We could have taken our supper in any of them, instead of here"

"I like it here," Brekonridge told him. "I prefer the food in a pub, and the warmth. Don't need linen tablecloths to eat here. Beyond that, this pub is closer to where I'm going tonight."

"You're going somewhere?"

"A Chartist meeting near here. Thought I would see if I can get in."

"I could go, too."

"No. There are limits, boy. I look like I belong there. You don't. Your hands are soft and your nails are clean. They'd never take you for a tradesman, and they'd bounce me for associating with you. You go back to the rooms and prepare for tomorrow."

"Tomorrow?"

"There's a lawyer named Lamond."

"Robert Lamond, yes. He was on the list Mr. M'Naghten gave you."

"I think I found out why he was included. When M'Naghten's rent was raised enough to allow him to register to vote, Lamond might have challenged it."

"How could he do that?"

"He's empowered by the Town Council and the Reform Act. He can challenge any voter registration."

"Do we know his party?"

"It's Glasgow. Tory, of course. He is considered one of the most ardent of party members."

"It would be interesting to find out what percentage of the challenges he filed were against Tories," Simon said.

"No records of the challenges are kept. They're either upheld or dismissed by the Registration Court. Most of the challenges are dismissed, but a few registrants are successfully blocked."

"And you believe Robert Lamond attempted to challenge M'Naghten's registration? Why? Because he was a Chartist sympathizer?"

"He might have been more. M'Naghten hired a Chartist agitator named Abram Duncan to work in his woodturning shop. Duncan is apparently well-known in these parts as a thorn in the Tories' sides. According to the current owner, this man Duncan was almost never at work, and when he was he spent the day spouting Chartist diatribes."

"You are surmising Robert Lamond knew of Duncan's employment by M'Naghten, and decided to…what?…punish him?"

"Obstruct him. Challenges must be backed by evidence. Gathering it takes time. The longer a challenge lasts, the longer the registrant is made to wait for suffrage. Perhaps, after enough time, the registrant becomes discouraged and abandons the petition. One or two challenges to Chartists won't take much of a bite out of the voting population. Challenge *every* Chartist sympathizer's registration, and before you know it your party is in the majority. But you missed the point, boy. Go back to what I said before, about Duncan's work habits." Brekonridge tapped at the side of his head. "Ask the next question."

"I don't understand, sir. What question?"

"For every answer, there is a next question. Knowing M'Naghten hired

Duncan and continued his employment, despite the fact Duncan was a poor employee, begs the next question."

"Why did M'Naghten hire him in the first place, and why did he not dismiss him after Duncan demonstrated his lack of diligence?"

"Exactly. But there's more. Let us say we do discover, upon your conversation with Robert Lamond tomorrow, that he challenged M'Naghten's voting registration. That begs the question…" He trailed off and waited for Simon to take the bait.

"Did he challenge M'Naghten because he knew him to be a Chartist sympathizer, or was the challenge due to the hiring of Duncan?"

"Of whom Lamond was almost certainly aware. Now. Ask the *next* question."

Simon stared into his stew. After a few seconds, he shook his head. "I am at a loss."

"There are several. First, was M'Naghten a Chartist—or at least a sympathizer—prior to hiring Abram Duncan? If he was, then he must have been aware of Duncan's politics."

"And, if so, why hire him, knowing it would not benefit his business?"

"The obvious first answer is he was providing some sort of camouflage for Duncan."

"You are suggesting M'Naghten hired Duncan to give him respectability in the community?"

"Yes. He's not an agitator or a rebel, he's a productive member of the town, working for the second generation of a respected family of woodturners. Now. Ask the *next* question."

After a few seconds, Simon said, "So…if I understand you, the next question would be who *else* benefitted from hiring Duncan?"

"Sir Isaac Newton postulated every action results in an equal and opposite reaction," Brekonridge said. "Everything we do impacts our future in one way or another, but it can also benefit or harm someone else. The most obvious results of any act are betrayed by the effect on the actors themselves, but the consequences emanate out from them like concentric waves on the surface of a pond."

"And sometimes the person impacted always expected to benefit."

"Yes!" Brekonridge said, before lighting his pipe. "If many people are impacted, it hides the benefit to the intended recipient. The needle in the haystack. Most incisive. Time may reveal the Middle Temple knew what they were doing when they admitted you at so young an age. Perhaps placing Duncan in the employ of M'Naghten was intended to benefit someone else. It served a purpose."

"There is the other possibility," Simon said. "M'Naghten hired Duncan, who was known to Robert Lamond as a Chartist agitator. When his rent was raised to the threshold for voting, M'Naghten applied to vote and was challenged by Robert Lamond, due to the fact M'Naghten had Duncan in his employ. M'Naghten did not know why his registration was challenged, but universal suffrage is a right claimed by the Chartists, and his right was therefore being impinged. He searched for other examples of discrimination and, in his imagination, he found them. They mounted one upon the other until he saw conspiracies everywhere. He visited one political official after another, complaining of persecution, but received no relief. Eventually, he believed the officials themselves were part of the scheme against him."

"And so he went to London to kill Robert Peel, to behead the entire Tory conspiracy and end his woes."

"It fits with the results of the interviews I had today with Police Commissioner Wilson and Sheriff Bell."

"Saw through your ruse immediately, did they?" Brekonridge asked with a smirk.

"How did you know?"

"These are senior officials in a city that has been highly organized for generations. They did not achieve their positions through sloth or gullibility."

"Then why did you tell me to lie about my purpose for visiting them?"

"It reinforced your youth and inexperience. You are obviously a gifted young man with an intellect that belies your years. Had you presented as that young man, it would have put the gentlemen you were interviewing on alarm. They are more likely to divulge information if they feel superior to you."

"Was it not as likely, if they truly believed I was a complete neophyte, they would simply lie to me and send me on my way?"

"It was possible, but I have come to the conclusion you know the difference between the truth and a lie. So, did either Commissioner Wilson or Sheriff Bell lie to you today?"

"I do not believe they did."

"And they both believe M'Naghten is dispossessed of his wits?"

"They do, and both readily indicated they would be willing to testify to it at M'Naghten's trial."

"Ask the next question."

"What? I'm overwhelmed with all the questions!"

"Why are they so willing to testify? It is a long way to London. Neither of these gentlemen has an obligation to M'Naghten. Moreover, how would they be served by M'Naghten being committed to an asylum? In fact, beyond M'Naghten himself, who would benefit from such an outcome?"

"You're suggesting the Tory officials in this city would benefit in some way from M'Naghten being insane?"

"I'm only tossing out possibilities, boy. Tonight you know a little more than you did this morning. Always ask the next question and follow it to its logical conclusion. A pattern will emerge from all those pieces of straw in the haybale. The patterns will lead you to your needle. Today, we only poked the haybale. Now we pull at its straw. I begin tonight by attending a Chartist meeting. You begin by returning to our rooms and getting ready for tomorrow's interviews. While you are at it, think on this. According to William Carlow, M'Naghten worked for several years as an actor. He was a great admirer of Macready's portrayal of King Lear and played the role a few times with a touring group of actors in the highlands."

"I have seen the play. King Lear slowly goes mad after giving away his kingdom."

"Yes. It would seem Mr. M'Naghten has some experience feigning insanity. Can you imagine what the *next* question is?"

Yes," Simon said. "I certainly can."

Chapter Twenty-Five

The Chartist meeting was held that evening at St. Andrew's-by-the-Green, the first Episcopalian church constructed in Glasgow, on the edge of the Glasgow Green where, in 1838, Dr. Arthur Wade had held aloft the People's Charter at a meeting of one hundred fifty thousand workingmen. The Episcopal Church in Scotland had long sympathized with the Chartists, and many locations welcomed Chartist and similarly-minded organizations to meet within their walls.

The church stood on a small plot of land behind a stacked-stone knee wall separating it from Greendyke Street. Its flat-faced two-story Georgian façade was wrought from stone, with huge gables at each side, and over thirty oversized windows to let in the daylight. It was not an impressive structure the way one might regard the Glasgow Cathedral. Its intent had always been to serve as a neighborhood parish church, which also made it a perfect location for out-of-the-way political meetings.

Gas-fired chandeliers and candle sconces lit the room cheerily. The pews had been cleared away, leaving an open area of oak floors and fluted Corinthian columns. At the top end of the congregation were three steps leading up to the sanctuary and an immense carved walnut pulpit. There would be no need for the pulpit this evening, as the speakers would simply stand at the top of the steps to deliver their orations.

Several dozen men had already assembled by the time Brekonridge strode through the door. He slowly worked his way toward a back corner of the room, which was a bit darker. More men filtered into the room over the course of the next quarter hour, until there were between two and three hundred milling about, talking excitedly among themselves. Smoke from a hundred pipes rose to the ceiling, pooled, and began to form a thick blue cloud.

These were hard men, who led hard lives. They were workingmen—stone masons, trench diggers, carpenters, sawyers, millwrights, molding makers, leather workers, coalmen, bakers, tailors, tanners, glaziers, and every other craft and trade in Glasgow. They were men with permanently calloused and stained hands, fingernails horned and cracked to the cuticle, skin leathered with age and exposure, constantly scabbed and scarred. They were men given to drink and smoking and sometimes fighting. They were better used to public house fare and ale from pewter tankards than restaurants with starched linen tablecloths. They were Britain's backbone and they gathered to demand their due rights.

A man wearing a long woolen coat and a weather-beaten top hat sidled up next to Brekonridge. The man's boots were filthy, and from the smell of him Brekonridge could tell he was a stableman.

"Quite the turnout, ain't it?" the man asked.

Brekonridge nodded, briefly making eye contact with the man. He hoped that would be enough to send the mucker in the direction of a more receptive audience.

"So, what's your trade, friend?" the man asked.

"Ship's carpenter," Brekonridge said brusquely, and it was not a lie. During the War of 1812, and after as a merchant seaman, Brekonridge had trained and served as a ship's carpenter. It was a trade he preferred, rather than dealing with the constant bravado of warfare. He was still as handy with an adze or a try plane as he was with a cudgel and handcuffs.

"Is that so! Well, it's nice to make your acquaintance. Healy's my name."

"And you muck stalls," Brekonridge said.

"That I do. And it's obvious how you know. You could say I take me work home with me. Have ye heard Mr. Cooper speak before? The man could light a fire under an iceberg, he could. You're in for a treat tonight, my friend."

Three men stepped up in to the sanctuary. One, between thirty-five and forty years old, was strongly-built, with shoulders as wide as an armoire. He had protruding ruddy cheeks and a pug nose. His hair was curly, pulled back into a queue. He was dressed in a suit fashionable five years earlier, and wore a bowler hat. He stood slightly back from the other two men, who apparently were in charge of the meeting. One of them stepped forward, stamped his feet two or three times, and raised his hands to get the attention of everyone in the hall.

Slowly, the din in the room subsided as the attendees turned toward the speaker, a thin man with short curly brown hair and eyes that seemed to see everything at once.

"It's wonderful to see so many of you come out tonight to hear our guest, Mr. Thomas Cooper!" the man exclaimed, and the crowd burst into a brief cacophony of hoots and applause. "As you all know, I am Abram Duncan, and before I ask Mr. Cooper to address us this evening, I should like to take a few minutes to pass along some important news. As you are aware, fifty-nine of our brethren go on trial for sedition and treason next month in Lancashire..."

As soon as Duncan introduced himself, Brekonridge focused in and tried to divine all he could from the man's speech and appearance. Carlow had said Duncan would milk the room for attention. Duncan craved notoriety almost as much as he did universal suffrage and a House of Commons made up of tradesmen. The way Duncan now waved his arms and allowed his voice to rise and fall in volume as he lauded the crowd with all the latest news from the Chartist trial, it was apparent he knew how to manipulate people.

"...All of these good men wish for nothing more than the decency of self-determination!" Duncan continued, as the men in the hall slowly surged forward. "And how does London respond? They prosecute us! They hold mass trials! They persecute us!"

Brekonridge's head snapped around toward the speaker. *Persecute.* The justification M'Naghten gave for shooting Edward Drummond. He wondered whom of the two—M'Naghten or Duncan—had uttered it first.

"We are the engine that drives the empire, my friends! Without the ache in our backs and the scars on our skin, Great Britain grinds to a halt. We demonstrated that with our general strikes, and in return our leaders are prosecuted. We need only look to our neighbors and former colonists in America to see what could be. There, every man may vote."

"Slaves can't," Brekonridge muttered, taking care nobody else could hear him.

"Every man in this room would lay down his life for the right to take this elementary role in the process of governance, the ability to fill out and cast a ballot. A simple thing. It takes no more than a minute, and yet it is fundamentally denied to eighty percent of British subjects! Are we living in medieval times, my friends?"

The crowd, as if rehearsed or in a responsive reading, responded with one voice, "No!"

"Are we serfs, to be lorded over by the fat earl sitting in his castle on the hill?"

"No!"

"Are we to be denied the universal human right of self-determination?"

"No!"

The volume kept increasing in the tiny hall, until it rang in Brekonridge's ears as he worked his way to the front.

"So, my fellow tradesmen and seekers of freedom, I ask you to welcome our extremely special guest. I am humbled to have Mr. Thomas Cooper here tonight to fill your heart with the spirit of liberty. Please, show the man he's welcome, lads!"

The crowd erupted in shouts and claps, some men whistling loudly and others stamping their feet. Within seconds, every other boot in the room stamped in time—*One, two, three! One, two, three!* Dust in the rafters, loosened by the vibrations of the Chartists' stomps, fell on the men who continued to cheer as they were pelted with fifty years of the church's detritus.

The men continued to press toward the sanctuary, creating an impassible mass of flesh. Brekonridge stood a full head higher than most of the men in the room, but their hats kept him from seeing the stage clearly, and he could not wedge himself through the crowd. The only option was to return to the outer edge of the mob and try to work his way around to the front that way.

The clamor in the room decreased as Thomas Cooper held up his hands to quiet everyone. As Brekonridge struggled to make his way forward, Cooper started his address.

"Thank you. Thank you, my Glaswegian friends, for your warm welcome. It is a great pleasure to address you tonight. Some of you may have seen me speak at other meetings and rallies, but the message is still a good one and worth the second hearing."

Applause again echoed against the stone walls and stained glass windows, egged on by Cooper himself, and then it died again.

"My friends, I am like you. I work with my hands. I don't know what various and diverse trades you represent, but I am myself a cobbler. Made these myself."

He pointed toward his shoes, and the crowd cheered.

"I also taught myself. I was never a shoemaker's apprentice, my friends. I learned through trial and error, and by observation and imitation..."

Brekonridge finally made it to the front of the room, only to find Cooper standing all alone in the sanctuary, three feet above the crowd, gesticulating wildly and regaling them with the story of his struggles with the intricacies of footwear. He could not find Abram Duncan anywhere in the group. Nor did he see the other man who had stood with Duncan and Cooper. Somehow, while he had attempted to maneuver his way toward the front, they had left.

He felt a draft of cool air to his right. An arched passageway behind the column at the front of the congregation opened to the street, and the breeze seemed to come from there. He made his way toward it, and found it was an access hallway to the back side of the sanctuary. The draft grew stronger and colder. The hallway was dark, with a glow of light toward the end. Feeling his way along the wall, he made his way to an exit door with three steps up toward the street. Two men stood outside the door. One smoked a pipe. Beyond the stone knee wall, Brekonridge saw Duncan and the other man climb into a carriage and close the door.

He started toward the steps, but the men stopped him.

"Where are you headed?" one of the demanded.

"I would have a word with Mr. Duncan," Brekonridge said, as he struggled against their grasp on his coat sleeves.

Duncan leaned forward in the carriage, glanced briefly at Brekonridge, and then leaned back again and barked an order. The horseman drew away from the curb.

"Guess he don't want to have a word with you," the man in the doorway said. "Why don't you go back inside?"

"My business is with Abram Duncan." Brekonridge wrenched one arm free and swung the second man into the first, causing both to tumble into the doorway. "I am not a man to be hindered."

He made his way to the top of the steps. By then the carriage had already disappeared around the next corner, and was moving at a steady clip toward the river. Brekonridge picked up his hat. The two men in the doorway slowly rolled to their feet. Brekonridge shot them a warning glance and they backed away. He put his hat on, cursed, and set off toward his lodgings on Clyde Street.

So disgusted was he at missing his opportunity to ask Duncan some questions, he never saw the stable mucker Healy, who followed half a block behind him.

Chapter Twenty-Six

Simon noted Brekonridge was out of sorts at breakfast the next morning. They sat in the dining room, enjoying a hearty meal of salt herring, thick bacon, porridge with cream and brown sugar, beans, mushrooms, Jerusalem artichokes, grilled onions, potatoes and toast. Both drank tea. Simon believed Brekonridge would have strongly preferred a tankard of ale.

"Did you learn anything important at the Chartist meeting last night?" Simon asked.

"Laid eyes on Duncan," Brekonridge grumbled, before stuffing a huge spoon of porridge into his mouth. "I imagined he would be larger."

"Were you able to interview him?"

Brekonridge shook his head and speared a piece of herring with his fork. "He left before I could."

"Perhaps you can locate him yet."

"Ah. That I will, boy. And when I do I'll be certain to find out why he evaded me last night. He saw me demand a moment of his time and had me delayed while he drove off."

"Surely he had no idea who you were. You've never met before."

"Looked pretty damned deliberate to me," Brekonridge said as he sliced a sliver from the bacon. "What's your plan for today?"

"I'll interview Sheriff Alison, and then move on to Robert Lamond."

"When you talk with Alison, ask him if he knows a hairdresser named Forrester."

"Why?"

"Forrester and M'Naghten were close friends. M'Naghten's landlady told me she was headed to Sheriff Alison to file a complaint about M'Naghten's strange behavior. On the way, she met with Forrester, who asked to accompany her. Forrester told her M'Naghten was daft, and he could help bolster her petition for assistance from the Sheriff's Court."

"Forrester also met with the sheriff?"

"No. Something about Forrester disturbed the landlady, and she told him she had to make a few other stops first. I'd be interested in whether Forrester ever made his own way to the sheriff. I'll ask him myself when I find him, but it's always useful to have both sides of a story. You know what to ask Lamond, right?"

"Voting registration challenges."

"Go about it generally, first. Don't dive right in talking about M'Naghten's application. For all we know, Lamond's quarrel wasn't with M'Naghten. This may be about Duncan. In fact, I am inclined to think Abram Duncan can answer a lot of our questions."

* * *

Sir Archibald Alison had been Sheriff of Lanarkshire for almost eight years, after applying to and being awarded the post by Sir Robert Peel following the death of the previous sheriff. Alison's qualifications for the post were relatively straightforward. As a baronet, he had the proper social standing. He had been called to the bar over twenty years earlier and had enjoyed a highly successful career as a barrister. His name had been mentioned as being on informal lists of potential future Solicitors-General.

He was a stout but not portly man. His face was classically defined, with a strong cleft chin, a beak-like nose and intense, piercing eyes. Shortly past his fiftieth year, his hair had receded from his forehead, but remained thick, wiry, and curly elsewhere. He was fond of sporting thick side whiskers, but left his upper lip and chin bare. His features, posture, and manner all indicated a quiet, distinguished responsibility. By all accounts, he was not a man to entertain guile.

"A frightening, awful business," Alison told Simon. "Sir Robert awarded me this position. I shudder to think that he could have been cut down so unfairly. I'm not certain why you are here. Your letter of introduction makes it clear you are working for the defense in this case. I am confused as to what assistance I may offer as a law enforcement official."

"We are gathering information in Glasgow regarding Mr. M'Naghten's past. Given the many witnesses present on Whitehall at the time of the shooting, there can be no doubt at all our client shot Edward Drummond. The question of his motivation remains. Specifically, as you have no doubt already surmised, my employers intend to demonstrate M'Naghten was insane at the time he committed the crime. That begs the question of whether he showed signs of mental disturbance during the months leading up to the killing."

"I am not aware of having ever met with young M'Naghten."

"Is it possible," Simon ventured, "that M'Naghten made a complaint with officials downstairs, with the expectation you would be made aware of it, and you simply never saw it?"

Alison tapped at the cleft in his chin and mused over the question. "It is entirely possible. When I was made Sheriff of Lanarkshire, the state of legal proceedings was in terrible shape. It took me almost a year to relieve the unheard cases. This is a new building, into which we only recently moved, and our record-keeping perhaps could benefit from better attention."

He called for one of his clerks downstairs. Simon heard the clomp of heavy boots on the stairwell. Allison had words with the clerk in the doorway.

"One of our clerks will look for a complaint," Alison told Simon after the clerk left.

"The date on it, if nothing else, could assist in formulating a chronology for Mr. M'Naghten's descent into madness. While your man is searching for the papers, might I ask you a related question? Mr. M'Naghten maintained a residence on Clyde Street, owned by a Mrs. Patterson. An associate interviewed Mrs. Patterson and was told she appeared here to seek help for her tenant because of his bizarre behaviors and thinking."

"Yes, I recall meeting with Mrs. Patterson. She did say her tenant was not in his right mind."

"And how was the matter resolved, if I may ask?"

"There was nothing for me to do. I took a report, of course, but commitment of the mentally deranged does not fall under the purview of the Sheriff's Court. I referred her to the Procurator-Fiscal…*if* she believed M'Naghten was dangerous and posed an immediate threat of bodily harm. Failing that, it was up to his family to deliver him to a proper asylum for treatment."

"And do you recall receiving a separate complaint about M'Naghten's behavior from a man named Joseph Forrester? I believe him to be a hairdresser."

"No. I am aware of Mr. Forrester and I can say he never appeared before me to swear a complaint or ask for assistance."

There was a knock at the door and the clerk entered, carrying a thin sheaf of papers. Alison dismissed him and examined the papers.

"I appear to have been mistaken," Alison said, after a few seconds perusing the documents. "Mr. M'Naghten filed a complaint against a number of Glasgow citizens, claiming they were following him and harassing him. The complaint was never passed along to my office, because the clerk who took it determined he was a madman and could be disregarded."

"May I see the list?"

Most of the names were those M'Naghten had already provided, with the exception that Sheriffs Bell and Alison and Commissioner Wilson did not appear on it. Apparently, Simon determined, they were added after M'Naghten received no relief from his tormentors and he became convinced the local court officials were bound up in the conspiracy against him. A few other names were also missing, including Lord Provost James Campbell and the local MP, Alexander Johnston.

The complaint was dated April 23, 1842. Over nine months before he stepped up behind Edward Drummond and fired a pistol ball into his back, M'Naghten had reported to the Sheriff of Lanarkshire that people were conspiring against him. Humphreys and Perceval would be pleased with this information.

Chapter Twenty-Seven

Finding Joseph Forrester was an easy task. He kept his hairdressing parlor only several doors from Mrs. Patterson's boarding house.

Brekonridge sat on a stone wall over the river, across Clyde Street from Forrester's parlor, smoking his pipe of hemp. He had waited for half an hour for the hairdresser to show up. It had been a cold business, as the wind off the river whipped around him, stirring what few leaves remained from the autumn around his feet. He ignored the cold. He was warm enough in his layers of woolen clothes, his belly was full from breakfast, and he had plenty of money in the bank. Getting paid to sit on a stone wall in Glasgow seemed, in retrospect, a relatively easy way to make one's way in the world. With the exception of a little cold wind, most things in his life were going as well as could be expected. The hemp did not hurt.

He passed the time reviewing what little information he had learned since arriving in the city and comparing it to the enormous list of things he did not know. In the course of some interview with some man he had not yet met, there would come a tipping point, that instant when all the random bits of information would fall into a pattern that would explain why M'Naghten had taken his fatal shot. Over the years, Brekonridge had learned not to force the moment. The understanding would come when it came, and the only way to urge it along was to acquire as much knowledge as he could regarding the life M'Naghten had led in Glasgow.

He had learned, also, to look for the picks in the fabric of understanding. Sometimes it was the contradictions that led to truth, not the consensus.

Warm was warm, fed was fed, and the view of the River Clyde was serene and relaxing, once you no longer smelled it, but after an hour Brekonridge determined the hairdresser was not likely to appear momentarily. He shuffled his day's schedule. Something William Carlow had told him had bounded around inside his head for most the night.

He pushed away from the stone wall and walked north, toward Cathedral Street, as a fresh flurry of snowflakes fell. It was a short walk, no more than seven or eight blocks back from the river. At Cathedral and Hanover, he found the Mechanics Institute. It was of relatively unimpressive size, only half again as large as St. Andrews-by-the-Green, but as he walked he discovered the façade of the building was a conceit and, while narrow, the institute ran back for almost half a block. The front of the building was a little more than two stories high, with the flat-faced Georgian architecture that had become all the rage across the country since the turn of the century. Two or three tradesmen stood outside at the bottom of three short deep granite steps that led to the doorway, the steam from their collective breaths coalescing into a cloud that enveloped their heads.

The temperature inside the building was agreeably warm, at least in comparison to the snowy chill outside. A man in his early sixties sat behind a desk in an alcove off the main hall. He was mostly bald, save for an inch-long fringe of white hair that ringed his head like an Olympic laurel. The effect of the hair and the woolen robes he wore to keep warm gave the impression of a tonsured monk.

"Can I help you?" the man asked. Brekonridge saw a nameplate on the desk. It read: *W. Ambrose.*

"Mr. Ambrose, I take it?" Brekonridge said.

"That is correct. Are you a member of the Mechanics Institute, sir?"

"No. I'm from London. I work for Humphreys and Perceval, solicitors. They are—"

"Providing the defense for Mr. M'Naghten," Ambrose finished, his eyes twinkling. "Are you by chance here regarding that case?"

"I am. You seem familiar with it."

"I'm an old man, sir. I have little to occupy my time except reading. I devour the London newspapers. They are so much more salacious than those in Scotland."

"You know M'Naghten?"

"Indeed. He was here regularly. Took a few classes and he was frequently in the library, reading. You are aware of the mission of the Mechanics Institute?"

"Not completely. I understand it is intended to provide educational services to tradesmen."

"In a broad sense, but there is more. So many of the industrial trades are conducted more by tradition than by modern scientific findings. By teaching our students as much about science and literature and mathematics as they can handle, we open their minds to scientific inquiry and thinking critically about the world. Their personal career explorations will be built on empirical knowledge rather than hearsay and tradition. The product will improve. Their standing in the community will improve. Everyone benefits."

"And it keeps them from killing one another in the public houses at night," Brekonridge said.

"Some benefits are unintended, but welcome."

"Beside greeting strangers from abroad, what is your position here?"

"I am the general secretary. I maintain records, schedule classes, keep track of attendance records, and issue diplomas."

"What do you recall about Mr. M'Naghten, other than his attendance and reading habits?"

"My acquaintance with Mr. M'Naghten was casual at best. I first became aware of him about three years ago. I believe he may have attended classes here for longer than that."

"How did he come to your attention? Was there some change in his behavior?"

"Not that I recall," Ambrose said. "It was a matter of frequent exposure. Many of our young men come once or twice, fail to see the advantages or opportunity here, and we never see them again. The regular students, those who attend most frequently, become familiar. I talk with them from time to time, and they tell me about their lives. I learn the most fascinating things talking to these boys."

"So, you saw no change in M'Naghten at all?"

"Not on the surface. Of course, we did not converse regularly. I tend to become friendlier with the lads who attend every night. Perhaps you should talk with Mr. Swanstead or Doctor Douglas."

"Who are they?"

"Mr. Swanstead is the curator and head librarian. As I mentioned, Mr. M'Naghten was most frequently to be found in the library, so Mr. Swanstead may have a greater familiarity with his behavior. Doctor Douglas teaches the anatomy classes in the evenings. I believe Mr. M'Naghten took several of them."

"Would these gentlemen be here today?"

"Doctor Douglas wouldn't. You might catch him at his surgery, or perhaps here in the evening after his class. Mr. Swanstead should be in his library. Have you seen it?"

"The library? No."

"Most impressive. We fill it with books from the Queen's grant. It's a marvelous resource for our young men. Most of them can't afford a subscription to a public lending library, but I daresay our collection rivals any you'll find there."

* * *

William Swanstead was tall and thin, not much older than forty, and appeared to pride himself in his dress. His hair was long and wavy, strawberry-blond in color, brushed back and held by a ribbon. His hands were long and elegant. His grip was tenuous as he shook hands with Brekonridge.

"So it's the M'Naghten case you're here about," Swanstead said, after escorting Brekonridge to a sitting area at one corner of the library. "How is the young man?"

"He appeared healthy and unharmed, if highly distressed. I have come to Glasgow to gather as much information on him as I can."

"What would you like to know?"

"How long have you known M'Naghten?"

"It has been a while. I met him in either 1834 or 1835, around the time he first started attending classes. He was an avid reader, which is probably why I became familiar with him."

"What sort of books did M'Naghten like to read?"

"It depended on what he was studying at the time. When he was taking Doctor Douglas's anatomy class, he would devour the books on biology. When his interests turned to philosophy, he would check out books on Aristotle, Descartes and Hegel. He was particularly fond of dramas and he occasionally read fiction. I would have to say his philosophy period was his longest and the one which he approached with the most vigor."

"Was he political?"

"Dear me, yes. Most of our students are tradesmen and craftsman and laborers. They are men who, as things stand, can never hope to enjoy the luxuries lavished on the privileged class. The best most of them can aspire to is a warm hearth under a roof that doesn't leak and a pleasant partner to dent the other side of the mattress. That was fine, for several centuries, but our students today are becoming impatient. They read in the Bible the meek shall inherit the Earth and they wonder how long they must wait for their bequest. Men like that are drawn to movements that promise a better life for all, regardless of whether they can actually fulfill the promise. M'Naghten was no different."

"You sound like a Chartist yourself."

Swanstead glanced around the empty library, as if wary someone might be hiding. "I sympathize with the circumstances these young men face. I share some of their desires for the future."

"Suffrage?"

"Of course. Universal suffrage seems the only answer."

"For women, too?" Brekonridge asked.

"Well," Swanstead said, "let's not get *too* ambitious, shall we? Yes, Daniel M'Naghten was political. So are a hundred other young men I could name as we sit here. It is their circumstances, you see. Political advocacy is their only real hope for a chance to move beyond their position in life."

"Were there specific men he spent more time with than others?"

"Mr. M'Naghten and Bill McLellan the blacksmith spent a great deal of time together. I even saw Mr. M'Naghten sitting and talking with some of our more notorious Socialists, a couple of men named Graham and Nockold. Real trouble, those two. Damned near anarchists. Seems to me M'Naghten was drawn to radical ideas endorsed by the young lions. Suffrage, representation in Parliament, reforming the taxation system. If a group espoused such goals, you were likely to see M'Naghten in their number. When he left, I thought perhaps he had sailed off to America or some such foolishness."

"You mean the first time he went away? In 1841?"

"Yes. Then, last year, during the spring, he returned, changed."

"In what way?"

"He was dressed better. Definitely smelled better. Even had clean fingernails. He went away as a woodturner, but returned as a dandy. There was more. He behaved differently. He always seemed to be looking over his shoulder. He became agitated and irritable with little provocation. There was a glassy look in his eyes. I don't know what sort of life he encountered in his travels, but I would have concluded at the time it did not agree with him."

"And that was in April or May of last year?"

"That's correct. He came back, acting strangely. He was here for five or six months, and disappeared again. The next time I heard of him was in the *Herald*, after he was charged with murder."

Brekonridge said, "Perhaps you did not hear this from M'Naghten himself, but has there been any talk among the students of taking violent action against the Prime Minister?"

"You are asking me to accuse our young men of treason!"

"Not at all. As you say, they are young and full of passion. Young men in a state of rage say things they do not mean and make plans which will never come to pass. But let us also suppose a young man who has been radicalized by ideas of rebellion overhears that conversation and takes it to heart. He may imagine becoming the hero to his entire pack of radicals by putting the plan into action."

"You are talking about ideas far beyond my ability to understand. I have no knowledge of the interior workings of the mind, especially the workings of a diseased mind. You are looking for an alienist, sir."

"I'm looking for answers. You have already alluded to an undercurrent of radical leaning within the Mechanics Institute. I do not wish to indict any of your students. I sympathize with the Chartist cause. I probably would not have taken this job if I did not. However, I have heard reports some of the students are actively seeking to turn the Mechanics Institute into a vehicle to promote their liberal causes."

"I have heard the same rumors."

"Are they realistic?"

"Who can predict the behavior of large numbers of disgruntled men in groups? For the most part, I believe it to be talk. For the rare student who feels he has nothing to lose and everything to gain, it might be taken seriously."

"Nothing to lose," Brekonridge repeated. "Yes."

Chapter Twenty-Eight

Robert Lamond was engaged in a legal partnership with Adam Monteith, as solicitors out of their office at 60 Ingram Street. Simon knocked on the front door and was escorted in by a clerk almost immediately. He asked to see Lamond.

Moments later, Lamond walked into the room to greet him. He was in his middle thirties, with a full head of thick auburn hair and a modest attempt at side whiskers that instead resembled thinning tufts of heather. He was of medium height, with rangy legs and a truncated torso. His breath smelled of brandy, only a little after one in the afternoon.

Simon presented his letter of introduction. Lamond barely glanced at it before handing it back.

"If you don't mind, I would prefer to have my partner, Mr. Monteith, sit in on our deposition."

"It's hardly a deposition," Simon countered. "I merely have a few questions."

"And should you subpoena me to appear in court at a later date, I should imagine those questions would be posed to me again. You aren't here out of blind curiosity, now, are you? You can call it Aunt Nancy's tea party, but it's still a deposition. I give you credit for trying to diminish it, however. A lesser man might be put off guard."

"I am grateful for your compliment—"

"I was speaking of myself. Mr. Monteith is waiting in my office."

The office was on the small side, perhaps only ten feet by fifteen, but it was comfortable and cheery. A desk made of oak had been placed in one corner, facing three velvet-upholstered chairs. A coal fire blazed in the fireplace, casting warmth across the entire room. Against the same wall as the door was a massive bookcase filled with leather-bound volumes.

Adam Monteith sat in one of the chairs but rose as they entered the room. He was slightly shorter than Lamond, but thicker, with jet black hair and dark eyes. He crossed the room and held out his hand, a serious look on his face.

"Adam Monteith."

"Simon Daughtrey, Mr. Monteith. We have a barrister on our defense team for Mr. M'Naghten named Monteith. I believe he is Scottish. Would you be related?"

"No," Monteith said abruptly, as he resumed his seat. He waited patiently for the interview to begin.

"I see," Simon said, "Perhaps we should get right to it. As I mentioned, we are representing Mr. M'Naghten in his upcoming murder trial in London. Another interviewer and I have been dispatched to Glasgow to learn as much as we can regarding M'Naghten's last several years here."

"You seem young for an attorney," Lamond observed.

"I am, in fact, not yet called to the bar. I have been admitted to the Middle Temple, and my studies continue."

"Such an important case, and they send a clerk," Lamond said to Monteith. "Should we feel offended?"

Monteith didn't change his expression.

"I am forced into an unfamiliar role," Simon said. "My intended duty was to maintain records of interviews conducted by our investigator. When we arrived in Glasgow, we quickly discovered an embarrassing wealth of people we would need to meet and a limited amount of time to collect our information before returning to London. I am required by necessity to assist in the interviews. Our primary investigator is busy elsewhere in the city talking with witnesses of higher priority."

Simon smiled sweetly, hoping his jibe had not been too direct.

"Ask your questions," Lamond said. "Mr. Monteith and I are busy, but we are always happy to carve out chunks of our day for a representative from

London, regardless of his lack of standing." He mimicked Simon's smile.

"Are you familiar with Mr. M'Naghten, sir?"

"Not directly. I am, of course, familiar with his name, and I believe I have had some dealings with his father of the same name, but almost all I know about the man is what I have read in the newspapers."

"Could you describe your political role in Glasgow?"

"To what purpose?"

"If I may say so without offending, Mr. M'Naghten has claimed publicly he shot Mr. Drummond due to persecution by Tories and others here in Glasgow. Before we left London, he fashioned a list of people in Glasgow whom he believes have conspired against him. Your name is on that list, sir. As Mr. M'Naghten's defense entails charges against the Tories, I wondered how your name came to be there."

"It's easy," Monteith said. "The man is deluded."

"A fact we intend to prove in court, and your saying so would be welcome testimony," Simon said. Monteith grimaced and Simon turned back to Lamond. "You are aligned with the Tories in Glasgow, are you not?"

"It's well known. I have served on the city council, and throughout the last decade I have been involved in the process of registering voters and getting them to the polls. My sympathies are entirely with the Tory faction and I see it as a civic duty to ensure as many Tory votes as possible are cast."

"How does one go about that, exactly?"

"There are a number of strategies. For instance, since one can vote upon paying a ten-pound-per-year rent, it is possible to buy up properties worth that amount and rent them only to loyal party members. As soon as they reach that rent threshold, they can register to vote."

"And you would never challenge the registration of a man who registers if you know him to be a Tory party member?"

"Why would I challenge a fellow Tory? Part of my job is to get as many of them to vote as possible."

"But you have challenged registrations from other parties. Is that not so?"

Lamond waved his hand in the air, as if swatting away a fly. "A few."

"You challenged over seven thousand registrations in 1832 alone."

"You come up with that number rather handily, I'd think."

"I have an excellent memory and a fair head for numbers," Simon said.

"A lot of good it did me. Only thirty or so of the challenges were upheld."

"But I would imagine a great many more were discouraged, and some lacked the resources to answer the challenge, and still others might have believed the challenge left them with no recourse. While only 'thirty or so' challenges were sustained, I would suspect your actions had no small impact on the turnout by the Whigs and Liberals in that election. Those *were* the registrations you challenged, were they not?"

"I won't deny it. I was within my rights. My office gave those rights to me as a result of the Reform Act. Nothing I did was in any way illegal."

"You must have been terribly inconvenienced by the rise of the Chartist movement."

"How so?"

"The movement is made up of tradesmen and craftsmen, most of them independent businessmen who rent their shops, rather than buy them. They are the ten-pounders who are likely to register to vote for the first time."

"A nuisance, I say," Monteith said.

Lamond held up a hand to silence him.

"You stated you try to enhance the numbers of Tory voters while limiting suffrage among other parties," Simon continued. "I will admit Glasgow is no great city on the order of London or Paris, but you have your fair share of people here. How does one keep track of which potential voters hold which political views? How would you know which voters to challenge, and which to let through?"

"Some you know by name and face and you know their leanings," Lamond said. "For the rest, it's a percentage game. Since, as you note, the majority of the ten-pounders are radicals who do not actually own land or property, it is an easy matter to challenge each and every one automatically. You will catch some loyalists in the net, but the eventual outcome will be you eliminate more of the opposition. The Tories who get caught up in a challenge need merely state they are Tories and the challenge will be removed."

"Is that fair?"

"All is fair in love and politics," Monteith quipped.

"Who cares?" Lamond added. "It is legal. That is all that matters. You should be in support of these actions, Mr. Daughtrey. You are educated, obviously privileged, no doubt from a fine London family. You are the picture of the status quo. Certainly, you would prefer to preserve our society as it currently stands. God, Queen and Country, right? Can you imagine a Parliament populated by shepherds and tanners and ironmongers? Why not let in sheep, goats and cattle, while you're at it? Let's face it, sir. The average laborer in England, Wales, and Scotland has the relative intelligence of a Yorkshire terrier. Put them in charge of the country? The notion makes me ill. I say we leave the management of the empire to men of breeding, education and traditional values. The laborers of the world enjoy their station as a result of their birth. It is dangerous to allow a man endowed of limited ability and intelligence to acquire too much power. They know not how to wield it."

"Having established your intent to limit the number of petitioners unsympathetic to the Tories, do you know whether you challenged Mr. M'Naghten's application?"

Lamond said, "I would presume I did, since I challenge every ten-pounder who applies. It is a logical conclusion his application was challenged. I simply have no memory of it."

"Are you familiar with a man named Abram Duncan?"

Monteith made a desultory sound. Lamond shot him a warning look.

"Of course," Lamond said. "Mr. Duncan is well-known in the Glasgow area. He is a Chartist rabble-rouser and a troublemaker. Were it left to me, he would be in prison or transported to Van Diemen's Land for treason and sedition."

"Mr. Duncan was employed by Mr. M'Naghten. Were you aware of this?"

"No," Lamond said. "Had I been aware, I would have put greater effort into suppressing M'Naghten's application."

"Because of his association with a known Chartist?"

"They are like roaches. They congregate in swarms. You find one, you'll find ten others. Apparently M'Naghten was running a nest of them out of his woodturning shop."

Simon paused for an instant. He looked first at Lamond, then at Monteith, and back at Lamond. Both seemed irritated, but also smug.

"I...I don't believe I mentioned M'Naghten ran a woodturning shop," he said. "When I asked you whether you knew M'Naghten, you said your only exposure to him had been in the newspaper. Strange you would recall a fact as obscure as his work from those articles."

"Like you, I have a good memory," Lamond said, rather facilely. "Have you acquired the information you sought? Mr. Monteith and I are quite busy, but we are anxious to ensure the fine firm of Humphreys and Perceval in London are satisfied with our cooperation."

"You may not have been aware of M'Naghten, but he obviously knew a great deal about you, enough to put you on his list of tormentors. What is your opinion on Mr. M'Naghten's claims of Tory persecution in Glasgow?"

"Poppycock. It's a humbug."

"Even though you said—had you known M'Naghten was a Chartist—you would have exerted greater effort to keep him from reaching a ballot box. Does that not seem like persecution to you? Singling out an individual for different treatment solely on the basis of his beliefs?"

"It is legal," Lamond said. "That is all that is important. I thought we had settled that. As for Mr. M'Naghten, your intent is clear, Mr. Daughtrey. Your defense team expects to prove insanity and spare M'Naghten from the gallows. Personally, I would prefer the punishment our beloved William Wallace endured, but we are civilized men, so I will settle for a short rope and a high scaffold. The only way we can hope to wipe out this infernal Chartist infestation is to burn it out, right to the roots. We start by showing sympathizers if they go to extreme measures to achieve their socialist and nihilistic goals, they will receive the harshest punishment possible."

Chapter Twenty-Nine

Having received directions from William Swanstead, Brekonridge made his way to Doctor James Douglas's surgery at the Royal Infirmary on Castle Street, next to the Glasgow Cathedral.

The Royal Infirmary was a huge five story hospital topped with the sort of cupola one would anticipate in a national government house. It contained two wings on each floor, divided by a central administrative structure.

When Brekonridge walked inside, he discovered that James Douglas maintained an office on the third floor. Brekonridge rapped on the door twice, and waited patiently in the hallway until a woman answered.

"Is there an emergency?" she said, as she surveyed her hulking visitor.

"Not a medical one, I am happy to report," Brekonridge. "I have traveled here from London, and I would appreciate a few moments of Dr. Douglas's time. It concerns one of his students from the Mechanics Institute."

James Douglas's office was not much larger than the waiting room, but it was much better appointed, with more comfortable furniture. Douglas himself was in his middle forties, and appeared to be in excellent shape. His face seemed to have an ever-present flush, so his cheeks and chin were constantly rosy. His hair was pewter-colored, worn long, and pulled back with a ribbon. A stray lock of it fell over his forehead. He wore wire-rimmed reading glasses, with which he apparently had been studying an oversized volume of a medical encyclopedia open on his desk. When Brekonridge entered, he stood and extended his hand. As they greeted one another, Douglas seemed to visually examine the burn scars at the side of Brekonridge's head.

"I smell burned rope on your clothing. You started using hemp to alleviate the pain of your burns, I take it," he said.

It was such an unusual and unexpected greeting, Brekonridge had to think for a second how to respond. "Yes," he said at last.

"And how does it work for you?"

"Are you asking as a physician?"

"More out of curiosity. I don't use the stuff myself. Never have. I do admit to taking a bit of cocaine from time to time, but only when I'm facing several days without rest. Have you tried it?"

"No."

"Quite remarkable stuff, actually. I suspect, like hemp, one develops a tolerance after some extended use and therein lie the seeds of addiction. You were most fortunate to find me in my office today. I've been on rounds since early this morning. We have a bit of a typhoid epidemic in Glasgow at the moment. Please do be careful what you eat and drink. Do you find the hemp muddles your thinking?"

Brekonridge tried to follow Douglas's leaps from subject to subject and noticed the physician's dilated pupils. Douglas, he deduced, had not been speaking casually about his cocaine use.

"No," Brekonridge said. "It opens it up."

"I don't understand."

"I have been blessed with the ability to maintain attention on a single matter for an extended period of time. My mind does not naturally wander. I may become obsessed with one explanation for a circumstance which, in my profession, may lead me to conclusions supported by available facts, but otherwise false. Hemp, in addition to its analgesic properties, enables me to consider multiple explanations for any single set of facts. It keeps me from becoming fixated on a single and possibly inaccurate solution."

"And what is your profession?"

"Thief-taker. Previously, I was a London police officer, and before that a Bow Street Runner. I have spent the last twenty years tracking malefactors and bringing them to the dock."

"And are you hunting some criminal today? Certainly it isn't me," the doctor said with an agitated giggle.

"Not at all. My journey to Glasgow is solely for the purpose of gathering information. I am working for the solicitors coordinating the legal defense of Daniel M'Naghten. I believe you are familiar with the young man?"

"Poor M'Naghten. Such a sad case. Huge potential in that lad, I can tell you, but he was born under the wrong roof. It is so hard to rise above one's given station in life, is it not? He attended a number of my anatomy seminars."

"How were his grades?"

"There were no grades. We aren't awarding medical degrees here. Most of the coursework is for the personal enrichment of our students, and I'm not even certain that term applies in Mr. M'Naghten's case. He never actually enrolled in my seminars. It isn't a requirement, after all. The theaters are open to all. We do provide certificates for registered students who complete the series. I suppose that would be the only reason to register, now that I think of it. To get a certificate."

"How did you find M'Naghten?"

"Intelligent. Inquisitive. Had a quick mind and an excellent memory. He asked a lot of questions. An instructor notices. I teach physiology, anatomy, and dissection. He was particularly interested in the anatomy and dissection classes. I recall talking with Mr. Lamond only the other week about him. You know, after he was charged with the murder in London. We talked about how unfortunate it all was. What a waste."

"Excuse me," Brekonridge interrupted. "Mr. Lamond?"

"Yes."

"Would that be Robert Lamond?"

"Yes. He's the Secretary for the Royal Infirmary. It's mostly an honorific, but—"

"And you talked with Robert Lamond about M'Naghten?"

"That's right. Why? Should I not have?"

"Not at all. I find it curious. Tell me, Doctor, had you noticed any changes in M'Naghten over the last couple of years?"

"It would be difficult to say. We only spoke about anatomy."

"Were there young men he spent a great deal of time with at the Mechanics Institute? People who might be able to describe his state over the last several years?"

"There's Forrester, the hairdresser."

"What about Abram Duncan?"

"I do believe M'Naghten and Duncan were acquainted in some way. They did not spend a great deal of time together at the Institute, at least not in my seminars. Duncan has never been in one of my classes."

"But you are aware of him?"

"I suspect everyone in Glasgow has heard of Abram Duncan. He's trouble, that one."

"Are you aware of any attempts on the part of the workingmen attending the Mechanics Institute to radicalize it in any way?"

"In truth, Mr. Brekonridge, I am only an adjunct faculty member there. I am not privy to all the internal politics of the place, but you can expect a great number of the students there are sympathetic to the Chartists, if not directly involved with them. It's the nature of the population."

"Part of my mission to Glasgow is to recruit witnesses to appear at M'Naghten's trial. Would you be available to appear to testify to his academic nature and his dedication to his studies?"

The physician blinked a couple of times, as if trying to understand the question.

"But, I am already appearing there as a witness," he said.

It was Brekonridge's turn to show confusion. "You are?"

"Yes. I mentioned my meeting with Mr. Lamond the other day. Apparently, he has been in contact with the prosecutors in the case. They are looking for people who can testify to young M'Naghten's clarity of mind. Mr. Lamond made all the arrangements. I have my train tickets already."

Chapter Thirty

Brekonridge and Simon sat eating inside a public house. They had arranged to meet in the early afternoon to catch one another up with their interviews.

"When I spoke with Doctor Douglas at the Royal Infirmary, he told me he had already been asked to appear for the prosecution at trial," Brekonridge said.

"It's to be expected," Simon said. "This is case of some notoriety. I would imagine the Queen and the Prime Minister have a great deal riding on it. What did you find?"

"A mixed bag. Some witnesses say M'Naghten has been in an emotional and mental decline for some time. Others have noticed no changes at all. I have two men from the Mechanics Institute who are willing to testify he was withdrawn and troubled over the last year or so, and had become increasingly disturbed in that time. What about Lamond?"

"The man is a most convincing liar. Not only that, he was arrogant and pompous. I took an immediate dislike to him and his slimy business partner."

"How could you tell he was lying?"

"There are body postures, ways of holding one's face, movements of the eyes."

"Like a bad cards player. What did he say about M'Naghten?"

"Almost nothing. Claimed to have no memory of the man, except what he had read in the newspapers after the arrest."

"Curious," Brekonridge said, after gulping some ale. "Lamond was most interested in M'Naghten when he spoke with Douglas at the Infirmary last week. From what Douglas told me, it was Lamond who arranged for him to appear at the Old Bailey."

"So my sense about Lamond lying was correct."

"It would appear so. What's the next question?"

"That's easy. We would next ask *why* Lamond lied."

"Well," Brekonridge said as he packed hemp into his pipe, "since your information suggests Lamond is not only a Tory but also dedicated to keeping Glasgow Tory; and since the Solicitor General represents the Tory Parliament in London and the Queen, who is decidedly behind the Tories, Lamond would likely seize on the opportunity to provide assistance, once presented."

"He'd be a fool not to, if he has any ambition."

"Following that conclusion, why lie? In your interview with him, he denied any interest in the case. Yet, a week ago he was recruiting witnesses for the prosecution. Curious."

"There's more. I asked specifically about Abram Duncan. Lamond displayed almost encyclopedic familiarity with Duncan's supposedly seditious activities in Scotland. However, when I asked whether he had singled out M'Naghten for challenge of his voting registration, he had no awareness of having done so. Later, however, he bragged about challenging every registration, showing little concern for whether Tories might be caught up in the net, because—in his words—Chartists are like roaches who live in communal nests. Following that logical course, if he considered one Chartist particularly egregious, he would be sure to make himself aware of all that man's acquaintances. He appeared to be especially vitriolic toward Abram Duncan."

"Meaning he should have been aware of M'Naghten, beyond what he read in the newspapers," Brekonridge said. "Another lie."

"Leaving us with the question of why, again."

"I have known men who lied for no reason at all. It appeared they lied because they had lost the capacity to be truthful. It was simply their nature to lie."

"Sometimes people lie to throw other people onto the wrong track, to divert attention from themselves," Simon offered.

Brekonridge held a match to his pipe, and exhaled a huge cloud of blue smoke.

"What if Lamond *did* single out M'Naghten for especially rigorous challenge to his voting registration, and in the course of doing so reinforced M'Naghten's burgeoning sense of persecution? When Lamond challenged his registration, M'Naghten, perhaps rightly, determined it was an act of persecution because of his Chartist ties."

"But Lamond admitted challenging every registration not overtly known to come from Tories."

"But not every potential voter he challenged was in the process of descending into madness. We keep thinking there is only one cause for M'Naghten's attack on Drummond. There may be many, working in consonance. Two or more storms combine into a cataclysm."

"You don't believe his madness resulted from actual persecution?"

"Not at first. He may well have been persecuted, as has every other Chartist in Scotland, but his defect of reason may have preceded it. Real persecution blended with his fantasies, and exacerbated his madness."

"And he tried to make that right by eliminating the man whom he believed at the center of the plot to persecute him. It is an elegant thesis, but does not explain everything we know. There is the other matter," Simon said.

"Which is?"

"The money. Where did M'Naghten get over seven hundred pounds? Your story has substance. One might even be able to sell it to a jury. But it doesn't explain M'Naghten's sudden windfall. I cannot imagine the prosecution will ignore it."

"No." Brekonridge inhaled again from the pipe. "The money is unexplained."

"Perhaps it is stolen."

"But from whom? A theft of that magnitude would certainly have made the newspapers around the time M'Naghten deposited it in the bank. That leads me to believe whatever the source the money, it was given willingly.

Which raises the next question."

"What did the person who gave M'Naghten the money get in return?"

Brekonridge took another draw from the pipe.

"We still don't know enough," he pronounced, after exhaling. "It occurs to me that a man of poor reason might make the perfect hired assassin. They are gullible, disposable, and plausibly deniable. Our primary mission appears to be working, as we have secured several witnesses willing to testify to M'Naghten's mental decline. The deeper we get into this, however, the greater I believe there is more to this crime than mere insanity."

Chapter Thirty-One

Brekonridge returned to Clyde Street to find Joseph Forrester's hairdressing salon open for business. Inside was a robust man, almost as tall as Brekonridge. He was barrel-chested, with thick arms and wrists, and was working on a white wig attached to a wooden bust.

"Can I help you?" he said, without looking up. His voice was soft and raspy, almost as if he were getting over an infection of some kind.

"Am I addressing Joseph Forrester?"

The man stopped his work and looked up. He had liquid blue eyes, and his dark red hair fell in curls around his face. "Aye. I'm Forrester. Have we met?"

"We have not, sir." Brekonridge introduced himself and explained why he was in Glasgow. Forrester listened attentively, then stepped to the door, turned the lock and placed a CLOSED sign in the window. Brekonridge considered several reasons why Forrester might do so, and he tensed to prepare for any contingency.

"Now we can talk privately," Forrester said. "And how is Danny faring in London?"

"As well as any prisoner can expect. Might I ask about your relationship with Mr. M'Naghten?"

"We're friends. I have known him for a number of years."

"Do you spend a great deal of time together?"

"I don't know what that means. We talk. We have dinner together. We go to meetings. He's a friend."

"How did you meet?"

"We were in the same theatre company, ten years ago. We traveled around, performing Shakespeare. Seemed so important at the time. Looking back on it, we were probably awful. But, people in the villages where we stopped weren't exactly used to Macready, were they? Danny acted. I did a few parts myself, but mostly I worked on makeup and hair and costumes. I seem to have a talent for that sort of thing."

"As you have known the man for over a decade, you would have noticed any changes in his thinking or his behavior over the last two or three years?"

Forrester gestured toward a pair of chairs closer to the fireplace. "Please, have a seat."

They both sat, and Forrester steepled his fingers, as if trying to project the image of engaging in some kind of internal debate.

"Danny was a sensitive boy," he said, finally. "Even back then. He craves attention. Under his father's roof, he was the bastard child, always beset with the impression that his value fell behind that of his father's legitimate children. When he came of age, his father refused to offer him a partnership. So, Danny decided to try his hand at the stage. We met shortly afterward. I remember how he loved applause, but could go into the darkest rage at a single boo or catcall."

"And recently?" Brekonridge asked.

"You want to know whether Danny showed signs of madness? I think he has always been a little mad. It has only been the focus of his madness that has changed from year to year. I have seen him struggle his way home from the Mechanics Institute with a barrow of books, all on the same subject. Once Danny was engaged with any subject—religion, politics, drama, even art and music—he would become obsessed by it. I can't think of anyone among my acquaintances who reads more. I think some of the books he read had greater impact on him than others. A lot of his ideas might have resulted from reading a book."

"What ideas?"

"You know. Radical ideas."

"Chartist ideas?"

"Chartist, Socialist, nihilist, all of them. I can recall, when we were playing the countryside, Danny talked about fairness and equality. Talked like a damned American, freedom of this and that, every man a king. We were in Oban, or it might have been Perth. Danny had a little too much to drink, and he stood on a bench and preached for ten minutes about universal suffrage. We had to drag him to the ground and back to our lodgings before the constables showed up. You ask me, Danny's always been a bit of a revolutionary."

"And yet, you remained friends."

Forrester leaned his chair back a couple of inches, until it contacted the wall. "Maybe I'm a bit of a revolutionary in my own way."

"You're familiar with Abram Duncan?"

"He worked for Danny as a woodturner. I think he's some sort of preacher now."

"You are not aware of his role with the Chartists?"

"It's a Chartist church he runs. There are a few of them scattered around the city. Chartists believed the Church of England was aligned with Parliament and therefore unsympathetic to Chartism. They decided to form their own denomination."

"And Duncan preaches at one of these Chartist churches."

"Arbroath, if I am not mistaken."

"Do you suppose I might find him there?"

"You might. He's active in Chartist rallies, and there's a lot of activity around Lancashire with the trial coming up, so he could be out of town."

"Do you have any estimate of Duncan's influence over M'Naghten?"

Forrester rubbed one side of his face as he thought. "Here's my belief. Danny has spent his entire life looking for a great cause to which he might attach himself. The more he read, the more disillusioned he became. The books weren't giving him what he wanted. Danny was likely to latch onto the first great movement that presented itself. Duncan may have provided access to that movement, but Danny was primed for it. You could not have authored a manifesto better suited to Danny's beliefs than the People's Charter. From the moment he read it, I think he was committed."

CHAPTER THIRTY-ONE

"You visited his boarding house?"

"A few times. I didn't spend a lot of time there. I don't think Mrs. Patterson likes me."

"Yet, when she was going to the sheriff to file a complaint about M'Naghten's behavior, you offered to help her and you said M'Naghten was daft."

"So, you've spoken with Mrs. Patterson? Sure. We met that day. She was distraught. I thought, if I help her, perhaps she will think better of me."

"You expected to curry her favor by indicting your friend?"

"I wasn't actually going to file a complaint. At the end of the day, it doesn't matter. She refused my help."

"Mr. Forrester," Brekonridge said, leaning forward in his chair. "Answer one question. Is Daniel M'Naghten actually daft?"

Forrester sighed and returned all four of his chair legs to the floor. "No more than he has been for as long as I've known him."

"And, as an actor, do you believe he has the skills to feign genuine madness in order to absolve himself of responsibility for his crimes?"

Forrester stood, walked to the shop door, and removed the CLOSED sign. He unlocked the door, and opened it.

"Perhaps he has. Mr. Brekonridge, nobody would like to see Danny spared the gallows more than I. However, I am not prepared to say my friend is truly insane, as much as saying it might help him. I'm busy, and you are keeping me from my work. I would ask you to leave now."

Chapter Thirty-Two

The Lord Provost in Glasgow served as the Queen's representative to the city. As such, his duty was to maintain relationships with authorities in London, entertain foreign and domestic dignitaries who visited Glasgow, host the Queen on her occasional visits to the Scottish countryside, and coordinate various national holiday festivals and events. As the Town Council went, so went also the Lord Provost. Since the Town Council in Glasgow was decidedly Tory, James Campbell was likewise.

Already in his middle fifties, Campbell was a man of relatively small stature, with short arms, short legs and small hands ending in stubby fingers. He had a prominent brow, a flat broad nose, full lips and a receding chin. His wildly curly hair was disappearing in disorganized clumps. What remained grew in uncontrolled brambles around his skull. He wore side whiskers which he had allowed to grow together all across the underside of his chin, leaving his chin and upper lip bare. Altogether, his appearance was more cartoon than natural. As if to counter his clown-like features, he had adopted a serious, almost funereal manner. He was dressed impeccably, and his office—situated as it was in a warehouse—was in remarkable order.

Simon introduced himself and gave Campbell the introduction letter.

"Yes. I recall young M'Naghten," Campbell said. His words came in bursts, interspersed with gasping inhalations. "I am familiar with his father, a well-known craftsman in town. The younger appeared right here, in my office. I think it was May of last year. It could have been early June. I can check my records if you need an exact date. He was a distraught man. He complained of all sorts of conspiracies against him."

"Did he outline the nature of those conspiracies?"

"I can retrieve my notes if you need to see them. He first said he was being persecuted politically. By the end of his story it seemed he had some fears of harassment from almost every organization in Glasgow, from the Town Council to the police to even the churches. He said spies followed him wherever he went, from the moment he left his home in the morning until he returned at night. He seemed to believe I could somehow bring this discrimination to an end. I hadn't the heart to tell him my office is largely ceremonial and I have no overt power to intervene in problems of his sort, so I told him I would do what I could."

"Which was next to nothing?"

"Of course."

"What did you make of his story?"

"He was obviously deluded. The sort of conspiracy he described would require so much coordination there would be no way to keep it a secret in a town the size of Glasgow. I even suggested to him he might be the victim of some strange malady that had clouded his thinking, and I asked him whether he had ever been treated as an insane person."

"How did he respond?"

"As if he had not heard me."

"You sent him away?"

"I told him I would do what I could. I wrote his father later that evening, as I am of long acquaintance with the man. I suggested we meet to discuss what to do about young Daniel. It never happened. After a week or so, I put the matter out of my mind. I never saw the youth again."

"But, in your estimation, M'Naghten was not in full possession of his faculties?"

"He was quite obviously a maniac."

"And yet, you did not approach the authorities on his behalf?"

"I felt it was his father's duty. Have you spoken with Reverend Turner? He has a church in Gorbals, but he conducts a great deal of business in Glasgow. I had occasion to speak with him last weekend. He had read the accounts of the assassination in London and recognized young M'Naghten's name. Apparently the young man, seeking divine intervention from his tormentors, had pled with Reverend Turner for assistance. You might speak with him."

"Do you have his full name?"

"Alexander Turner. He lives on Kingston Place in Gorbals. Number Fourteen."

* * *

Gorbals was across the Clyde River, a short walk across the Bishop's Bridge. Kingston Place was three streets back from the river. Simon knocked on the door at Number Fourteen. It opened almost immediately. A man wearing a clerical collar peered at him.

"I was headed out when you rang," the man said.

"Are you Reverend Turner?"

"I am. Can I help you in some way?"

"I met with Mr. James Campbell, the Lord Provost. He suggested I might wish to have a talk with you."

"Are you in some spiritual or physical crisis?"

"Only an intellectual one. I represent Humphreys and Perceval, Barristers, in London. They are providing the defense for Daniel M'Naghten in the killing of Edward Drummond."

Turner stared at him from the doorway. "I knew I shouldn't have mentioned that to Campbell."

"I only have a few questions."

"Well, I am in a hurry. I need to get to the Infirmary to see a parishioner. If you wish to walk with me, I will try to answer your questions."

They started north, toward the Bishop's Bridge.

"You are a Presbyterian cleric?" Simon asked.

"Quite so."

"And I am led to understand the M'Naghtens are in your congregation."

"The elder M'Naghten. I am most familiar with him. I had never met young Daniel. It is my understanding they had a falling out almost a decade ago. Something about the family business. Daniel, the father, had never mentioned his…eh, illegitimate son. I met the younger Daniel about eight months ago, more or less. Might have been the middle of May, since I seem to connect the event with an especially important wedding I conducted around the same time, and that was mid-May. He appeared in my church office asking for assistance."

"Of what sort?"

"He seemed terribly troubled. He said he was being spied upon, He had nobody to trust, because everyone he turned to seemed to be part of some vast conspiracy to ruin him. From what I could tell, he suspected almost every man of wealth or position in Glasgow as being allied against him. He appeared to be wrestling with the most frightening demons."

"Demons?"

"Of the imaginary sort. He seemed most beside himself."

"What did he expect you to do about it?"

"I'm not certain. That was never made entirely clear. It certainly appears as if he imagined the entire world to be a threatening place."

"Did he seem panicked or frightened?"

"Absolutely. There was sweat beaded on his face, and his hands trembled horribly. He looked like a man facing immediate execution."

"You don't believe his behaviors might have been feigned?"

"Not unless he was a championship-class actor."

"How did you resolve his visit?"

"I didn't. After raving for several minutes, he left on his own accord. I had no opportunity to counsel him or offer advice. After he left, I contacted his father and suggested in the strongest possible terms he should consider placing his son in an asylum, where he most undoubtedly belonged. Anyone could tell the poor boy was delusional. It was only a matter of time before he lost control and…"

"Hurt someone?" Simon finished.

"Yes. That is precisely what I was about to say. Seems prophetic, in retrospect, doesn't it?"

"And you are completely convinced? When Daniel M'Naghten appeared before you last year, he was not in his right mind?"

"I was convinced enough about it to alert his father to the fact."

"I would like to ask you to testify in the trial next month. Like you, we at Humphreys and Perceval are convinced M'Naghten killed Edward Drummond in the throes of a defect of reason so profound he was unaware of the true nature of his act. Your testimony could keep an unfortunately deranged man from going to the gibbet, sir."

Turner stopped and thrust his hands into his coat pockets. He turned back toward his house, and then toward Bishop's Bridge, as if trying to make a momentous decision. He sighed, his breath fogging in the frigid winter air.

"Yes," he said. "I am obligated. Perhaps if I had done more than send a note to the boy's father, that poor man in London might still be alive. I don't see how killing young M'Naghten would make that right. I'll testify."

Chapter Thirty-Three

Brekonridge arrived back at the lodgings on Clyde Street to find Simon bent over a sheet of paper at the table, writing with a steel nib pen.

"What are you up to, boy?" he asked.

Without looking up, Simon said, "It might be easier to track Mr. M'Naghten's decline into madness if we had some sort of chronological depiction of the events that took place in his life."

Brekonridge leaned over and looked at the paper. Simon had fashioned a ruled line along the bottom edge, and had put dates below the line, month and year.

"Why January, 1838?" Brekonridge asked, pointing to the beginning point of the line.

"First, because we have no witness accounts providing information relevant to an insanity defense before that date. Second, because in January of 1838, the rent on Mr. M'Naghten's shop rose to twelve pounds a year, which qualified him to register for the vote."

"You believe that's the event that started M'Naghten's decline?"

"Perhaps it accelerated it. I cannot find anything more relevant at an earlier date."

"This is impressive. Are you sure you're only nineteen years old?"

Simon smiled and looked up from the paper for the first time. "I'll be twenty soon."

"You're going to need more paper. I went back to Mrs. Patterson's lodging house this afternoon after interviewing Joseph Forrester."

"Why?"

"Something Forrester told me didn't sound right. I needed clarification from Mrs. Patterson to ensure I heard her correctly. In the course of our talk, I asked her if she knew where M'Naghten had lived before he came to her house. She told me about two previous addresses. One belonged to a tailor named Hughes. The other was operated by a Mrs. Dalgliesh. I visited Mr. Hughes in his tailor shop."

"What did he tell you?"

"It seems M'Naghten lived in his house as a tenant from about 1834 until he moved in with Mrs. Patterson. About a month before M'Naghten moved to Mrs. Patterson's house, he approached Hughes and demanded to know whether people had been talking about him behind his back."

"When was that?"

"March, 1835. Almost eight years ago, M'Naghten was already expressing suspicions others were persecuting him."

"I believe the French call the condition *paranoia*," Simon said.

"There's more. According to Forrester, M'Naghten engaged in strange behavior as far back as a decade ago, when he was an actor. Lamond's challenge of M'Naghten's suffrage may have only been on the wrong side of the fulcrum upon which his sanity had teetered for years."

Simon leaned back in his chair and crossed his arms over his chest. "The two sheriffs, the commissioner of police, even a pastor. M'Naghten appealed to each of them for assistance. For some of them, there was nothing they could do personally and M'Naghten interpreted their inability to help as persecution. Each one, with the exception of Lamond, seems genuinely remorseful they were unable to see the violent potential in him. Some tried to enlist the aid of M'Naghten's father, but beyond that they were powerless to rid him of his delusions. The very men M'Naghten blamed for his persecution appear to be the most sympathetic toward his tragic circumstances. It leads one to wonder whether there was such an attempt at systematic persecution."

"I've spoken with the man. He accused me of persecuting and tormenting him only an hour or so after we met. He was convincing. If I slapped a white wig and a false beard on him, M'Naghten could be a fair-to-middling Lear, a role, I might add, he has played to some effect in the past. I've also spoken with M'Naghten's friends and other acquaintances, the people he saw every day. Some deny he has any overt mental problems at all. Others report he was peculiar, but not demonstrably dangerous or frightening. Only his landlady says he was daft. Every one of his friends, however, agreed he was a radical. His accused tormenters regard him with sympathy. His supposed friends offer opinions sure to end in M'Naghten's trip to Tyburn Tree. Peculiar. Perhaps M'Naghten was only mad in the presence of certain people at certain times. Let's look at your chronological line again, this time with a more cynical eye. When did M'Naghten first approach the authorities for relief?"

"Here," Simon said, pointing to May of the previous year. "He met with Reverend Turner, Sheriff Bell, and Police Commissioner Wilson last May. Sheriff Alison believes he saw M'Naghten in June."

"Yet your record goes back all the way to 1838, with the presumption M'Naghten's madness was precipitated by political persecution on the part of Robert Lamond. My information suggests not only M'Naghten was acting strangely long before he was privileged to register, but he also expressed radical political leanings long before he manifested these feelings of paranoia."

"You realize, of course, you are postulating a set of conditions that actually favors the prosecution?"

"That's of no consequence. As I recall, the defense is not required to share inculpatory evidence with the prosecution."

"That is correct."

"So we are free to speculate. I think it is important, if only for my own peace of mind, to explore all the possible explanations for the tragic meeting of M'Naghten and Drummond on Whitehall three weeks ago. Because, there is another glaring complication in this case, for which I have yet to receive an adequate explanation."

"That being?"

"The money, boy. Where did that damned seven-hundred-fifty pounds come from? Follow me closely on this one. It occurred to me this afternoon while I was walking."

"And smoking hemp?"

"What of it? When did the money first appear?"

"August, 1841. He deposited the money at the London Stock Bank."

"But the money was in the Glasgow and Ship Bank when he was arrested."

"He arranged for a transfer in May of 1842."

"From the London Stock Bank, to the Glasgow and Ship Bank, yes. Does that not seem strange to you?"

"In what way?"

"Well, at the same time M'Naghten was dashing around town, screaming to every authority he could collar that spies followed him into the privy and disturbed his sleep at night, he had the presence of mind to initiate a transfer of his funds from the London Stock Bank to the bank here in Glasgow. Does that not strike you as somehow uncharacteristic of a lunatic?"

"It is inconsistent with my understanding of lunacy."

"M'Naghten sold William Carlow the woodturning shop in August of 1841."

"The same time M'Naghten made his first deposit of seven-hundred-fifty pounds at the London Stock Bank."

"Yes. Except, Carlow only paid eighteen pounds for the shop. He considered it quite the bargain."

"Perhaps M'Naghten saved the rest during the years he operated the shop."

"We've recently come through years of hard economic times. I would be shocked if the shop makes a profit larger than fifty pounds a year even now. There wasn't enough time for M'Naghten to acquire that much money. He was, however, in a great hurry to sell the shop, which he let go for a fraction of its value. A large fraction, to be sure, but at a great discount. Ask yourself why, boy."

"He was assured of not needing the proceeds of the shop to survive," Simon said.

"My conclusion precisely. He came into possession of a large sum of money and divested himself of his business as quickly afterward as was possible. Here," Brekonridge said, stabbing at August 1841 with his finger. "Wilson."

"Yes," Simon said. "That was about the time M'Naghten first complained to Police Commissioner Wilson he was being harassed by priests. Within a week or so, he returned, complaining Tories had joined in with the clerics."

"And, yet, Carlow did not report any alarming behavior from him at the same time. Do you see the inconsistencies here? He appears deranged around some people, and perfectly normal around others. And why the gap in time between his complaints to Wilson in August 1841, and his flurry of complaints to other officials in May 1842?"

"That's easy. He was in London."

"Living with Mrs. Dutton, on Poplar Row. Yes. See? There's this gap between August and the next May which has almost no information in it. Sergeant Shaw's interview revealed that, during the first time he was in Mrs. Dutton's house, M'Naghten was social, engaging, and gregarious. She said he was among the kindest and gentlest of men and he carried bread crumbs in his pockets to feed birds. It was only after he returned to London in November that she noticed he was more distant and solitary. We know M'Naghten claimed in August, to Commissioner Wilson, that he was being persecuted by an array of Tories and clergymen. By September he was in London, seemingly the life of the party, and remained there until April of last year, when he returned to Glasgow. Immediately upon his return, he dashed desperately from pillar to post, complaining of harassment by an army of oppressors. I am puzzled. Is there a form of insanity that exists only in one geographic location? If not, we must start sending madmen from all over the Continent to London for its curative effects."

He pulled his pipe from his pocket and lighted it. Immediately, the room was filled with the acrid scent of hemp.

"That begs the next question," he said, after exhaling.

"Why return to Glasgow?" Simon said.

"Exactly. The man was wealthy. Why return to a city where you can reliably anticipate merciless persecution?"

"There was something here he wanted or needed."

"What? He didn't work during the time he was here last year. He had almost no contact with his father. Seemingly, he spent all his time at the Mechanics Institute. Why come back here?"

Brekonridge stepped over to the window and looked down on the Clyde River, as he tried to digest all the information he'd acquired.

"The Queen," he said at last, without turning away from the window.

"What?" Simon asked.

"Mrs. Dutton in London said M'Naghten had described his intense interest in the Queen's visit here last summer. He was ill, shortly after his return to London last November, and in his fevered delirium he talked about following the Queen around when she was in Scotland."

"That was August of last year, was it not?"

"Yes. Put the Queen's visit on your chart, for last August. So, after a perceptible eight-month period of lucidity in London, M'Naghten returned to Glasgow in April. The faculty at the Mechanics Institute and his friends in the city all stated he looked healthy and well-dressed after his short sojourn. Even so, within three weeks, he was again wildly delusional, banging on every Tory official's door begging for relief from his persecutors. His tirades run into June. What happens next on your chart?"

"M'Naghten purchases his pistols."

Brekonridge did turn around at that. "Say that again."

"In July. M'Naghten entered a gunsmith's shop in Paisley, run by a Mr. Martin, and asked about purchasing a pair of pistols. Martin said M'Naghten actually wanted a matching pair, but he ultimately purchased the unmatched pair on the condition that, should he return, Martin would sell him a match to the larger of the two. M'Naghten paid 17 shillings for the two pistols, a powder-flask, percussion caps, and several pistol balls."

"Months before his eventual return to London, but only days before Queen Victoria made her visit. The pieces are beginning to fall together, Simon, but I don't think your employers are going to like the way they arrange themselves."

"You called me Simon."

"Beg pardon?" Brekonridge said, his attention broken.

"You've never called me Simon before. It's always 'boy' this and 'boy' that. You just called me Simon."

"Did I? Can't imagine why. Can't imagine it will happen again. Have you eaten?"

"Yes."

"I haven't and I'm hungry. I'm going out to find some food and think this through some more. You did a good job with this chronological chart, Simon. It clarified a great deal in M'Naghten's case, even if it did raise more questions."

"You did it again. Called me Simon."

"So I did. I shall endeavor not to make it a habit. I'll return before midnight."

Brekonridge pulled on his greatcoat, scarf, and John Bull hat and headed back to the streets. The winter sun was almost down entirely. Chandlers walked from post to post, firing gaslights to illuminate the streets. A frigid winter wind swept down the Clyde River, bringing with it the odor of rotting fish and sewage, and it caused Brekonridge to pull his coat more tightly around him. A clipper ship slid by on the river, sails flapping in the wind, headed from the port back out to sea. Couples, holding one another close, traversed Bishop's Bridge over the Clyde between Glasgow and Gorbals.

What Simon had said worried him. The boy was right. He was being paid—and paid handsomely, he reminded himself—to do a specific job. When he picked up a warrant at the Bow Street Station, he never worried about whether his quarry might have been falsely accused. He did not consider possible innocence before clapping irons on some poor suspect's wrists. While he was old and cynical, he did depend on the courts to sort things out properly in the end. If they did not, it was on their heads.

He also harbored concerns about guilty men walking out of the court free. The idea the woodturner might successfully evade the hangman's noose due to his talent at feigning insanity rankled him. He remembered how M'Naghten had behaved in his prison cell. Brekonridge would have sworn on the spot the man was deranged. Something about the look in his eyes, the furrow in his brow and the rage in his voice had presented a perfect depiction of madness. He had only witnessed such a display once before.

Brekonridge had enjoyed the privilege of attending William Macready's performance as King Lear at Drury Lane. He recalled how he had been drawn in by the master's portrayal of a descent into lunacy. He remembered reading in a magazine, days later, how the great actor had declared, *"Madness in a crystal jar is the best sort of talent an actor can have."* A great actor must keep his lunacy stored and locked away—as in a crystal jar—only to be taken out and worn like a mask as the demands of a character required.

Was that what M'Naghten had done? He had also played Lear, after all. Others who had seen him had said the man was more than adequate to the task. Was he good enough to persuade the Glasgow authorities he had disposed of his reason?

Brekonridge was no expert when it came to diseases of the mind. For all he knew, there could be a form of insanity that came and went like the ebb and flow of tides, and if M'Naghten was truly afflicted with such a horrible disease, he might in fact have acted out of genuine terror when he killed Edward Drummond. Sending such a man to the gallows would be the cruelest of travesties.

Nothing he had learned thus far, however, better explained the existence of over seven hundred pounds in M'Naghten's bank account than a murder for hire.

Brekonridge was so engrossed in his internal debate, he failed at first to notice the man who fell into step behind him. The man followed, at a cautious distance, for almost three blocks, before hastening his step and catching up with the thief-taker.

Walking downwind, Brekonridge smelled the mucker before he heard the approaching footsteps. As Healy caught up, Brekonridge called behind, "Something I can do for you, Mr. Healy?"

"A ship's carpenter, eh?" the man said as he pulled alongside Brekonridge. "In a pig's eye. What are you? Some sort of policeman?"

"I don't see it is any of your concern, sir."

"I've been watching you since the meeting the other night. You have been a busy man. Yet, I have not seen you venture within seven blocks of the port. Your clothes do not belong to a sailor. I believe you are in Glasgow on some other business."

"Again, my business is my own, and at the moment my business entails finding my dinner."

"Do you have five shillings?"

"For what?" Brekonridge asked, becoming irritated.

"Information. After you left Mr. Forrester's shop this afternoon, I took the opportunity to pop in and have a chat with the man. You're here about Mr. M'Naghten, are you not?"

"Why do you ask?"

"Five shillings, and I will take you to a person who can tell you whatever you want."

"Unlikely. No offense, Mr. Healy, but I know nothing about you other than your aromatic profession."

"All I ask is the promise. If you are unhappy with the outcome, you owe me nothing. What could be fairer?"

Brekonridge stopped walking and looked at Healy. Five shillings. With a hundred sovereigns waiting for him back in London, what did he have to lose?

"Where?" he asked.

"Come with me."

The stable mucker told him to turn up the next street, and they walked uphill from the river toward the university and the Mechanics Institute. They had gone four blocks when Healy pointed toward an alleyway.

"We cut through there," he said. "The place we're headed is on the next block. It's a short lane between cross streets."

Brekonridge shrugged and turned into the alley. Healy led him, two paces ahead. They had not walked ten yards before something hard and heavy struck Brekonridge across the middle of his back, driving the air from his lungs. He stumbled to his knees, gasping for breath. Before he could roll over to defend himself, his arms were pinioned behind him and a burlap sack was tossed over his head. He felt a rope cinch around his neck, securing the bag, and two stout sets of arms drag him to his feet. He started to struggle, and was rewarded by another thump across his back. He felt irons encircling his wrists, and the metal-on-metal sound of them being screwed shut.

"Don't make a fuss," a deep voice with a strong Scottish brogue said. It wasn't Healy. "You stay calm, and you might make it home tonight."

From inside the sack, he heard the clops of horse hooves. Once he was steadily on his feet, the men on either side crab-walked him back toward the end of the alley.

"Step up," the voice said. "We're entering a carriage. No questions now. Keep your mouth shut and we'll be where we're going in a few minutes."

Brekonridge lifted his foot and tried to find a step into the carriage. After several false starts, he located it. The two men on either side of him lifted him up, and pushed him inside. He rolled onto the floor and tried to get to his feet again.

"No you don't," the voice said. "Wouldn't look good for us to roll around the streets of Glasgow with a hooded man sitting in the window. You stay on the floor."

The ride took several minutes, during which nobody in the carriage spoke. Presently, the horse slowed, and the carriage came to a halt. Brekonridge was pulled to his feet, none too gently.

"Be careful," the voice said. "Don't want you to fall on your face. You let us guide you to the ground."

"When this is done, I will find you. This will be squared," Brekonridge threatened.

They pulled him toward the carriage door and physically lowered him to the ground. Once on the cobblestones, his captors took him by the arms and led him away from the carriage. He heard a door open, and a wave of warm air hit his hands. They helped him up two steps, into a building. Almost immediately, they turned him around.

"There's a chair behind you," the voice said.

"Take off the manacles," Brekonridge demanded, as he collapsed into a heavy wooden straight-backed chair.

CHAPTER THIRTY-THREE

"I don't think so. Not yet."

The cord around his neck was loosened, and the burlap pulled from his head. The room was dim, illuminated by three or four candles. He blinked a couple of times as his vision swam into focus. The chemical stench told him he was at a tanner's shop. A table had been placed in front of him. Two men sat behind it, peering back. He recognized both of them as the men who had shared the stage at the Chartist meeting.

"Good evening, sir," that one said. "My name is Abram Duncan."

Chapter Thirty-Four

"I believe you have been asking about me." Duncan wore a waistcoat but no jacket or overcoat. His collarless shirt was stained around the neckline by sweat. He had not shaven, and his curly hair was rumpled as if he had recently gotten out of bed.

The other man, who had also been on the stage at the Chartist meeting, sat silently, but his eyes roamed over Brekonridge's frame as if measuring him for a coffin. He was tall and lanky and, like Duncan, did not wear a jacket. Brekonridge, now free from the sack, found the temperature in the room stifling.

"I'm hot," he said. "If you will remove the manacles I can take off my coat."

Duncan gave a signal, and Brekonridge felt stout, rough hands manipulate the cuffs. After a few seconds, his hands were free. He stood slowly, as to avoid alarming his captors and provoking them to violence, and slipped off his heavy woolen overcoat.

"I had a hat," he said. "I happen to like it."

One of the men who stood behind him passed it over Brekonridge's shoulder. Brekonridge placed it on his folded coat on the table and sat.

"It wasn't necessary to abduct me," he said.

"There are spies everywhere," Duncan said. "I have no intention of winding up in the dock like Feargus O'Connor and his fellows in Lancashire. Why have you been asking after me?"

"I was hired by the firm of Humphreys and Perceval in London to find witnesses in Glasgow for Daniel M'Naghten's trial. Your name came up in the course of the investigation."

Duncan appeared to relax a little, but the other man continued to stare at Brekonridge intently.

"I won't appear at any trial in London," Duncan said.

"I'm not asking you to, at least not yet. It's no matter to me. All I want is information."

"About Danny?"

"Mostly. I know you're Duncan, from the meeting the other night. But who are you?" Brekonridge asked the tall man.

"My name is John Gordon."

"The foundryman," Brekonridge said.

"Have we met, sir? I believe I would have recalled it."

"Your name came up in my conversations with other witnesses. William Carlow told me about you. I believe you work at Laing and Son, and you have been close to M'Naghten yourself."

Gordon leaned over and whispered to Duncan. Duncan addressed the men standing behind Brekonridge and told them to wait outside.

"I apologize for your rough treatment," Duncan said. "Healy was concerned you might be trying to infiltrate the Chartist movement with aims to create dissension. As you may be aware, these are hard times for dissidents."

Brekonridge rubbed his wrists, which had chafed under the cuffs. "People who challenge the status quo seldom find the road smooth."

"This much is true. What do you want to know about Danny?"

"You're the first friend of his who hasn't asked me how he is faring in Newgate Prison."

"We know he is well. We have people in London who have kept us abreast of his condition. And what is the posture at Humphreys and Perceval regarding Danny?"

"They intend to prove he is insane. It is the only way to keep his neck from getting stretched."

"And you? Do you also believe in Danny's insanity?"

"I have questions."

"Will anyone care about your questions?"

"Probably not. What about you? Do either of you have doubts about M'Naghten's reason?"

Duncan stood and walked over the to a window that overlooked a quiet lane. "Danny is searching for something I do not believe he will find. He wishes to see a world that is more equitable and inclusive. Like most Chartist sympathizers, he correctly believes far too much power has been vested in the ruling classes, and the common man has little say in the conduct of the country's business."

"You called him a Chartist *sympathizer*. Is he not actively involved?"

"He never completely committed to the People's Charter, or any other organization of which I am aware. I believe, and this is only a belief, that his actual goal is to hamper the Tories in any way he can, using any vehicle that might permit his success."

"Because of persecution," Brekonridge said.

"Who knows? I have heard there is a great deal of rancor between Danny and his father, who is well-known to be devoted to the Tory cause. Perhaps his sentiments are driven by nothing more prosaic than to achieve some sort of revenge against his da."

"For refusing to bring him into the business?"

"For treating him like a bastard child under his own roof. Old man M'Naghten would barely have been aware of Danny's existence if the boy's mother had lived." Duncan turned away from the window and faced Brekonridge again. "I like Danny. I really do. I don't trust him, certainly not enough to allow him inside the inner circle of our operations in Glasgow."

Brekonridge turned to Gordon. "What about you? How do you regard the man?"

"He is lost," Gordon said. "He only knows he wants something, but he isn't certain what it is or how to obtain it. Is he insane? Perhaps. I am not qualified to say. I do know he sees the world as a dangerous and foreboding place."

"When he was arrested, he had almost seven-hundred-fifty pounds in the bank."

Duncan said, "I can read your suspicions, Mr. Brekonridge. You think someone in the Chartist movement hired Danny to murder the Prime Minister?"

"The notion had crossed my mind."

"As it has mine, I'm sorry to say. If you think I or my companions had anything to do with it, you are sorely mistaken. Contrary to the ravings of the Tories, there is no such thing as monolithic Chartism. There is no central control, no vertical hierarchy. Nobody is in charge. In fact, there is a schism at the present time. One faction prefers to foment change through the political process, slowly increasing numbers of Chartist sympathizers in Parliament. The other is more…impatient. They seek change through any means necessary. General strikes have not gotten us the attention and change we seek, so some of our number have suggested taking more radical, violent action. I represent the first faction. I truly believe, however, neither of us would stoop to assassination as a means to our ends."

"Who would?"

"I have no idea."

"I spoke with Mr. Swanstead at the Mechanics Institute," Brekonridge said. "He mentioned two socialists with whom M'Naghten was familiar."

"Yes," Duncan replied. "Colin Graham and Angus Nockold. I remember them."

"Mr. Swanstead believes them to be anarchists. What do you think?"

"Graham is reasonable," Gordon said. "A coal miner, if I remember correctly. He's intelligent. Nockold is a hothead. He flies off the handle with the least provocation. They are a strange pair."

"They spend a great deal of time with one another?"

"I couldn't say."

"Do you think they might have been involved in the attack on Drummond?" Duncan asked.

"I don't know," Brekonridge told him. "But the things you do not know are often among the most important. Perhaps I should return to the Mechanics Institute and have a word or two with Mr. Graham and Mr. Nockold."

"Don't bother," Gordon said. "They've left. I haven't seen them in at least a month. I overheard a conversation between two of their friends suggesting they had taken off for France, but I can't confirm it."

"One more thing," Brekonridge said. "Did either of you spend time with M'Naghten last spring? Say, around April or May?"

"Of course," Duncan said.

"How was his demeanor? Did he ever talk about being followed around town by spies?"

"No," Gordon said.

"That's not entirely true," Duncan said. "He inquired whether people had been asking about him. I think it was May of last year when I ran across Danny on Argyll Street. He was agitated. Kept looking past me, over my shoulder, toward the next corner. I asked him what he was looking for, but he only said he was expecting to see someone. That's when he asked me whether people had been talking about him."

"Besides agitation, did he appear to be reasonable?"

"As much as ever. If you're thinking Danny was hired to kill Peel, I can assure you we weren't involved. I apologize for the rude way we brought you here. With the trial in Lancashire upon us, one can never be too careful."

Brekonridge stood and slipped on his heavy woolen coat. He slid the John Bull hat onto his head and said, "I'll take my leave, if you'll tell me which direction will lead me back to Clyde Street."

"Turn right outside the door, and it will take you directly to Hope Street. Turn right again and you'll be at Clyde Street in about five blocks."

Brekonridge pulled five shillings from his pocket and stacked them on the table. "For the stable mucker, Healy. I promised him this money if the information was helpful."

Brekonridge stepped outside, where two burly men stamped their feet and rubbed their hands together to ward off the cold. He looked back and forth at them.

"What did you hit me with?" he asked.

The man on the right reached under his jacket and pulled out a ship's belaying pin.

"You're a sailor?" Brekonridge asked.

"I was, once upon a time."

"As was I," Brekonridge said. "Served in His Majesty's Navy. Was a powder monkey in the battle of New Orleans. Did you ever see action at sea?"

"Naw. I was on a merchant ves—"

Brekonridge's fist blurred out in an overhand arc and slammed into the man's face, bursting his nose and lips, and sending gouts of blood into the snowbank at the curb. The man collapsed to the ground, howling and clawing at his face with his gloved hands.

"You've seen action now," Brekonridge said. "I'll be pissing pink for a week. I figure we're even." He picked up the belaying pin and turned to the other man, who slowly backed away.

"I got no quarrel with you, sir," the man said. "I did what Mr. Duncan told me."

"Walk, and keep walking until I can't see you," Brekonridge ordered. The man slouched away, careful not to show his back. Once he had put safe distance between himself and Brekonridge, he turned and ran. Brekonridge pointed the pin at the man lying in his own blood in the snow.

"I'll keep this," Brekonridge told the man "Never know when it might come in handy."

"It's yours," the man said, the words bubbling through his split lip. "Just don't hit me again."

Brekonridge secured the pin inside his jacket and turned toward Hope Street.

Chapter Thirty-Five

"Time to go home," Brekonridge announced as he walked in the door of the lodging he and Simon had rented.

"Why?" Simon asked. "Is there trouble?"

"We've learned everything there is to learn here."

"But I still need to interview the Procurator. We haven't spoken with everyone on M'Naghten's list."

"We've spoken to enough. We have multiple officials who will testify to M'Naghten's benefit, for what it is worth."

"I don't understand."

Brekonridge dropped his greatcoat on the bed, and tossed his hat on top of it. He twisted his torso, first left and then right, and winced at the pain in his back where the man had cudgeled him.

"I met with Duncan and that foundryman, Gordon. They knew M'Naghten as well as anyone in Glasgow and they didn't think he was insane. In fact, with the exception of Mrs. Patterson, I can't locate any of M'Naghten's intimates in this city who can verify that theory."

"We should keep searching."

"Don't you understand, boy? Have you been listening? The only people in Glasgow who will help find M'Naghten insane are the officials he approached for help."

"What about William Carlow? Didn't he say M'Naghten had acted strangely when he lived here last?"

"And he also said he did not believe the man was out of his wits. Is there some sort of madness that only manifests itself on one side of the street, but not the other? If there is, I have never heard of it. We have already established M'Naghten was ostensibly insane in Glasgow but not in London. Now we discover he was only mad in the presence of some people here but not others. Ask the next question."

"Why?"

"Precisely. Either the man is possessed of a most curious form of derangement, or he is malingering. If we rule out the impossible disease, we are left with fakery. Ask the next question."

"What did he get out of his bizarre behavior?"

"Given we know he killed Edward Drummond, a fact which is incontrovertible, we can presume he intended to do so all along. He made complaints of persecution to local officials prior to the Queen's visit last year. I believe he planned to feign madness in Glasgow to provide him with a perfect excuse and a way to avoid public execution. He failed or lost his nerve with the Queen, and so decided to murder the Prime Minister in London instead. With meticulous efficiency, he identified the exact officials who would provide him with the best testimony to his madness, and visited each of them, raving about Tory persecution. Then it was back to London, his insanity defense ensured, to do in Robert Peel. The list I found under the floor in his rooms wasn't comprised of conspirators against him. It was his witness list for the trial. Fool that I am, I let him manipulate me in prison, giving me the exact same list, knowing I would interview them. This one is a clever bird. I can find no other explanation."

Simon sat back, his brow furrowed, and drummed his fingers on the table. Finally, he slapped the wooden tabletop with his palm.

"You go back to London. I'll stay here and interview the Procurator. I can do that tomorrow, and I'll follow along. Mr. Cockburn is not going to be happy with your report."

"I'm not in the business of pleasing Mr. Cockburn. I will not present a pack of lies to him simply to justify the payment he agreed to provide for my services. I came here to find the truth. If Humphreys and Perceval insist on pursuing an insanity defense, they will have to do it without me. I'll write up my conclusions here You interview your witnesses, Simon, and after you've secured their agreement to appear at trial, we'll take the first train back to London."

Chapter Thirty-Six

As Simon had predicted, Alexander Cockburn was not amused. Simon and Brekonridge arrived back in London and had took a carriage directly to the Newgate Street offices of Humphreys and Perceval. There, Simon presented his list of witnesses who had agreed to testify for the defense. Brekonridge detailed his theory of the murder, going back to the unexplained appearance of M'Naghten's seven-hundred-fifty pounds. As he outlined his hypothesis, step-by-step, Cockburn's eyes narrowed, until it appeared he had quite drifted off to sleep. Only the occasional guttural *"Mmmm"* betrayed his consciousness and his attention. When the thief-taker was finished, Cockburn stood, his expression demonstrating no emotion at all, and left the room.

Brekonridge looked over at Simon and raised an eyebrow. The youth shrugged his shoulders.

"I can't tell," Simon whispered. "He's a strange duck."

They sat in near-silence, the hulking thief-taker and the beardless boy, waiting for something to happen. Outside, several carriages passed by, the clopping of horses' hooves resonating off the glass in the windows. Finally, they heard boot steps. Cockburn re-entered the room, along with William Corne Humphreys, who carried an envelope.

"So this is your investigator?" Humphreys said as he surveyed Brekon-ridge.

Brekonridge stood and faced the solicitor. "Vicar Brekonridge. Late of the Metropolitan Police Force."

"*Very* late, I'd say. It's been years since you wore a badge and carried a clacker."

"True, sir. I presume Mr. Cockburn told you of my findings in Glasgow."

"He did. I cannot say I am completely satisfied. That is the trouble with the truth, is it not? It may be verifiable, but it is not always convenient. This is yours."

He handed the envelope to Brekonridge.

"My payment?"

"Inside is a bank draft for one hundred fifty pounds."

"My fee was only a hundred."

Cockburn and Humphreys stared at him.

"I see," Brekonridge said. "You still intend to pursue the insanity defense."

"We do," Cockburn said. "Your assistance in this matter is appreciated, but no longer required. Consider the extra fifty quid a bonus."

"To keep me quiet."

"We have a duty to our client, Mr. Brekonridge. Duty supersedes any other factor."

"Including the truth?"

"Truth is ethereal, sir," Humphreys said. "It varies based on the perspective of the beholder. Recall the famous fable about the blind men and the elephant."

"It would have to be some elephant for a blind man to miss *this* truth," Brekonridge observed. "But worry not. I can keep a secret as well as any man for the right price. After all, we know M'Naghten killed Edward Drummond. I would imagine it only matters to the poor man's family why, and whether he swings for it or spends the rest of his life in an asylum."

"Oh," Cockburn said, "It matters to a great many more people. But it need no longer matter to you. Thank you for your services. I wish you a good day, sir."

He shook Brekonridge's hand. The thief-taker put on his John Bull hat and left the room.

Back on the street, he opened the envelope and inspected the draft inside. The bank was only two blocks away. He could live for quite a long time on the money from this job, without having to chase malefactors all over

London. He had visions of Mrs. Langtry, sweet-smelling soap, a hot bath, a hearty meal, and who knew what else?

He needed to make an important stop along the way.

Whistling an ancient sea shanty, he strode off toward Paternoster Square.

* * *

M'Naghten sat on his bed, his back against the wall, staring off into space. He did not, at first, acknowledge Brekonridge's entry. The thief-taker gestured to the guard to close the door and leave them alone. As the cell door slammed shut, Brekonridge sat at the battered wooden table and examined the prisoner.

"Did you know?" Brekonridge said. "In antiquity, when a man made delusional exclamations or experienced hallucinations, his fellows would treat him with a process called trepanning?"

It was a most curious question, and for the first time M'Naghten looked in Brekonridge's direction. "I do not know that word," he said, almost a whisper.

"In trepanning, they take a razor-sharp obsidian stone, keen as broken glass, and peel away the scalp over the top of the skull. Then, using a pointed piece of stone, the prehistoric surgeons would drive a hole through the skull into the brainpan to release the demons they believed to live there. Tell me, sir. Were I to crack open your skull, what sort of demons would escape, do you suppose?"

"You speak in riddles."

Brekonridge leaned forward. "You may believe you have fooled everyone. I know better. When I was here last, I promised I would go to Glasgow and find the truth behind your persecution. I have returned, and your story is as obvious to me as the clouds in the sky outside."

"I am in your debt," M'Naghten said. "You agree I was pursued relentlessly by my enemies?"

"Hogwash. Your *enemies* displayed nothing but the greatest pity for your circumstances."

"They are devious to a fault. Can you not see their treachery? They damn me with faint pity, after driving me to madness. Even in this prison there are spies working against me. I awake at night and find them peering at me through the peephole in the door, or lying on the ground and watching me through the port they use to slide in my meals. There is no place I can go to escape their relentless persecution."

"I am familiar with your act, Lear. If I allow you to run on with your performance, is it inconceivable you will, at some point, utter *'Thou hast pared thy wit o' both sides and left nothing in the middle?'* Shall we go to such lengths, or shall we begin again with truth?"

M'Naghten visibly relaxed. "What would you have of me, sir?"

"What is real."

"That I cannot give you. My future is fixed either on the gallows or the asylum. There is no other path for me, and in truth I do not know yet which I prefer. Reality to me is all in the past. I have lived the life I was given. What remains is waste and waiting for death, either soon or later. What profit would there be in giving you the truth you desire? It would not change my fate."

"It would satisfy my curiosity."

"Seek your enlightenment elsewhere. I will not play your fool. I am tired. Please leave."

"Not before I know the truth."

"You will sit in this cell until hell cracks open."

"So be it. I brought a book to pass the time." He pulled a small volume from his jacket pocket, and settled into his chair to read.

"You carry a book with you everywhere?"

"Hardly. Only when I expect to counter boredom."

"And what are you reading today?"

"Why do you ask?"

"I spend every day and every night in this cell, staring at the walls. It becomes tiresome. I am curious."

"As am I. Who paid you the seven hundred fifty pounds?"

"Who wrote your book?"

CHAPTER THIRTY-SIX

"It's *Voyage of the Beagle*. Charles Darwin."

"Ah. Then Charles Darwin paid me. There. Your curiosity has been satisfied. You may be on your way and leave me to mine."

"All right, then," Brekonridge said, lying the book on the table. "Last July you purchased two pistols from Martin the gunsmith in Paisley."

M'Naghten was silent.

"You needn't deny it," Brekonridge said. "Martin has already confirmed it."

"I deny nothing," M'Naghten said. "You did not ask a question."

"You are correct. My apologies. When confronted by your landlady, Mrs. Patterson, about these pistols, you claimed that you intended to shoot birds. This came as something of a surprise to her, since you were well-known to carry dried bread around to feed the birds. Did you in fact tell her you intended to shoot birds with these pistols?"

"I do not recall. It is possible."

"Because you are in the habit of shooting birds?"

"Not at all. I merely say it is possible that I said as much, because Mrs. Patterson told you I did. I have no cause to doubt her veracity."

"So, if you did tell her you intended to shoot birds, you were lying."

"I should like to hear the reasoning behind that conclusion." Slowly, M'Naghten relaxed, releasing his knees and stretching his legs out again.

"Quite easily done. One does not shoot birds with a pistol ball. It is uneconomical and it usually spares the bird everything except a fright. Paired with your obvious love for our avian friends, your story seems unlikely. You will grant me this point?"

"As I cannot recall having made such a statement, but trust Mrs. Patterson's memory implicitly, I would have to grant it without reservation."

"Thank you. Having rid ourselves of the canard of bird-hunting, Mrs. Patterson's question remains unanswered. For what purpose did you acquire the pistols?"

"You know the answer. I was being persecuted. I wished to protect myself."

"Against people in the streets of Glasgow who followed you everywhere."

"It can be demonstrated by evidence."

"That's the problem," Brekonridge said. "It cannot. We spoke with many people in Glasgow, and none of them could corroborate your story. Nobody ever reported seeing you being followed, harassed, bullyragged, taunted, spat at, or even looked upon sidewise. The only person who ever reported your harassment was *you*. But we will put that aside for the moment. There is another issue of concern. I would agree that Glasgow is no London or Paris, but it is not a tiny hamlet either. You have lived there for your entire life, have you not?"

"With the exception of the time I spent in London, yes."

"And, yet, you were unable to recognize or identify by name a single member of the crew who tormented you? You reported to the police commissioner and the sheriff that you saw these people constantly and that they were priests and police officers, yet you were not able to provide a single name for them to investigate."

"They were furtive."

"Still, the timing intrigues me. You purchased the pistols in July. I believe the Queen and Sir Robert Peel visited Scotland only a few days later. Your landlady in London, Mrs. Dutton, said that you took great interest in that visit. Here is what I think happened. In the summer of 1841, someone paid you over seven hundred pounds to kill Sir Robert. You knew what the consequences would be, so you concocted a clever attempt to portray yourself as insane, drawing on your experience playing King Lear, in hopes that you would be exonerated at trial. For some reason, you missed your opportunity in Scotland, and so you returned to London, where you botched the job by shooting the wrong man."

"Are you certain you are working for my defense?" M'Naghten asked. "That story does not put me in a favorable light at all."

"In truth, no. I no longer work for Mr. Cockburn. I lied my way into the prison to see you tonight because I do not believe the picture Mr. Cockburn will paint of you in the courtroom is an accurate one. I wished to interview you once more, to see if I could draw the truth from you."

"You have wasted your time. I have told the truth repeatedly. I do appreciate the company, however. Might I ask you for one small favor before you go?"

"I hadn't planned on leaving quite yet."

"I think you are. You see, in a few seconds I shall scream. The guards will come, and I shall tell them that you have no legitimate reason to be here, as you are no longer employed by my attorney."

"I see," Brekonridge said. "And this favor?"

"Leave the book?"

"What?"

"Your book by Mr. Darwin. I was immersed in books in Glasgow. They are my solace. I miss reading intensely. I am immensely bored here. I wish for something with which to pass the time, and the book would be greatly appreciated. I would be so appreciative, that I might forget to scream."

Brekonridge glanced at the book on the table and back at M'Naghten. Then he chuckled.

"The book, then. You're clever, Mr. M'Naghten. I'll grant you that."

He banged on the cell door three times. When the guard opened it, Brekonridge left the book on the table and started to leave. As he reached the doorway, he looked back. "I will know the truth," he said. "One way or another, I will."

"Perhaps," M'Naghten replied. "But you will learn nothing more from me."

Chapter Thirty-Seven

Elizabeth Ann Louisa Dalley Godfrey—"Dalley" to her friends—was twenty-five years old, a mother for three years, and hopelessly devoted to Alexander Cockburn. They had never married, despite producing a daughter together, because it had never occurred to Cockburn to propose. Dalley was content with their inconstant and unpredictable relationship. As a former stage actress, whose brief but stellar career on the boards had ended with her pregnancy, she was accustomed to nontraditional arrangements between lovers. She knew her daughter's father, sixteen years her senior, engaged in other dalliances—as did she— but as long as he provided for young Louisa and for herself, she blithely overlooked them. Cockburn extended her similar courtesy.

As she had told a close friend and confidante a year earlier, "Mr. Cockburn may nibble around town, but he knows where to come for a feast."

At the end of February, 1843, with no sign of spring yet visible, Alexander Cockburn was in the midst of a veritable banquet. He had brought Dalley and their love child Louisa to Wakehurst Place in Sussex, which he had let for a week from the family who maintained it. It was one of Dalley's favorite spots, with vast gardens through which she could wander with Louisa.

Louisa was in the company of her nanny. Dalley lay naked in a gargantuan, ornately carved Louis XIV bed on the third floor of the manor, one leg languidly stretched across Alexander's thighs, the perspiration on their bodies slowly drying in the warmth from the roaring fireplace several feet from the footboard. The aroma of their lovemaking hung in the air like a musky cloud. She had been with many men over the previous decade, but none of them had ever aroused her like the man she called her "little bantam."

At the moment, the little bantam stared at the ceiling, one arm resting under Dalley's head and shoulders like a fleshy pillow. She caressed his chest and allowed her gaze to wander out the immense casement windows, where snow fell gently, muffling all the sounds of nature across the immense estate.

"When must you leave?" she asked.

"In the morning. The trial begins in five days. Most of the preparation is completed, but I must meet with my fellow defense barristers to coordinate the order of witnesses. Will you miss me terribly?"

"No more than I would miss my own heart," she said.

"Were it up to me, my darling, I would stay on here forever. Have I ever mentioned how I detest London?"

"Only every day since we met."

"It's so…stodgy. Everything is about class. The people are obsessed with wealth and status. Mr. Dickens is precisely on target, you know. He has captured the tragedy of class in London most ably."

"Thank goodness for Bohemians like us," she joked. She rolled over, until she was nearly lying on top of him. As always, it amused her that she was substantially taller, so as she lay her head on his chest her breasts became a convenient resting place for his manhood. She also knew he enjoyed the disparity in heights, as he had often joked in an affected Cockney accent—among his closest confidantes—*"Nose-to-nose, me toes is in it. Toes-to-toes, me nose is in it!"*

The first time he said it to Dalley, she nearly passed out laughing.

"Will you be required there long? How many days do you expect the trial to last?"

"Four days to prepare, and on Friday we begin testimony. I would be shocked if the trial should run for more than two or three days. We should finish testimony on Saturday, with good luck. The real question is how long it will take the jury to reach a decision."

"Are you confident you can spare him from hanging?"

"Confident? Certainly. I have an infinite reservoir of confidence. Assurance? Not so much. Any time you challenge orthodoxy and precedent, you accept the risk a jury will reject it."

"And if you cannot prove him insane?"

"He'll hang, miserable fellow, and the most horrible consequences will follow. This country is a powder keg. The fuse is Daniel M'Naghten and fifty-nine other Chartists on trial in Lancashire. Once the trial is completed, how would you feel about a holiday?" he asked.

"Any particular spot?"

"Have you been to Italy?"

"That old place?" she joked. "You don't fool me, you know. You are worried M'Naghten might be convicted and you fear we might get caught up in the aftermath. How adorable, you want to go to such lengths to protect us. You do love me, then?"

"With unending devotion. You are my absolute favorite, you know."

"And you are very high in my top five." She nibbled at his shoulder. "Italy sounds wonderful, especially the south. I am so exhausted by the unending British winter. My fingers and toes are tired of being cold."

"Capri. Have you seen it?"

"Never. Is it lovely?"

"Breathtaking."

"Then we must go. Will you have to leave so early in the morning?"

"I think so. It's a long way to London. I hope to return by the middle of the next week."

"I suppose you will find some company there in the duration. I hope she is ugly, with warts all over her face."

"Oh, no, my dearest. She's quite a lovely person. You would like her."

She slapped at his flank and they embraced so strongly it seemed they might pass through one another. He kissed her over and over again as they tickled and giggled, and finally they collapsed and stared into each other's eyes.

"I shall be far too busy to allow my eye to wander," he assured her. "I do appreciate the permission."

She held up her left hand. "No ring. No demands."

"No. No demands. We remain together because we wish it and for no other reason. Now, let's get some sleep. Breakfast tomorrow will find me far down the road."

***

Sir Robert Peel arrived at 10 Downing Street on Monday, February twenty-seventh, to find Home Secretary James Graham waiting sourly for him. He gestured for Graham to follow him and they made their way to Peel's office.

"You have some report, I take it?" Peel said, as he settled into the high-backed leather chair behind his desk.

"It concerns the Chartists trial in Lancashire, Mr. Prime Minister. I am happy to report we have secured the testimony of two highly placed members of Feargus O'Connor's Chartist faction to testify against their fellows. William Griffin and James Cartledge."

"And what is the substance of their testimony? Is it quite damaging?"

"It will suffice. However, trying fifty-nine men simultaneously is a risk."

"If we tried them separately, it would take so long we might find some of them convicted under a new monarch."

"In that case, we must expect some percentage of the accused parties will be acquitted."

"As long as O'Connor is held accountable for the Plug Plot Riots. That is the important point," Peel said.

"And what then, sir?"

"I don't follow."

"What is to be done with O'Connor and his fellow convicted Chartists after the trial? My concern is over the long-term potential for them to become a rallying point for their fellows in Scotland and Wales to engage in similar disruptions in protest of severe punishment. Were O'Connor and his lot to be imprisoned, can you imagine the impact on the country if the Welsh coal miners were to go on a general strike in protest?"

"They could be transported. I hear Van Diemen's Land can use able bodies. Within a few months of sailing, they'd be forgotten."

"I had another notion. Presuming O'Connor and his principals in the Irish Chartist organization are convicted, and the testimony to be provided by Cartledge and Griffin makes that a near certainty, perhaps sentence might be suspended at the Queen's pleasure."

"A conviction without punishment? I fail to see the deterrent."

"It's a conviction with punishment *deferred,*" Graham said. "Should these troublemakers rise up against the Crown again, they would be subject to the full penalty for their treason. No trial required. The Attorney General's delegates could meet with the defense counsel and present a…a *deal* of sorts. They accept the inevitable conviction and a suspended sentence in return for the convicted members of O'Connor's gang making public statements of remorse and gratitude to the Queen."

There was a knock at the door and the assistant entered with a tea tray. He poured a cup for each of the men in the room and retired back to the hallway, closing the door behind him.

"I think I understand," Peel said, after taking a sip. "Whilst the Crown can boast of having dealt fairly with these radical rebels, it can also diffuse the political impact in the countryside."

"We give the appearance of cracking down, but minimize the potential for backlash and further uprisings," Graham said.

"An iron fist in a velvet glove. It is an interesting notion. Let me think about it and get back with you."

"While I am here, might I bring up another pressing matter? It's about the Daniel M'Naghten trial this week. I have been informed Mr. Cockburn intends to make a plea of insanity. I believe, given the opportunity, the prosecution could demonstrate conclusively M'Naghten not only killed Mr. Drummond, but he was paid to do so. The case can be made."

"And the consequence?"

"M'Naghten would be hanged. This is not only a case of murder, it also comprises treason. There can only be one penalty. The loyalists in England would not stand for transportation or imprisonment. Even if we can quell the backlash from the Lancashire trial, executing a man whose act was fully informed by his Chartist and radical beliefs could result in riots."

"What is the solution?"

"I believe I have come up with a strategy that could serve both justice and peace."

"Please, elaborate."

Graham told him.

Peel was about to respond, when there was another knock at the door. The assistant entered and handed a note to the Prime Minister. He read it and placed it on his desktop.

"Speaking of Her Majesty," he said. "She wishes to go for a carriage ride this morning, and Prince Albert is presently in Wales. I have been summoned to Buckingham to accompany her in his stead. You are the Home Secretary and in charge of legal matters in the courts. Discuss your ideas with the Attorney General and the Solicitor General and decide how you would prefer to proceed. I should caution you, however. Should your machinations backfire, I cannot protect you from the consequences. Have we reached an understanding?"

"It appears we have," Graham said.

Chapter Thirty-Eight

It was a meteorological rarity in London—a sunny and relatively warm day in late February. Crowds going about their daily business along Constitution Hill near Buckingham Palace stopped and took notice as the Queen's royal carriage rolled by. Former soldiers and sailors saluted her. Gentlemen doffed their hats, and some of the women—despite the fact they were in a public space and decorum could be foregone—affected a slight curtsey.

The carriage itself was a grand affair, with red enameled sides polished to a mirror-like gloss, the royal crest and coat of arms attached to the door on both sides, and the convertible top pulled down to allow the people to admire their monarch. The carriage was drawn by two magnificent Arabian stallions, their bridles bedecked with plumes rising above the tops of their heads like feathery geysers.

While unseasonable, the temperature outside was still crisp, so the Queen had dressed to accommodate, in a rich emerald green velvet gown and cape with a sweeping hat to match. As always, she had brought along her bullet-resistant parasol. Adding to her brilliance was the fortune in jewels she wore—a diamond and ruby pendant on a gold chain and a huge diamond brooch. On a previous sojourn, Peel had remarked about them, more out of concern for her safety than for public appearance.

"Nonsense," the Queen had told him. "There is no longer an imperious monarch, Sir Robert. There is, however, an imperial one. The Queen is a symbol to her people, a barometer, if you will, by which they measure the strength and financial health of the empire. As I ride the streets of London, the people see the empire is strong and prosperous, and they are at ease. Besides, I do adore pretty things."

It reminded the Prime Minister that, while she was the queen of a vast empire, Victoria was also a twenty-three-year-old woman who, up until only a handful of years before, had led a remarkably sheltered life.

Today she seemed content to take in the sights and sounds and questionable air of London. They rode in silence for almost a quarter hour, the Queen occasionally pausing to wave at her people as they stopped to pay tribute to her. They happened across a prominent member of the House of Lords strolling with his wife and Victoria ordered the carriage to stop for a moment so she might greet him—and to allow him to pay her a compliment.

When they got back underway, the Queen asked, "What news from Lancashire?" It was not necessary for her to ask in greater detail. The only matter of great importance in Lancashire was the upcoming Chartists' trial.

"The Attorney General assures me they have put together a thorough prosecutorial case. Mr. Pollock believes he can secure convictions for a little over half the defendants. Perhaps two-thirds."

"The measure is unimportant. What is important is the recognition that fomenting riots and general strikes in Britain is tantamount to treason."

"About that, Your Highness. I spoke this morning with Mr. Graham. We both fear issuing too severe a punishment against these Chartist gentlemen might precipitate resentment among their followers. We discussed some options which could both send a message that the behavior is intolerable, but at the same time mollify the mob."

"I'm listening," she said, as she smiled and waved at a crowd of children who had assembled from the park along Constitution Hill.

"The Home Secretary suggested that, upon conviction, we issue stiff penalties, including prison time, to be served at the Queen's pleasure."

Victoria stopped waving and turned back to Peel.

"I am not sure I understand the purpose of issuing a sentence not imposed."

"It would be under specific circumstances. In essence, the men would walk around for the rest of their days with the threat of imprisonment hanging over their heads. The message would be clear. Engage in economic warfare with the Crown and your life will never belong fully to you again."

"And I could revoke my leniency at any time?"

"The sentence is *'at the Queen's pleasure,'* Your Highness."

Victoria crossed her hands in her lap, and stared straight ahead, ignoring onlookers who waved to get her attention.

"The idea appeals to me," she said at last. "And I see your purpose here. It allows the Crown to appear both strong and merciful simultaneously, and could discourage a retributive outbreak among the radical factions. I see no reason why we could not proceed, presuming Mr. Pollock can get the convictions."

"He will get a great many."

"As to the matter of your late secretary," Victoria continued. "What is the posture of the trial at this point?"

"It should be short," Peel said. "The Solicitor General is conducting the prosecution, and of course there can be no doubt young M'Naghten committed the shooting. He was witnessed by dozens of people."

"And the defense? I am distressed to learn it is to be conducted by Mr. Cockburn. He is, regrettably, in line for the baronetcy. It is an accident of his birth, over which I have no control. However, I have refused several requests for peerage on his behalf, due to his deplorable moral character. You are aware he has at least one child out of wedlock?"

"I have been so informed."

"He is undeniably brilliant, otherwise I never would have appointed him a Queen's Counsel. I am also aware he is a trickster. His courtroom theatrics have brought some degree of ill repute on him, regardless of how successful they may have been. Do you think he has a chance of bringing Mr. M'Naghten an acquittal?"

"It is my understanding that he intends to bring an insanity defense. In my experience, such pleas are seldom successful. The rules for insanity established by Lord Hale in the last century have remained un-assailed."

"That is a comfort," the Queen said.

"And, yet," Peel continued, "once a case is put into the hands of a jury, almost anything is possible."

"The attack on Mr. Drummond and its tragic outcome are unacceptable. I am distressed at the impunity with which disgruntled individuals have taken their frustrations out on my own person and on other high government officials. I shall be incensed at any outcome in the M'Naghten trial which does not result in the assassin's execution. General strikes are one thing, and I can recognize the value of lenience in dealing with their instigators. Regicide and murder are quite another. I am not inclined to offer any mercy to Mr. M'Naghten. He must be made an example to others who might attempt to overthrow the government by violence."

* * *

When Alexander Cockburn arrived at the Newgate Street offices of Humphreys and Perceval, he was surprised to find them nearly empty. A fire crackled in the conference room hearth, and young Simon was present to admit him to the building. After taking Cockburn's coat, Simon retreated to prepare a tea tray for the Queen's Counsel. When he returned, Simon discovered Cockburn had strewn papers all across the three-yard conference table and was bent over at one end of the table examining a list of names.

Simon placed the tea tray on a side table and waited for Cockburn to acknowledge him. After almost a minute, he cleared his throat. Cockburn looked up.

"Yes?" he said.

"Will there will be anything else, sir?" He expected Cockburn would dismiss him with a wave of his hand. Instead, the barrister stood and straightened his waistcoat.

"Why, yes, Mr. Daughtrey. A few moments of your time?"

"I have no other responsibilities this morning but to but attend you, sir."

"Please, take a seat."

Nobody had ever asked Simon to sit at the conference table. Reluctantly, he slid a chair from the table and gingerly lowered himself into it. Almost to his surprise, no lightning flashed from the ceiling to smite him.

"Your reports from Glasgow are impressive," Cockburn began. "Unless you have the soul and creativity of a novelist, your accounts of the interviews you conducted with the Glasgow officials are remarkably complete. You must have a top-shelf memory."

"I have been informed my memory is out of the ordinary, but I have nothing with which to compare it. I am gratified you find my work helpful."

"And, yet, as I recall, your intended role in Glasgow was only to accompany Mr. Brekonridge and collate the records he produced. Might I inquire at which point you abandoned the role of clerk and assumed that of detective?"

Simon felt the flush that spread across his cheeks. "I… overstepped my authority. It was at Mr. Brekonridge's suggestion, but I assume full responsibility. I was completely able to refuse him and I did not."

"I see," Cockburn said. "And why did Brekonridge press this responsibility upon you?"

"He believed I would be more likely to beguile the authorities, due to my youth and my apparent and obvious inexperience."

"Whilst he spent his time interviewing the common laborers and craftsmen."

"Yes, sir."

"With whom, as a man used to the vernacular of the streets, he would be more likely accepted and effective."

"Yes again, sir."

"And the two of you, together, completed your interviews in only three days?"

"I'm sorry, but is there a problem with the reports? Should we have spent more time working on them, or perhaps we might have interviewed even more of M'Naghten's—"

Cockburn held up his hand, and his face broke into a smile. "Relax, Mr. Daughtrey. I am not criticizing your work. In fact, I am impressed beyond my expectations. I understand you have been admitted to the Middle Temple."

CHAPTER THIRTY-EIGHT

"Correct, sir."

"Are you quite comfortable with your situation here at Humphreys and Perceval?"

Simon squirmed in his chair. Such questions simply weren't asked by people from outside the firm, certainly not of nineteen-year-old clerks.

"I…I don't know how to answer your question, sir. Messrs. Humphreys and Perceval have been good to me. They have encouraged my studies, and Mr. Humphreys was instrumental in my admission to the Middle Temple."

"What I am about to tell you is strictly confidential. But I like you, boy, and I think it is in your best interest to know certain things. Within the year, the firm of Humphreys and Perceval will be dissolved."

Cockburn might as well have leveled a pistol at Simon and pulled the trigger. He could only stare, dumbfounded, at the Queen's Counsel.

"Mr. Perceval's gambling debts," Cockburn continued. "He does not believe Mr. Humphreys knows, but people have approached your senior partner with demands. In order to protect himself, Mr. Humphreys intends to break the partnership with Mr. Perceval and venture out on his own. Needless to say, many of the employees here will be left in the cold."

"I don't know why you would tell me such a terrible thing!"

"To prepare you for what is to come. Forewarned, a bright, industrious, self-motivated young man such as yourself might prepare for the eventual cataclysm by finding another situation which is more advantageous to you."

Cockburn, amused, watched as a panoply of emotions crossed Simon's face—fear, dread, shock, and even a little confusion. Finally, there was a hint of hopelessness. Nineteen years old, a brilliant future ahead, and now it all crumbled before him.

When he could contain himself no longer, Cockburn said, "You could, for instance, come to work for *me*."

There was sharp rap at the door downstairs. Thinking it might be one of the other barristers, but dearly wishing to pursue the notion Cockburn had presented, Simon was torn between duty and opportunity. In the end, duty won out.

"Please, excuse me," he said, and dashed down the stairs to answer the door.

Moments later, he reappeared in the conference room with an envelope his hand.

"It was a messenger," he said, handing the envelope to Cockburn. "For you."

Cockburn broke the seal and read the message inside:

> *Mr. Cockburn—*
>
> *If it is not inconvenient, might you come to my office at Buckingham Palace at your earliest opportunity. I have a matter to discuss with you which I believe may be in our mutual interests.*
>
> *Yours-*
> *James Graham*
> *Home Secretary*

"Is it important?" Simon asked.

"It has every appearance of being so. If I am not mistaken, the Home Secretary wishes to engage in a little *ex parte* communication regarding Mr. M'Naghten's case. What do you make of that?"

"He is worried about losing," Simon said.

"Or perhaps he wishes to make a deal, avoid the trial altogether. In any case, when the Home Secretary summons, one is rather obligated to accept the invitation."

"Now?"

"No better time. My fellows on the defense team appear in no hurry to meet. I might as well conduct some business in the interim."

"I'll retrieve your coat and summon a cab."

"The coat is fine, but I'll walk. It's a lovely day."

Simon brought Cockburn his coat and hat and helped him dress to leave.

"Sir, about what you mentioned earlier," Simon said, brushing some lint from Cockburn's top hat. "You said something about…about…"

"Coming to work with me?" Cockburn examined himself in a cheval mirror. "What of it?"

"Were you serious?"

"I am always serious, young man, when discussing business. You would have to leave London, I'm afraid. I can't abide the place for longer than a few days. Don't fret. I wouldn't demand you abandon the city until you've finished your studies in the Middle Temple. Afterward, you'll come to clerk for me in the west, until you are called to the bar, at which time we will make you an associate. How does all of that sound?"

"I don't know what to say."

"Say whatever you like, as long as it includes the word *yes*. There is no future for you at Humphreys and Perceval, and I would not like to see such a disaster befall a young man with your potential. Think it over. We'll talk again after the trial."

Chapter Thirty-Nine

Cockburn had not been untruthful when he told Dalley that she would like the woman he kept in London. His paramour was a delightful, lively young lass, only recently turned twenty, and surprisingly creative in her attentions.

Those attentions, however, were wasted on him as the day of the trial dawned. He awoke shortly before sunrise, roused by a growing sense of urgency in his bowels. The young woman snored softly beside him, naked under the duvet, unaware of his distress. There was no question of it. He was going to be ill.

He rolled out of the bed and dashed to the privy at the end of the hall, as he doubted the capacity of his chamber pot and did not wish to expose his mistress to the indignity he knew would very shortly follow. There, he was seized by the most exquisite spasms of agony for almost a half hour, with little relief. As he sat and waited, sweat popping on his brow, he became aware of a tightness in his stomach that rapidly bypassed queasiness directly to nausea.

He tried to recall what he might have consumed the night before that could produce such acute and overwhelming misery.

"Damnation!" he cried out, as he tried to determine which end of his digestive tract required the most urgent attention. "The worst possible time!"

He could see light begin to penetrate the jamb of the door. In only four hours, he was scheduled to try one of the most taxing cases of his legal career, and for the moment he might as well be chained to his privy.

* * *

Friday, March third, 1843, was a blustery day, as the world turned relentlessly toward spring. In London, astronomers were excited about a new comet which had been discovered only a few weeks earlier and which promised as it grew in magnitude to become a major celestial spectacle.

While the trial of Daniel M'Naghten was not scheduled to begin until ten o'clock at the Old Bailey, potential spectators queued up near the courthouse shortly after sunrise. Newspaper accounts of the prospective showdown between some of the greatest legal minds of their generation had spurred sensation-seekers to take their chances on snatching up one of the few seats available. Many of the seats had been sold by brokers and were already reserved. Even so, carriages choked Grace Church Road all the way up Ludgate Hill. Few of their occupants stood any chance of acquiring a gallery seat in the courtroom, but they all wanted to be part of the great event.

Vicar Brekonridge, despite having been discharged by Humphreys and Perceval, had pulled strings with his friends at Bow Street to obtain a seat. Likewise, as an employee of Humphreys and Perceval, Simon Daughtrey was granted one. They spied one another as they entered the Criminal Courts building and immediately conspired to sit together to watch the fruits of their investigative labors.

They arrived in their seats shortly after nine. A few minutes later, a gentleman sat directly in front of them. He was young, barely out of his twenties, and had shoulder-length wiry hair made even more bedraggled by the electricity in the dry winter air. His alert eyes scanned the room. He was dressed neatly in a fashionable suit with a brocaded silk waistcoat. He removed his short hat and placed it in his lap.

Simon elbowed Brekonridge gently, pointed discreetly at the gentleman, and whispered, "Dickens."

"The writer?" Brekonridge whispered back.

"No, the bellows mate. Of course, he's the writer. I hear he has taken a special interest in this case."

Dickens turned around to face them. "You may also report I have exceptional hearing," he remarked, and then saw Brekonridge's face and winced. "We have met before, sir. Have we not?"

"We may have crossed paths, sir, but I do not believe we travel in the same circles."

"You are the thief-taker from Bow Street, if I am not mistaken."

"I am, sir."

"Have you some relation to this case?"

"Mr. Brekonridge did the investigatory work for the defense in Glasgow," Simon said.

"Indeed," Dickens said. "I think I'd like to hear more."

"You will," Brekonridge told him. "It will all be in the testimony."

"Are you planning a novel based on the M'Naghten trial, Mr. Dickens?" Simon asked.

"Not specifically. I am attracted to all tragedies and misfortunes. While I may draw inspiration from them, I do not write biographies. Some snippets of the proceedings may show up in a future work, however. I find the idea of prosecuting a man who is unable to fully understand his circumstances compelling."

"Well, I can tell you I'm enjoying *Martin Chuzzlewit*. I cannot wait for the next installment."

"That would make one of us. I cannot say I am pleased with either the reception or the proceeds from that book."

"Can you tell us what you will write next?"

"A Christmas story, I think," Dickens said. "However, I have not yet started it. My plans might change. Who knows? Perhaps this trial will inspire me to write a murder mystery. What say you, Mr. Thief-Taker? We should meet over a tankard or two one day. I imagine you are a treasure trove of stories." Dickens smiled and scanned the room again, as if trying to commit it to permanent memory so that he could describe it in print.

* * *

Having donned his robes and wig, Alexander Cockburn joined his similarly attired team of attorneys at the defense table, to the right of the judges' bench. His face was drawn and haggard under the powdered wig. His hands shook as he took his seat.

"Are you ill?" Clarkson, seated next to him, asked.

"A bad oyster, I believe," Cockburn said. "I am in considerable distress, but the trial is the important thing. I'll muddle through. Today is mostly prosecution witnesses in any case."

A figure clad entirely in black, her face shadowed behind a darkened veil, appeared in the gallery doorway.

"Drummond's sister," Clarkson told him.

Anne Eliza Drummond, as a family member of the deceased, was afforded a prime viewing space behind the defense table. She was accompanied by her brother Charles, on whose arm she weighed heavily as he escorted her to her seat.

Within minutes, the gallery filled, with some persons forced to stand at the back. A bailiff entered the courtroom and commanded all rise for the introduction of the justices.

The court was presided over by a triumvirate of justices, led by Chief Justice Nicholas Conyngham Tindal. Nearing his seventies, Tindal was a dour man with sleepy eyes and heavy jowls. As was custom for justices and barristers alike, he had covered his otherwise bald head with an elaborate curled and powdered wig, which seemed to itch him horribly, if one was to judge by the way he constantly fidgeted at it and scratched at his scalp through it. His fatigue after a long and eventful life at the bar was evident.

On each side of Tindal sat the other judges in the case, Justices Coleridge and Williams.

John Taylor Coleridge, the nephew of the great poet Samuel Coleridge, was regarded more as a scholar than as a barrister. Already in his middle fifties, his face remained largely unlined and youthful under his massive wig. His hands, being the only thing besides his face the court could see, were slight and graceful with long thin fingers. He was known to take voluminous notes with a graphite pencil.

Of the three judges, only Justice John Williams was a cypher for Cockburn.

In general, it was speculated Williams had attained his silk robes more through his connections to the estimable Justice Tindal than he had through his own energies and endeavors, and therefore Cockburn was satisfied that, as Tindal ruled, Williams was sure to follow.

After the justices were seated, and the gallery had also returned to their seats, Justice Tindal asked the recorder to call the case.

Cockburn noted, when M'Naghten was led into the courtroom, how many in the gallery expressed surprise at how youthful the prisoner looked. M'Naghten was still in his late twenties, with a broad open face and eyes downturned at the corners, but the man led out to the dock by the bailiffs looked small and helpless and almost juvenile. Cockburn hoped to use the woodturner's young features to his advantage.

M'Naghten's head swiveled as he took in the courtroom, the justices, the jurors, and the huge crowd who had gathered to watch the spectacle. The bailiffs deposited him in the dock, where he stood, his hands trembling as they grasped the walnut railing.

"The prisoner having declared his innocence in this case, the court will hear evidence from both the prosecution and the defense in turn," Tindal announced. "Gentlemen of the jury, I would implore you to attend most carefully to the testimony to be presented by the witnesses, as it is on that basis you must decide this case. Evidence will first be presented by the prosecution. Bailiffs, please bring a chair to the dock for the prisoner, as it does appear this will be a lengthy proceeding."

The larger of the two bailiffs hoisted a straight-back oaken chair into the dock, and M'Naghten thanked him pleasantly enough before sitting. Almost instantly, his chin fell to his chest.

Simon leaned toward Brekonridge. "Is he…sleeping?" he whispered.

"He shows every indication."

In fact, as Solicitor General Follett gave his opening arguments—the only arguments traditionally made by barristers in open court—M'Naghten began to snore lightly, much to the amusement of the spectators in the gallery.

Chapter Forty

Richard Jackson was in his late sixties, but still active and robust. He took his seat in the witness box and waited patiently for Solicitor-General Follett to arrange his papers on the lectern. Almost absently, Follett launched into his questions.

"Are you familiar with the victim in this case?"

"I have served the Drummond family as an apothecary for many years."

"Were you summoned to Mr. Drummond's side on the day of the shooting?"

"I was sent for to attend him at the Drummond banking-house in Charing Cross."

"Upon arriving at the Drummond Bank, what did you find?"

"Mr. Drummond was in great pain but struggled mightily to avoid showing it."

"What action did you take?"

"I am not a physician, sir. I did not feel I was competent to treat him. I recommended his immediate removal to his own residence."

"How was Drummond transported?"

"By carriage. I accompanied him there, in case I might be of any small service until the physicians could be summoned."

"And were they summoned?"

"Shortly after we arrived at Mr. Drummond's home. The ball was extracted the same day, within an hour after the injury was received."

* * *

Despite being close to sixty years of age, Dr. George James Guthrie remained vibrant and active. His gaze was direct and steady. Not a tall man, he appeared larger than his actual height due to his bearing and posture. He mounted the witness stand at the Old Bailey and waited patiently for Solicitor-General Follett to collect himself at the lectern.

"Your name?" Follett asked.

"Dr. George James Guthrie."

"And your profession?"

"I am a surgeon."

"Could you, for the benefit of the court, outline your training and area of expertise in your field?"

"I was trained at the Royal College of Surgeons beginning in 1801, when I was sixteen years of age."

"Is that not considered young to be entered into such a profession?"

"I have been told I was a precocious child," Guthrie said. The courtroom erupted in polite but obvious laughter, and Chief Justice Tindal allowed it to subside naturally before he gaveled for order.

"And after your matriculation at the Royal College?"

"I served as a military surgeon during the Peninsular campaign in Iberia."

"During that episode of your life, did you treat men suffering from gunshot wounds?"

"Many. I wrote and had published a monograph on the subject, entitled *On Gunshot Wounds of the Extremities.*"

"So, it would be correct to state you are no stranger to the treatment of firearms-related injuries."

"I am intimately familiar with such matters."

"And he isn't ashamed to say so," Brekonridge whispered to Simon in the gallery. For an instant, he imagined he saw Justice Tindal giving him a warning look, but as quickly as it flashed across the judge's face, it disappeared.

Follett asked, "And of your career since leaving the military?"

"I am on the council of the Royal College of Surgeons, and have served twice as its president."

Follett allowed the weight of Guthrie's statement to settle on the jury before continuing. "Could you describe the events that transpired between January twentieth and January twenty-fifth of this year?"

"I was called in to see Mr. Drummond about five o'clock on the evening of the twentieth of January. I found Dr. Bransby Cooper there, who had examined the wound before my arrival; but as he had not found the bullet, we at once proceeded to make a further examination. We turned Mr. Drummond upon his back, and found the ball in the front, about half an inch below the skin."

"Did you surgically remove the ball?"

"It was taken out by a lancet, as I had not had time to assemble my surgical tools before being summoned to the Drummond house."

"What was Mr. Drummond's condition?"

"Quite grave. I have no hesitation whatever in saying his death was occasioned by the wound."

"Did Mr. Drummond have much chance of survival following his grave injury?"

"It was certainly a mortal wound," Guthrie responded. "I never knew a person to recover from such an injury made by a pistol ball."

* * *

Dr. Bransby Blake Cooper, while still in his early fifties, had given way to the pleasures of lavish food and drink, so his skin was sallow and his jowls had a pronounced droop. Even so, his strong chin, full lips, long nose, and deep blue, sad eyes were still considered attractive by most women and men who met him.

His reputation as a surgeon was spotty at best, but through social and political connections and the benefit of having been the nephew of the great surgeon, Astley Cooper, he had enjoyed a long a successful career providing medical services to the families of the most highly placed members of the British government.

Horatio Waddington, the first of Follett's team of prominent prosecutors,

249

stood and approached a lectern in front of the prosecution table. A short, rotund man, he appeared even more sphere-like with his body wrapped in the barrister robes and his head covered with a short, white, powdered wig. His tenor voice was soft and punctuated by the occasional wheeze as he tried to draw breath to speak.

After establishing Cooper's credentials, Horatio Waddington launched into an examination of Cooper's recollections on the treatment of Edward Drummond.

"I attended Mr. Drummond, in conjunction with Dr. Guthrie and other medical gentlemen. I was present when the ball was extracted."

"Do you concur with Dr. Guthrie? Once shot, Mr. Drummond's fate was sealed?"

"I perfectly agree with Mr. Guthrie with respect to the nature of the wound, and have no doubt whatever it was the cause of death."

"Perhaps a stronger, more athletic man might have survived?"

"I have no intimate knowledge of Mr. Drummond's physical state prior to the shooting," Cooper answered. "I would suspect the subsequent infection of peritonitis was the likely cause of his death, and such an infection was both inevitable and ultimately incurable."

"But you have no doubt, as a physician and surgeon, that it was the bullet that caused the death of Edward Drummond?"

"Not a doubt in the world," Cooper said.

* * *

Solicitor General Follett again took the lectern and addressed both the justices at the bench and the impaneled jury. "Some of you esteemed gentlemen may labor under the impression the prisoner was driven by demons of madness to suppose killing the Prime Minister would salve his psychic wounds. The prosecution would like to disabuse you of these notions. The next witnesses will demonstrate the prisoner meticulously planned his crime, and exerted great effort preparing for the day he would encounter Edward Drummond on the street at Whitehall. The prosecution calls John Drake to testify."

John Drake in his dark blue overcoat appeared somewhat drab. He wore the same uniform coat he had worn the day before on his patrol near Whitehall. If one had looked closely enough, it would have been possible to see the stain left from a dribble of mustard. Even so, Drake attempted to affect a sense of authority as he took his place in the witness stand. He was addressed there by Russell Gurney.

"I am a police constable of the A division, and in the months of December and January last I occasionally was on duty at Whitehall," he said.

"In the course of your patrols along Whitehall, did you have occasion to encounter the prisoner?" Gurney asked.

"I noticed the prisoner frequently near the corner of Downing Street, loitering about between the third and fourth, up until the twentieth of January last."

"Can you state why your attention was drawn to this particular man?"

"Some of the blokes in the Council offices didn't like him hanging about on the steps of the building."

"And your response to their concerns?"

"I had a word or two with the prisoner about it on Wednesday, the eighteenth of January."

"Two days before the shooting of Edward Drummond," Gurney clarified.

"That's right. I walked up and I said to him, *Some of the gentlemen inside have been speaking to me about your standing on the steps.*' "

"How did the prisoner reply?" Gurney asked.

"As if he didn't care. He said, *Tell them it is a notion I have taken.*' As he was committin' no crime, I told him to be about his business, but there was nothin' else I could do."

"Did you encounter the prisoner again?"

"On that same day, at the corner of Downing Street."

"What was the nature of that encounter?"

"He asked me to take a glass of ale with him."

A wave of whispers ran through the gallery, punctuated by no small number of giggles. A stern look from Justice Tindal brought it to a quick conclusion.

"I declined it, of course," Jones added. "Wouldn't be seemly, me a man in the uniform of the police, takin' a pop in broad daylight."

"How did he respond to your refusal?"

"Why, he asked me if I would take a gin."

This time, the gallery erupted into outright laughter. Tindal rapped a gavel several times to bring it back to order.

"Well," Jones said, seemingly oblivious to the disruption, or perhaps playing to it. "That I also declined. I left him for that day, and on the following day I saw him between one and five in the afternoon, at the corner of Downing Street."

"Did you speak with him then?"

"I did, sir. He asked me if I would have something to drink, and I said, *'No, thank you.'*"

"He asked you to drink with him again?"

"He did. Seemed most intent on it. Never met a man so thirsty."

Another round of laughter echoed through the courtroom, but ended itself before Tindal was forced to bring it to a halt.

"He said, *'Why won't you?'* and I replied, *'If any of my people see me I shall get into trouble.'*"

"Did you see the prisoner again?"

"Not until the next day, at the station-house, in Gardener's Lane."

"No further questions," Gurney announced.

Chapter Forty-One

"The prosecution calls Mr. John Gordon," Follett announced, as he relinquished the lectern to Horatio Waddington. As had been his habit almost all day, Alexander Cockburn had declined to cross-examine Officer Drake.

When Follett called Gordon to the stand, Simon felt Vicar bristle beside him.

"I had no idea Gordon would be testifying," Brekonridge whispered. "Who is he?"

"A compatriot of Abram Duncan. When I was abducted by Duncan's men in Glasgow, Gordon was there. He is bound tightly with the Chartist resistance in Glasgow and a long-time friend of M'Naghten. Duncan was adamant that he would not testify. I presumed Gordon would avoid it as well. What in hell is he doing testifying for the prosecution?"

"We shall soon see," Simon replied.

"Could you describe your relationship with the prisoner in the dock?" Waddington asked Gordon.

"I have known M'Naghten about six years. He was working in the same close with me when I knew him. We did not work together. He was working for himself. I was manager for Laing and Son, and occasionally employed the prisoner as a day laborer."

"In what business is Laing and Son?"

"It is a foundry. We cast bronze, mostly, but also copper and brass. When M'Naghten abandoned his career as an actor, he sought some more lucrative employment. For a while, I gave him work in the foundry."

"When did this business relationship end?" Waddington asked.

"When he established his woodturning business. I continued to employ the prisoner on an occasional basis, as needs warranted, when he went into business for himself."

"Were your other interactions with the prisoner an occasional thing, or did you see him more often?"

"I saw the prisoner twice or thrice a week during the whole of that time. I paid him money and he gave me receipts for the same."

"Were you socially engaged, or was your relationship merely in the course of business?"

"I was not in the habit of visiting him. I was not generally acquainted or intimate with him. We communicated only on matters of business."

"He's lying," Brekonridge whispered to Simon. "They were fast friends in the Chartist society and at the Mechanics Institute."

Dickens turned around and glanced at Brekonridge. He pointed to his ear and smiled, then jotted in his notebook.

"Have you had any meetings with the prisoner outside of Glasgow?" Waddington asked Gordon.

"I came to London in November last. While strolling, I met the prisoner in St. Martin's Lane. I shook hands with him, and asked him why he was in London. Instead of answering, he asked *'What do you here?'* and I replied, *'In search of employment.'* He said, *'I am also in search of employment.'*"

"Were you surprised to find him in London?"

"I did not know he was in London until I met him there. We walked on together and passed by the Horse Guards and down Parliament Street. I know Sir Robert Peel's house, from an earlier visit to London. We passed that on our way to Westminster Hall. I told him it was the house was where Sir Robert Peel stayed."

"How did the prisoner respond?"

"He said, *'Damn him, sink him!'*"

"How was his voice?"

"He was furious. Mr. M'Naghten is most commonly soft-spoken, but when he saw the Prime Minister's home he became incensed."

"Something is wrong," Brekonridge whispered. "I asked Gordon directly in Glasgow whether he had witnessed any violent inclinations toward the Prime Minister. He denied them. He lied."

"What can you do about it?" Simon whispered back.

"Time will tell, boy."

Dickens smiled and wrote furiously.

"He's lying," Brekonridge whispered. "I will know why."

* * *

"The prosecution calls Mr. Joseph Forrester," Waddington said, after relieving Cockburn at the lectern.

In the gallery, Brekonridge suddenly became alert. Forrester had not mentioned to him in Glasgow that he planned to testify. He wondered how the hairdresser had received a summons to appear as the large red-headed man took his place in the dock.

"For the record," Waddington said, "could you describe your relationship to the prisoner?"

"I have known the prisoner for a number of years, but we were separated from one another for many of them, until the last eighteen months."

"Did you visit with him frequently?"

"I knew him when he lodged at Mrs. Patterson's, in Clyde Street, Glasgow, and I have visited him there."

"When you visited with the prisoner, did you commonly have long conversations?"

"We used to talk together, but upon no particular subject beyond the mere occurrences of the day."

"During the eighteen months during which you most recently had the prisoner's acquaintance, did you form an opinion regarding his mental state?"

"I never saw anything in his manner which led me to think he was not in his right senses, or he was wrong in his intellect."

"No further questions, Your Honors," Waddington said, and he backed away from the lectern.

Brekonridge noted there was some sort of disturbance at the defense table. William Clarkson leaned over to Cockburn and whispered quickly. Cockburn shook his head. Clarkson attempted to assert himself more directly, but Cockburn dismissed him with a wave of his hand. Clarkson shook his head and stood to make his way to the lectern. Cockburn slouched in his chair, his hands crossed over his midsection. He appeared to be in even greater physical distress than earlier.

Clarkson cleared his throat. "Ah, Mr. Forrester, to…to clarify, you have been acquainted with Mr. M'Naghten for a number of years."

It was obvious Clarkson would have preferred that Cockburn conduct the cross-examination, Brekonridge mused.

"That is correct," Forrester replied. "However, there was a long period, up until a year and a half ago, when we were separated by our circumstances."

"And, during that last year and a half, could you estimate the number of times you have been in his company?"

"I don't know. Twenty. Perhaps thirty. Perhaps more."

"So, you have spent anywhere from forty to eighty hours in the man's company."

"That would be a dependable estimate," Forrester said.

"During those many hours, you state you saw nothing of concern in his thinking or his behavior?"

"I never suspected there was anything wrong in the prisoner's mind."

"So, you have never had reason to believe Mr. M'Naghten might have issues with his reason?"

"Never."

"Yet, by report, you have referred to him on occasion as daft, have you not?"

"Sir?"

"According to an affidavit by Mrs. Patterson, M'Naghten's landlady in Glasgow, she was on her way to make a complaint about M'Naghten's bizarre behavior and fantasies to the sheriff in August of last year. Along the way, she encountered you, and according to her you referred to Mr.

M'Naghten as daft, and asked whether you could accompany her to the sheriff to lodge a companion complaint."

"I have spoken to Mrs. Patterson on several occasions respecting the prisoner. One night she told me she was surprised I said he was right, as I had once said he was wrong, but I denied having said anything of the sort."

"So, you deny telling Mrs. Patterson Mr. M'Naghten was daft, as she reported?"

"I do deny it."

"And the cock crowed." Brekonridge whispered to Simon.

"Because, according to another affidavit from James Wilson, the baker, you also stated to him you considered Mr. M'Naghten to be daft," Clarkson continued "Is that not correct?"

"Neither did I ever tell Wilson that M'Naghten was daft."

"Never?" Clarkson probed.

"Not in my memory."

"And the cock crowed twice," Brekonridge whispered.

"Could you explain to the court how you came to provide your testimony here today?" Clarkson asked.

"It never occurred to me I should like to come to London as a witness. The captain of the Anderston police first came to me upon the subject."

"You did not approach him?"

"No. He came to my shop, and asked me whether I knew anything about M'Naghten. I told him all I knew."

"Did you have contact with any other officials in Glasgow before coming to London to testify in this case?"

"Only Mr. Lamond."

"Could you clarify the identity of Mr. Lamond for the benefit of the court and the jurors?"

"Mr. Robert Lamond. He's a solicitor in Glasgow."

"Is it not true Mr. Robert Lamond is also a primary operative for the Tory government in Glasgow?"

"I suppose. I had never met with the man before I was asked to testify here."

"Never?"

"No. I never offered myself as a witness to anyone else."

"Were you interviewed by a representative of the defense in Glasgow?"

"I was. A Mr. Brekonridge, I believe."

"And, in the course of that interview, did you not say M'Naghten was always a little mad?"

"I think Mr. Brekonridge misheard me. I would never say that about Daniel. It simply isn't the case."

"And the cock crowed thrice," Brekonridge said to Simon. "The man has done nothing but lie on the stand."

"What can you do about it?" Simon whispered back.

"Time will tell, boy," Brekonridge repeated. "Time will tell."

* * *

The prosecution completed its case with a review of M'Naghten's bank records, but without establishing the source of his remarkably large amount of cash. That struck Brekonridge as odd, since—as Solicitor General Follett had established they would discount any claims to insanity the defense might make—it seemed to the advantage of the prosecutors to establish an alternate motive for murdering Edward Drummond. By not claiming M'Naghten committed the shooting for hire, they missed an important opportunity to nail M'Naghten to the wall.

As Follett announced the prosecution was ready to rest its case, Chief Justice Tindal turned to Alexander Cockburn at the defense table.

"Is the defense prepared to move forward with their witnesses?" he asked.

Cockburn rose at the table, but appeared disinclined to make his way to the lectern.

"With the permission of the court, I would humbly request we adjourn for the day and take up the defense case on the morrow. With all due respect, I have been taken with a severe indisposition, which I hope will be resolved by tomorrow morning. In addition, we have a great many witnesses to present, and I fear it would be impossible to close the proceedings this evening in any case."

Tindal leaned forward, as if attempting to examine the Queen's Counsel from across the gulf of the courtroom floor. "Should we adjourn at once, are you quite certain the remainder of the case for the defense might be accomplished within the compass of tomorrow?"

"Were we confined to testimony for the defense alone, I could say with confidence we will complete all testimony tomorrow. I cannot say how much time the prosecution may wish to take for cross-examination."

Williams and Coleridge leaned in, and the justices whispered back and forth for a few seconds. Finally, Tindal tuned his attention back to the courtroom. "Whatever the consequences, the Court will at once adjourn proceedings in this case. We will reconvene tomorrow morning at nine o'clock, at which time we hope the counsel for the defense will be in better disposition."

"I'll see you later," Brekonridge said to Simon, as the justices rose to leave the courtroom

"Where are you going?"

"I have unanswered questions. Things are not as they seem."

Chapter Forty-Two

The front door of Richard Jackson's apothecary shop was a sturdy oak affair, topped with a Palladian stained glass transom arranged to depict a beaker flask, a set of scales, and various other implements of Jackson's trade. The stained glass in late afternoon, with the sun beating down from the west, cast multicolored beams of light across the tiled floor of the shop. To his right, as he entered the store, Brekonridge saw a heavy counter with a wavy glass front, behind which were stored bottle upon bottle of potions, panaceas, poultices, and powders, all labeled with the manufacturers' trademarks and claims of miraculous properties. A set of brass scales sat in the middle of the counter. Behind the counter, shelves reached from floor to ceiling, bowed under the weight of hundreds of jars and bottles from which the apothecary could find the ingredients for almost any remedy of the day—calomel to purge the bowels, tartar emetic to cure alcohol addiction, quinine for malaria, tincture of mercury to rid oneself of syphilis, and any number of other poisons which, administered in the most sparing of doses, were believed to resolve common physical complaints.

An ornate, hand-painted sign to the side of the front counter read "Teeth Carefully and Painlessly Extracted." Reflexively, Brekonridge probed one of his back-bottom molars with his tongue, as it had been bothering him mildly but chronically for some time, but he decided he had no desire to have it pulled in a strange apothecary shop in St. James' Parish.

He recognized Richard Jackson immediately. The chemist was behind another counter to the left of the door. This counter was smaller and served as a compounding station. Jackson was deeply immersed in conversation with a gentleman.

"It was quite an interesting experience," Jackson said as Brekonridge walked in the door. "Thirty years serving as a chemist to the upper crust and I never once set foot in the Old Bailey."

"Were you nervous?" the customer asked.

"Not half as nervous as old Bransby Cooper or George Guthrie must have been. After all, I only tended to poor Mr. Drummond until they could take over. It was their treatment that…" he stopped, suddenly aware Brekonridge was in the shop. "I'm sorry, sir. Is there something I can do to help you?"

"No rush," Brekonridge said. "Please, complete your business with this gentleman. I can wait."

"I was leaving," the customer said. Jackson handed him a wrapped package. The customer tipped his hat to Jackson and Brekonridge before leaving the shop.

"I hope I didn't run him off," Brekonridge said. "I really am not in any hurry."

"It is of no consequence. We had concluded our business and were passing the time of day. How can I help you, sir?"

"Hemp. My local chemist is presently out of stores. I use it for…" He drew fingers across the scar tissue mottling the right side of his head.

"I see. Gets tight, does it?"

"From time to time. I am beset by headaches. The hemp helps."

"I am certain it does. But have you considered laudanum as an alternative?"

"Clouds the mind," Brekonridge said. "I need to stay alert. Besides, laudanum binds me up."

"Not a problem. We could set you up with some mercury chloride to resolve that pesky side effect."

"No need. I find the hemp does quite nicely, with no need for me to take any other medicines. Do you have any in stock?"

"Why, of course. I recently received a shipment of the finest air-cured ganga from Assam, on the Indian subcontinent. Do you take is as a tincture, or do you smoke it?"

Brekonridge pulled the pipe from the inside pocket of his jacket. "I smoke."

"Would you prefer it in a jar, or simply boxed?"

"Boxed will be fine."

"I'll pull it together immediately."

Brekonridge dropped coins on the counter as Jackson pulled a die-cut merchandise box from under the counter and folded it into shape to carry the hemp. He placed the folded box on one side of the scale and a one-ounce weight on the other, and pinched buds from the jar to drop them into the box until the scale was level. He dropped another bud into the box.

"For the weight of the box," Jackson reassured Brekonridge. "You are a new customer. I would not wish you to walk away feeling short-changed."

"I appreciate the consideration. You mentioned you were in court at the Old Bailey today?"

"Why, yes. Have you been there before?"

"Once or twice. Called to testify, were you?"

"A most disconcerting experience. It was in the course of a murder trial. Are you familiar with the shooting of Edward Drummond, the Prime Minister's secretary?"

"Certainly. It's been in all the papers."

"Well, it was the trial of his killer, a man named M'Naghten."

"Strange that an apothecary might be called to testify in a murder trial.."

"I have been a friend of the Drummond family for many years. On the day poor Mr. Edward was shot, I was the first called to tend to him. Once Mr. Edward was removed to his quarters in Grosvenor Place, proper surgeons were available to tend to him."

"Cooper and Guthrie."

"You know them?"

"You mentioned their names to your customer."

"You don't miss much, Mr...."

"Brekonridge," he said, extending his hand. Jackson took it, with a firm grasp. "Other people have commented on my powers of observation in the past. I must admit I am unaware of them myself, much as one might take the ability to hear for granted, compared to a deaf man."

"No man ever fully appreciates his own talents, I suppose," Jackson said as he tied the box closed with a length of twine.

"How true. Might I ask? You mentioned earlier you were nervous taking the stand, but not as nervous as Drs. Cooper and Guthrie. Why might that be?"

"All I did was patch Mr. Drummond's wound securely enough to allow him to be transported to his quarters from Charing Cross. It was Cooper and Guthrie who actually killed him."

Brekonridge felt his heart quicken and a rush of blood flow through his body. "What a curious statement," he said, trying not to reveal his excitement. "I was under the impression the pistol ball took his life."

"It probably would have, in due time. We shall never know, shall we? Too much bleeding. At least, that is the impression of Mr. Drummond's sister, who was in this shop only two days back."

Brekonridge recalled seeing Anne Eliza Drummond in the courtroom at the Old Bailey, still dressed in mourning black, her face covered with a netted veil that failed to hide the scorn and revulsion she directed toward M'Naghten as he sat, complacent, in the dock.

"In the course of our conversation, Miss Drummond described the treatment administered by the doctors, which seemed to me most extreme. A quart taken on Saturday and another two on Monday? The body can only hold so much blood and relieving a man of three quarts in two days seems excessive."

"I was a naval sailor," Brekonridge said. "Many years back. Fought in the Battle of New Orleans."

"Did you? Most impressive."

"Not at the time. I saw men hit with grapeshot. They lost a phenomenal amount of blood and still lived."

"It's like milk, I hear," Jackson said. "You spill a little and it spreads to look like a flood. I daresay you could use the blood in a single person to paint the walls of an entire room, and still have some left over."

"No doubt, though I find the imagery disturbing. Thank you for providing my medication."

***

Doctor Elias Sullivan maintained a surgery on Bedford Avenue, several blocks from Brekonridge's rooms in Bloomsbury. As it was late on a Friday afternoon, the doctor looked surprised when Brekonridge stepped into the parlor.

"Mr. Brekonridge!" he exclaimed. "Did we have an appointment?"

"I'm sorry. We did not."

"Is there some emergency?"

"Not a medical one, I am happy to say."

"Well, while you are here, let's take a look at your progress."

He directed Brekonridge toward another chair which benefitted from better light, then examined and palpated the mottled and bubbled scar tissue on the side of the thief-taker's head.

"Yes, yes. The healing is obviously complete. Do you experience much pain?"

"The scar tissue feels tight sometimes."

"It is a shame," Sullivan said as he inspected his work. "I believe there will come a time when we can replace burned skin with fresh, leaving almost no scarring. Sadly, you were born into the wrong time, my friend."

"The time in which I live suits me in other ways. Actually, I came here to probe your expertise."

"Does this have something to do with one of your cases?"

"In fact, it does. Can you tell me precisely how much blood the human body holds?"

"It depends on the size and girth of the person, but a person your size would carry between five and six quarts. The average is between four and five, but as I have remarked on other occasions, you are not average."

"So, a man in his middle fifties, of slight stature, might have no more than five quarts available to him?"

"At most, I'd imagine."

"And," Brekonridge continued, "how long after a substantial loss of blood does it take to replenish the supply?"

"How substantial a loss are we describing?"

"Let's start with a quart."

"Almost a fifth of the body's volume for most people," Sullivan said. "The plasma—the fluid which carries the blood cells—would replenish in, say, forty-eight hours. But blood is much more than the fluid in which it is suspended. There are red cells and white cells and all sorts of other materials, all fundamental to maintaining life. When you lose a quart of blood from the body, you remove all of the components, and they are not immediately replenished. Instead, when the plasma is replaced, the vital components I've mentioned are diluted for a considerable period of time."

"And what would be the effect on the person who has lost that considerable volume of blood?"

"He would feel weak. He may experience light-headedness or even fainting upon standing. His resistance to infection would be compromised."

"For how long?"

"Weeks. He would gradually feel better, but the effects would be longstanding."

"I see," Brekonridge said. "Now, let's say that man loses a quart of blood on Monday. If I understand you correctly, the fluid would be replaced by Wednesday."

"More than likely, but not the vital bodies in it."

"So, what would happen should that man lose two more quarts on Wednesday, after having lost a quart on Monday?"

"The man would die," Sullivan said, without hesitation.

"It's that cut and dried?"

"Exsanguination has been carefully studied. Let us assume your gentleman in question loses a quart on Monday. While the volume of plasma will be replaced by Wednesday, the important vital cells would not. So, by Wednesday, our unfortunate patient would have, perhaps, three quarters of his necessary blood cells. When you remove two quarts more, you are, conservatively speaking, removing two-fifths of his blood volume, or forty percent. That means you are removing forty percent of the seventy-five percent remaining, or—"

"Thirty percent," Brekonridge said.

"That was fast."

"I was always good with numbers. So you are stating, in our hypothetical case, the man would lose fifty-five percent of his blood cells within forty-eight hours."

"Your mathematical calculations are correct. Such a loss is not compatible with life."

"What would be the physical effects on the individual?"

Sullivan settled back into his chair. "Prior to death, the heart would beat faster. The person would feel faint and might become delirious. He would lose the ability to clot. Any scratch or cut or even a bruise could prove fatal. He would breathe more quickly to compensate for a sense of respiratory insufficiency and oxygen starvation. The patient would likely pass in and out of consciousness. Eventually, the heart, no longer able to serve its own needs for oxygen, would beat erratically before stopping altogether."

"I see," Brekonridge said, as he steepled his fingers and tried to digest all the surgeon had told him.

"Why do I imagine we are not discussing a hypothetical situation?" Sullivan asked.

"Perhaps because you are an astute and intelligent man," Brekonridge said.

"And I am no fool. What you are describing is aggressive blood-letting in a potentially fatally infirm patient."

"I have another hypothetical situation for you. Say a man has been shot, in the back, by a pistol at close range. The ball penetrates the back, travels in a downward and forward direction, breaking a couple of ribs in the process, and lodges in the diaphragm."

"I'm following you so far."

"Is this a survivable injury?"

"I fancy a glass of whiskey. Can I offer you one?"

"I am a Scotsman, sir," Brekonridge said. "And I will never turn down an offer of drink."

Sullivan crossed the parlor to a cabinet, from which he extracted a bottle of rye and poured an inch into each of two glasses. He handed one to Brekonridge and took the other back to his chair. He sipped, impolitely smacked his lips, and placed the glass on the table next to him.

"You're working on the Edward Drummond case, are you not?" he asked.

Brekonridge tried the rye. He was more a scotch man himself when he wasn't drinking ale, but the liquor was more than satisfying. Dr. Sullivan, he surmised, had excellent taste.

"I've been working with the defense team assembled by barristers Humphreys and Perceval for the last month, mostly in Scotland."

"And the trial of the man who shot him is taking place as we speak, is it not?"

"It is."

"And, I believe, Doctors Cooper and Guthrie were scheduled to testify for the prosecution this afternoon."

"They did."

"Hence, your sudden curiosity regarding the practice of phlebotomy. Am I to understand you correctly? Guthrie and Cooper drew three quarts of blood from Mr. Drummond in less than forty-eight hours?"

"That was their testimony."

"Then they killed him. I know both men. Guthrie is sober and deliberate. He would never do such a thing of his own volition. Cooper…well, that's a different story. Comes from a family of exceptional surgeons, but I do not believe he inherited the talent. His intellectual skills are not at issue, but he is also impetuous and reckless. Sometimes he can see no further than the current crisis. He drains a bog only to find himself standing in quicksand. It must have been Cooper who pushed Guthrie to comply with this irresponsible treatment option."

"If they considered Mr. Drummond's injuries to be inevitably fatal, would such bloodletting be a reasonable option?"

"Replacing one form of assured death with another? I fail to see the benefit. But, as to whether the injury suffered by our unfortunate Mr. Drummond would in fact have been ultimately and inevitably fatal, I'd have to say no. It may not have been, in and of itself, the direct cause of death. You say the pistol ball broke some ribs?"

"That was the report."

"And it lodged in, or on the diaphragm?"

"I can't recall completely. Both Guthrie and Cooper appeared to believe, at least in their testimony, the wound was mortal."

"If the ball did not penetrate the diaphragm, and did not injure surrounding organs enough to promote the deposit of digestive fluids into the peritoneal cavity, such a wound might be survivable. This is all conjecture, of course. In the absence of having access to the living patient myself, I would only be guessing."

"I see. However, there is a slim possibility Mr. Drummond did not die as a result of being shot, but rather as a consequence of his treatment by Drs. Cooper and Guthrie."

"That would be a reasonable assessment."

"Which would produce reasonable doubt in a jury." He drained the glass of rye and held it up to Sullivan. "I thank you for your hospitality. I must hurry along. I need to meet with the Queen's Counsel."

"I do hope you will return and tell me how this story turns out."

"If I'm right," Brekonridge said, "You'll read all about it in the *Times* in a day or so."

"I may wish to write a monograph on the subject. *What Killed Mr. Drummond? The Lead or the Lancet?* What do you think?"

"We live in a litigious society. I think you should write it anonymously," Brekonridge said.

* * *

At the Newgate Street offices, Alexander Cockburn sat patiently, if uncomfortably, and listened as Brekonridge outlined the information he had received from his interviews with Richard Jackson and Elias Sullivan.

"In other words," Brekonridge said, "what actually killed Edward Drummond was the aggressive bleeding, not the wound inflicted by Daniel M'Naghten."

"I think I understand your argument," Cockburn said, "and I appreciate the distinction. However, the bleeding would not have been necessary had M'Naghten not shot Drummond in the first place."

"Which would make him guilty of assault, and perhaps even manslaughter, but not premeditated murder."

"Despite the fact he clearly approached Mr. Drummond with the specific intent of shooting him?"

Brekonridge looked back and forth at Cockburn and Simon. For an instant, he felt as if the world had been turned on its side.

"You were hired to defend M'Naghten," he said.

"I was hired to keep him from the gallows," Cockburn said.

"Demonstrating he was not immediately responsible for Drummond's death would do exactly that!"

Cockburn placed both hands on the meeting room table and stared at the thief-taker. "Your services were discharged upon your return from Glasgow. What right have you to go nosing about in this business now?"

"I have unanswered questions."

"Which are none of your concern. Is there not some warrant outstanding over at Bow Street you can obtain to satisfy your curiosity? Are there no thieves left in London for you to apprehend? Why poke around in this business now, on the eve of a verdict? What right have you, sir? What right?"

"The right all men should enjoy when placed in the dock. Fairness at trial. Can you tell me, if this new information were presented on the stand, it would not leave the jury in such a state of quandary and doubt they would have no choice other than to acquit M'Naghten?"

"They may. And at what cost? Daniel M'Naghten did shoot Edward Drummond. Of that there is no doubt. He purchased two pistols and carried them to Whitehall with the intent of killing. He spent weeks watching officials travel to and from Downing Street. This was a premeditated act and Edward Drummond lost his life."

"Which may not have occurred had he received competent medical assistance!"

"*May*. There is no assurance…" Cockburn stopped and crossed his hands over his belly, his face screwed into distress by his dyspepsia. When he spoke again, his voice was quieter and his tone more measured. "Sir, there is no point in this argument. Accusing these fine surgeons would serve no purpose. Do you know Doctor Guthrie is a favorite at Her Majesty's court? Taking the blame from M'Naghten and placing it on these two fine physicians does not fit in with the narrative of this trial."

"The narrative?" Brekonridge asked, incredulous. "I have recently read the American Poe's novel **The Narrative of Arthur Gordon Pym**. In that case, the *narrative* was a fiction. Are we discussing such a narrative here?"

Cockburn held up a hand. "No. I'm not doing this. I thank you for your contribution once again, Mr. Brekonridge. To say you are thorough would be an understatement and perhaps an insult. You are fastidious to a fault in your investigations, damn your eyes. That was why I enlisted your aid in the first place, but your job here is done. There are forces at work in this case you cannot be aware of and which dictate the course we are to follow. I can say no more than that."

"There is no need," Brekonridge said. "I understand completely. Consigning M'Naghten to Bedlam and throwing away the key solves a great many problems for both sides of the courtroom, does it not?"

"I have no desire to continue this conver—"

"And I can imagine why. Thank you for your time and for M'Naghten's money, sir. Maybe I'll trot on down to Bow Street. See if they have a warrant for some lowly pickpocket who needs snatching. I'm certain a person of such standing will inconvenience nobody's *narrative*."

He placed the John Bull hat back on his head, wrapped his scarf around his neck and walked out of the building.

He had not gone half a block before he heard a voice call out behind him. He paused until Simon caught up. The clerk was still wearing his light outer jacket but no greatcoat, despite the fact it was below freezing and flurries of snow fell over the rooftops and spires of central London.

CHAPTER FORTY-TWO

"You'll catch your death, boy," Brekonridge said.

"What did you mean in there?" Simon asked.

"You haven't figured it out yet?" They arrived at the entrance to a public house. "Come along inside, Simon. It will be warm by the fire. I will not carry the weight of your death from exposure on my conscience."

Moments later, they sat by the inglenook, a cheery fire warming them. A woman brought them each a tankard of ale.

"No cawl?" Simon asked, nodding toward the cauldron bubbling lazily in the inglenook.

"I've lost my appetite."

"So, explain."

"The game is rigged, boy."

"What do you mean?"

"Weren't you in the courtroom? I could have sworn you sat right next to me. There was never any intent to place M'Naghten's neck in a noose. Not on either side."

"I don't understand. The prosecution—"

"—scrupulously avoided every opportunity to demonstrate M'Naghten planned this murder for months," Brekonridge finished. "Where were the questions about the money in M'Naghten's bank account? We have already determined he didn't acquire it through his business. The only logical explanation was he was hired to kill Peel and botched the job. Yet, Follett and his sterling barrister companions failed to explore that in any way other than to establish the money existed. Why?"

"According to you, because they didn't want M'Naghten to hang, either."

"Ask the next question."

Simon took a sip of the ale and placed the tankard back on the rough-hewn oak table. "Why?"

"Now, propose an answer." Simon stared into the fire for a few minutes before Brekonridge lost his patience. "Oh, come on, boy. It's as plain as the nose on your face. Did you read the newspaper this morning? The trial in Lancashire?"

"Yes, I read it. It appears they will be convicted."

"Not all of them, but yes, a great number of them will be found guilty. Peel and his friends at Whitehall, not to mention the crowd at Buckingham, have enough on their plates already. If the prosecution were to demonstrate radicals hired M'Naghten to assassinate the Prime Minister, what do you think would happen?"

"He would be hanged."

"Yes, but think beyond the hanging. What happens next?"

"I don't understand."

"M'Naghten swinging from the end of a rope makes him a martyr. Add to that a few dozen Chartists facing the next several years of their lives in prison after the Lancashire trial, and you have the makings of the sort of nastiness our French brothers endured only half a century ago. The folks at Downing Street aren't fools. They can see this as well as I. Had M'Naghten only succeeded in wounding Drummond, he could be socked away, forgotten, in a cold prison cell for years. But Drummond died, and unless M'Naghten is found insane, there would be no option but the gibbet for him, as there is no doubt he fired the fatal bullet."

"*If* the bullet was indeed fatal," Simon said.

Brekonridge watched as an expression of revelation transformed the boy's face. "Now you understand. Cockburn said Drummond's death coming as a result of careless medical care didn't fit the narrative he was trying to establish. What narrative? M'Naghten is insane. Cockburn not only wants to spare M'Naghten's life, as any reasonable defense attorney might. He also wants to set a precedent. He wants to demonstrate Lord Hale's interpretation of insanity no longer holds. He wishes to be the man who rewrites common law, and he can only do that if M'Naghten is found insane."

"An insanity judgment is, in effect, a win for both sides," Simon said.

"Truth be damned."

"But...but, that would mean..."

"I believe you have already asked the next question."

"That would mean, at some point, the prosecution and the defense had to come to some sort of agreement as to how the trial would proceed." He leaned forward and dropped his voice. "I shouldn't tell you this, but several days before the trial the Home Secretary invited Mr. Cockburn to a meeting at Buckingham."

"That's when they must have struck a deal," Brekonridge declared. He emptied the tankard and slammed it down on the table. Several other people in the tavern glanced at him nervously. "We've all been played for fools. God! How weary, stale, flat and unprofitable seem to me all the uses of this world!"

"You…you quoted Shakespeare!" Simon exclaimed.

"What? You think, because I dress in old clothes and walk around with a face that frightens children, I don't read? I am not educated? I may have spent the better part of my youth as a carpenter's mate and powder monkey in His Majesty's navy, but I know a thing or two. I'm fed up, Simon. I'm done in. I have spent the last twenty years associating with thieves and blackguards and murderers, and it wears on me like a poorly fitted pair of shoes. I ache. I yearn for a place of beauty and consolation. I think, quite soon, I might hie abroad for a spell."

"Where would you go?"

"America, at least for a while. There are opportunities there. It is a huge country, stretching for thousands of miles from the centers of population along the eastern coast. There is plenty of space for a man to get lost, places where one could go and not see another human—saint or criminal—for years."

"No," Simon said. "Not you."

"Time will tell. Time will tell. Run along now. Go back to your warm offices. I intend to stay by this fireplace and drink myself into oblivion."

Chapter Forty-Three

Sheriff Henry C. Bell somehow managed to walk the tightrope between being both grotesque and resplendent. As portly and ugly as ever, he had managed to procure a fine new suit of clothes from a prominent haberdasher in London and seemed pleased with himself as he ascended to the witness box after being called by Monteith.

Monteith said, his Scots accent thick as porridge, "Could you describe the nature of your acquaintance with Mr. M'Naghten, the prisoner?"

"I do not know him personally, but he strongly resembles…and I believe him to be…the person who called upon me some time ago."

"Can you be more precise regarding the time he came to meet with you?"

"I think it must be about nine or ten months."

"So, May or June of 1842?"

"That would be correct."

"Can you tell the court why Mr. M'Naghten visited you?

"He complained to me about harassment by a system of persecution, for which he could obtain no redress whatever."

"Did he detail the nature of that persecution?"

"Not at first."

"And how did you answer his request for help?"

"I told him he must be laboring under some erroneous impression, and advised him, if he had any criminal charge to make against any person, to go to the Procurator-Fiscal, or if his complaint was of a civil nature, to apply to some man of business. He said it would be perfectly useless to make any such application and he went away."

"Did you form an impression with respect to the state of the prisoner's mind?"

"I concluded he was not right in his intellects."

"Could you be more precise? In what way was he not right?"

"I concluded he was laboring under some extraordinary delusion, and I made a remark to that effect to my clerk."

"No further questions," Monteith declared. He stole a quick glance at the prosecutors' table, but none of the barristers rose to cross-examine the witness.

* * *

Simon had not been able to interview Alexander Johnston when he and Brekonridge were in Glasgow. Johnston had been in London at the time, attending a session of Parliament. He was a member of House of Commons from Kilmarnock Burghs, which included Glasgow.

Johnston was in his early fifties but looked much older. It was obvious he suffered from some sort of chronic malady. He was thin, and his eyes were rheumy. He walked with the aid of a cane. His voice was weak but understandable.

"I know the prisoner at the bar. He called upon me a twelvemonth ago," Johnston told William Clarkson. "Prior to that, I knew nothing of him."

"Why did he appear before you?"

"He complained of being subjected to an extraordinary system of persecution and wished for my advice as to the best method of getting rid of it."

"Did he describe the details of that persecution?"

"He said he had for a considerable time been persecuted by the emissaries of a political party, whom he had offended by interfering in politics. He also complained of being attacked through the newspapers, and said the persons of whom he complained followed him night and day. They had destroyed his peace of mind."

"Did he identify the party he held responsible for his persecution?"

"He said he was hounded by the Tories."

"And how did you respond to him?"

"I reasoned with him, and told him I thought he must be mistaken. While I am at political odds with my fellow authorities in Glasgow, I hold them all personally in high esteem. They are, most uniformly, good men with good intentions and I cannot imagine they would engage in the systematic harassment of a single individual. I assured Mr. M'Naghten nobody followed him about, and advised him, if he received any annoyances, to apply to the captain of police."

"What was the impression left upon your mind by that interview?" Clarkson asked.

"I thought what he stated was his firm conviction, though I did not give it any credence."

"Was that your last encounter with him?"

"No. A month after the last interview, I received a letter from the prisoner, reiterating the same complaints and begging of me to intervene in his behalf; to that communication I wrote the letter produced."

Clarkson held up a letter he had brought from the defense table so Johnston could see it clearly. "Is this the letter you wrote to Mr. M'Naghten?"

"It is."

Clarkson addressed Chief Justice Tindal. "We propose now, my lords, to put in and read the letter this witness, no less than a member of the House of Commons, wrote to the prisoner."

Tindal, without consulting with the associate justices, said, "Be it so."

Clarkson handed the letter to the clerk of arraigns, who stood and read it aloud to the jury and to the public sitting in the gallery:

> *"Reform Club, May 5, 1842.*
>
> *Mr. D. M'Naghten.*
>
> *Sir,*
>
> *I received your letter of the 3rd of May, and am sorry I can do nothing for you. I fear you are laboring under an aberration of mind, and I think you have no reason to entertain such fears. I am, etc—*

Alexander Johnston."

* * *

The Reverend Alexander Turner of Gorbals looked as sour and as discontented as on the day Simon had interviewed him a month earlier. He scanned the crowd in the gallery until his gaze landed on Simon, who was sitting next to Vicar Brekonridge. Turner's eyes narrowed and his face screwed into a grimace.

Simon leaned in Brekonridge's direction and whispered, "I don't think he likes me."

"If it comes to blows, I think we can take him," Brekonridge answered.

"I am minister of the parish of Gorbals, near Glasgow," Turner replied to William Clarkson's first question.

"And, do you recognize the prisoner in the dock?"

"Seven or eight months ago, I recollect the prisoner calling upon me at my residence. He told me he was the son of Mr. M'Naghten, the turner, who was a member of my congregation. He reported being persecuted by a number of persons who constantly followed him about and who annoyed him in various ways. As he could not get rid of them, his life was rendered perfectly miserable."

"Did he relate to you any of the measures he had employed to rid himself of these persecutions?"

"He told me he had called on the Sheriff and likewise upon the Procurator-Fiscal, but they refused to do anything for him."

"Did you arrive at any impressions regarding his mental condition?"

"I observed he appeared to be laboring under a great degree of excitement. I thought he was insane. In consequence of that interview, I called upon his father a day or two afterwards, and told him the young man ought to be put under restraint."

"No further questions," Clarkson said.

Waddington elected to handle the cross-examination. "Reverend Turner," he said from the lectern, "can you recall the approximate date of the conversation you had with the prisoner?"

"To the best of my belief, that conversation took place about seven or eight months ago."

"During the summer?

"Yes. I believe it was either May or June, now that I think of it more closely."

"And what were the results of your pleas to the prisoner's father?"

"The fact we are here today suggests my efforts were fruitless."

* * *

As the morning edged on toward lunchtime, more of M'Naghten's Glaswegian defense witnesses took the stand. Each reported the same disturbing paranoid behavior from M'Naghten the previous year. One after another recounted his descriptions of a vindictive plot to ruin his life.

Brekonridge's stomach had just begun to grumble with hunger when Tindal turned his attention to the defense table. "Mr. Cockburn, do you anticipate a great many more witnesses?"

Cockburn stood at his table. "Your Honors, Commissioner Wilson concludes our witnesses from among Mr. M'Naghten's acquaintances. We have yet to present expert testimony from various medical professionals who have examined him."

"Do you have many?"

"Enough to fill the afternoon, Your Honors."

"Do you believe you could complete testimony from your physicians this afternoon, were we to take a short recess for lunch?"

"In fact, Your Honors, I was about to make that request."

"So ordered. This Court will recess until one-thirty this afternoon, at which time we will conclude testimony in this case."

Chapter Forty-Four

Brekonridge and Simon strolled up Ludgate Hill after court adjourned for lunch.

"It's looking good for Mr. Cockburn," Simon said. "I daresay he will rewrite the law on insanity today."

"Good for him," Brekonridge said. "And the only victim is the truth."

"Saves Mr. M'Naghten from a noose, if it works. That is something."

"And leaving poor Mr. Drummond un-avenged. Hello. What's this?"

He grabbed Simon's arm and pulled him into a doorway.

"What the devil…"

"Shh!" Brekonridge pointed up the hill toward two people standing by the roadside and arguing, waving their arms and pointing fingers.

"It's Forrester," Brekonridge said quietly. "The man he's engaging is John Gordon."

"So?"

"The cock crowed, boy. Remember? Forrester and Gordon both lied on the stand, several times. Now they're arguing. I would like to know what they're saying."

"Why?"

"Perjury is never undertaken blithely. People perjure themselves for a reason. Perhaps they are discussing that reason as we speak."

"Aren't those the men you said lied in court yesterday?" a voice said behind them. Brekonridge whirled to find Dickens standing behind them.

"Your hearing is impeccable," Brekonridge said.

"My reason isn't bad either. Why did you say they lied?"

"Mr. Brekonridge interviewed them in Glasgow," Simon said. "The stories they told there didn't match their testimony today."

"I think this is a story I'd like to hear," Dickens said.

"I am too occupied at the moment to tell it," Brekonridge answered impatiently. "Perhaps another time."

After a few seconds, the pair of witnesses stopped arguing and proceeded on their way up Ludgate Hill.

"Let's follow them," Brekonridge told Simon. "Perhaps they'll meet up with someone interesting."

"Might I tag along?" Dickens asked.

Brekonridge considered waving the writer off, but then thought better of it. "Why not? The more people surrounding me, the less likely they are to imagine they're being followed."

Keeping a respectable distance behind, Brekonridge, Simon, and Dickens tracked the pair up the hill to Fleet Street, where they saw the men enter the Ye Olde Cock Tavern on the north sidewalk.

"Wait here," Brekonridge told his companions. He left them sitting on the steps of a tenement and crossed the street to access the close behind the tavern. He sidestepped piles of oyster shells and other refuse and snuck through the back door, where he found a pantry separating the main room from the stores and kitchen. Fortunately, the kitchen was empty. He made his way toward the pantry and looked over the tavern itself for Gordon and Forrester. He found them sitting over tankards of ale with a third man whom Brekonridge did not recognize. They did not seem happy to be in each other's company.

Brekonridge returned to Simon and Dickens, across the street.

"I need your help," he said to the youth. "Forrester and Gordon know me from Glasgow. They don't know you. I want you to take a seat near them and try to hear what they're saying."

"Might I be of assistance?" Dickens asked. "I have a good memory for overheard conversations. You'd be amazed how often I've used them in my writing."

"The boy's memory is sharp as well," Brekonridge said. "And your face is not unfamiliar. We'll wait here."

"This is madness," Simon argued.

"Not for me, it isn't. I have unanswered questions. Now go, boy. Do it."

Simon gave the thief-taker a resentful look before he crossed the street and entered the tavern.

Chapter Forty-Five

Huddled figures sat in the far corner, talking animatedly.

"An ale, please," Simon said to the man tending the bar. He took his drink and sat as close to the men as he dared without causing suspicion. It was so early, there were only eight people in the place, so it was easy to eavesdrop.

"…nothing for it," Forrester said, finishing a sentence. "What's done is done."

"But nothing's been done," the stranger said. "Peel is alive. The Tories still control London and Glasgow, and we are bedeviled by their spies. How are we to rally around a lunatic? What sort of cause is that to rouse the masses to action? He made a hash out of it. Who cares about some secretary? By next week, people will have forgotten the case entirely."

"Forrester is right, Nockold," Gordon said, the disappointment evident in his voice "Some games are wins, some are losses. I hear things are going badly for O'Connor and his lads in Lancashire. If the court decides to imprison the lot, we have a new rallying cry. The Lancashire Boys!" He held his tankard high in a toast.

"The Lancashire Boys!" both Forrester and Nockold said, grimly meeting the salute. A couple of heads in the tavern turned their way, but Simon maintained his attention on his mug of ale. He did, however, recognize the name Nockold from his Glasgow notes. The man was a noted socialist in the Mechanics Institute.

After a gloomy interim in which the trio stared off into space, each ensconced in his own private worries, Nockold said, "So, back to Glasgow, then?"

"The sooner the better," Forrester said.

"How will you present this to Duncan?" Nockold said to Gordon.

"Keep plugging," Gordon said. "Abram has the best of intentions, but he lacks long-range perspective. He would be satisfied with suffrage and a few seats in the House of Commons. *Small steps* he is fond of saying. *Work within the system.* He fails to see the only way to extend all rights to all men is through massive acts of resistance. You were right to have me get close to him. Over time, he has come to trust my judgment. If I push him the right way, he will see larger action is required."

"I'm off to Wales," Nockold said. "There are coal miners there who need organizing. Colin will join me in a month or so."

Simon presumed Nockold was referring to Colin Graham, another socialist from the Mechanics Institute.

"It's as Robbie Burns once uttered," Forrester said, affecting the strongest Edinburgh brogue he could muster, "the best laid schemes o' mice an' men gang aft agley."

"The truth it is," Gordon said, raising his tankard. "To missed opportunities, my friends."

"Missed opportunities," the other two echoed, before banging their pewter mugs together.

They changed the subject to football, and shortly after that, Simon rejoined Brekonridge and Dickens in the doorway across Fleet Street.

"They were part of it," Simon said, partly winded with excitement. "Whatever *it* was. They never came right out and said they had sent M'Naghten to London to kill Sir Robert, but they sure were disappointed at the outcome."

"Who was the third one?"

"Nockold."

"The socialist?"

"Yes."

"Very curious. In Glasgow, Gordon told me Nockold had disappeared, perhaps even moved to France. Now here they are, together, in London."

"And Nockold seems to have won Gordon over to the side of violent insurrection."

"Contrary to Abram Duncan's goals. Duncan told me there was a schism in Chartism, moderates versus radicals. If his closest confidante, Gordon, has been coopted by the radical fringe, then everything else he's said is compromised."

"Strange he would come all the way to London for the trial when he wasn't called as a witness."

"Keeping an eye on his investment, perhaps. He may have feared M'Naghten would panic in the dock and give up his backers."

"Well, whatever they were doing here, Forrester obviously knows more than he said in court. He's knee deep in whatever plot Gordon and Nockold hatched."

Brekonridge clapped Simon between the shoulder blades. "Good work, boy. Head on back to Humphreys and Perceval. Tell them I may have word for them shortly."

"What word? The trial will be over this afternoon."

"But the truth is still out there. I mean to find it before the cock crows again."

* * *

Brekonridge waited in the shadows with Dickens, several blocks south. The wind had changed over the course of the afternoon, and mist hung heavily in the air around them. Fog rolled in from the river.

"It is a dangerous business you pursue," Dickens observed. "And yet, I perceive you are, at heart, a man of peace."

"Do you?" Brekonridge said absently, his eyes riveted on the door to the tavern.

"You remind me, physically, of one of my characters. Bill Sikes. But he was roughhewn to the bone. I suspect there is some treacle underneath your crust."

"Little enough."

"Tell me about the boy."

"Simon? I suspect he will be a fine man one day."

"But you toss him into harm's way."

"Simon was in no danger. Nobody would pay him any mind."

"Exactly what do you suspect of the men in the tavern?" Dickens asked.

Brekonridge rubbed his hands together to ward off the advancing cold that accompanied the fog. "Someone paid M'Naghten over seven hundred pounds. I suspect, like M'Naghten, they anticipated the victim to be Peel."

"You know what you're suggesting?"

"Aye. Conspiracy. Treason. There is a contingent within the Chartist movement that sees violence as an acceptable means to the end of suffrage and freedom. They have factored the cost of murder against the value of achieving their goals, and the goals have won. The socialists and anarchists have been allies for a long time and are also willing to sacrifice lives to achieve their goals. Any of them could have paid M'Naghten. If it can be proven by evidence, they are as good as dead already."

Dickens chuckled. "Think so, do you?"

Brekonridge turned to him. "You don't?"

"I'm just an inveterate scribbler," Dickens said. "But I've observed enough bare-knuckles prizefights to recognize when the fix is in."

"How do you mean?"

"There can be no doubt that M'Naghten murdered Mr. Drummond. It is evident your employers—"

"—*Former* employers," Brekonridge corrected.

"All right, then. Your former employers obviously intend to demonstrate M'Naghten's mental incompetence. One might imagine the prosecution would prefer to test the limbs of Tyburn Tree against Mr. M'Naghten's neck. They don't seem enthusiastic about it, though. Do they?"

"They don't. You're right. The trial is fixed. I discovered that only yesterday. Mr. Cockburn has struck a deal with the Home Secretary. For whatever reason, the Home Office has determined that England would be better served with M'Naghten in Bedlam."

"It makes sense," Dickens said.

"Aye. In Bedlam, M'Naghten cannot become a martyr to the Chartist cause. The Crown has chosen the path of least resistance."

"I was right about you," Dickens said. "I may wish to interview you at length on another occasion. I believe you would be a rich trove of material for my stories."

"You overestimate me," Brekonridge said. "And, in any case, the work I do thrives on my anonymity. It helps if people don't see me coming. Being the subject of one of your little tales might make me famous, at the cost of my livelihood."

Eventually, Nockold, Gordon and Forrester exited the tavern, shook hands, and set off in their separate directions.

"Follow Forrester," Brekonridge said, pointing toward the large redheaded man.

Forrester turned up Fetters Lane at St. Dunstan-In-The-West Anglican Church, and strolled past the house where Samuel Johnson had lived and written a century earlier. Forrester stopped there and spent a minute or two viewing the property. The speed at which he walked indicated he might be sight-seeing rather than heading toward a specific destination. That suited Brekonridge's purposes as he and Dickens strolled casually, an unobtrusive distance behind.

The afternoon sun cast long shadows across the narrow streets lined with multi-story buildings. Fog descended on the city, rising from the Thames and spreading across the boroughs like a moist blanket. Brekonridge could see candles and gas lamps glow in windows.

Near Bartlett Court, Forrester hailed a carriage and stepped inside. Brekonridge spotted another carriage rounding the corner, and he hailed the driver as Forrester's carriage left the curb. The second hack driver pulled alongside Brekonridge, who opened the door and pushed Dickens inside.

"Follow that carriage!" Brekonridge barked at the driver, a rotund man in his forties, sporting military sideburns, and who stared at Brekonridge as if Prince Albert himself had hailed him.

"Do what now?" the man inquired.

"Were my instructions unclear? See that carriage?" He pointed toward Forrester's cab.

"I reckon I do!" the man said.

"I wish you to follow it."

"For what purpose?"

"What?"

"Well, it ain't every day that some ruffian hires me to pursue another carriage, is it?" the man said. "For all I know, there's someone in that carriage who you wish ill. You might just shove a blade in him and run off, and who's left holding the bag then? Archie Brownlee, that's who."

"Mr. Brownlee, I am a thief-taker, and the man in that carriage may be in the act of committing a crime."

"Well, that's no skin off my nose, is it? An' all I got is your word for it? Seems skinny reason to put myself in a compromising position, it does."

"Look," Brekonridge said. "I don't have time to...oh, to hell with it. Move over."

"Say what now?" Brownlee protested.

"As an officer of the court, previous of the London Metropolitan Police, I commandeer this carriage." He had no such power. It was a bold lie, just big enough to work. Brekonridge climbed into the driver's seat and grabbed the reins.

"I protest, I do!" Brownlee said.

"You can come with me or stay here," Brekonridge said.

"I'm not letting you drive off with my carriage, I ain't!" Brownlee said.

"With me it is, then."

Brekonridge snapped at the reins, and the horse took off up the street toward Forrester's carriage, which already receded into the distance, becoming a blurry shape in the fog.

"I must protest!" Brownlee shouted. Brekonridge transferred both reins into one hand and clapped the other calloused palm across Brownlee's mouth, silencing him.

"Look, mate," Brekonridge said. "The point here is to *not* get noticed."

Forrester's carriage took a right at Bartlett Court, and ran due east until it reached a minor lane where it turned left toward Fetters Lane. The fog grew thicker, and visibility decreased to mere yards. Brekonridge snapped at the reins again, and the horse leapt forward, the clopping of its hooves making a staccato beat that echoed off the bricks of the buildings that flew by.

Just as Forrester's carriage swam back into view, it sped up and began to pull away once again.

"Damn," Brekonridge muttered. "He knows we're after him."

He urged the horse on, and within seconds both carriages careened down residential streets at breakneck speed. Brownlee's horse had the advantage, however, and Forrester's carriage began to back toward Brekonridge.

"I'm giving you back the reins, Archie," Brekonridge said. "You pull alongside that carriage, and I'll jump across to stop the driver."

"You'll...*what?*" Brownlee exclaimed.

"Did I mumble?"

"I will not do such an insane thing. You must be mad!"

"There's a sovereign in it for you."

Brownlee smiled.

"Well! Why didn't you say so? Gimme them reins!"

Brownlee took over the carriage as Brekonridge climbed forward on the roof, watching Forrester's carriage as it slid back toward them, its horse not up to the task of holding off Brownlee. The clopping of hooves had turned into a pounding snare drum beat. Brekonridge could smell the musk of the horses' sweat as Brownlee's carriage slowly drew alongside the other. As soon as he found the opportunity, Brekonridge launched himself into the space between them, and spread out as he landed on the roof. Immediately, the driver pulled back on the reins and stepped on the brake. Taken off guard, Brekonridge rolled toward the front of the carriage roof. At the last second, he grasped the reins to prevent himself from falling in front of the carriage. Brownlee's carriage sped past them up the next hill, slowing as it went.

"Are you crazy?" the driver yelled. "You could've killed us both, ya damn fool!"

Brekonridge jumped to the ground, yanked open the carriage door, grabbed at the Forrester's coat, and pushed him against the wall.

"Welcome to London, Mr. Forrester," he growled.

"You!" Forrester said. "I thought I was being robbed!"

"I have no need of your money. I will know what your business is with Gordon and Nockold and I will know why you lied on the stand."

"I didn't—"

"Don't compound one lie with another! You said in Glasgow you told Mrs. Patterson M'Naghten was daft. In court, you denied it. In fact, you denied several facts on the stand. Then, you met with two radicals from Glasgow at that tavern, Gordon and Nockold. One's a Chartist, the other is a socialist."

"They're *both* socialists," Forrester said. "Gordon plays both sides of the track. He keeps an eye on Abram Duncan, and he has the man's ear."

"And you?"

"I owe you no explanations."

"You admit lying on the stand?"

"I admit nothing. You'll either have to kill me or let me go."

Brekonridge still had the belaying pin stuffed in the lining of his coat. He pulled it out and pressed the thick end up under Forrester's nose.

"Maybe I'll beat the truth out of you. Who hired M'Naghten to kill Robert Peel?"

"I have no idea what you're talking about. I told you in Glasgow that Danny was always a little crazy. It was a notion he took on himself."

"That won't play. There's no adequate explanation for his newfound riches. Business wasn't that good. Someone paid M'Naghten. I know he was close with Nockold and his fellow socialist, Graham, at the Mechanics Institute. You lied on the stand, and the next day you were bending an elbow with Nockold. That says you know more than you're divulging. Who paid M'Naghten?"

"You're deluded. We're three strangers to London who happen to know one another in Glasgow. It's natural for us to commiserate over our fallen friend."

"Except you weren't commiserating over him. You made a toast to 'missed opportunities,' and you lamented you had 'lost' this game…the game being Peel's assassination."

"You…you heard? How could you?" A light of recognition appeared in Forrester's eyes. "The boy. The one who sat near us. You sent him?"

"I'm asking the questions here. Explain what you said in the tavern!"

Quicker than Brekonridge imagined possible, Forrester grabbed the belaying pin from his grasp and tossed it deep into the fog. Before it even left his hand, Forrester brought the other fist up into Brekonridge's midsection at the base of his ribs. The result was paralyzing, as if all the breath had been sucked from his body. Brekonridge was not accustomed to being at a disadvantage in a fight, but Forrester was as large and as strong as the thief-taker, who discovered instantly he could neither breathe nor lift his arms. He collapsed to the ground, bracing himself with his hands and knees to keep his face from the pavement. Forrester took the opportunity to kick him again in the midsection, compounding the original injury. Completely unable to breathe, Brekonridge rolled onto his back and waited for Forrester to administer the *coup de grace*.

Instead, Forrester bolted toward the next side street, and disappeared into the billows of fog.

Brekonridge's ability to breathe slowly returned and he realized he wasn't terribly injured, other than the insult to his pride. He slowly made his way to his feet and braced himself against the brick side of the building as Dickens ran up to him.

"Well," Dickens said, "that was exhilarating. Perhaps, as a *digestif*, we might consider a cockfight."

Brekonridge scowled at him, picked up his hat, and started the long trudge back toward the Old Bailey.

* * *

Brekonridge and Dickens barely made it back to the courtroom before the justices returned and called the trial back into session.

"What happened to you?" Simon asked, noting the dirt on Brekonridge's coat.

"A dustup with Forrester. I'll explain later."

Alexander Cockburn took the lectern and called, as the first physician witness, Dr. Edward Thomas Monro.

Monro was a jovial man in his middle fifties, of average height and build, with an open, friendly face. His balding head was ringed with curly graying hair, accented by mutton-chop whiskers. He wore neither a mustache nor a beard. His aquiline nose, strong chin, thin lips, and dark brown eyes gave him an overall handsome appearance, even at his advanced age.

Cockburn said, "I believe, Dr. Monro, you have had great experience in lunacy?"

"I have devoted myself entirely to the subject for over thirty years."

"In what capacity, sir?"

"I am the Principal Physician at the Royal Bethlem Hospital, a position I have held since 1814. My father held the position before me and I studied in his shadow for several years before I took the position upon his death."

"Have you had occasion to examine the prisoner?"

"I have. I was requested to visit him during his confinement in Newgate, for the purpose of ascertaining his state of mind."

"When did that examination take place?"

"On the eighteenth of February."

"I believe there were some other medical gentlemen who accompanied you?"

"We all saw the prisoner together."

Cockburn took a moment to review his notes before asking, "What did the prisoner say in answer to the questions put to him?"

"The prisoner said he was persecuted by a system or crew at Glasgow, Edinburgh, Liverpool, London and Boulogne. He had no peace of mind and was sure it would kill him; it was a grinding of the mind. He stated in Glasgow he observed people in the streets pointing at him and speaking of him. They said, *'That is the man, he is a murderer and the worst of characters.'* He believed everything was done to associate his name with the direst of crimes."

"Do you think your knowledge of insanity enables you to judge between the conduct of a man who feigns a delusion and one who feels it?" Cockburn asked.

"In the course of my practice at Royal Bethlem, I have on occasion encountered a poor soul who desperately believed he might find respite from the cold streets by posing as insane. I have found every one of them out in short order."

"Do you consider the delusions described by the prisoner were real or assumed?"

"I believe the prisoner shot and killed Mr. Drummond whilst under a delusion. He looked upon the assault itself as the crowning act of the whole matter—the climax, if you will—as a carrying out of the pre-existing idea which had haunted him for years. He saw it as a final solution to his problems."

"Is it consistent with the pathology of insanity that a partial delusion may deprive the person of all self-control, whilst the other faculties remain sound?"

"Certainly. Monomania may coexist with otherwise general sanity."

"You are familiar, I take it, with Lord Hale's treatise on insanity?"

"Intimately."

"And your response to it?"

"Lord Hale, and his treatise, were of their own time. Our understanding of defects of reason has grown exponentially in the interim, thanks in large part to the work of Dr. Pinel in Paris, and of my father and myself, if it does not seem boastful to say so. Contrary to Lord Hale's hypothesis, I have frequently known a person insane upon one point to exhibit great cleverness upon all others not immediately associated with his delusions. I have seen clever artists, arithmeticians and architects, whose minds were disordered on only a single point, but otherwise completely able to manage their affairs competently."

"And, would any evidence in the course of this trial disabuse you of the notion that exactly such a set of circumstances existed in the case of Daniel

M'Naghten?"

"The evidence which I have heard in court has not induced me to alter my opinion of the case in any way."

"Thank you, Doctor," Cockburn said. "No further questions, Your Honors."

Follett took his place at the lectern for cross-examination.

"I should like you to acquaint the Court with the exact form of the question you put to prisoner M'Naghten which had a reference to his firing the pistol at Mr. Drummond. Did you ask him if he knew whom he fired at?"

"I think he was asked the question more than once. He hesitated and paused, and at length said he was not sure whether it was Sir Robert Peel or not."

"Did Mr. M'Naghten say he would not have fired if he had known it was not Sir Robert Peel?"

"No, I think he did not."

"What was the form of the question which related to his firing at Sir Robert Peel?"

"I think the question was, *'Did you know whom you were firing at?'* In reply, he observed, *'He was one of the crew that had been following me.'* "

"Do you mean to say, Dr. Monro, you could satisfy yourself as to a person's state of mind by merely going into a cell and putting questions to him?"

"In many instances."

"Is it not necessary to examine the bodily symptoms in these cases; for instance, the pulse?"

"Yes, sometimes."

"And, in the case of Mr. M'Naghten?"

"I did not feel his pulse, neither did I lay much stress upon the appearance of his eye."

"Do you always assume the party tells you what is passing in his mind?"

"Not at all. I have known patients to lie most comfortably in my presence."

"Earlier, you departed in substance from the established standards for sanity as espoused by the late, esteemed Lord Hale. I would like to explore this is greater detail. What do you mean by insanity? Do you consider a person laboring under a morbid delusion of unsound mind?"

"I do."

"May insanity exist with a moral perception of right and wrong?"

"Yes. In fact, I would suggest that it is common."

"A person may have a delusion and know murder to be a crime?"

"It is my considered opinion, based on a lifetime of experience and study, that a person may be of unsound mind, labor under a morbid delusion, and yet know right from wrong. In many respects this was the case with the prisoner."

"No further questions," Follett said, before returning to his table.

Cockburn requested the opportunity to redirect, which Tindal granted.

"You suggest, Dr. Monro," Cockburn said, "that a person might labor under a particular form of insanity without having his moral perceptions deranged. For illustration, a man may fancy his legs made of glass. There is nothing in that which could affect his moral feelings?"

"Certainly not. Presuming, in fact, his legs were *not* made of glass, he would be merely delusional."

"And you have not the slightest doubt M'Naghten's moral perceptions were impaired?"

"No. There is no doubt in my mind. Mr. M'Naghten knew the exact nature of behavior he engaged in when he shot Edward Drummond. He knew what he was doing was morally wrong. His perception of right and wrong are unmolested. At the time, he saw no other option available to him in order to disabuse himself of his persecutors."

"His *perceived* persecutors?"

"That is what I intended to say," Monro concluded. "He believed he was acting in self-defense, and no argument could have convinced him otherwise."

* * *

After excusing Dr. Monro from the witness stand, Cockburn handed the lectern over to William Clarkson, who called Sir Alexander Morrison to the stand. Morrison was a tall, thin man with a horse-like face and a mass of dark, curly hair framing his clean-shaven features. He spoke with a pronounced Scottish accent.

Clarkson said, "I believe, Dr. Morrison, you were one of the gentlemen who saw the prisoner in conjunction with Drs. Monro, Sutherland and Bright?"

"I did."

"You have been in Court during the whole of the day?"

"I have."

"Were you present during the entire examination of the prisoner in Newgate?"

"I was."

"After that examination, did you arrive at any conclusion as to the prisoner's state of mind?"

"I did."

In the gallery, Brekonridge leaned toward Simon and whispered, "Talkative fellow."

Without thinking of the possible physical consequences, Simon elbowed the thief-taker to silence him.

Clarkson continued, "Please state to the Court what your impression was."

"Mr. M'Naghten was insane."

"After having heard the evidence adduced this day in Court, has your opinion undergone any alteration?"

Morrison crossed his hands in his lap, and attempted to put himself at ease in the stand. "I am of the same opinion. The prisoner was insane at the time he committed the act with which he is charged."

"You have heard, I believe, all the evidence of Dr. Monro?"

"I have."

"Do you concur with him in the view which he has taken of this case?"

"I do."

"The prisoner's morbid delusions consisted in his fancying himself subject to a system of persecutions?"

"Yes. That was the peculiar cause of his insanity."

"What effect had this delusion upon his mind?"

"It deprived the prisoner of all restraint or control over his actions."

"Do you speak with any doubt upon the point?"

"Not the slightest."

"You have had, I believe, considerable experience in these cases?"

"I have devoted my attention for nearly half a century to the subject of insanity."

"No further questions," Clarkson said, retiring to the defense table.

Solicitor General Follett conducted the cross-examination. "Do you think the prisoner of unsound mind?"

"I do."

Brekonridge whispered, "And he also believes words are shillings, as freely as he spends them."

Simon squeezed Brekonridge's arm, as Tindal again shot a warning glance in their direction.

Follett said, "It is your contention his delusion consisted in his fancying himself persecuted by a number of persons?"

"Yes," Morrison replied.

"Based on your own questioning of the prisoner and observing the questioning by others?"

"Yes," Morrison said. "That is the case."

* * *

Henry Bodkin called William M'Clure to the stand. M'Clure was in his middle fifties, but retained strikingly handsome features belying his age. His hair was full and dark, and his face relatively unlined. Brekonridge looked around the gallery. The few women who had chosen to attend the trial appeared to be jostling one another to bring attention to the new witness. They all looked most taken with him. Even Anne Eliza Drummond had raised her veil for a better look.

"You are a surgeon, living in Harley Street," Bodkin began.

"I am."

"Have you been in practice for many years?"

"For the period of thirty years."

"And did you take part in the examination of the prisoner at Newgate Prison on February eighteenth?"

"I did."

"Do you consider the delusions under which M'Naghten is laboring to be real or feigned?"

"He believed they were real. He had no doubt on the point."

"Did you consider the prisoner to be suffering under a delusion?"

"Yes."

"Looking at the history of the case, the evidence adduced, as well as the melancholy termination, what opinion do you entertain of the state of the prisoner's mind?"

M'Clure considered the question before answering. "When he fired at Mr. Dummond, the prisoner was suffering from an hallucination which deprived him of all ordinary restraint."

"No further questions," Bodkin said to the justices on the bench.

Follett resumed his place at the lectern. Since the luncheon break, none of the other prosecuting barristers had addressed any witnesses. Follett clearly wished the fate of the Crown's case, for better or worse, to rest on his head.

"Did you ask the prisoner if he knew whom it was he fired at?" Follett asked.

"I did not." M'Clure responded. "That was asked by Doctor Monro."

"Did he not say, if he had known it was *not* Sir Robert Peel at whom he fired, he would not have shot Mr. Drummond?"

"He did not say so."

"Most curious," Simon whispered to Brekonridge in the gallery.

"I agree. He keeps asking this question, as if he has information that, at some point, M'Naghten made such a statement."

"If so, he certainly didn't make it to his doctors," Simon said.

"Or they have conspired to keep it out of the court record."

"Why would they do that?" Simon asked.

"Ah. That is the next question, isn't it?"

* * *

Alexander Cockburn called Dr. William Hutcheson to the stand. Unlike the medical men who had preceded him, Hutcheson was youthful, only in his middle thirties. He dressed like a dandy, but his features were stern and solemn. His flaxen hair was cut so it fell in thick, clumpy waves above his ears, and a stray lock kept falling across his forehead.

Cockburn opened the questioning. "You are, I believe, physician to the Royal Lunatic Asylum at Glasgow."

"I am."

"When did you see Mr. M'Naghten?"

"I visited him whilst he was confined in Newgate Prison, in conjunction with the other medical men."

"What was the prisoner's state of mind?"

"I found him laboring under a morbid delusion."

"Were the delusions feigned or real?"

"They were real."

"What effect had they upon his mind?"

"They deprived the prisoner of all control over his actions."

"Do you think he had lost all self-control at the moment he fired at Mr. Drummond?"

"I do. I consider the act flowed immediately from the delusion."

"No further questions, my Lords," Cockburn said.

Again, the Solicitor General elected to conduct the cross-examination. "Dr. Hutcheson, do you mean to say the delusion prevented the prisoner from exercising *any* control over his actions?"

"I said the act was the consequence of the delusion, which was irresistible. The delusion was so strong that nothing but a physical impediment could have prevented him from committing the act. He might have done the same thing in Glasgow if the disease of the mind had reached the same point.

I do not think it would have been within his power to resist any impulse springing from the morbid delusions under which he suffered."

"Divesting your mind of all the evidence you have heard, and all the facts connected with the case, and forming your judgment on the examination to which you subjected the prisoner, what would be your opinion of his state of mind?"

"I should have no hesitation in certifying he was a dangerous lunatic."

Chief Justice Tindal interrupted Follett's line of questioning by holding up a hand and turning to the witness on the stand. "Nothing which you have heard during the last two days has altered your mind on the subject?"

"He has the same reservations as I," Brekonridge whispered to Simon. "Why did only the officials in Glasgow and the physicians at Newgate see these symptoms, and not those closest to M'Naghten in Glasgow?"

Hutcheson cleared his throat. "My opinion of the prisoner's insanity is the same."

"The prosecution has no further questions," Follett said, as he stepped away from the lectern.

Cockburn rose immediately to his feet. "Dr. Hutcheson, when patients exhibit symptoms similar to those which the prisoner manifested, they are generally placed under restraint?"

"Yes. Such symptoms often gradually develop themselves, whereas many have these delusions for some time and are harmless, until they may suddenly impel them to the commission of crime."

"No further questions," Cockburn said.

Chapter Forty-Six

The testimony continued throughout the remainder of the afternoon. The fog rolling in from the Thames thickened and the light in the courtroom faded as one after another physician presented by the Queen's Counsel testified M'Naghten was evidently insane at the time he discharged his pistol into Edward Drummond's back. They all had come to the same conclusion. M'Naghten labored under delusions of persecution so strong, he believed his only relief from oppression was to kill the man he encountered on Whitehall near Charing Cross.

Dr. J. Peter Crawford, of the Andersonian Institute in Glasgow, testified the former woodturner was indeed insane. He was seconded by Dr. MacMurdo, the surgeon assigned to Newgate Prison; and by Dr. Ashton Key, a surgeon at Guys Hospital. As Cockburn paraded his seemingly endless list of physicians who had tended to, or evaluated, M'Naghten, the crowd in the gallery became restless. The testimony had become more like a litany or responsive reading than the electrifying, scandalous revelations they had expected.

Late in the afternoon, William Clarkson called Dr. Forbes Winslow to the stand. Winslow, only thirty-three, was a short, portly man with a balding pate and a pronounced overbite that only accentuated his receding chin.

"I believe, Doctor Winslow, that you are a surgeon, residing in Guildford-street?"

"I am."

"You are the author of the *Plea of Insanity in Criminal Cases*, and other works on the subject of insanity?"

"Yes."

"I think, Doctor Winslow, you have been in court during the whole of the trial, and have heard all the evidence on the part of the Crown and for the defense?"

"I have."

"Judging from the evidence which you have heard, and drawing on your widely-acknowledged expertise in the nature of insanity, what is your opinion as to the prisoner's state of mind?"

"I have not the slightest hesitation in saying he is insane and he committed the offense in question whilst afflicted with a delusion under which he appears to have been laboring for a considerable length of time."

Clarkson was about to ask another question, but Chief Lord Justice Tindal raised his hand to stop him. "Dr. Winslow, will you repeat what you have just stated?" Tindal asked.

"In my opinion, based on all the testimony I have witnessed over the last two days, there is not a shadow of doubt in my mind the prisoner, Mr. M'Naghten, was laboring under such a defect of reason at the time of the murder that he was incapable of controlling his actions. There is no other explanation except he is insane, and has been for a considerable period of time."

"Please resume, Mr. Clarkson," Tindal said.

"My Lords, I have no further questions for this witness," Clarkson replied.

"Mr. Solicitor General?" Tindal called out.

Follett, sitting at the prosecutors' table, looked fatigued and defeated. Even he, at that point, could read the handwriting on the wall.

"The prosecution has no questions of this witness," he said, dejectedly.

"In that case," Clarkson said, "the defense would like to call Dr. Barnabus Phillips, a surgeon at Westminster Hosp—"

"Before you do so," Lord Chief Justice Tindal said, raising his hand again. "Mr. Cockburn, do you anticipate a great many more medical witnesses in this case?"

Cockburn held up a sheet of paper, and made a show of reviewing it. "I believe we may need to examine five or six more, my Lord."

Tindal directed his attention to the prosecution table, where Follett sat, his face sallow and slack. "Mr. Solicitor General, are you prepared, on the part of the Crown, with any evidence to combat this testimony of the medical witnesses who now have been examined? Because we think, if you have not, we must be under the necessity of stopping the case. Is there any medical evidence on the other side?"

Slowly, knowing his race was run, Follett stood at the table and faced the justices. "My Lords, I must say there is not."

Tindal addressed the jury. "Gentlemen, the evidence on the part of the defendant, and more particularly the evidence of the medical witnesses, is sufficient to show this unfortunate man, at the time he committed the act, was laboring under insanity; and, of course, if he were so, he would be entitled to his acquittal. I have undoubtedly been struck, and so have my learned brethren, by the evidence we have heard from the medical persons, as to the state of the mind of the unhappy prisoner. It seems almost unnecessary I should go through the evidence. If you think you ought to hear the evidence more fully, I will state it to you and leave the case in your hands. Probably, however, sufficient evidence has now been laid before you, and you will say whether you want any further information."

The jury foreman, William Routledge, stood and said, "We require no more, my Lord."

"If you find the prisoner not guilty on the ground of insanity, then say so, and proper care will be taken of him."

After conferring briefly with his jury colleagues, Routledge turned again to face the justices. "We find the prisoner *not* guilty, on the ground of insanity."

The courtroom erupted into chatter. Anne Eliza Drummond, still clad entirely in black, stood immediately and retreated from the courtroom. Witnesses later reported she departed with a satisfied smile on her face.

Chapter Forty-Seven

The knock came early the morning after the trial. Brekonridge lay in his bed, snoring soundly, when the echo of unfamiliar boots on the stairwell awakened him. He grabbed a cudgel made from the crook of a larch from under his bed. There was a sharp rap on his door.

"Open in the name of the Queen!"

Wearing only the linens he had not cast onto a chair next to his bed the night before, Brekonridge quickly jumped into his trousers. The loose cotton muslin undershirt he had worn while sleeping would have to suffice for upper body wear. He crossed the main room of his lodgings, the cudgel secreted behind his back, and cracked the door. Two soldiers stood outside in the hall.

"You are Vicar Brekonridge?" one asked.

"I am. What of it?"

"You will come with us."

"Am I under arrest?"

"If you were, we would not be here. We are not the police. Please dress quickly. You are summoned to meet with a high government official."

Half an hour later, after he had dressed hastily in the clothes he wore for thief-taking, Brekonridge was escorted into the Admiralty. The soldiers stood on either side of him as they stepped up to the main entrance and took a stairway to the third floor. There, they traversed a long hall until they reached the door at the end. One soldier knocked on the door while the other ushered Brekonridge inside. The soldiers remained outside, apparently to stand guard.

The room was a small office, furnished simply with a desk and several chairs. A Union Jack stood in one corner and a painting of the young Queen Victoria decorated the wall. A pair of windows behind the desk revealed a courtyard and gardens beyond, as bright sunlight flooded the room. A man stood in front of the window, gazing out over the gardens, his hands clasped behind his back. He turned. He was tall and lanky with a handsome face and a sly smile.

"Would you have a seat, Mr. Brekonridge?" he said. "I am James Graham, the Home Secretary."

"I recognize you well enough. I apologize for not dressing better. Your friends outside did not afford me time for a decent bath and to rummage through my closet for my Sunday finest."

"It is I who must apologize for getting you out here so early on a Sunday morning. It suited my purposes to conduct this meeting while most of London is still abed. For the same reason, we are meeting here at the Admiralty instead of at my own office. I am told you made the preliminary investigations for the defense team in the M'Naghten case."

"I did."

"And you attended the trial?"

"I was in the gallery. Sat behind Charles Dickens."

"And, now the verdict has been pronounced, how do you feel?" Graham asked.

"Like a tennis ball, struck first one way and then the other. I do not care for the sensation. Was it you who rigged the trial with Cockburn?"

Graham's eyebrows raised slightly. His smile disappeared, replaced with the slightest sneer. "The outcome served a number of purposes," he said.

Brekonridge chuckled, which appeared to confuse Graham.

"You find that funny?" he said.

"I said the exact same thing to Cockburn myself recently."

"I would be interested in your interpretation."

"No, you would not. You only wish to know whether I have found you out. However, to satisfy your curiosity, it is my impression M'Naghten was paid to kill Sir Robert Peel and bungled the job. Drummond actually died as a result of misadventure on the part of his surgeons, not from M'Naghten's pistol ball. Men of the stature of Doctors Guthrie and Cooper are never held responsible, so M'Naghten should have swung for killing Drummond, but you, a staunch member of the Tory party, and I, a Chartist sympathizer, both know what the result of that decision would have been. It was efficacious to find M'Naghten insane, when we both know he is not, because it gives everyone an escape route."

"Except the Queen. I can tell you she is quite livid over the verdict."

"Drummond's sister appeared overjoyed," Brekonridge said. "To each his or her own. I also think I have discovered M'Naghten's co-conspirators, for what it is worth."

"And they would be?"

"A man named John Gordon, a socialist who has infiltrated the Chartists in Glasgow. Another openly avowed socialist named Nockold. And a man who claimed to be M'Naghten's friend in Glasgow, a fellow named Forrester. I confronted Forrester yesterday. He as much as admitted the plot."

"In so many words?"

"By what he didn't say."

"I see," Graham said. "I suppose I should admit my admiration for your deductive skills, and your perseverance. However, I am quite happy to disabuse you of one notion."

As if on cue, there was knock at the door. It swung open and Joseph Forrester walked into the office. Instead of the common clothes he wore in Glasgow, he was dressed in a fine red jacket and tight white breeches. He wore a high felt top hat.

"A pleasure to see you once again, Mr. Brekonridge," he said. "I am sorry it must take place under such surreptitious circumstances. I do hope you were not injured during our discussion yesterday."

At first, Brekonridge was shocked to see the hairdresser in the London office of the Home Secretary. Then, he understood. "Ah, yes," he said. "I believe you would be an expert in surreptitious dealings."

Forrester addressed Graham. "I told you he had a quick mind."

"You're a Tory spy," Brekonridge said.

Forrester made a small bow. "I owe you a degree of gratitude. When you accosted me and accused me of taking part in a plot to assassinate Robert Peel, you lent me greater credibility."

"Some hairdresser," Brekonridge said as he touched the tender area on his chest where Forrester had struck him.

"Actually, I am," Forrester replied. "Almost everything I told you in Glasgow was the truth. I did tour with M'Naghten's acting troupe a decade ago, before I was recruited by the Home Office. Daniel and I were friends, at least as close a friend as Daniel will allow anyone to be. We do believe there was a plot to kill the Prime Minister and Daniel was to be the instrument of that assassination. We also believe, as do you, that someone paid him over seven hundred pounds to do it. However, I have probed them thoroughly, and I can assure you it was not Nockold and Gordon."

"Who, then?"

"We have no idea," Graham replied. "It could have been a physical force branch of the Chartists, the group represented by Feargus O'Connor and his compatriots on trial in Lancashire. It could have been the Anti-Corn Law League. M'Naghten visited Boulogne last year. Perhaps his bounty was French money. We're still trying to find out ourselves."

"So, I was right all along? M'Naghten isn't insane?"

"I said I told you the truth back in Glasgow," Forrester replied. "Remember when I told you Daniel had always been a little mad?"

"I do, and I recall you perjuring yourself on the stand over it."

"That was necessary."

"And was it necessary to lie about asking to accompany Mrs. Patterson to Sheriff Alison's office and saying M'Naghten was daft?"

"It was. Sheriff Alison knows my true role in Glasgow. Daniel was my friend. At the time, I had no reason to believe he might be dangerous. He was simply…peculiar. I did not wish to see any harm come to him. It was necessary to lie on the stand. My words were to become public record. If Daniel was hired by one of the groups I am attempting to infiltrate, it would not do to be on record as having believed their hired killer was a lunatic."

"It appears," Graham interjected, "two things are equally true. First,

M'Naghten was recruited by someone to kill Sir Robert. Second, even if he is not truly mad, there is strain of mental aberration in him which the people who hired him hoped to exploit."

"It gave them the ability to deny their part in the killing," Brekonridge surmised.

"Precisely," Graham said.

Forrester said, "Danny saw bogeymen in every closet and spies behind every window. He believed the government in London was engaged in a conspiracy to prevent workingmen from accessing the quality of life enjoyed by the upper crust."

"Aren't they?" Brekonridge said. "Were it not so, Parliament would have addressed the People's Charter."

"A matter of interpretation," Graham said, sounding peeved.

"I sought to protect Daniel from the possibility Sheriff Alison might put him in restraints, Forrester explained. "Now I wish Alison had committed him. At the very least, Edward Drummond might still be alive. I shall regret my error for the rest of my days."

"So you also believe he was faking when he visited all those officials in Glasgow?"

Forrester shrugged. "I saw him play Lear. I know he can portray madness most effectively, perhaps because he is so close to it in reality. Faking now fits in with the narrative."

"The narrative," Brekonridge said. "Cockburn used that same phrase when I confronted him. It is all about making the official story consistent."

"History is written by the victors," Graham replied. "They control the narrative. At this moment in history, the government in London has two primary concerns. The first is keeping the peace. The second, as the case in all governments, is retaining power and control. When radical elements threaten both objectives, we must take action to diffuse their impact. Finding M'Naghten insane does precisely that."

"Truth be damned," Brekonridge said, bitterly. "You had the Solicitor General ignore important evidence, allowing Cockburn and his team the upper hand."

"We convinced Mr. Follett that, regardless of Her Majesty's immediate wishes, it would suit the Queen's long-term goals better if M'Naghten did not become a symbol to those who would gladly bring her down. He was left to his own discretion as to how he might bring that about. Mr. Brekonridge, I have divulged to you a state secret of the highest priority, so high even the Prime Minister and the Queen are unaware of it. When you inserted yourself into affairs, it threatened the work Mr. Forrester has done to uncover plots like the one involving Mr. M'Naghten. It is of the utmost importance you drop your inquiries and your accusations. You are too close to the truth, and some truths should remain hidden for the greater good. Please, tell me, is there any incentive we could offer that would convince you to keep your confidence?"

"In other words, how large a bribe am I willing to take to walk away?"

"In the interest of maintaining security in the realm."

Brekonridge mulled the situation over. The only sound in the room was the ticking of a wall clock and the occasional clop of horse hooves on the road outside.

"I believe I have a solution that will satisfy everyone concerned," he said, "For some time now, I have entertained the notion of emigrating to America."

Chapter Forty-Eight

1864

For twenty-one years, Royal Bethlem Asylum, also known as Bedlam, had been the only home Daniel M'Naghten had known. He spent each day in a cell barely nine feet by eleven in size, furnished with a trundle bed and a crude wooden table and chair. His mattress was made of straw, replenished once a year.

No attempts were made to restore his presumed lost sanity. Treatment at the time for the criminally insane still consisted largely of confinement for the protection of the masses. His basic nutritional and medical needs were tended to, and he was offered poor opportunities at recreation in keeping with the new humane protocols for managing the mentally deficient, but in every other way his life became an unending series of sunrises and sunsets, demarked only by the crossing of shadows on his cell wall, with nothing between them but boredom, isolation and his own brooding.

As time passed, he became the model of a compliant, obedient inmate. He did as he was told, and over the years he obtained more and more freedom to explore the limited confines of his new world.

Ten years after entering Bedlam, he took up knitting. At first he was permitted only the crudest of needles, purposefully blunted to prevent injury to himself or others. Eventually, he was able to acquire proper needles and his craft improved.

He came to be on friendly terms with his guards and with the supervisor on his wing, who would drop by and talk about matters of the day. In 1850, the supervisor visited and told him Sir Robert Peel had died. The former Prime Minister, who had kept his promise to his beloved wife and retired from public office in 1846, had gone out riding in Westminster and had been thrown from his horse on Constitution Hill. The horse had, in righting itself, rolled over Peel, inflicting fatal injuries.

If the news had any impact on M'Naghten, it was not evident. He accepted it as a matter of course and quickly moved on to a new subject.

M'Naghten, in twenty-one years, had never spoken publicly about his crime. From time to time, some investigator or reporter would visit to engage him in the subject, but M'Naghten simply refused to talk.

With time, M'Naghten's forced indolence led to excessive weight gain. His face grew square and jowly. His attention faltered and sometimes he forgot why he was hospitalized in the first place.

"I must have done something terrible," he said to one interviewer. "to wind up in such a place as this." But he did not elaborate.

With the gain in weight and lack of consistent exercise, M'Naghten's heart grew weak. His ankles swelled at night, and he felt feeble and listless.

In 1864 he received a respite. The superintendent at Bedlam visited him in his cell to tell him a new hospital for the criminally insane had been erected at Broadmoor. The archaic, fifteenth century edifice at Bedlam had become inadequate to meet the needs of its inmates. The Broadmoor facility was airier, more modern and better equipped. M'Naghten, at Her Majesty's pleasure, was to be relocated to the new facility.

For the first time in twenty-one years, M'Naghten stepped outside the confines of Royal Bethlem Hospital, his hands and feet bound in manacles. He was escorted to a train to be transported. For the first time in twenty-one years, he listened to the warbles and cries of birds in the trees and felt unfiltered light on his face. For the first time in twenty-one years, he saw people going about their daily business around Victoria Station, dressed in intriguing clothes.

"Women are most daring these days, I perceive," he said to the man who sat next to him on the train. "It would appear life has changed considerably since I was out and about."

On the way to the train, the carriage passed along Whitehall and the exact spot where he had fired on Edward Drummond. If he recognized the location, he did not let on.

He arrived at Broadmoor, still dressed in the rude clothes issued to him at Bedlam, with his only possessions—three skeins of yarn, a pair of knitting needles, and a small bundle of books. Within minutes, he was escorted to his new cell, which he was delighted to discover included a window through which he could watch the outside world for the first time in two decades. He sat on the bed and wept.

* * *

April 1865

Vicar Brekonridge stood outside the Bloomsbury house, waiting.

Well past seventy years of age, he was no longer the imposing thief-taker he had been. He still stood taller than most men, but his step was slower, aided by a cane, and his vision dimmed. He had recently begun to wear glasses. As his face had drawn long, losing the fight with gravity, he had surrendered to vanity, and now wore a wig when walking in public. For the first time in nearly three decades, he now could stroll the marketplace without the worry of frightening young children. In fact, he had discovered some of them regarded him as some sort of fairy-tale giant. His obvious disfigurement concealed, children now flocked to him as he strolled, wanting to examine his large hands and feet as if he were some sort of curiosity.

His escape to America had proven profitable, if not entirely happy. Bankrolled by the Home Office, Brekonridge had traveled west, into the new frontier that stretched three thousand miles to the Pacific Ocean. The vastness of the continent and its diversity of plant and animal life beckoned him and left him astounded when he compared it to the relatively miniscule island of his birth. While he enjoyed several harrowing adventures in his travels, he was disappointed to learn that, wherever he went, human avarice and cruelty preceded him. He sought isolation and peace, but found it nowhere. He returned to New York to discover that his investor there had made him an enviably wealthy man. Yet, his heart pulled him toward home.

He returned to London in 1847 and had been back less than a month when Alexander Cockburn called on him. Cockburn had work for Brekonridge, if he was inclined to accept it. Brekonridge took the job, which led to another, and another, and across the years the two had developed a close working relationship. Over two decades later, and despite the fact Cockburn was now the Lord Chief Justice in London—an appointment approved by Queen Victoria only with the greatest reluctance—Brekonridge remained uncertain whether he fully trusted the man. On the other hand, his payments were never late. That was enough on which to build their armistice.

Mrs. Langtry died in early 1860. She had promised Brekonridge he would always keep his three rooms, but he was dumbfounded to discover she had left him the entire building, and two others. In addition to his investment fortune and his income from investigations he had conducted for Cockburn and others, he also found himself a landlord and property owner. As a consequence, his bank account grew precipitously, and in 1865 he was a remarkably wealthy man.

A carriage pulled alongside the Bloomsbury house. The footman opened the door to admit Brekonridge. When he stepped inside, he found Alexander Cockburn facing him.

The Lord Chief Justice had definitively aged. His nose had become a beak. His earlobes dangled as if they might flap in the wind. His face was covered with dark blotches and liver spots. The skin on his hands looked like crepe paper. He was shortly past sixty, but the years and dissipation for which he was widely noted had been less than kind.

As the carriage pulled away from the curb, Cockburn said, "Have you read the papers?"

"Not today," Brekonridge said.

"The war in America is over. A peace agreement was signed at someplace called Appomattox Courthouse, in Virginia."

"Who won?"

"The Union. It seems the states will not be torn asunder after all."

"And slavery is ended," Brekonridge said. "High time."

"It is a great thing, bought at enormous cost. I daresay America will reverberate from this war for years to come."

"Growing pains," Brekonridge said.

"Too true. You saw George Perceval died?"

"I did."

"Perceval, Humphreys, Peel, Tindal, Graham, Forrester. The list seems endless. We may be the only people left alive who recall the M'Naghten trial."

"Or at least the truth of it. The Queen still lives."

"There is that. She will outlive us all, I believe."

"We are too stubborn to die. I don't miss any of them."

"Even Simon?"

Brekonridge smiled. "I do miss Simon. He was a stout lad."

"You had a great many adventures together."

"More than I'd care to count."

"I suspect it should not be so long before you and I must also stand before our maker and account for our sins."

"Speak for yourself, sir. I have lived my life unencumbered by deities, and I have no desire to wrestle with them from the grave."

They rode on in silence for a while. Brekonridge watched the world go by through the carriage window. It seemed he did that more and more of late—watch the world go by.

"I ran across an interesting case at the Old Bailey the other day," Cockburn said.

"No," Brekonridge replied. "Thank you."

"I wasn't suggesting you investigate it. I only thought you'd be intrigued by the puzzle."

"I am no longer interested in crime and punishment. I suspect we all face our peculiar punishments in short enough time. Life has a way of balancing the scales before it lets you leave. I wish to spend what little time remains in peace and quiet contemplation."

"I won't tell you then."

"I am in your debt."

In early afternoon, they arrived at Broadmoor Hospital, an imposing red-brick affair comprised of multiple three-story towers joined by ground-level walkways. The windows were all topped by half-round transoms that allowed plenty of light inside. The grounds were meticulously maintained, with gardens and lawns on which benches erected for visitors and inmates to sit in the sunlight. It was wholly different than the horrifying asylum at Royal Bethlem.

They were greeted at the front office by the current superintendent, a lively middle-aged man who sprinted up to greet them.

"How is he?" Cockburn asked.

"Not well. I fear he is in a decline. This may be your last opportunity to visit."

"What is the nature of his illness?" Brekonridge asked.

"It's his heart. It simply isn't strong enough to sustain him much longer."

"And his spirits?" Cockburn asked.

"They are high, for his condition. He knows he hasn't long to live and I believe he regards it as a happy liberation."

The superintendent led Cockburn and Brekonridge down several halls, until they reached a small open area furnished with comfortable chairs and tables. They found a short, portly man with burst cheek veins and close-cropped, greasy hair sitting there, slowly knitting.

"Mr. M'Naghten," the superintendent said. "You have visitors."

M'Naghten looked up at them. His eyes were rheumy. He cocked his head to the left as he examined them.

"It is Mr. Cockburn and Mr. Brekonridge, is it not?" he asked. His voice was as soft as it had been at his trial over two decades earlier, but also now wheezy and interspersed with occasional gasps for air. "How generous of you to come so far."

The two visitors took seats.

"How are you treated?" Cockburn asked.

"Poorly. I am constantly hectored by the guards. They do not afford me the least privacy. My only consolation is it is not Bedlam. I do enjoy the sunlight here."

Cockburn produced a package he had brought from the carriage. "I have some books for you. The latest works, the most popular in London."

"You are too kind." M'Naghten placed a hand on the bundle and caressed it gently. "I have so few diversions here and I do enjoy reading, even if my eyesight betrays me these days."

The three sat and conversed for almost an hour, when Cockburn declared they would have to leave quickly if they hoped to return to London by nightfall. He apologized to M'Naghten for the inability to stay longer.

"I am grateful for the time we had," M'Naghten said.

Brekonridge told Cockburn, "I shall be along shortly. I would speak with Mr. M'Naghten about a private matter before I leave."

Cockburn bowed and shook M'Naghten's hand before heading down the corridor toward the exit. Brekonridge leaned forward in his chair, balancing his weight on his cane, and peered into M'Naghten's eyes.

"You are not long for this world," Brekonridge said.

"Neither of us is, I'd imagine. But you are correct. I am not the man I was even a month ago. I feel my time is nigh."

"I would ask you one more time. There is no consequence on Earth that can be visited on you as a result of your reply. You are beyond man's law now. My curiosity remains. Who hired you to murder Robert Peel?"

M'Naghten had knitted constantly throughout the visit. Now, he smiled slyly and placed his work on the table to face Brekonridge directly.

"It is quite useless to talk to me on that subject. You know fully well I have resolved long ago not to say another word about it. It would be most childish to pursue the matter further. We have run this conversation into the ground over the years."

"There can be no profit in maintaining the charade," Brekonridge pleaded. "The question has vexed me for decades. I know the seven hundred fifty pounds was blood money, given to you in payment for assassination. I only wish to know who paid it. What if I were to promise never to divulge your answer to any living person?"

"Do you recall Benjamin Franklin's admonition? A secret between two men might be kept only if one of them is dead? I believe we shall shortly see whether Mr. Franklin was correct." M'Naghten settled back into his chair and picked his knitting up from the table. "It may well be that you and Mr. Cockburn are among the few men on this planet whom I might call friends. As a friend, I would ask you to indulge me in this one matter. I have so little in this life I can call my own. Please allow me to take this knowledge with me into the hereafter. Permit me to keep my one great secret. It is all I have left that I can call truly my own."

Brekonridge, bracing himself with his cane, slowly rose to his feet and looked down on the pitiable woodturner. "All right, then," he said. "Your secret is safe, damn you. I hope we shall talk again."

"Unlikely," M'Naghten said. "But if we do, it will be welcome."

Brekonridge placed a reassuring hand on M'Naghten's shoulder. M'Naghten barely acknowledged it, and kept knitting.

Brekonridge emerged from the hospital to find Cockburn standing next to the carriage.

As the driver pulled away, Brekonridge stared down at his companion.

"So," he said, "Tell me about this case which caught your attention."

Acknowledgements

Vicar Brekonridge is a work of fiction, based on actual historic events. With the exceptions of Brekonridge, Simon Daughtrey, Mrs. Langtry, Doctor Elias Sullivan, Healy the stable hand, Albert Camp, the tanner Bouton, Jericho Pratt, and Matthew Mark Luke John Mayhew, all of the characters in this novel existed in real life.

Vicar Brekonridge's occupation of thief-taker was not unusual in the 1840s, though Brekonridge is undoubtedly among the most distinctive individuals in that profession. Broadly speaking, thief-takers were part bounty hunter and part private detective, though neither term existed in the first half of the nineteenth century. Their duties ranged from assisting police officers in the apprehension of criminals, to acting as private agents for victims of crime, to—in some cases—shaking down wanted criminals as a form of extortion. In reality, the role of thief-takers varied from one individual who took up the profession to another. Each thief-taker acted out of a personal code of conduct, from noble to nefarious. One notorious example of the latter, Jonathan Wild, amassed a small fortune by turning in members of his own band of thief-takers, many of whom were eventually hanged at Tyburn Tree.

In the middle eighteenth century, Henry Fielding penned a series of diatribes decrying the unregulated nature of thief-taking and called for a better-organized group of citizen law enforcers to take the place of private vigilantes. Those screeds resulted in the formation of the Bow Street Runners. Originally six in number, they were London's first professional police force, though in this case the word *professional* might not completely describe their activities. Prior to Fielding, some of the original Runners had made a living as private police, apprehending miscreants for a fee and delivering them to magistrates for prosecution. Even after Fielding established the Bow Street Runners, the members did little in the way of official regular patrols in neighborhoods. Instead, their primary duties were to serve warrants issued by sworn magistrates and bring accused criminals back to London to stand trial. The Runners—a title largely disparaged within the organization, but no better alternative was ever suggested—had arrest and detention powers. Instead of taking private payments for their services they were compensated directly by the Bow Street Magistrates on a case-by-case basis. When Robert Peel initiated the formation of the London Metropolitan Police in 1834, many of the Bow Street Runners were incorporated into the force, including Vicar Brekonridge, who had been a Runner for seven years after leaving his youthful career as a sailor.

While Elias Sullivan is a fictional character, the monograph he wanted to write: *"What Killed Edward Drummond, The Lead or the Lancet?"* did appear under the anonymous byline of *"An Old Army Surgeon"* in 1843, published by Simpkin and Marshall of Fleet Street. In my fictional universe, Doctor Sullivan took Brekonridge's advice to submit the article under a pseudonym.

Writing a piece of fiction based on actual events entails an enormous amount of research. I am indebted to Richard Moran, PhD, of Mount Holyoke College, the author of *Knowing Right From Wrong*, the definitive nonfiction examination of the M'Naghten trial. His exhaustive analysis of the evidence provided (and not provided) in the M'Naghten trial, and the sociocultural, economic, and political conditions of early Victorian Great Britain that contributed to the murder of Edward Drummond, was of inestimable value in writing this novel.

I should also note that the £750 discovered in Daniel M'Naghten's bank account was completely factual, and that nobody has yet been able to determine, over the last 180 years, exactly where the money came from, or how it came into M'Naghten's possession. Dr. Moran believes, as I have stated in this fictionalized account of trial, that it was payment for a botched assassination. £750 in 1843 would be the equivalent of approximately $120,000 USD today, so it was no mean sum at M'Naghten's disposal. It is likely that such an amount could pay for a lavish court defense even today.

The way the M'Naghten trial ended has long been a source of controversy. Judge Tindal, according to the official trial transcript, apparently truncated the defense's parade of expert medical witnesses, satisfied that Queen's Counsel Cockburn had adequately demonstrated M'Naghten's insanity, and instructed the jury to act on that determination. While this would be an egregious act in a modern courtroom, apparently it was not unusual for Old Bailey justices to instruct juries on how to rule, mostly because juries of the day tended—like today—to be comprised of people who weren't cagey enough to get out of jury duty. Even so, Tindal's precipitous conclusion to the trial reinforces Dr. Moran's and my contention that an agreement had already been reached between Home Secretary Graham—who oversaw all court activity—and Alexander Cockburn. To preserve public security, it was important that M'Naghten be found not guilty by reason of insanity, regardless of the Queen's wishes.

Likewise, I would like to thank Paul Thomas Murphy, whose book *Shooting Victoria: Madness, Mayhem, and the Rebirth of the British Monarchy* provided most of the background on the wave of assassination attempts that took place in London prior to Edward Drummond's death.

Dr. Moran and Mr. Murphy both wrote their books prior to the availability of the Internet, and the vast trove of minutiae that this medium now makes available. For instance, most of the testimony during the trial is drawn directly from the transcript of the actual trial of Daniel M'Naghten in 1843. Some testimony was cut from the trial testimony and instead used in dialogue during the Glasgow investigation, which means that some of that dialogue was the original person's actual words.

I would also like to acknowledge the contributions of the following:

Richard M. Bousfield and Richard Merrett, for their 1843 work *The Trial of Daniel M'Naghten For the Murder of E. Drummond*, which provided a firsthand account of the proceedings at The Old Bailey in this case, including a full transcript of the trial itself.

The Post Office Annual online, which provides scanned copies of the original London and Glasgow street directories, from which I gathered most of the information on various characters' real-life addresses and occupations.

The Old Bailey Online, which provided numerous details on the workings of the British legal system in 1843.

The Open University Online, for its detailed examination of Queen Victoria's attempts to deal with the Chartist uprisings across Great Britain in the late 1830s and early 1840s.

Along with countless individual, obscure, arcane, and fascinating websites dealing with trivia such as the recipe for Irish cawl, men's and women's fashions of the period, London open markets, the British railway system, and any number of other details that helped bring this story to life.

I am indebted to my beta readers: Karen Lynn Fry, Russell Fry, Pat Reck, Alan Kaplan, Jann Briesacher, and Mike Flannigan. Huge thanks to Deni Dietz and Derek McFadden for early developmental editing, and to my editor at Level Best Books, Harriette Sackler. Also thanks to Kevin Burton Smith and Daniel Stashower for providing cover blurbs for this novel.

Finally, I want to thank my greatest fan—my lovely wife Elaine, who has traveled this writing journey with me, every step of the way. Without her, none of this would make any sense at all.

WH December 1, 2021

About the Author

Richard Helms is a retired college professor and clinical/forensic psychologist. He has been nominated five times for the Killer Nashville Silver Falchion Award, with one win; eight times for the SMFS Derringer Award, winning it twice; eight times for the Private Eye Writers of America Shamus Award, with a win in 2021 and another in 2022; twice for the ITW Thriller Award, with one win; and twice for the Mystery Readers International Macavity Award, which he won in 2022. He is a frequent contributor to *Ellery Queen Mystery Magazine*, along with other periodicals. His story *"See Humble and Die"* was selected for inclusion in Houghton Mifflin Harcourt's *Best American Mystery Stories of 2020*, edited by C.J. Box and Otto Penzler. *Vicar Brekonridge* is his twenty-third novel. Mr. Helms is a former member of the Board of Directors of Mystery Writers of America, and the former president of the Southeast Regional Chapter of MWA. When not writing, Mr. Helms enjoys reading, travel, gourmet cooking, simracing, hanging with his grandsons, and rooting for his beloved Carolina Tar Heels and Carolina Panthers. Richard Helms and his wife Elaine live in Charlotte, North Carolina.

SOCIAL MEDIA HANDLES:
www.facebook.com/rickhelms051

www.twitter.com/rickhelmsauthor

AUTHOR WEBSITE:
www.richardhelms.net

Also by Richard Helms

Geary's Year (1981) World Karting Magazine (serialized)

Geary's Gold (1984) World Karting Magazine (serialized)

Joker Poker (1999) Back Alley Books

The Valentine Profile (2000) Mystery and Suspense Press

The Amadeus Legacy (2000) Mystery and Suspense Press

Voodoo That You Do (2001) Back Alley Books

Bobby J. (2002) Barbadoes Hall Communications

Juicy Watusi (2002) Back Alley Books (Shamus Award Finalist)

Wet Debt (2003) Back Alley Books (Shamus Award Finalist)

Grass Sandal (2004) Back Alley Books

Cordite Wine (2005) Back Alley Books (Shamus Award Finalist)

The Daedalus Deception (2009) Back Alley Books

Six Mile Creek (2010) Five Star/Cengage Mysteries

Thunder Moon (2011) Five Star/Cengage Mysteries (Silver Falchion Award Finalist)

The Unresolved Seventh (2012) Five Star/Cengage Mysteries (Silver Falchion

Award Finalist)

The Mojito Coast (2013) Five Star/Cengage Mysteries (Shamus Award Finalist/Silver Falchion Finalist)

Older Than Goodbye (2014) Five Star/Cengage Mysteries (Silver Falchion Award Finalist)

Paid In Spades (2019) Clay Stafford Books (Shamus Award Finalist)

Brittle Karma (2020) Black Arch Books (Shamus Award Winner)

Doctor Hate (2021) Black Arch Books

A Kind and Savage Place (2022) Level Best Books/ New Arc Books

www.ingramcontent.com/pod-product-compliance
Lightning Source LLC
Chambersburg PA
CBHW050008120726
47903CB00006B/1688